REGENCY
Scandals

Sophia James

MILLS & BOON

Mills & Boon, an imprint of Harlequin (UK) Limited,
Eton House, 18-24 Paradise Road, Richmond, Surrey TW9 1SR

REGENCY SCANDALS © Harlequin Books S.A. 2011

The publisher acknowledges the copyright holder of the individual works
as follows:

High Seas to High Society © Sophia James 2007
Masquerading Mistress © Sophia James 2007

ISBN: 978 0 263 88739 6

052-1011

Harlequin (UK) policy is to use papers that are natural, renewable
and recyclable products and made from wood grown in sustainable
forests. The logging and manufacturing processes conform to the legal
environmental regulations of the country of origin.

Printed in the UK
by CPI Mackays, Chatham, ME5 8TD

High Seas to
High Society

For Pete, my pirate!

Chapter One

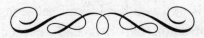

London, May 1822

Asher Wellingham, the ninth Duke of Carisbrook, stood in a corner with his host Lord Henshaw, and watched a woman sitting alone near the dais.

'Who is she, Jack?' he asked with feigned casualness. In truth he had noticed her as soon as he had walked into the salon, for it was seldom a beautiful woman wore such a plain gown to a ball and then sat alone looking for all the world as if she was actually enjoying her own company.

'Lady Emma Seaton, the Countess of Haversham's niece. She arrived in London six weeks ago and every young blood has tried to strike up some sort of relationship with her since.'

'Arrived…from where?'

'Somewhere in the country, I would presume. Obviously she has not seen a London stylist—I've never seen hair quite like it.'

Asher's gaze travelled across a thatch of blonde curls barely restrained by hairpins. A home-fashioned coiffure, he surmised, and executed badly, yet the whole effect of sun-bleached curls threaded with gold and corn was unsettling.

People seldom surprised him. Or intrigued him.

But this girl with her lack of self-consciousness and her fashion faux pas had succeeded. What woman, after all, ate her supper whilst wearing her gloves and licked the end of a silk-covered finger when the jam of a sweet biscuit stained it.

This one did.

Aye, this one did not nibble on the food as every other female in the room was wont to do, but piled the plate before her from the tray of a passing waiter as though her very life depended on it. As though it might indeed be a good deal of time until the next course showed itself, or as if, perhaps in her old life, in some country village, she had not had as much food as she had needed and could barely believe that she was being offered such bounty here.

He saw others looking her way and felt vaguely irritated. The buzz of whisper had grown as she stood, tall and thin, the hem of her gown reaching a good inch above the line that would have been decent and at least three inches above the length that was now in vogue.

He could hear the conjecture and the whispers all around, even if she did not seem to, and he wondered why the hell it should concern him anyway, but there was something about her. Some hint of familiarity. Some elusive memory of fellowship that could not quite be shaken. How could he know her? He tried to determine the colour of her eyes, but from this distance he could not. Turning, he cursed the Countess of Haversham for being remiss in seeing to her niece's wardrobe and hairstyle, and left Lady Emma Seaton to the circling society wolves.

The room was crowded with men and women chatting at great speed and without pause, the music from a stringed quartet hardly discernible across the din.

Emerald frowned and sat, closing her eyes in order to listen better. People here did not seem to appreciate music, did not seem to understand that, when silence threaded the undertones, sound could be better heard, melody enhanced.

The music was unfamiliar, an English tune and lightly woven. She could almost feel her harmonica at her lips, notes soft across whisper-swelling seas. Jamaica crowded in like an ache.

Nay, she mustn't think of this, she admonished herself, drawing her body more upright in the chair and forcing herself to observe the pressing crowd around her.

This was her life for a time.

England.

Her hands fingered the silk gown that swathed her from head to foot and, raising the third glass of fine champagne to her lips, she swallowed quickly. Good drink dulled her anxiety and heightened other senses. Sound. Smell. Feel. Every pore in her body longed for sun or wind or rain upon it, to break free of her high-waisted frilled bodice. To lie on summer-warm sand or in the wild grasses on the rise above Montego Bay or to dive deep into an azure sea, down and down until the bubbles tickled greenness and the other world was lost.

Letting out an audible sigh, she schooled her thoughts. 'No more memories,' she whispered beneath her breath and was pleased when her aunt sat down on the spare seat opposite. The paleness in her face, however, was alarming.

'Are you quite well, Aunt?'

'He is here, Emmie…' Miriam could barely enunciate the sentence.

'Who is here?' She knew which name she would hear even before her aunt spoke.

'Asher Wellingham.'

Panic raced across fear and anger.

Finally, he had come.

Weeks of waiting had strained her nerves almost to breaking point and the advances of the men here had become increasingly more difficult to discourage. But had he seen her? Would he remember?

Placing her glass upon the table, she refused more from a circulating waiter and her hand strayed to her hair to tuck in an errant curl. Please God, let it be enough, for, if he recognised her, everything would be lost.

'Where is he?' She hated the tight nervousness she was consumed with.

'Over in the corner by the door. He was watching you before. Watching closely.'

Resisting a strong urge to turn around, Emerald summoned up every reserve she had. 'Do you think he suspects?'

'No, for if he did he would have you dragged out of this place immediately, and hanged in the gallows of Tyburn as the daughter of a traitor.'

'He could do that?'

'Oh, you would be surprised what he can do, Emmie, and do with the impunity of a lord who thinks himself so utterly and morally right.'

'Then we must hurry to complete that which we came here to do. Now, look across at him. Slowly,' she added as her aunt's head jolted around. 'Is he carrying a cane of any sort?'

Emerald held her breath as her aunt looked. Could it really be this easy?

'No. He has a drink in his hand. Wine, I think and white.'

She tried not to let her frustration show.

'At least it will not mark this gown.' She had three

dresses, procured from the second-hand markets in Monmouth Street, and with a dire lack of funds for any more, did not want this one ruined by a stain that she could never remove.

'Oh, my dear. Surely you do not intend to just bump into him? He would know a sham when he saw one, I am certain of it.'

'Do not worry, Aunt Miriam. I have done this before in Kingston and in Port Antonio when Beau wished for an introduction to some well-heeled stranger. Here it will be easy. Just a small push. Enough at least to allow me the beginnings of a conversation and the chance to be included for a while within his circle of friends.'

'This is the Duke of Carisbrook. Do not underestimate him as your father did.'

Emerald drew in a breath. Beau had become careless but she would not be. Standing, she bent to loosen the silver buckle on her left shoe. The little details needed to be right. She remembered Beau telling her this over and over again.

Asher Wellingham was still speaking with the host when she came in from behind, falling deftly against him. Her small shriek was inspired, she was to think later, for the Duke's reflexes were quick and he had turned to reach for her as she began to lose balance. If the material of her skirt had not caught at the heel of her shoe, she would have been all right. And if the small man beside him had been stronger and kept his feet, all three of them would have stayed upright. But with the highly polished floor and her soft leather soles she could not gain traction and so she simply let herself fall, the splash of wine cold against her skin.

She heard the gasps all around her as the strong arms of the Duke of Carisbrook came under her waist and knees, the black of his superfine jacket soft against her cheek. He was lifting her up against him. Easily.

She felt her own intake of breath at exactly the same moment as she registered the steady beat of his heart, and when his fingers brushed against her bodice, her whole world tilted. Dressed in these ridiculous clothes, the soft swell of her breasts was highly visible and she was taken aback with what she saw in Asher Wellingham's eyes as he carried her from the ballroom. This close, the light brown was webbed with a fine and clear gold and an undeniable masculine interest. For just a second shock disorientated her and everything became immeasurably more difficult.

'You fainted,' he said as he placed her on a sofa in a room away from the dancing. His voice was deep, the finely tuned vowels of privilege easily heard on the edges and his glance held more than a sting of question. With his dark hair slicked back at his nape and his brandy-coloured eyes, the Duke of Carisbrook was unforgettable. A man with legendary confidence and enough gall to pursue her father across three oceans.

And kill him!

Bitter anger congealed with an age-old hurt and, raising the pitch of her voice into something that she hoped resembled embarrassment, she brought her fingers to her mouth.

'I'm utterly and dreadfully sorry,' she gushed, pleased when her sentiment sounded so genuine. 'I think it must have been the heat in the ballroom or perhaps the crush of people. Or the noise, mayhap…' Uncertainly she stopped. Was she overdoing the feminine penchant for histrionics with three excuses all rolled into one? Exaggeration was dangerous, but, dressed in this bone-tight gown and these flimsy, useless shoes, it was also surprisingly easy.

With a quick movement of her fan she hid her eyes and regrouped her defences, every pore in her body aware of the Duke of Carisbrook, and every problem she now had a direct result of his actions. Swallowing a snaking thread of guilt, she was pleased when he stepped back.

'Was it you who caught me, your Grace?'

'It was more a case of you bouncing off the frail old Earl of Derrick and landing in my arms.'

She tried to look mortified while thinking what hard work it was to be so perpetually sorry, or eternally grateful, and of a sudden the whole charade of being here seemed impossibly more difficult. She didn't belong, couldn't understand the rules or nuances and every instinct told her to be wary. It was anonymity she needed to maintain—if questions were to be asked, they would need answers and she could not give those without endangering everyone she loved. Even the thought made her tremble. 'Where is my aunt?'

'The Countess has gone to find you a shawl for your dress.'

Swinging her legs down off the sofa, Emerald tried to rise. 'If I could stand…'

'I think that it may be wiser to stay still.' His words were husky and her pulse spiked sharply as he placed his finger across the veins of her left wrist. Listening for the beat, she thought weakly, and wondered what he would be making of the pace.

When he smiled she knew. Not a man to incite an insipid reaction from any woman, she determined, not even one as badly turned out as she was. Pulling away her hand, she fanned her face in an exact impersonation of the girls she had watched in many a crowded salon across the past month. 'I am seldom so very clumsy and I cannot think what it was that made me trip…' Lifting the hem of her gown, the loosened silver buckle caught the light. 'It must have been this, I wager…' She let him absorb this and was pleased to see Miriam return, a shawl across her arm and her expression drawn. Lord Henshaw accompanied her.

'Are you feeling better, my dear? You could so easily have knocked your head in the fall and the wine has quite ruined your gown. Here, lean forward and I will wrap this about you.' A bright flame of red-gold material was fastened quickly, although Emerald had had enough of being the wilting centre of attention and stood.

'I will be more careful in future and I thank you for your assistance.' She had to look up at Asher Wellingham as she spoke and, at five foot ten inches in her bare feet, this was not an occurrence that she was often used to. When his eyes caught her own she wished suddenly that her hair was longer and that her gown was of a better quality.

No. No. No.

She shook her head. None of this made sense. Asher Wellingham was her enemy and she would be gone from England as soon as she found what it was she sought. It was the heat in this room that was making her flush and the shock of the fall that had set her heart to pounding. If only she could escape outside and take a breath of fresh air or feel the wind as it made its path along London's river, a hint of freedom on its edge.

Raising her voice to the discordant and high whining tone she had perfected under the tutelage of Miriam, she pushed into her cause.

'I suspect that it was the soles of my shoes that made me falter and the floor itself is highly polished. I do hope that the gossip will not be too unkind.'

'I am certain that it shall not be.' His tone was flat.

'Oh, how very good of you to say so, your Grace,' and although the flare of darkness in his eyes was intimidating she made herself continue. 'Whenever things went wrong at home, Mama always said the strength of a woman's character was not in her successes, but in her failures.'

The tilt of his lips was not encouraging. 'Your mother sounds like a wise woman, Lady Emma.' The sentiment lacked any vestige of interest and she knew that he was fast approaching the end of his patience.

'Oh, she was, your Grace.'

'Was?'

'She died when I was quite young and I was brought up by my father.'

'I see.' He looked for all the world like a man who'd had enough of this discourse, though innate good manners held him still. 'Rumour has it that you are from the country. Which part exactly do you hail from?'

'Knutsford in Cheshire.' She had been there as a child once. It had been summertime and the memory of the flowers of England had never left her. Her mother had pressed one in the locket she now wore. A delphinium, the sky blue dimmed under the onslaught of many years.

'And your accent. I can't quite place it?'

The question startled her and a vase balanced on a plinth near her right hand toppled. A thousand splinters of porcelain fell around her feet. Bending to pick some up, the china pierced through her glove and drew blood.

'Do leave it alone, Emma. This is hardly proper.' Miriam's reprimand was sharp and Emerald froze. Of course, a servant would tidy up after a lady. She must not forget again.

'Is it expensive?' More to the point would she have to pay for it?

Henshaw stepped forward. 'The plinth was shaky and I have never been overly fond of ornate things.'

Wellingham's bark of laughter behind him worried Emerald; looking around, she could also see that this last statement was patently false. Everything in this room was overly embellished and elaborately decorated. Still, given the fact that eighty pounds and a few pieces of jewellery were all that stood between her and bankruptcy, she could hardly afford to be magnanimous.

'I am so terribly sorry.' Desperation stripped her voice to its more familiar and husky tone. She wanted to be away from here. She wanted the wide-open spaces of Jamaica and enough room to move in. She wanted to be safe with Ruby and her aunt and far, far away from a man who could ruin her completely.

But she needed the cane first.

Without the cane, nothing would be possible. Squeezing her eyes together, she was pleased to feel moisture. These Englishmen loved women who were fragile and needy. She had seen this to be true ever since she had arrived here. In the ballrooms. In the drawing rooms. Even in the park where women sat beside their men and watched them tool horses Emerald thought so docile that a child in Jamaica might have managed them. It was just the way of things in England.

She was surprised, therefore, by the Duke of Carisbrook's withdrawal. She had done something wrong, she was sure of it, for his amusement now fled and awkwardness hung between them. Re-evaluating her options, she bit at her lower lip. He was not as the others were here. In looks. In temperament. In size.

Damn it.

Another month and her funds would be spent. Another month and the servants they had hired would be demanding payment and all of London would despise them.

For herself the prospect was not as daunting as the effect such hatred might have on her aunt, for Miriam was old and deserved some comfort in her last years, and her title, although venerable, carried little in the way of income.

Money.

How she hated the fact that it always came back to that. If it had been just her she would have managed, but it wasn't just her anymore. She shivered and pulled the shawl more firmly around her saturated bodice. 'It's cold.' She needed to think, needed to mull over the reaction that the enigmatic Duke seemed to inspire in her, needed to get away and re-think her strategies in this endlessly grey and complex land.

'I will have a footman call up my carriage.' Asher Wellingham was turning even as Miriam stopped him.

'It will not be necessary, your Grace. We are quite able to procure a hackney.'

Emerald, however, having suddenly devised a plan, jumped in.

'We shall be delighted to accept your most generous offer, your Grace, and I trust that the time taken should not inconvenience you.' She glanced at the ornate clock on the mantelpiece. 'Twenty past one, sir. You should have your conveyance back easily before the clock strikes two.'

His shadow dark gaze ran across her. Taking in everything she suspected, and finding her lacking. Face. Manners. Dress. Hair.

'Then I will bid you both good evening.' As she watched him go, she noticed for the first time that he walked with a limp.

The cane, she thought. The cane with the hidden treasure map that Beau swore concealed a fortune. The cane she had come to London for in a last bid to shake off the debtors from her heels and reclaim at least a little of life as it had been.

Doubt passed across her, but she dismissed it. She

had to believe in the story Azziz had heard twelve weeks ago in the taverns of Kingston Town. The story that the Duke of Carisbrook had been seen in London using a distinctive carved ebony cane.

Her father's cane, encrusted with emeralds and rubies, the secret catch hidden beneath an overhanging rim of ivory.

Lord, it was all so nebulous, but she had to have faith that it was here, because if it wasn't…? She shook her head. Hard. The alternative didn't bear thinking of and with the covering of darkness the night was still long.

Long enough to waylay a duke?

Her first real chance?

Dressed as a lad, she might be able to shake some clue from Wellingham as to the whereabouts of the map, and if Azziz accompanied her…? Excitement flushed her cheeks as she threaded her hand through her aunt's and helped her from the room. All they needed to know was the location of the cane. With this in hand they could find it and be gone from England on the next outgoing tide. Disappearing was easy when you had the promise of enough money to cover your tracks.

Chapter Two

Two hours later the carriage she had been waiting for thundered out of the Derrick town house, the heavy velour curtains on each side drawn. Signalling to Azziz to urge the team forward and follow, Emerald searched for a place to cut the conveyance off, though as it turned into the docks on the south side of the river, she bade him to hang back.

'What is the Duke doing here at this time of night?'

She asked the question of Toro, who sat beside her, and when he shook his head the ring in his left ear gleamed in the moonlight.

'The tide will be up before morning. Perhaps he means to take ship somewhere.'

Puzzlement was replaced by surprise as a woman she had not seen before climbed down from the now-stationary coach.

No, not a woman, but a girl, she amended, and hardly happy at that. The older man who met with her had his fingers tightly about her forearm and he wasn't looking pleased as they walked to the porch of a shabby doss-house and stopped. Or at least the girl stopped. Emerald could quite plainly hear her speaking.

'I do not think this is the place we want, Stephen. You cannot mean to have brought me here.'

'It is just for tonight, Lucy. Just until I can find ship on the morrow.'

'Nay. You promised we would be wed first.' Her distress was increasing. 'If my brother found out I have come to this place…' He did not let her finish.

'I did not force you into the carriage, Lucinda. You came, I thought, of your own free will. An adventure, you said, to spice up the boring routine of your existence. Now come along, for we do not have all night.' His words were slightly slurred.

'Are you drunk?' The young woman's consternation was becoming more obvious as the driver of the Wellingham coach joined them.

'The master would be most displeased, my lady. My instructions were to take you straight home.'

'I shall be with you in a moment, Burton. Please, could you wait in the carriage?'

The servant wavered, plainly uncertain as to what he should do next and his hesitancy fired the younger man into an angry response. Without any warning, his fist shot out and the driver fell dazed onto the pathway.

'Come, my love, no servant should question a lady's motives and we have waited long enough for this chance.'

Emerald grimaced. She had heard that tone before and knew what was to come next. A young and inexperienced girl would have no idea how to counter such overt masculine pressure. And would suffer for it.

Breathing out, she pushed forward, signalling to Toro and Azziz to stay behind.

'Let her go.' Her voice was as low and rough as she could make it, the glint of her sharpened blade in the moonlight underlining the message.

'Who the hell are you?'

Ignoring his question, she addressed the girl. 'Think hard and long before you accompany this gentleman, miss, for I think he is not as reputable as you might hope. If I were you, I would take the safer option and return home.'

Emerald tensed as the one named Stephen came towards her and, slipping her blade into the intricate folds of cravat at his neck, she held him still. 'I would advise you, sir, to keep very quiet as to the purpose of this night's excursion. Put it down to folly if you like or to the effects of strong drink, but know that even a small whisper of what has transpired here could be dangerous to your well-being.'

'You would threaten me?'

'Most assuredly I would.'

He moved suddenly, the heel of his hand striking Emerald's cheekbone before she brought the hilt of her knife up hard against the soft part of his temple. He crumpled quite gracefully, she thought, for a tall man and did nothing to cushion his fall. The startled eyes of the girl came upon her and unexpectedly Emerald felt the need to explain away her actions.

'I'd had enough of his questions.'

'So you have killed him?'

'No. Simply wounded his pride. In much the same way as he has wounded yours, I suspect.'

'He was not the person I thought him to be and I can't imagine what may have happened if you had not come along, Mr…?'

'Kingston.' Emerald's heart sank as small, cold fingers entwined around hers.

'Mr Kingston.' The young voice sounded breathless and when Emerald tried to disengage her hand the girl began to cry, tiny sobs at first and then huge loud wrenching ones until the patrons spilled out from a nearby tavern. Emerald was now in a quandary. She was hard-pressed for time and the dawn was not far off and yet she could not just abandon such innocence either.

'How old are you?' she said roughly as she hailed Azziz and waited as he turned the hackney.

'Seventeen. I shall be eighteen, though, in three

months and I am indebted to you for your help. If you had not come when you did, I…' Tears rolled down her cheeks and splattered on the yellow silk of her gown.

Oh, dear God, Emerald thought, her own twenty-one years seeming infinitely more worldly. By seventeen she had sailed the world from the Caribbean to the Dutch East Indies, the promise of death dogging her at each and every mile. By seventeen her innocence had long been robbed by circumstance. The thought made her head ache. England was like a hothouse, she suddenly decided, its people so sheltered from reality and difficulty that they were easily hurt. And broken. Like this girl. By small contretemps and silly mistakes.

'If you had not been here…' Lucy began again. 'My brother warned me to have nothing to do with the Earl of Westleigh…said I should stay away from him…insisted that I did not even talk with him.' Her sobs were lessening now and her voice levelled out from panic to anger. 'It was the forbiddenness I think that made him interesting.' She looked down at the man prostrate at her feet. 'Certainly here I can see no redeeming quality, save for the waistcoat, I think.' She finished on a teary giggle. 'I always liked the way he wore his clothes. By the way, I am Lady Lucinda Wellingham. The Duke of Carisbrook's youngest sister.'

Emerald stilled a sharp jolt of surprise. Carisbrook's sister? Lord, what was she to do now? The thought that perhaps she could use Asher Wellingham's sibling as a hostage did cross her mind, but she dismissed this in a moment. For one, she doubted she could stand the company of such a watering pot for any great length of time; for two, she reminded her of a golden retriever they'd had once at St Clair. All gratitude and shining devotion.

No, the girl must be returned post-haste to her brother; if luck held, he might as yet still be at Lord Henshaw's soirée. She could be in and out of the Carisbrook town house without having to speak to a soul, for, damn it, she did not dare to chance any encounter with the Duke. Not dressed like this in the full light of his home.

'Do you know my brother, Mr Kingston? He will be most eager to see that you are compensated for the time and trouble you have taken and I think really that you would like him for he is as practised at the art of fighting as you appear to be and….'

Emerald held up her hand and was glad when the inconsequential chatter finally ground to a halt. She had to think. What was the way of things here? Would it be suspicious to merely drop the girl off at her door? She shook her head and determined that it most probably would be. She would have to play the damn charade out and escort Lady Lucinda home. If Toro drove the coach, he could leave it for the Carisbrook servants to deal with and then rejoin Azziz and her in the hackney.

A compromised solution, but it would have to do. Turning away from the gathering crowd of interested onlookers, Emerald helped the injured driver gain his footing on the carriage steps and was thankful to close the door behind the Wellingham party.

The twelve-hour candle on the library mantelpiece was almost gutted. Another night gone. Relieved, Asher unwound his cravat and threw it on the table. His jacket followed.

Shaking his head, he caught the movement of it in the mirror above his oaken armoire. His eyes were rimmed with darkness.

Darkness.

Frowning, he reached for the brandy, rolling the glass in his hand before swallowing the lot. A quick shot of guilt snaked through him, for he had promised himself yesterday that he would stop drinking alone.

Just another broken vow.

He laughed at the absurdity, though the sound held no humour, and as he settled to what brandy was left in the bottle the image of Lady Emma Seaton in his arms came to mind.

She had smelled nice. Neither perfumed nor powdered. Just clean. Strong. And she had particularly fine eyes. Turquoise, he determined, frowning as the same vague shift of memory he had felt on first seeing her returned.

She was familiar.

But how did he know her? An unusual face. And different. The mark that went through her right eyebrow and up under her fringe was strange. If he were to guess at its origin, he would have placed it as a knife wound. But how could that be? No, far more likely she had been whipped by a branch while riding or tripped perhaps in her youth and caught a sharp edge of stone. He liked the fact that she made no effort to conceal it.

The ring of the doorbell startled him and he checked his watch. Five o'clock in the morning! Surely no acquaintance of his would turn up here at this time and uninvited? Lifting a candle, he strode into the front portico to hear the quiet weeping of his sister.

'My God. Lucy?' He could barely believe it was her as she threw herself into his arms.

'What the hell has happened? Why were you not in the bed you were bound for when you left the Derricks' two hours ago?'

'I…Stephen…met me…in a place…by the port. He said we would be married and instead…'

'Stephen Eaton?'

'He said that he loved me and that if I came to him after the ball tonight he would speak of his feelings. But the place he expected me to accompany him to was hardly proper and then he almost killed Burton…'

'He what…?' Asher made himself simmer down.

Redress could come later and calmness would gain him quicker access to answers than rage. 'How did you manage to get home?' He was pleased when his sister did not seem to notice the pure strain of fury that threaded his words.

'A man came with a knife and knocked Eaton out. He put us all in the coach and his driver brought us straight home. A Mr Kingston. He did not know you, for I asked, and his accent was strange.'

'Where is he now?'

'Just gone. He followed us back in a rented hackney and said he would not stay, even though I tried to persuade him differently. He said something of another engagement and promised to send word as to how he could be contacted.'

Asher caught the eyes of his butler and indicated that someone follow the hackney. Blackmail was often a lucrative business and he did not want to be without the facts. Everybody in this world wanted something of him and he could not contemplate this Mr Kingston to be the exception. Still, at least he had brought Lucinda home. And safe. For that alone he would always be grateful.

Gesturing to a maid hovering by the staircase, he bid her take his sister up to bed. He was glad when Lucy went quietly and the sounds of her crying subsided.

It took twenty minutes for Peters to return and the news was surprising.

'The gentleman went to the Countess of Haversham's town lodgings, your Grace. Got out of the hackney and sent it on before disappearing into the house. He had a key, for I tarried to see how he gained entrance. I left Gibbon there to trace his steps further should he surface again.'

'Very good.' Dismissing the messenger, Asher went back into his own study. Emma Seaton and the Countess of Haversham. What did he know of them?

Both niece and aunt were newcomers to London. Miriam had been here for a year and Emma merely a matter of weeks. Both had gowns that had seen better days and the look of women who dealt daily with the worry of dwindling funds, and Miriam kept neither carriage nor horses.

Would they have a boarder living with them as a way of bolstering finances? Or could Emma Seaton have a husband?

And now a further mystery. A young man who would rescue the sister of a very wealthy man and wait for neither recompense nor thanks. A mysterious Samaritan who scurried away from what certainly would have been an honourable deed. In anyone's eyes.

Something wasn't right and in the shadows of wrongness he could feel the vague pull of danger, for nothing made sense. Instinctively his fingers closed hard against the narrow stem of his glass and he sucked in his breath. Harnessing fury. Calculating options.

* * *

Emerald pulled the curtain back from her bedroom window on the third floor and cursed. The man was still there and she knew where he had come from.

The Duke of Carisbrook.

He had sent someone after her and she had not bothered to check. Stupid, stupid, stupid mistake, she thought, banging her hand against her sore head and roundly swearing.

She should have sent the conveyance on to some other street and then made her way home undetected. She would have done so in Jamaica, so why not here? With real chagrin she stripped off the boy's clothes and rearranged her blankets beside the bed, glad to lay her head down, glad to close her eyes and think.

What a day. Nothing had gone easily and she did not know the next time she might be in contact with Asher Wellingham.

Close contact.

She remembered the feel of his finger across her pulse. A small touch of skin that fired her blood. The trick of memory and circumstance, she decided. After all, she had gone to sleep every night for the past five years with those velvet-brown eyes and hard-planed face etched in dream.

The same dream.
The same moment.
The same beginning.

So known now that she could recall each minute detail, even in wakefulness. The sounds, the smell, the sun in her eyes and the wind off the Middle Passage of Turks Island at her back. And a thousand yards of calico luffing in the breeze.

She shook her head hard and made herself concentrate on the sounds of London and on the way the lamp on her side table threw shadows across the ceiling. She would not think of Asher Wellingham. She would not. But desire crept in under her resolution and she flushed as a thin pain entwined itself around her stomach and delved lower.

Lower.

She thought of the bordellos that had dotted the port streets of Kingston Town and wondered. Wondered what it would be like to draw her hands through night-black hair and beneath the fine linen of his shirt. Imaginary sinew and muscle made her pulse quicken and she turned restlessly within the bedclothes, any pressure unwelcome on heated skin.

Her eyes flew open. Lord, what was she thinking? Dread and the cold rush of reality made her shiver.

Asher Wellingham.

Her enemy.

Her father's enemy.

Anger and hurt surfaced and she reached for her wrapper. She would never sleep tonight. Adding another log to the fire, she took a book from the pile beside the chair, 'The Vanity of Human Wishes' in Latin, from Juvenal's satires.

She remembered Beau teaching her the conjugations of complicated verbs from books bound in heavy velvet. Books he had been taught from when he was a child.

A half-smile formed.

Once he had been a patient man. And a good father.

And while she knew he was no angel, he had not deserved the revenge the Duke of Carisbrook had exacted upon him. A calculated retribution timed when the *Mariposa* limped home from a storm in the Gulf of Mexico. Asher Wellingham had come in quickly with three times the manpower and demolished the smaller boat with military precision. Boom-boom, and the masts had gone. Boom-boom, and the front of the brigantine had been holed with a volley of cannon fire.

Azziz had told her the story later when he had been returned to Jamaica on the Baltimore clipper that had picked them out of the sea. The English duke had not given her father the chance to jump, but had demanded a duel on the foredeck of the sinking ship.

And a minute was all it had taken. One minute to run her father through the stomach.

Emerald felt tears prick at the back of her eyes. Her father had lived by the sword and died by it, but there had been a time when literature and classics and music were more important.

When her mother had been with them! When the family had still been whole. When St Clair had been their home and the *Mariposa* was another man's ship.

Gone. Long gone.

In the depths of longing and promise. And false, false hope.

And it had been a struggle ever since.

With care she replaced the book on the shelf and stood back, distancing herself from the pain of memory, regathering strategies and garnering strength.

Retrieve the cane and return to Jamaica.

Simple plans and the revival of a proper life. Ruby and Miriam and St Clair. Home. The word filled her with longing, even as the amber-fired eyes of Asher Wellingham danced before her. Beguiling. Intriguing. Forbidden.

Shaking her head, she sat down in the chair by the fire and watched the shadows of flame fill the room.

Chapter Three

Asher Wellingham came to Haversham House early the next morning and hard on the heels of a note he had sent. And he came alone.

The drawing room where Miriam and Emerald sat to receive him had been hastily tidied and what little furniture they had in the house had been brought down to fill out the spaces left from an auction they had held almost two months prior in York. Quietly. Secretly. The recompense they had gathered from the exercise had reflected the clandestine nature of the adventure. Still, money could be translated into food and beggars could not be choosers. At least they still had the silver tea service, placed now on a side table.

This morning Emerald wore her second-best gown of light blue velvet with lace trimming around the neckline and an extra petticoat sewn into the base of the wide double skirt for length. On her head she wore a matching mobcap, the scratchy lace making a red rash on the soft underside of her throat. If she had had her potions from home, she might have been able to ease the itchiness. The names on the bottles in the London apothecaries were indecipherable.

Indecipherable!

Everything here seemed that way. Medicines. Places. The weather. People. The Duke of Carisbrook.

'Ladies.' This morning his voice was underlaid with both tiredness and purpose. 'I have come to you this morning on a rather delicate manner.' He cleared his throat and Emerald caught a hint in his eyes of what she could only determine as uncertainty, though the impression was fleeting before the more familiar and implacable urbanity returned. 'I was wondering whether it would be possible to speak with the young man who resides here with you.'

'Young man?' Miriam's response wavered slightly.

'The young man who helped my sister yesterday evening. My servant followed him when he did not stay to be thanked, and it was to this house that he returned. This morning at around the hour of five after sending his carriage on.'

Miriam looked so flabbergasted that Emerald felt bound to break across her silence. 'Perhaps he means Liam, Aunt Miriam?' she prompted and hoped that her aunt might take the hint, though as blankness and silence lengthened she realised she would have to brazen this out by herself. 'Yes, it must be Liam that you speak of. My cousin. He was here for two days only and left this morning for the country, but I shall tell him that you came to relay your thanks. Now,' she added as if the whole subject was decidedly *passé* and she wanted no more discussion, 'would you like tea?'

The Duke's returning glance was so cold that Emerald felt her heart tremble, and his voice when he spoke was fine edged with anger.

'My sister said Mr Kingston had an unusual accent, Lady Emma. Would this accent be the same one as your own?'

'It is, your Grace.' She did not elaborate, but as he swiped his hair back off his face she saw that the two last fingers on his right hand were missing and the stumps where they once had been were criss-crossed in scar tissue.

He has become a ruthless warrior because of the actions of my family.

She made herself stop. She could not feel sorry for a man who had stalked her father and run him through with the sharp edge of his sword. More than once, it was said. And more than what was warranted.

Warranted?

Therein lay the rub. She had heard the story of Asher Wellingham's hatred for her father from every camp except his own. And if life had taught her anything it was the fact that things were seldom black and white. Aye, grey came in many shades. Her father's dreams. Her mother's disappearance. Her own childhood lost between the scramble for easy gold and the rum-soaked taverns of Kingston Town.

Lord, she had to be careful. She had to appear exactly who it was she purported to be or else he would know her. Expose her. Consign Ruby to the care of the nuns in the Hill Street Convent for ever. Ruby. Her heart twisted as she remembered the last sight of her little half-sister being bundled away by the dour and formidable Sister Margaret. How long had it been now? Over a hundred days. The time of passage to England and the weeks waiting for Carisbrook to appear. Without the map she could provide neither home nor sustenance, the squalor of the Kingston Town port streets no place for a fey and frightened child of eight.

Accordingly she schooled impatience and, catching the rough gist of her aunt's conversation, observed the man opposite carefully.

This morning he was dressed in fawn trousers and a brown jacket, the cravat matching his white shirt loosely tied in a casual style she had not seen before. With one long leg crossed over the other, he gave the impression of a man well used to power and unquestioned authority and his confidence was contagious after years of living with a father who had little of either.

Damn it, but she must not think like this either. Beau's choices had been foisted on him by his own self-doubt and excessive introspection. If at times he had made decisions that were suspect, he had still tried through it all to provide a home for her and Ruby. A home Asher Wellingham had shattered when he returned to the Caribbean bent on revenge.

Revenge.

His revenge and now her revenge? And what difference lay between them as the thin veneer of right and wrong tumbled under the greater pressure of need? She shook her head and poured the tea. When he stood to take the cup from her, their fingers accidentally met, and everything slowed.

Time.

Breath.

Fear.

The beat of her heart narrowed as she felt the warmth of his skin. Reaching out, she grabbed the arm of the sofa. To stop herself falling. Into him. For ever.

Whatever was wrong with her? She was acting like the simpering misses so prevalent in London and she did not even recognise these constant, damning blushes that seemed to consume her from head to toe. Her resolve firmed.

'Excuse me,' she said when she saw his pupils widen. 'The accident at the ball yesterday has left me rather poorly…' Leaving the explanation in mid-air she noticed that he had placed his cup on the side table as if making ready to catch her again.

Poorly?

When in her life had she ever used such a word? In the fading light of day she suddenly saw herself as he would see her. Vulnerable. Delicate. Feminine. She almost had to repress a smile. So easy to make men believe exactly what you would want them to. So simple to become a person of such little account. Lifting a fan from the table next to her, she was pleased for the cooling breeze it engendered and used the moment to take stock.

Asher Wellingham was older and harder now and the icy brittleness that coated his eyes was disconcerting. Here, in the blandness of a London drawing room, she could feel a barely concealed danger, a thread of the warrior only lightly clothed beneath his well-pressed jacket and pantaloons. Untamed. Ready to pounce should she put a foot wrong. Oh, God, she blanched, she had already put a foot wrong, last night in her haste to get home, and she was worried by the way he watched her now.

How could he not *know me?*

She almost smiled at the whisper of the words as she took a sip of sugary tea, the quick infusion of sweetness bolstering her confidence further. With the practice of one well used to schooling her expression into the shape of something she wasn't, she placed her hand across her mouth and stifled a yawn. Effortlessly.

Asher watched Emma Seaton with an ever-growing feeling of speculation. He could not understand this woman at all. Nothing about her quite made sense. She still wore the same gloves she had had on last night, which was odd given that they were stained. And this morning, although the scar above her eyebrow was still unhidden, a nasty bruise on her cheekbone had been smothered in thick beige face paint in an attempt to conceal it. From whom?

'You have hurt yourself?'

'I fell against the side of a door. Miriam treated it for me just an hour ago and I hoped it was not too…too noticeable.' Her hand hovered across the mark and he was touched by the movement. She wore the oldest clothes he had ever seen a woman dare to at any social occasion and her hair today was as badly tended as it had been yesterday. Yet she was embarrassed by the bruise upon her face? Nothing about Emma Seaton made sense.

Nothing.

She always wore gloves. She had the same accent as the mysterious and absent Mr Kingston. And she was frightened and decidedly delicate.

Looking around him, other things jarred. The furniture was as badly down at heel as her clothing, yet in the shelf by the window sat well over a hundred books, leather bound and expensive. Kingslake. Wordsworth. Byron and Plato. English was the predominant translation, though many were embellished with the script of the Arabian world. Who the hell here would read those? Defoe stood in company with John Locke, non-conformist authors who chided the establishment with an underlying hint of something darker.

Could the books be Liam Kingston's? He was about to question the Countess on the matter when the doorbell rang and his sister and her maid swept in.

'I am so awfully sorry to just drop in on you like this, Lady Haversham, but I had to come. I am Lady Lucinda Wellingham, and I was informed that Mr Kingston returned home here last night. After he helped me?' The final enquiry was murmured somewhat breathlessly. 'It's just that I would so like to thank him, you see?'

Asher crossed the room to stand by his sister. 'Liam Kingston has departed, Lucinda. Back to…?' His voice was filled with question.

'His home.' Miriam's hesitation shrieked volumes.

'But he will return?' Lucy could barely contain her interest.

'I do not think so. No.' Emerald had regained her wits now that Lucy Wellingham's face held not even the slightest hint of recognition. 'He is married, you see, and his wife is from America. From Boston. She wants to move back there as soon as she has had her fourth child.'

Lucinda paled noticeably. 'Married with four children?' She gawped. 'But he hardly looked old enough.'

'Oh, people are always saying that to him. Are they not, Aunt?' Desperation lent her voice credence and she was pleased to see Miriam nod vigorously. 'Perhaps in the dark you did not see him properly.'

The Duke of Carisbrook's face was inscrutable, though his sister insisted on some recompense. 'We are going to Falder next week, Asher. Could we not invite the Countess and her niece? As a means of saying thank you.'

Emerald's heartbeat accelerated at the question.

'Indeed.' His reply could hardly have held less of a welcome, but, seeing the glimmer of opportunity, she seized upon it.

'We would be delighted to visit your home, Lady Lucinda. Why, I could hardly think of anywhere I should rather go.'

A way into Falder. A first unexpected providence. And although Emerald wished that he could have shown more enthusiasm for the promise of their company, she was not daunted. One night. That was all it would take.

'And your cousin, Liam Kingston, would be most welcome,' Lucinda added, 'for I should deem it an honour to thank him for his assistance in person.' She gripped her brother's arm in entreaty and Asher Wellingham inclined his head in response.

'Bring him along by all means, Lady Emma, for

a man who can dispose so summarily of the Earl of Westleigh and deliver my sister home without recompense is to be much admired.'

The thought did cross Emerald's mind that his voice had an odd edge of question to it but she couldn't be certain, for he did not look at her again before gathering his sister's hand into his own and politely bidding them goodbye.

As they heard his carriage pull away, Miriam began to smile. 'I would say that went very well, would you not, my dear? Aye, very well indeed.'

Emerald crossed to the window and looked out.

Very well?

She wondered if her aunt needed new glasses and smiled at the thought before gingerly touching her own throbbing cheekbone.

'What do you know about the Countess of Haversham, Jack?' Asher leaned back in a chair in his library and drew on his cigar. He'd barely managed an hour of sleep last night but, with his body mellow with brandy, the peace here was pleasant. For just a moment the familiar anger that haunted him was quieter.

'Her husband, Matthew, died from heart failure five years back and it was said that his gambling debts were substantial.'

'So the Countess sold off the furniture to pay her creditors?'

'She what?'

'Sold off the furniture. I was at the Haversham town house in Park Street this morning and there were three chairs and a table in one room and little else in any of the others.'

Jack leant forward, intrigued. 'That explains the gowns they wear then. And the niece's hairstyle. Home-done, I would wager, and by her very own hand, though there was something Tony Formison told me yesterday that did not ring true. He said that Lady Emma had not come down from the country at all, but had arrived a few months ago aboard one of his father's ships with two black servants and a number of very heavy-looking chests.'

Asher began to laugh. The books he had seen in the drawing room? They were hers? 'Formison was on the docks when she arrived?'

'Aye, and he said that he could have sworn her hair was longer.'

'Longer?'

'To her waist according to Tony, and looking nothing like it appears to now.' He stood and retrieved his hat from the table beside him, bending to look at the label on the bottle as he did so. 'It's late and long past the time that I should have been home, but you always have such fine brandy, Asher. Where's this one from?'

'From the Charente in France.'

'A boon from your last trip?'

Asher nodded. 'I'll have some sent to you, but in

return I want you to find out from Formison exactly where the boat that brought Emma Seaton to London came in from. Which port and which month.'

Jack's eyebrows shot up.

'Ask discreetly and in the name of precaution, for I don't want problems resulting from this information.'

'Problems for Emma Seaton or problems for yourself? I thought you seemed rather taken by her at my ball.'

'You misinterpret things, Jack. I put my arms out and caught her as she threw herself against me. Hard, I might add, and with none of the wiles that I am more used to. Before she had even hit the floor she had her eyes open; there was a calculation there that might be construed as unnerving.'

Jack began to laugh. 'You're saying she may have done it on purpose?'

'I doubt I'll ever know, though a betting man would have to say that the odds were more than even.' The humour faded quickly from his eyes as he continued. 'Besides, I am too old to fall for the tricks of a green and simpering country miss.'

'You're thirty-one and hardly over the hill and Lady Emma is…different from the others…less readable. If you are not interested in her, then I sure as hell am.'

'No!' Asher was as surprised by the emotion in the word as Jack was, and to hide it he collected the remains of the brandy and corked the top. 'For the road,' he muttered as he handed the bottle to him, swearing quietly as the door shut behind his departing friend.

Emma Seaton.

Who exactly was she? For the first time in a very long while a sense of interest welled to banish the ennui that had overcome him after Melanie's death.

Melanie.

His wife.

He fingered the ring that he wore on his little finger, the sapphires wrought in gold the exact shade of eyes he would never see again. Her wedding ring. His glance automatically went to the missing digits of his other hand. With good came bad.

He frowned and remembered his return to England after a good fourteen months of captivity. Any innocence he might have been left with had been easily stripped away. He was different. Harder. He could see it reflected in the face of his brother and in the eyes of his mother and aunt. Even his impetuous sister was afraid, sometimes, of him.

Running his hand through his hair, he frowned. Brandy made him introspective. And Emma Seaton touched him in places that he had long thought of as dead.

It was the look in her eyes, he decided, and the husky timbre of her voice when she forgot the higher whine. She gave the impression of a frail and fragile woman, yet when she had fallen against him at the ball he had felt an athletic and toned strength. The sort of strength that only came with exercise or hard work.

He was certain that the mishap had been deliberate and he tried to remember who else had been standing beside him. Lance Armitage and Jack's father John Derrick, older men with years of responsibility and solid morality behind them. Nay, it was him she had targeted and now he had asked her to Falder.

On cue?

No, that could not possibly be. He was seeing problems where none existed. The woman was scared of her own shadow, for God's sake, and unusually clumsy. She was also threadbare poor. A wilder thought surfaced. Was she after the Carisbrook fortune? A gold digger with a new and novel way of bagging her quarry? He remembered the countless women who had tried to snare him since Melanie's death.

Lord, he thought and lifted a candlestick from the mantelpiece before opening the door and striking out for the music room. Melanie's piano stood in a raft of moonlight, the black and white keys strangely juxtaposed between shadows. Leaning against the mahogany, he pressed a single note and it sounded out against the silence, a mellow echo of vibration lost in darkness.

Like he was lost, he thought suddenly, before dismissing the notion altogether. He was the head of the Carisbrook family and everybody depended on him. If he faltered…? No, he could not even think of the notion of faltering. Carefully he replaced the lid of the piano across the keys. Dust had collected upon the hinges and had bedded into the intricate inlaid walnut that spelled out his wife's initials.

Ash unto ash, dust unto dust.

Tomorrow he would inform his housekeeper to instruct the staff to clean the music room again. It had been too long since he had forbidden its use to anyone save himself. And his wife would have abhorred the fact that her prized piano had sat unplayed for all these years.

Still, he could not quite leave the room, an essence of something elusive on the very edges of his logic.

Something to do with Emma Seaton. Her turquoise eyes. The scar. The sound of laughter against the sea.

The sea?

Was he going mad? He crossed to the window. Outside the night was still. Dark. Cold. And the cloud that covered the moon made his leg ache, shattered bone healed badly into fragments.

Fragments.

They were all that was left of him sometimes, a shaky mosaic of loss and regret.

'God,' he whispered into the night. 'I am becoming as maudlin as my mother.' Blowing out the candle, he resolved to find some solace in his library. At least till the dawn when he could sleep.

Azziz returned to the house in Park Street just before midnight, and Emerald hoped that this time he had been careful to scour the neighbouring roads to make certain he was unobserved.

'I have heard word on the docks that McIlverray is on his way to London, Emmie.'

'Then he knows about the cane—why else would he come?' She frowned; this news put a whole different perspective on everything. Karl McIlverray, her father's first mate, was as corrupt as he was clever and had a band of loyal men who followed him blindly. Any intelligence circulating the docks of Kingston Town usually ended up in his ears and Karl McIlverray had been with her father long enough to put two and two together. He would know exactly what was inside the cane.

Damn, it was getting more and more complicated and she wished for the thousandth time that her father had kept the treasure in the vault of a bank or in a safe where it could have been more easily accessed.

Time. It was slipping away from her.

How long before he arrives?'

'A week or even ten days—the storms out in the Atlantic might slow them down, if we are lucky. I'll leave a man in place to make certain we see them before they see us.'

'And you?'

'Toro and I will come to Falder. We can camp somewhere close and keep an eye on things.'

Emerald was not certain as to the merits of the plan for they would be easily seen in the English countryside around the house. But if McIlverray came, she would need to be able to summon help, and quickly. She imagined the aristocratic Carisbrook family coming face to face with any of them and her heart pounded. And if someone innocent got hurt because of her…! She could not finish.

She had to be in and out of Falder quickly and on a boat back to Jamaica, making sure in the interim that Karl McIlverray had word of her movements. Another more worrying thought occurred to her.

'What if the cane is back here in London?'

Azziz frowned. 'It wasn't in the house a month ago when Toro and I searched it.'

'But he may have brought it with him this time. The limp still troubles him.'

'Have you seen him use a cane at all in public?'

'No.' She began to smile. 'And I do not think that he would. Each time I have been in his company he is careful that others may not notice the ailment. A cane would only draw their attention to what he seeks to hide.'

Privacy. Sanctuary. She sensed these things were important to the enigmatic Duke of Carisbrook and her spirits lifted.

'Miriam and I are due to leave for Falder soon and I can search the house easily under the cover of night.'

'The Duke of Carisbrook does not strike me as a man who could be easily fooled.'

'How does he strike you then?'

'Tough. Dangerous. Ruthless. A man who would have little time for lies.'

'Then I must be out of Falder before he knows them as such.'

'Do not underestimate him, Emmie.'

'You are beginning to sound like Miriam.' She smiled and laid her hand on his arm, her fingers tightening as she remembered all the other times in her life she had depended on Azziz. If she lost him too…? If anything went terribly wrong…? As she tried to banish fear she was consumed by sadness. When was the last time that she had taken a breath in joy and let all of it out again?

She could barely remember.

Her father's death, Miriam's agedness, and a debt that was increasing with each and every passing day. She could go neither backwards nor forwards and the options of anything else were fast shrinking. What happened to people who ran out of money in London? She shook her head in fright.

The poorhouse took them.

The place of liars and cheats.

A liar. It was who she had become. If she could

find the map, she could fashion a home. Not a grand one, but a for-ever place. A place to stay and grow and be. A place like St Clair. She closed her eyes against the pure thread of desperation that snaked itself around her heart, because she knew that the old house was gone, up in flames, the living embodiment of the McIlverray hatred for her father. And grounded perhaps on a sense of justice, for Beau had promised Karl McIlverray far more than he had ever delivered.

She let out her breath. Beau had promised everyone more than he had ever delivered and she needed to make it right.

Right?

If she hadn't been so worried, she might have smiled at the thought. Right? Wrong? Good? Bad? She remembered Beau's interpretation of law and doubted that Asher Wellingham's would be even remotely similar. Enormous wealth and righteous morals were easy when you were not staring down the barrel of a gun and saying what you thought the bearer would most like to hear.

Lies and deception.

It was all that she was left with as truth withered under the harsher face of reality.

Azziz pulled his blade from the leather sheath at his shin and wiped it with an oiled rag from his pocket. The movement caught her attention.

The sheer danger of it all was no longer as exhilarating as it had once been. Now, instead of seeing the adventure in everything she saw the pitfalls, and an encounter with McIlverray worried her a lot more than she allowed Azziz to see that it did.

Was she growing old?

Twenty-one…twenty-two in six months. Sometimes now she caught herself looking across at other women her age as they walked the streets with husbands and children at their side.

She tried to remember what her own mother had looked like, tried to remember the touch of her hand or the cadence of her voice and came up with nothing.

Nothing. The emptiness of memory caught at her with a surprising melancholy. To distract herself, she began to speak of the entertainment for the following night.

'There is a party at the Bishop of Kingseat's that I am indebted to attend. Lady Flora has been generous in her friendship…' She faltered.

'Will Carisbrook be there?'

'I think so.'

'Miriam said he seemed interested in you. If he should find out even a little—'

'I know,' she interrupted Azziz before he went further and was glad when he left the room for the kitchens on the ground floor to find his supper.

Chapter Four

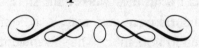

At a gathering at the home of the Bishop of King-seat the following evening, Asher again met Emma Seaton. The result, he suspected, of their encounter at Jack's ball and the host's wife's penchant for matchmaking. If he had liked the Learys less he might have left on some simple pretence, but George had been a good friend to his father and Flora was a woman of uncommon sensitivity.

Today, as Flora Leary turned to attend to a question another guest had asked of her, Emma Seaton looked rather nervous. Asher saw that the lace on the top of one of her gloves had been badly mended and that the gown she wore was at least a size too big. The colour was odd too. Off-brown and faded in patches. None of this seemed to faze her, though, and her confidence in a room full of well-dressed ladies was endearing. The bruise on her cheek was barely visible today.

'Lady Emma. You look well.'

'Thank you, your Grace.' Folding down the sleeve of her gown to cover the torn lace, she took a sip of the orgeat she was drinking. 'I was certain that Lady Flora had mentioned just a small gathering?'

He looked up. Only forty or fifty people milled around the salon.

'At Falder a little supper would constitute thrice this number,' he remarked and she coloured. But it was not embarrassment that he saw in her eyes when she met his glance, but irritation.

Sea blue.

Her eyes were turquoise and outlined with a clear sea blue. Here in the light it was easy to see today that which he had missed yesterday.

'My family was a quiet and modest one. My father was religious, you see. Very religious. And time spent in the company of others was time that he could not spend in prayer.'

'A devout man, then?'

She nodded and fiddled with the fan she held. 'With an equally devout family.'

'You are Catholic?'

'Pardon?'

'Catholic? The persuasion of your beliefs?'

'Oh, indeed.'

'And which church do you attend in London?'

The fan dropped out of her hands and onto the floor, surprising them both. As he leaned down to fetch it for her, she did the same and her bodice dipped in the middle.

She wore nothing beneath. No stays. No chemise. No bindings. Two beautifully formed breasts topped with rosy nipples fell into his sight and were gone again as she righted herself.

He felt his body jolt in a way he had not felt for years and shifted his position to better accommodate the hardening between his thighs. God, he was at the house of a bishop and the woman next to him was completely naked under her ill-fitting dress. He could barely believe it. Heat and lust made the cravat he wore feel tight and he was annoyed when Charlotte Withers, a woman whose company he had once enjoyed, came over to him.

'It has been an age, your Grace, since I have seen you in London. I had heard that you were here and I suppose on reflection you were down for Henshaws' ball. The evening before last, was it not, and all the gossip of how the Duke of Carisbrook was cajoled into falling for the wiles of a green and fainting country miss.'

'Not a faint, but a fall,' he returned and moved forward, pleased to see a blush mark Charlotte's cheeks when she saw who stood next to him.

'Lady Emma! I did not realise you were here and I apologise for any hurt you may have suffered from my careless remarks. Are you quite recovered from your mishap?'

'I am and I thank you for your concern.' Emma Seaton's reply contained no little amount of irony.

'Your accent eludes me,' Charlotte remarked as she recovered her equilibrium. 'Where exactly are you from?'

'My mother was French.'

Asher frowned. She had answered another question without telling anyone anything.

'So it is your father who is related to the Countess of Haversham?

'Was. He died last year from the influenza. A wicked case it was, too, according to the doctor; it took him a long time to succumb to the effects of the infection. One moment hot and the next cold. Why, I pray nightly to the Lord above that I should not see another soul die in such a way.'

'Yes. Quite.' Charlotte looked away to the riper pickings of Percy Davies who had come to her other side and Asher, while silently applauding Emma Seaton's skilful evasion, decided to up the stakes a little.

'Charlotte Withers is a notorious gossip and an inveterate meddler. If you were to entrust any secrets to her I am certain that they should be all over town by the morning.'

As the colour drained out of Emerald's cheeks, the smile he gave her was guarded.

Could he be warning her? For just a second she wanted to fold her fingers around his and pretend that

he offered protection. Here. In London, where each
battle was carried out with words and sly innuendos.
Where the people said one thing and meant another.
She didn't understand them. That was the trouble.
She had come to England woefully unprepared and
desperately different. It showed in her accent, in her
clothes, in the way she walked and moved and sat.

Pity.

She had seen it written all over his handsome face
as his glance had brushed over the torn lace on her
glove and the generous fitting of her gown. Pity for
a woman who, when compared with the other refined
beauties, personified by the likes of Lady Charlotte,
fared very badly. Gathering her scattered wits, she
tried to regroup.

'Secrets?'

'My sources say you arrived in England not from
the country, but from Jamaica?'

She laughed, congratulating herself on the inconsequential and tinkling sound. 'And they would be
right. I came back to England after sorting out my
father's possessions when he died, and setting his affairs into order.'

'Your father was a scholar?'

A scholar? Oh God, what was he referring to now?
And just who were his sources? She was pleased
when Lord Henshaw caught her attention.

'Lady Emma. Are you feeling better?'

'Yes. Very much better, thank you.' Such a polite

society, Emerald thought, as she gave him her answer. Such a lot unsaid beneath every question. She pulled her fingers away and laid her hands against the voluminous skirt of her gown.

'Did you hear of Stephen Eaton's problem the other night, Asher? He met with footpads by the dockside and has a wicked lump on his head. The local constabulary are out in force to try to find the culprits. Word is that it's a shocking state of affairs when a gentleman cannot even ride around London without being robbed and beaten.'

'He is saying he was robbed?'

'Yes, though I cannot work out for the life of me what he was doing at that time and in that part of London, given he had left my ball only an hour or so earlier. His watch and pistol were taken and a ring he wore upon his hand that was a family heirloom. Diamonds, I think. He plans to spend the next few months abroad to recover from the assault, his mother says. I saw her this morning.'

'A fine scheme. I hope he takes his time to make a full recuperation. If you see his parents, do acquaint them with my sentiments, and say that I was asking after him.' Pure steel coated his words.

'I will do just that. Does your sister know of his mishap?'

'My sister?'

'Lucinda. She has danced with him at several parties and I thought perhaps there was a special friendship…'

Jack's voice tailed off. Emerald was certain that he had just put it all together and also deduced that this was neither the time nor the place to discuss such things. She saw him chance a quick look at Charlotte Withers behind him before he changed the subject entirely.

'My oldest sister was hoping to visit Annabelle Graveson next month, Asher. How is she keeping.'

'Very well.' His tone was amused as he finished off his drink. 'You will meet the Gravesons this weekend at Falder, Lady Emma.'

'Are they relatives, your Grace?'

'No. Annabelle Graveson was married to my father's friend. When he died, he asked me to watch over the affairs of his wife and son.'

Jack Henshaw joined in the conversation. 'The old Duke was a philanthropist and Asher has inherited his own bevy of needy folk.'

Asher said nothing, but Emerald could tell that he was not happy at his friend's summation of duty. Interesting, she thought, for a man who professed to caring for little as he held the world at bay.

Looking around, she noticed an attractive dark-haired woman whose eyes were fastened on the Duke of Carisbrook, but if he felt her regard he gave no indication of it as he leant towards her as if to shelter his words from the others around them.

'Eaton is using the ploy of a robbery to ease his guilt, I would suspect. Though there is another explanation. How honest is your cousin?'

'As honest as I am, for the ten commandments were the bread and butter of our childhood.' She felt the distinct turn of guilt in her stomach.

'You never lie?'

'My father taught us the importance of truth and honesty.'

She forced back conscience and stiffened when he reached for the locket dangling on a long chain about her neck.

'Is this some family crest?'

'My mother's,' she replied softly and deposited the golden trinket down again between her breasts, glad when he did not pursue the topic.

'Who was French?'

She looked at him blankly. 'Pardon.'

'You said that your mother was from France.' He was so close she could have reached out a finger to run along the hard cut of his jaw.

'I did? Yes, of course I did. Because she was.' Lord, this lying was eating at her composure and she felt sweat in the palms of her hands.

'*Êtes-vous originaire du sud ou bien du nord de la France?*'

What was it he had said? Something of north and south. This much she had translated, though the other was lost to her.

'*Oui.*' She chanced one of the ten or so French words she actually knew and was disconcerted by the amusement scrawled on his face.

'And honesty was as important to your mother as it is to you?'

'Yes, your Grace.'

'Admirable,' he returned and as his eyes glanced across the loose material of her gown she felt the skin on her nipples pucker and folded her arms. She should have worn her underclothing, but it felt so much better without it.

'It is seldom one meets a woman of such high moral fibre.'

The blood rushed into her face. 'I will take that as a compliment, your Grace,' she said simply.

His laughter brought the conversation around them to a noticeable quietening and as she looked up the hostess, Lady Flora, caught her eye and smiled broadly. Emerald observed that the green-eyed beauty standing next to their host didn't look anywhere near as friendly as she posed a question.

'I hear that your newest ship is ready for a launch here in London, your Grace. What is it to be called?'

'The *Melanie*.'

An inexplicable tension filled the room.

Who was Melanie, she wondered, and what was she to Asher Wellingham? Someone important, no doubt. Someone he loved?

But where was she now?

The Bishop of Kingseat raised his glass.

'To the *Melanie*, then. May she ride the waves long and true and be as beautiful as her namesake.'

There it was again. Her namesake? Interest flared as Asher acknowledged the toast and drank and Emerald was struck by the difference five years had made in the lines of his face.

Hardness and distance.

For some reason the thought made her unfathomably sad and when the topic turned to dancing she was pleased, for it gave her time to compose herself.

Half an hour Emerald stood alone near a pillar that led off to a balcony. Asher Wellingham was across the other side of the room with the beautiful green-eyed woman draped across his arm. From this distance the darkness of her carefully coiffed hair was exactly the same shade as his. The memory of her own hair was sharp and she raised her hand to pat down the short errant curls.

Two ladies behind her were talking about the Duke and she turned so that she could overhear them more easily.

'If only he would look our way, Claire. Just once. Would it be considered rude, do you think, to raise one's glass and smile at him?'

The other girl began to laugh. 'Oh, you would never do that, surely. Imagine what he might think of us.'

'It is rumoured that he will go to India next month. Let us hope that he does not meet the ghost of the pirate Beau Sandford on his travels.'

A loud squawk of titillation brought the Duke's glance their way, and Emerald tensed. Hearing the name of her father here disorientated her because it was so very unexpected. Her heartbeat accelerated when she saw the subject of the girl's conversation start towards her.

'Lady Emma? Would you walk with me for a moment?'

'Walk with you?' Her astonishment was such that she forgot to use her carefully perfected girly voice.

'There is a balcony just here overlooking a garden. I thought it a good place to talk and I have something for you.'

More of an order than a request. She ignored the arm he held out and hoped that he had not seen the imprinted adulation on the faces of the young women around her. His arrogance was already legendary enough.

The balcony was open at one end and she welcomed the quietness of it. A group of other people stood near the French doors that led in from the main room; pausing by the railing she waited for him to speak.

'Lucy gave me something to give to you and I had my man return home for the letter when I saw that you were here tonight.' He dragged a sealed envelope out of his pocket. 'It is for your cousin, Liam Kingston. A letter of thanks, I should imagine but Lucinda is young and impressionable, so if the correspondence seems exaggerated in places—' He stopped as she held out her hand and his fingers inadvertently touched her own. She shivered. Even here in the most public of places and with the simplest of contacts she was vulnerable. Hoping that her face did not hold the same expression as the vacuous women inside, she tucked the letter unread into her reticule.

'If Mr Kingston could find it in him to send a reply and state his circumstances, I would be grateful. Seventeen-year-old girls have a propensity for imagination, you understand, and I would like the matter resolved.'

There it was again. Responsibility and control. Important to a man like Asher Wellingham and something he rarely let go of.

What would happen if he did let go of it? a small voice questioned. As the blood hammered in her temples she turned away to give herself a moment to recover and his next words came through a haze.

'Would it be possible for you to give me his direction? When I am next in his part of the world I could call in on him and give my thanks.'

Lord!

What address could she tell him? She knew no one in the Americas. A happier thought surfaced. Perhaps Azziz had contacts...

'I will write it down for you and have it delivered.'

He shook his head. 'You will be in Falder in two days. I can wait until then.'

The strain of the supper waltz rent the air.

'How is it that I know you, Lady Emma? Have we met before?'

'Are you familiar with Cheshire, your Grace?' She was relieved when he smiled at her question and shook his head.

'No, but I do not think the memory of you lingers from England somehow...'

Desperate to take his mind from recollection, she locked her hand on his and asked him to dance, completely ignoring the look of astonishment on his face.

His body melded against her own and found the rhythm of the music with much more finesse than she did. Leaning into him for just a moment she closed her eyes.

Wishing.

Wishing that she was a well-born lady and that he might like her just a little. Wishing that things could have been different between them and that all he believed of her was true.

Asher felt her relax against him and pulled her closer. He had not asked anyone to dance with him since Melanie.

In truth, he had not asked Emma Seaton to dance with him either and yet here she was, the warm whisper of her breath tantalising in the folds of his neck. Close. Unexpected. Had she not listened to gossip?

A quick glance at the interest on the faces of others made him wary and he pulled back, the distance between them wider now.

'You are new to town, Lady Emma. If you want your reputation to stay intact, it might be as well to avoid me as your supper partner.'

'And why would that be, your Grace? The girls who stood behind me inside would have liked an introduction and they looked innocuous enough.'

He began to laugh. 'Where were you schooled?'

She was taken aback. 'In a convent. Why?'

'Because your vocabulary is…surprising.' Emerald sensed a new emotion in him that was difficult to interpret. 'Have you had any offers yet?'

'Offers?'

'Of marriage. Isn't that why you have come to London?'

The blood drained out of her face.

'You did not know this to be the Season? The time for men to choose from the year's débutantes.'

'Men like you?' she countered and tried to sound indifferent.

'If you had been listening to the gossip, you would know that the state of holy matrimony is something that I have become adept at avoiding.'

'Oh. I see.' The uneasy sensation of being played for a fool suddenly overcame her. 'Then you will be pleased to know that I am not on the look out for a husband either, your Grace.'

'Really.' His brows raised. 'What are you here for then, Lady Emma?'

Two things hit Emerald simultaneously. The lazy devastation of his smile and the husky timbre of his voice. Her spine tingled with an odd and lonely pain as she remembered a younger Asher Wellingham standing on the transom of his ship, eyes blazing under the emotion of a high-seas' battle and releasing her from the sharp tip of his sword only when he determined her not to be the lad he thought she was, but a girl. And now here in the ballroom of a beautiful English house she understood what she had only half-known then.

The Duke of Carisbrook was an honourable man and one who respected the codes of England's aristocracy. Gentlemen did not hurt women. Even ones who could wield a weapon with as much finesse as any man aboard the *Mariposa*.

'I am here to see to the welfare of my aunt. She is old and lonely and I am the very last of her family.'

'And very deaf?'

'Pardon?'

'Deaf. Hard of hearing. A woman who would sleep through the night no matter what might happen in her house.' A glint in his eyes softened the insult. 'Your cousin, Liam Kingston, for instance, keeps hours that a poor sleeper might find tiring.'

Despite everything she laughed. 'And for your sister's sake it is just as well that he does.'

'Indeed,' he returned. 'A lucky coincidence that.

What was your cousin doing following the Caris-brook coach in the first place?'

'Pardon?'

'My driver noticed a carriage dogging his heels through the city streets. On memory he would say it to be a hired hack and I know that your aunt does not keep a conveyance.'

She was silent. Lord, he had worked it all out with little more than a passing clue.

'Perhaps he was mistaken. Liam has only recently come to London and I can think of no reason for him to be following your sister.'

'Can you not? Then perhaps it was me he wanted.'

'And what would my cousin want with you?'

'That's the same question I have been asking myself these past few days.' His voice was laconic.

'And did you find an answer, your Grace?'

'I did not, Lady Emma.'

Leaning back, the lights glinted off his timepiece and threw refracted rainbows across the floor at his feet. Danger and stealth. And manners. Was there ever a combination quite so appealing?

'My cousin is a wealthy and respectable married man.'

'So you say.'

'Who makes his money from cotton,' she continued, not liking the disbelief she could so plainly hear in his voice. 'He would have no need for blackmail, if that is what you are suggesting.'

'I suggested nothing.'

'Or kidnapping,' she continued and then bit down on her lip. Lord, she was being drawn into showing her cards by a master. The thought had her temper rising. Dredging up every skill she had ever shown in acting, she plastered a smile on her face.

'Why, your Grace, it is really too bad of you to jest me, for surely that is what all this is.'

'Assuredly,' he returned, bowing as the music stopped, implacable politeness replacing the humour. 'Although sometimes I greatly doubt that you are quite as vapid as you make out to be.'

Emerald's heartbeat faltered at the tone and without even trying she could see the lonely mantle of distance that lay between him and everyone, keeping them back and away.

Cross this line and be damned.

The missing fingers and his limp underplayed the jeopardy, but she could not afford to let her guard down.

Supper had been set up on a long table to one end of the salon, and Asher led her over to join the Learys and Jack Henshaw and Charlotte Withers at one of the smaller tables around it. After finding them each a plate of food, he sat down beside her and the topic turned to music.

'Do you have a speciality, Lady Emma? An instrument that you play.' Flora Leary's eyes were full of interest.

'No. I am afraid not.' She did not imagine that the harmonica was the sort of instrument the Bishop's wife would be thinking about.

'Can you sing?'

'No.' God forbid that she should have to stand in front of this crowd and croon a bawdy number learnt at the knees of sailors who had never so much as graced a salon even a quarter as reputable as this one. 'My father was a man who believed music to be a facet of the Devil's mind. A religious man, you understand, of strong beliefs and an utter conviction in the rightness of them.'

'Not an easy man to live with, then.' Asher joined in the conversation and an undercurrent threaded his words. 'What is it that you are well versed in?'

Emerald struggled to think up accomplishments that would be acceptable to this company. 'I am a proficient rider and excellent in the preparation of meals.'

The heavy silence around the table lengthened as she realised the extent of her mistake.

'Surely you mean the planning of menus, Lady Emma? A most salutatory undertaking. Why, I remember my mother enjoyed the art of putting together meat and wine. It quite took up much of her time before a grand meal. Was it that sort of thing you meant, my dear?' The kind and gracious Lady Flora gave her an easy way out and she gladly took it.

'Yes. Just exactly that.'

Lady Charlotte leaned forward and laid her fingers along the line of Asher Wellingham's arm. 'Your brother Taris was always a connoisseur of fine wines, your Grace. How is he? Has his sight improved?'

'Markedly.'

'Well, that is the most pleasing news I have heard in a while. Tell him I was asking after him, and if he is down in London in the near future…'

'I will.'

Emerald felt that something was not quite as it should be. She knew that Taris was Asher's brother, for Miriam had given her a vague outline of his immediate family. But the fact that he had some problem with his sight had not been mentioned at all and the mask that shuttered any trace of emotion on the Duke of Carisbrook's face was intriguing.

A brother with a sight problem and a woman named Melanie who, apart from being beautiful, was also absent from his life. He had many secrets and held every emotion beneath a rigid self-control.

Discipline and governance had etched a hard line between his eyes, puncturing a face of pure masculine beauty into something less easy—whenever she was near him she felt a pull of sadness, the world stretched out of shape. Even here in the bland world of London society he did not relax as the others did, but looked around.

A constant check on safety.

She was certain that if someone had come up unexpectedly behind him he would have used the small knife hidden in the folds of his jacket. And used it well. She smiled. It was intriguing, this mix of mannerisms. The crest of ducal importance counterpoised by a dangerous fighting ability.

She had seen it, after all, and knew what he was capable of. Knew too that these people who fawned over his title and wealth had absolutely no idea: the wash of blood and guts across the deck on the high seas and the wailing agony of hurt.

Her life.

His life for a time.

For the time it had taken her to extinguish honour and send him hurtling downwards into the boiling anger of the ocean.

Asher instructed his driver to go fast through the dark London streets and, opening a window, enjoyed the breeze on his face and the sky above his head. Dotted with stars tonight, he mused. A small respite in a month of rain. His brother would be pleased, for watching the heavens through the telescope he had had shipped over especially from China was a passion he could still enjoy. He grimaced. But for how long?

Taris's sight was worse. He admitted it to himself and cursed Charlotte Withers for asking. Emma Seaton would be at Falder the day after tomorrow and he did not want her to know the extent of the problem.

He wanted no one to know.

He wanted to keep the world away from his brother until he could fashion a solution. Until he knew for certain what it was they were facing. Total loss of sight? Partial vision?

If only Taris had not come out to the Caribbean to find him after the ransom note had been sent. If only he had stayed here in England and left the danger of rescue to others. No, he could not think like that. Taris had come and he had been saved. The high price of his brother's sacrifice paid ever since with his own crippling guilt over his brother's blindness.

'God, help me,' he whispered to a deity that to-night felt close, though the vision of Emma Seaton's lack of underclothing juxtaposed strangely against his request, and for a second amusement filled the more familiar void of loneliness.

Her soft skin on her right breast had been marked with an indigo tattoo. A butterfly. Tiny. Delicate. Unexpected.

Curiosity welled. An emotion he had not felt in years. It was a relief to laugh. Even to himself out here in the night.

Emma Seaton.

Her hair was curly when it was loosened from the pins that tightly bound it. Stray tendrils had worked themselves free at her nape and the ringlets that hung only to her collar were tightly coiled. Red-blonde hair and turquoise eyes. And a body well endowed with the curves of womanhood.

He shook his head and rubbed at the stiff muscles on the back of his neck. He had enjoyed tonight. Enjoyed her humour and her candidness. Enjoyed the view of sun-warmed skin that lay beneath her loose bodice and the feel of her in his arms as they had danced.

What would she look like in silks and satins and with her hair dressed by the best of London's hair salons?

He swore roundly. He had seldom kept a mistress in the way other men of the *ton* did. Oh, granted he had occasionally used the services of select women who could be relied on for their discretion, yet tonight, with the dull ache of sexual frustration seeping through his bones, he wanted more.

The image of two rosy-tipped breasts came to mind as the bells of Westminster rang out the hour of one across the slumbering city, and he smiled into the darkness as his horses slowed at the corner between Pall Mall and St James's Square.

Opening Lucy's letter on her return home, Emerald found the missive to be full of the adolescent adulation Asher Wellingham had spoken of. After memorising the note for future reference and consigning it to the fire, she walked across to the window to watch the sky.

Tonight the heavens were clear, a half-formed moon low in the eastern horizon and climbing. It would rain tomorrow, she suspected, for a cloud of mist encircled the glowing crescent and the air had a tang of moisture in it.

She wondered where the Duke of Carisbrook was now. Entwined in the arms of the green-eyed woman, she guessed, and wondered why she found the thought so irritating.

Asher Wellingham was nothing to her.

She would be in and out of Falder in a matter of days, hours even, if her searching went to plan. And then she would be gone. Away from here. Away from him.

Her mind wandered to the feel of his arms around her waist as they had danced tonight, the soft music between them. She had leant her head against the superfine of his jacket and breathed in.

'Lord,' she said aloud and swore roundly. Is this what England was making her? Soft? Needy? Dependent?

She was her father's daughter with years of fighting imbued in her blood and drawn upon her skin. Her finger went to the mark that intersected her right eyebrow and travelled beneath her fringe into her scalp. Black Jack Porrit and his men off the coast of Barranquilla in the winter of 1819. She would never fit in here and before the first whisper of her parentage surfaced in London town she would need to be gone.

With resolve she stripped off the gown and arranged her blankets beside the window overlooking the street.

Across the city the bells peeled in the night. Two o'clock. Burrowing down, she whispered the name of her sister into the darkness.

'Soon, Ruby. I will be home soon. I promise.'

Chapter Five

Miriam and Emerald arrived at Falder just as a rain shower departed and the sun tinged the clouds off the wild coast of Fleetness Point.

Falder.

To Emerald it was the most beautiful land she had ever seen, soft green hills with glades of trees colouring the lay of the fields. Everything about it was appealing. The isolation. The strength. The way the valleys dipped to a sea that was cold and free and deep. She could smell the sharp taste of salt on the wind and hear the lonely voices of the gulls.

Home. Home. Home.

Falder beckoned to her in a doleful wailing chant. Breathing in, she caught her reflection in the window of the coach and screwed up her nose. Would she ever get used to the shortness of her hair?

'If the master of Falder discovers any more about

us we will be tossed out in a minute.' Miriam fidgeted with the thin silk strap of the little reticule she carried. 'And if you think to dress in your lad's clothes and scour the house at night, I should warn you of the dangers in it.'

Taking a deep breath, Emerald rubbed her palms against the rough wool of her cape. 'Would you rather I took a knife to his throat, Aunt?' Today, in the light of what she had to pretend, she could not find it in herself to be kind.

'You would kill him?'

'No, of course not,' she answered back and swallowed down chagrin. Lord, did Miriam truly think that she was capable of slitting the jugular of an unarmed man?

'Beau made some stupid mistakes, Emerald. And I would say his biggest one was not dispatching you to England the moment your mother left.'

'I think sometimes you are too hard on my father—' she began, but Miriam would have none of it.

'You were six and he was away as often as he was not.'

'I had Azziz and St Clair.'

'Pah! That huge house and a boy who barely spoke the English language. You think that was a suitable home?'

'It was my home.' How often before had they had this very same conversation?

'Your home? With a bevy of Beau's good-time girls and barely a night without some drunken orgy?'

'He missed my mother.'

'Missed her money more like.'

Emerald frowned. This was a tangent she had not heard before. 'Money. My mother had money?'

Miriam paled. 'I promised my brother that I would never talk of that time. He wanted you to be free of the restraints and vagaries of society and I promised him my silence.' Shifting in her seat, she crossed herself and Emerald saw the glimpse of a tear. 'He was a man who demanded too much sometimes. Even of me.'

'I do not even have a name to remember her by, Miriam. Can you not give me just that?'

'Evangeline.'

When the dark eyes of her aunt met her own she felt a heady dizzy sense of shock.

'Evangeline.' She whispered it, turning the word on her tongue. Savouring it. At last a name. 'Like an angel?'

Miriam's deep frown was not quite what she had expected. 'Your mother found life away from England difficult, and my brother would not have been the easiest of husbands. But he was your father and my brother and one should never speak ill of the dead, God bless them all.'

As the silence lengthened Emerald knew that she would hear no more.

* * *

Falder was a revelation. An uninhibited and magnificent hotchpotch of architectural styles, it sat above a river on a hillock completely surrounded by grassland. Part-Scottish baronial, part-Gothic and part-English manor, its many turrets and gables dominated the landscape around it and proclaimed not only great wealth, but a long lineage of generations of Carisbrooks who had all added their mark to it.

As the carriage clattered in across a pebbled drive, she looked up and hoped that there were not too many other guests here this weekend, for she was beginning to feel that she could not brave another round of social niceties.

A bevy of servants were at the front entrance to meet them, their faces stiff with the rigours of servitude; she refrained from meeting their glances, reasoning that such folk might be better at recognising a faux lady should they come across one. The thought made her frown. Circumstance had robbed her of being gently reared, but her birth was hardly dubious. Beau had been a lord before he had become a pirate and the title of Lady was hers to rightly use. She took the arm of her aunt and started up the staircase.

Asher Wellingham was waiting in a small blue salon directly off the portico. Beside him another tall man stood.

'Was your journey here pleasant?' The Duke asked the question in a voice that was measured.

'Thank you, yes, it was.' Emerald helped Miriam to a chair on one side of the fireplace and arranged a woollen blanket across her lap. Her aunt looked pale and tired and old, a woman whose secrets had leached the lifeblood from her soul. Her father's sister, her only relative left save for Ruby. In the unfamiliarity of Falder she was suddenly dear. Standing, she draped one arm protectively across Miriam's frail shoulders as Asher Wellingham apologized for his mother's absence— she was indisposed—and introduced his brother.

Taris Wellingham wore thick glasses and stood with his hand against the end of a large armoire. The identical sense of danger that cloaked his brother cloaked him and he had exactly the same shade of hair: midnight black. She waited for him to give his greeting, but he did not.

'Taris had an accident off the coast of the Caribbean. You may need to come closer.' The Duke's sentence was offered so flatly that Emerald's mouth widened at the rudeness.

'I am sorry—' she stammered loudly and was cut off.

'My brother is not deaf.' A sense of challenge filled the room, unspoken and sharp. Miriam pushed back in her chair, but Emerald took two steps forward and waited as opaque eyes ran across her. She had a feeling he saw more than she wanted him to.

'Your voice holds the accent of a place very far from here, Lady Emma?'

She stayed silent, loath to lie to a man who had been so badly hurt, the scar across his forehead dissecting his left eye and running down the line of his cheek. The mark of a bullet! No small accident this one. Could he have been another casualty of her father's? The thought worried her unduly and she was relieved when a maid offered them a drink.

Miriam preferred lemonade, but Emerald chose white wine; taking a sip to calm her nerves, she made herself stand straighter, caring little for her added height.

'Asher tells us that your cousin Liam saved our sister from ruination.' The line of Taris's eyes did not quite meet her own.

'Well, I would hardly say ruination.'

'Would you not?' Asher Wellingham's question was underlaid with anger. 'Your cousin is a hero, albeit a reluctant one. What ship did you say he took to the Americas?'

'The *Cristobel*,' she returned without pause, glad that she had taken the time before coming up to Falder to check the shipping schedules, though as she gave the name another thought surfaced. What if he checked the passenger list and found no mention of Liam Kingston and his family? Or worse—what if he discovered that she had been into the shipping office making enquiry as to the departures?

Complicity and subterfuge.

She had a feeling that the Duke of Carisbrook would take badly to them both and she was being increasingly drawn into a web of deceit.

A sennight, she mused. Seven days to find the map and leave. If she were quick, everything would be feasible, but if she were not...?

'Your house is beautiful,' she said as her eyes scoured this room and the next one for any sign of what she was after. 'How many rooms does it have?'

'One hundred and twenty-seven,' Lucinda supplied the information. 'We have two libraries and a ballroom and Asher has just had a new fencing room added to the eastern wing that was built three years ago.'

Filing away the information, Emerald thought she should perhaps start looking over the new wing, although the salons radiating out from this room looked promising. She would start here tonight and then plan a general widening of her search as a grid, so that no room would be forgotten.

Two hours later she was ensconced in a bedchamber overlooking the front drive of the house. Miriam was in the room next to her and had used a headache as an excuse to take herself to bed. Emerald hoped that she was not sickening with a cold, or worse; wandering over to wide doors curtained with billowing yards of soft fabric, she opened the latch. Sun-

light streamed in unbroken across a balcony draped
in ivy. Walking outside, she was perfectly still. The
sound of long beaching waves rolling in from the
northern seas could be heard and, if she stood on her
tiptoes, there in the distance, between the crease of
two green hillocks, she saw the ocean, dancing and
sparkling in the sun. The ocean. Her ocean, the warm
blue of the Caribbean mixed with the wilder grey of
Fleetness Point.

A noise had her looking down as Asher Wellingham rounded the corner on a large horse. Moving
back into the room, she watched him until he was out
of sight, the fluid muscle of his racing stallion reflected in the surface of the lake as he passed it, a dark
shadow against a darker line of the trees.

He was a man who did not seem to fit into the
strict regimens of London's manners or its rules, a
duke who seemed more dangerous than he had any
right to be, and more menacing. She smiled. Now
there was a word that described Asher Wellingham
exactly.

Menacing.

And she would need to be very, very careful.

He was dressed in black at dinner and his hair was
wet. The length of it was intriguing. Too short to be
easily tied into a queue, but far longer than most other
men of the *ton* wore theirs.

As they filed in to the dining room, Emerald

found herself seated to Asher's left, his sister acting as hostess, in his mother's continued absence,
at the foot of the table with Taris to her left. An older
couple made up the numbers, near neighbours invited for the evening, for Miriam had decided not
to come down and had asked to have a tray delivered to her.

'Is your room satisfactory, Lady Emma?' Lucy
asked as the steaming plates of food were brought to
the table. Beef, pork and chicken. When her stomach rumbled she pushed down on it hard and hoped
that nobody had heard.

'It's very beautiful and I can see the ocean from
the balcony,' she added, frowning as Asher looked up
sharply. Tonight he looked tired. She saw that he was
drinking heavily, saw too the gesture Lucy made to
the servant behind to bring her brother a carafe of
water. He didn't touch it.

'Emma hails from Jamaica,' he said as the silence
grew.

The man named William Bennett nodded. 'I was
there once, a long time ago. Did you know a family
by the name of de la Varis?'

'No, I don't believe so. My father was an invalid,
so we were quite insular.' For a second she wondered
how it would be best to keep track of all the lies and
decided that later she would write out her fabrica-
tions in a diary. Relaxing into the role, she picked up
her confidence and continued. 'My aunt and uncle

lived close by and I had Liam, of course. My cousin,' she qualified as the man looked puzzled.

'And your own mother?'

'Oh, she was a beautiful woman. Evangeline.' Emerald enunciated the newness of the name lovingly and just the saying of it conjured up a golden-haired beauty to stand alongside her sick but handsome father. She smiled. She had always filled her world with dream people. When her mother had gone. When her father had returned with yet another woman whom he insisted she call mama.

Dreams had saved them all and made them whole and good and true. It was not so hard here to imagine cousins or a beautiful mother who had not deserted her.

'Liam is about your age, then?' Lucy's query was strongly voiced. Of all the Carisbrooks she was the most inquisitive.

'No, he is a little older,' she replied evasively, trying to remember the exact number of offspring she had invented for her fictitious cousin. Would 'a little older' render such children possible? Had she said four?

'And did he like to read, Lady Emma?' Lucy continued.

'Like to read?' Danger spiralled.

'I think my sister is referring to the books in your aunt's drawing room.' When Lucy smiled and nodded, interest sharpened in his eyes. 'Miriam does not strike me as a scholar of Arabic philosophy.'

'And you think that I would be?' She forced a laugh and was rewarded with a *frisson* of uncertainty. 'Indeed, your Grace, the books were my father's.'

'Ahh, yes of course. The devout and invalided scholar?'

Emerald wondered at the edge of disbelief she could plainly hear and was relieved when Lucinda again garnered her attention.

'I should like to sketch you while you are here, if I may, Lady Emma.'

Emerald looked up sharply. Was she jesting? Dangerous ground this. She didn't know quite how to answer. How easy would it be for Lucy to fathom the memory of Liam Kingston in her face? 'Are there many of your works here at Falder?'

'That one is mine.' Her hand pointed to a large watercolour above the fireplace depicting the castle and Emerald caught her breath.

'You have a considerable talent. Do you sell them?'

'No, but I gave Jack Henshaw one once as a gift and Saul Beauchamp. Asher's friends,' she clarified as Emerald looked puzzled. 'I have not mustered up the courage to show them further, but if you would like a look at some other portraits I have done I would be more than pleased to show you.'

Portraits? Of her brother, perhaps? Emerald felt a rising interest until she saw the dark anger that coated Asher Wellingham's eyes.

She was pleased when the servants began to clear away the plates and the women were able to repair to the smaller salon.

Taris sat against the window and placed his hand on the cold hard surface of the glass. From where he stood, Asher could see the outline of mist that surrounded his print. He wondered just how much of it Taris could also see. Today he had tripped over a stool in the study. A year ago he would have walked straight around it.

'Emma Seaton is not as she seems.'

Asher stiffened and waited for clarification.

'No, she is stronger than she pretends to be. Much stronger.' He paused for a moment before continuing. 'Describe her for me, Asher. What does she look like?'

'Her eyes are the colour of the sea, she has the shortest hair I have ever seen on a woman and she never removes her gloves.'

'Why not?'

'God knows why, for I certainly don't.'

Taris began to smile. 'And her face?'

'You could see nothing of her?'

'I could hear that she is beautiful.'

'That she is.'

Taris's sudden laughter unnerved him. 'And when was the last time you thought a woman beautiful?'

As Asher walked away from a discussion he did not want, he fingered the sapphire ring he wore on his little finger and cursed his brother.

Chapter Six

Emerald dressed in black trousers and a jacket, stuffing a candle and tinder box into its deep pockets. It was already after three and the last sounds of people moving had been well over an hour ago.

She had memorised the layout of the rooms that she had been in, but was glad for a full moon. The light slanted against her as the curtain opened and she stepped out on to the balcony.

Night time.

She had always loved the darkness, even as a child, and here the sounds of the countryside after the stuffiness of London were welcomed. Shimmying down the ivy that hung from the latticed balcony, she crept around the edges of the lawn, careful to walk where the vegetation overlaid the grass so her footprints would not show. At the wide door that accessed the library from the garden she paused and drew out a piece of wire. Slotting it into the lock, she was glad to hear the mechanism turn and the portal spring open.

One minute at most.

Letting herself into the room, she stood against the velvet curtain and waited until her eyes had become accustomed to the darkness before lighting the candle.

Bookcase upon bookcase greeted her, the leather-bound copies of a thousand volumes lending the musky scent of learning to the air. Her fingers ran across the embossed titles closest to her: Milton, Shakespeare, Webster, Donne and Johnson. A library that embraced great authors and their ideas. She wondered which of the Carisbrooks was the reader and guessed it to be Asher, the thought making her smile.

A low shelf to one side of the room caught her attention. Rolls of paper were stacked against a cupboard and behind them there was an alcove containing other things. Umbrellas, parasols and walking sticks.

Her heart began to hammer. Could it be this easy? She held her breath as she sorted through the objects. A stick of ebony, another of some fragrant wood and a third handmade, using the shiny limbs of birch. Her father's cane with the map inside it was not among them. Neither was it in the next room nor the next one.

Some time later she knew that she would be pressing her luck to keep searching. Already she had heard the stirrings of the servants in the kitchens and knew very soon other maids would come to set the fires or draw the curtains. Creeping out of the room she was in, she found herself in a smaller salon with a row of windows gracing one wall—it was then that she saw it.

The first light of pale dawn slanted across a portrait. A portrait of the Duke of Carisbrook and a woman. Her Grace, Melanie, the Duchess of Carisbrook, the title written beneath it said, and she was beautiful.

Melanie. As in the ship that was ready to launch in London? Asher's wife? A red-haired beauty with eyes the colour of midnight. Emerald could not keep from studying the face.

What had happened to her? Where was she? The date on the painting was from ten years ago and she would have been merely the age that Emerald was now. Who could she ask? Lucinda, perhaps. Quietly, of course. She ran her fingers across the thick swirl of paint that made up a brocade skirt and looked again at the painting. Asher Wellingham's hair was short and he was young. As young as his wife and in love. She could see it in the light of his eyes and in the way his hand curled around hers, holding them together in an eternal embrace.

And the ring that Melanie Wellingham sported on her marriage finger was the same ring that Asher Wellingham now wore on his little finger.

An unexpected noise to one end of the room had her turning and she left the house with only the slightest of whispers.

Asher stood against the door to the small salon and watched Emma Seaton blow out her candle and slide through the opened window with all the expertise and finesse of a consummate thief. Hardly a noise, barely a footprint. He had thought her an intruder at first until the light from the flame had thrown her high cheekbones into relief.

What the hell was she doing here? He walked across to stand where she had just been, in front of the picture above the mantel, and his heart wrenched with sadness.

The wedding portrait painted just after they had returned from their honeymoon in Scotland. God. It had been so many years ago now he could barely recognise the man he was then. Cursing, he turned away and went to the window, watching as a shadow, black against the pearly dawn, flitted around the edge of the house leaving no trace of its presence. No sign of what he could not believe that he had seen.

Who was she?

A thief? A robber? Something more sinister?

Another wilder thought surfaced. What had Lucinda said of Liam Kingston? Tall. Accented. Thin. *Emma Seaton.*

Hell! There was no Liam Kingston. It had always

been her. The Countess of Haversham had certainly appeared bemused by Emma's insistence on a cousin. And now he knew why.

He almost laughed at the ruse and would have marched to her room then and there and confronted her had not another thought stopped him.

She had saved his sister.

She had risked her own life for the well-being of a stranger. The bruise on her cheek. Her embarrassment. Her ridiculous story as to how it had happened.

She had saved Lucinda from certain damnation and ruination and she had demanded nothing in return.

Why?

He would find out.

But first he had to determine whether Lady Emma Seaton posed a danger to his family. Starting from today.

The Duke of Carisbrook was still at the table when Emerald went down to breakfast later that morning. Folding his paper, he waited as she gave the hovering servant her preference of beverage.

'I trust you slept well last night.'

She smiled at his query and helped herself to a slice of toast from the rack in the centre of the table. 'Oh, indeed I did, your Grace. It must be the country air.' She yawned widely.

'And your bed was comfortable?'

'Very.'

'You were not disturbed by any noises in the night?'

She gave him a sideways look to determine where this line of questioning might be leading. 'No, I certainly was not. Why, as soon as my head hits the pillow I am generally asleep and stay so until the morning.'

'You are most fortunate, then.'

'You do not sleep well?'

'I don't.' He raised his cup of coffee to his lips and peered at her over the rim. When his eyes locked on to hers, it was she who looked away, making much of buttering her toast. He might suspect her, but that was all. And tonight, forewarned of his lightness of sleep, she would be far more careful in her searching.

'I was planning a ride across the fields of Falder. Would you like to accompany me? Lucy has a spare riding skirt and jacket and you will find anything else you need in the room off the stables.'

'I'm not certain. It has been a long time since I was on a horse.'

'We will go slowly, Lady Emma.'

Emerald frowned, for beneath the outward affinity there was a look that held a hint of something much darker. A rage kept only in check by a steel-strong will. She tried to keep the conversation light.

'Lucinda said your mother resides here in Falder

but I have yet to meet her. She also said that the Dowager Duchess enjoys keeping bad health.'

He smiled at that, the white of his teeth startling against the tan on his face.

'That she does. Lucinda surprises me sometimes with her insights into others. Take your cousin for instance.' A gleam of something she could not quite interpret danced in his eyes. 'Liam Kingston. She saw him as an honourable man. A man who would not lie. A trait of character to be commended in a person, would you not say?'

'Indeed, I would.' She hoped he did not hear the waver in her voice.

'Indeed, you would,' he repeated and lifted a silver knife to take jam from the pot before him. He used his left hand for almost everything, she noted. Writing. Smoking. Eating. The hand that was not ruined.

Her mind went back to the day they had boarded his ship and she took in a short breath. He had once been right-handed. She was certain of it. The enormity of the realisation made her stiffen. When had the accident happened? Lord, not straight after she had toppled him overboard? Surely not right then.

'My family is extremely important to me, Lady Emma, and as the head of the house it is my duty to see that they remain safe.'

'I see.' The beat of her heart was twice its normal speed and rising.

'I'm glad that you do.' The smile that he gave her did not reach his eyes.

'Good morning.'

Lucinda's voice had Emerald turning in relief. Asher's questions had an edge to them that she didn't understand—it was as if he was furious at her. An awful thought surfaced. Could he have seen her last night? She had heard a noise as she had left the small room off the library, though she was certain that if he had seen her she would hardly be sitting here and being served a very substantial breakfast. With growing unease she looked across at Lucy.

Today Asher's sister was dressed in a deep-blue riding habit and had a wide smile on her face. A complete and utter contrast to her own, she supposed, and was unreasonably tired by such innocence and openness.

Petty, she knew, and belittling to honour. Taking a breath, she tried to rally.

'Are you joining us for breakfast, Lucy?' Asher asked as he pushed out a chair for his sister.

'No, I have already eaten. Taris said you would be going into the village this morning and I thought to ride with you, for I am spending the day with Rodney and Annabelle Graveson. Will you be leaving soon?'

'As soon as we have breakfasted.'

The cold lash of his eyes gave Emerald the feeling that he was ordering her to go with him for this had nothing to do with choice. Swallowing her gall, she squared her shoulders and faced Lucy. If the Duke of Carisbrook meant to confront her, she would rather the scene take place away from Falder. 'Your brother mentioned a riding habit of yours that I might use?'

'Of course. Come with me now and we can find it—I have just the colour to go with your hair. Dark green—have you ever worn that colour? You tend more to the pastels, you see, and I thought really the deeper shades might just suit you better. The tone of your hair is unusual. Not quite blonde, but not red either. Do you take after your mother?'

Shaking her head at all the questions, Emerald followed Lucy from the room, glad to have a genuine reason to leave.

An hour later they were wending their way into Thornfield. After a shaky start Emerald had picked up her old skills in riding and was enjoying the freedom of being on horseback. Lucinda beside her chatted about her childhood; in front of them Taris rode a little further back from his brother. She could see how he concentrated on the path before him and on the sounds of the horse's hooves upon the road. Lucy sometimes called out to him, warning him of an incline or of a particularly deep ditch.

Asher gave him nothing. No help. No leeway. She wondered what it was Taris had been doing off the coast of the Caribbean when he had lost his sight.

Thornfield was beautiful. A village set beside the sea with a main road sporting a number of shops and many well-built houses, round a deep harbour where a ship was moored.

As Asher dismounted and helped his sister down, Emerald was already fastening the reins of her horse and looking towards the ship.

'It is yours?'

'Ours,' he amended. 'She's the *Nautilus*, built for the Eastern Line and due out to India at the end of the month to fill a silk contract we have in Calcutta.'

'She's beautiful. What does she draw?'

'You know something about ships?'

Cursing her slip, she lied easily. 'Liam was always interested in ships, so I suppose some of his knowledge must have rubbed off on to me.' Deliberately she turned away from the harbour and perused the inn, glad that the brim on the hat she wore was wide, for she doubted she could have hidden the longing she was consumed with.

To set foot on a ship again. To ride in the winds of a wide-open sea with the smell of salt and adventure close to the bone. To climb up the rigging of an eighty-foot mast and hang suspended against the blueness of a horizon that stretched for ever.

A voice calling to them brought her from her thoughts and she looked around to see a man hurrying forward.

'I had hoped to see you here today, your Grace,'

he said when he was upon them. 'There was a break-in on the *Nautilus* last night, though from what I can gather nothing was taken. But the lock on the main cabin door was forced and a few papers shifted.'

'Did anyone see anything untoward?'

'No, nothing. Davis heard noises after midnight and thought it was me checking on the ropes.'

'Set a double shift tonight, then,' Asher ordered, 'and have Silas bring his dog back on board.'

Emerald stiffened as his eyes raked across her and again she felt some sense of complicity and an uncertainty that was hard to pin down. Had Azziz and Toro frisked the ship already? It could well be possible. She had determined to contact them tonight and let them know of the new plans Asher Wellingham had set in place to guard his ship when the arrival of a beautifully dressed woman in her forties made her turn. At her side there walked a boy, his eyes firmly fixed on Lucinda.

'I didn't realise that you would be up for the week, Asher.' The woman smiled, looking at Emerald and waiting for an introduction.

'Lady Emma Seaton, meet Lady Annabelle Graveson and her son, Rodney. Emma is newly come to London to stay with her aunt, the Countess of Haversham.'

'Miriam of Haversham?' Her glance sharpened on the locket around Emerald's neck; if she had been pale before, now she was even more so.

'You are her niece?' Her fingers pulled at the lace around her collar before her eyes rolled up and she fell into the arms of Asher Wellingham.

Again, Emerald thought.

How tiring it must be to for ever have collapsing women swoon around you. This faint, however, hardly looked like the one she had pretended in the Henshaw ballroom. It was obvious that Annabelle Graveson was truly ill for her face had taken on a greenish-grey pallor and sweat covered her brow.

Asher Wellingham hardly seemed fazed as he lifted the woman up effortlessly and led the small contingent into the inn, where a space was cleared on a cushioned seat.

'Fetch some water and give us some room,' he ordered and the innkeeper wasted no time in doing as he was bid.

Rodney stood at the foot of his mother's makeshift bed. 'She said that she felt ill this morning, but I didn't think she meant this ill.' Emerald noticed Lucy's hand resting on his shoulder, trying to give him comfort and almost laughed.

This ill?

The woman was probably just hot or the stays binding her stick-thin waist were too tight. Already she was coming to. She thought back to the aftermath of battles aboard the *Mariposa* when sailors had sat in silence against the bulwarks and nursed broken bones. Or worse.

But this was England, she reminded herself, where a faint still retained an important place in the whole scheme of things. A vivid reminder of the place of fragile women.

She watched as the woman sat herself up and wiped her brow and upper lip with a delicate hanky she had extracted from the sleeve at her wrist.

'Oh, my goodness,' she said, repeating it over again as she looked around the group. 'I said to Rodney this morning that I was not feeling up to a jaunt into the village. My stomach, you understand. It is rather unpredictable and yesterday the cook served a strong soup that I can only surmise was badly made. Old meat, if I were to hazard a guess, or fungi plucked from a place it should not have been. Rodney, where are you?'

'I am here, Mama.' He did not move and Emerald looked away when she perceived that both Annabelle Graveson and her son were watching her, their blue eyes a mirror copy of each other's.

Asher, as usual, had taken charge, ordering large platters of food and wine and making certain that Taris was aware of the fare that was placed before him. Glancing across the room, she saw a group of young men looking her way, but the scorching glance of the Duke of Carisbrook discouraged them.

She almost smiled. How easy it must be to slip into the role of a protected woman.

How simply easy.

Lucinda. Annabelle Graveson. They let him take charge without even noticing what they had given up.

'Are you at Falder for long, Lady Emma?' Rodney Graveson was sitting on her left side, next to Lucinda.

'For a week. My aunt, the Countess of Haversham, is here, too, but she has been laid low by a cough and has taken to her bed. Perhaps you know of her—your mother seems to.'

'Mama seldom travels outside of Thornfield these days, but I have heard her mention that name.'

He blushed, his fair hair standing out against the colour, but he did not look away and Emerald liked him for it. Once, years ago, she too had been cursed with such shyness and Rodney Graveson seemed like a kindred spirit and in desperate need of friendship. Looking up, she caught Annabelle Graveson watching her.

'What is it you are speaking of with Lady Emma, Rodney?' Her voice was high and the colour in her cheeks was better.

'He was just asking me how long I planned to be here for, Lady Annabelle.'

'Oh, I see. And your answer?'

'Seven days, I think.'

'Then we shall have you over to Longacres for dinner next Sunday. Asher will bring you. About six.'

She did not ask the others at the table, which struck Emerald as both odd and rather impolite, and the Duke of Carisbrook's perfunctory nod was such that she wondered if he meant to honour the invitation at all, but as she felt the squeeze of Rodney Graveson's hand against her own beneath the table she was touched by his gesture and hoped that it would be possible to go.

Two hours later, after saying goodbye to the others Emerald sat on Hercules and picked her way down the incline behind Asher Wellingham on his tall black stallion. Lucy had stayed in Thornfield with the Gravesons and Taris had met a friend at the tavern and had decided to embark on a game of chess. Emerald wondered whether the whole thing had been a set-up, for Asher Wellingham seemed very keen on riding back with her and left as soon as the first opportunity presented itself. She also wondered as to the propriety of being alone with him, but dismissed that notion with indifference. Her reputation here was unimportant—she would be gone from England as soon as she found the cane.

The sea lay before them and, licking her lips, she could taste the salt. Here the sand was not fine and white, but grey and coarse, the pebbles mulched by the movement of this lonely, lovely coast. The sea. Her heart sang at the joy of being beside it again. If this was my home, she thought, I should never leave it.

After the warning at breakfast Asher Wellingham

had seemed withdrawn and quiet. He did not tarry or offer her any explanation of beaches, cliffs or field.

His land, she thought.

If he loved Falder, it was not obvious.

'What is the peninsula in the distance?' she asked as the sun lit up a long low tongue of land to their left.

'The Eddington Finger,' he said promptly. 'Though my great-great-grandfather always called it "Return Home Bay." The last sight of Falder lands as he left the coast, I suppose. He was a sailor with a love for adventure.'

He stopped as they cantered down on to the sand and dismounted and the image of an old duke naming the place made Emerald laugh.

'What was his name? Your great-great-grandfather's name,' she qualified when he looked puzzled.

'Ashland. My father was Ashborne and his father Ashton, all derivatives of the original family name of Ashalan. It is tradition.'

'Tradition.' Longing welled on her face. She was certain he must have seen it and was surprised when he smiled. It made him look younger, as young as he had looked on his ship off Turks Island with the sea winds at his back. As young as the man staring out from the portrait in the small salon with a loving wife on his arm.

Desire snaked through caution and she was shocked by the heavy hammering of her heart. She, who had been around men all her life. Handsome men. Dangerous men. But none like this one. None who had haunted her dreams for five long years with his velvet eyes and night-black hair. None who spoke of a family name that they could trace back through the generations and whose ancestral seat rivalled that of any lord of the realm.

Responsibility and place.

A combination that became all the more appealing with the land of his birth at his back and the full blue day upon his face. Her own shifting lifestyle completed the equation. What must it be like to have your children run in the same fields as their children and their children's children? Oh, tradition was sweet when you had never had it.

The silence between them stretched in an endless vacuum as he helped her dismount and she felt a breathless shiver of wonder. Did he feel it too? How could he not? She was shocked at her thoughts, shocked at the sheer bald desire for his touch. Schooling herself to wait as he tethered the horses to a branch, she was surprised at his first question.

'What were you doing in the blue salon last night, Lady Emma?'

'Last night?' She hoped the slight catch in her voice would be interpreted as chagrin rather than the bone-deep fear she was suddenly consumed with.

'Last night when you slipped through the rooms of my house in the guise of one suspiciously similar

to the description my sister gave of Liam Kingston.'
He was very still.

'I am not certain what you mean.' With her back
against the wall she couldn't afford to give an inch.

He changed tack, easily. Distrust coated his words
and was seen in the hard planes of his face. 'What is
it you want from me?'

'Want from you? Nothing, your Grace. And there
is a simple explanation for last night. I have never
slept well since my father's passing. Sometimes in
the dead of night I wander...'

'Dressed as a boy and moving in and out of the
house like a shadow. I think not.'

One hand encircled her wrist and she felt the same
bolt of awareness that she was almost becoming used
to in his company.

'Are you a thief?' he asked quietly, his thumb ca-
ressing the sensitive skin at her wrist.

'No.' The touch of his breath across the sensitive
folds of her neck nearly undid her.

'A spy, then? Who sent you here?' His fingers
tightened. Not a harsh hold, but a tempered one. She
knew he must feel the hammering pulse beneath his
fingers.

'No one.' She could barely get the words out.

'I do not believe you, but if you are in trouble I
could help.'

It was the last thing she had expected him to say.
He hardly knew her and yet here he was offering

his assistance. Another responsibility. Another needy supplicant. Another duty on top of all his other duties. Pride made her shake her head and she saw a distinct flicker of relief.

'You are a guest here at Falder and my sister would be disappointed, no doubt, if I packed you off before your due date of departure. But if you sleep-walk again, Lady Emma, take warning, for I shall not be as lenient as I have been this time. Do I make myself clear?'

'Perfectly.'

'Then I'm glad of it.' Again, his thumb traced the blue veins on the thin skin of her wrist and she felt her world throb. When she looked up, there was muted calculation in his eyes and a worm of worry niggled.

Had he used the caress as a means to an end by underlining his threat with a promise? Admiration surfaced in equal proportions with ire. Such cunning would not be out of place on board the *Mariposa*, for with it he had gained exactly what he wanted.

And all without raising a finger. She was too much her father's daughter not to applaud his craftiness.

Taking her reins when he offered them back, she walked her horse down towards the water, the mist of salt enveloping the beach with an opaque whiteness. A wilder bay than she was used to, and colder. Shivering, she bent to pick up a shell and the sound inside as she raised it to her ear was exactly the same as it was at home.

For a second she felt displaced, uncertain, lost in the pull of what had been taken from her, and drawn to the man who now came to stand beside her, his cheeks lightly spattered with the mist of ocean. If she had been braver, she might have leant forward and touched the wetness, felt the swell of cheek beneath her fingers, and understood what it was that she could now only guess at. But she was not brave. Not like that. Not here with the wide brim of her hat tugging in the wind and the fullness of her riding skirt unfamiliar around her legs.

Don't. Don't. Don't.

She recited the word over again and again beneath her breath, trying to incite some sort of sense in her actions. Trying to make herself step back from him, out of reach, out of harm, out of temptation. But when his thumb came up to caress the sensitive skin on her bottom lip, she closed her eyes and just felt.

For once.

For this once.

For the time it took to run her tongue across the length of skin and bring his flesh into her mouth.

'Lord, what you do to me.' The darkness in his eyes was bottomless as his lips slanted down across her own, the hunger in them easily definable in the afternoon grey. Just the two of them with the damp rivulets of water running beneath her feet, and the green lands of England all around. Just the two of them coming together along the full lines of their bodies and pressing hard.

And then there was nothing.

No today or yesterday, or tomorrow with its sharp uncertainty.

Just him. Just the warmth of skin against the cool of the rain and the burning fiery want that consumed her. She did not notice when he cast aside her hat, loosening the curls to his touch. All she knew was urgency and want and need.

A man's touch. On her woman's body. The living reality of her countless dreams. She felt the puckering of her nipples and the clench of an almost-pain between her legs.

More. More.

Everything, she longed to whisper, everything, and when he drew away she tried to hold on, tried to take his mouth in the same way that he had taken hers, but he stopped her simply by pulling her against him, head firm beneath his chin, fitting well into the spaces of his body.

'Emma.' Whispered. Barely there.

The frantic beat of his heart against his throat told her that he was as affected as she was. Not all one-sided, then, not all her fault. She could not find it in herself to raise her eyes to his.

'I'm sorry. That should not have happened.' His voice was husky. 'There is no excuse at all. I should not have—' He stopped and the shrill cry of a gull could be heard over the silence.

He was sorry? She stiffened. An apology. For this?

Every man she had ever known in her life would have taken what it was she had just offered and be damned with what happened next. But not Asher Wellingham. No, not him. Confusion ripped through guilt and sheer embarrassment chased hard on the heels of that.

Lord. What now? When she felt his hands slacken she stepped back and reached for the bridle, angry at the help she needed to mount and pleased when he did not speak again as he handed her her hat. Did not explain. Did not even try to draw level with her as they cantered along the beach and up into the valley that led to Falder Castle.

Gaining her room she laid her head back against the solidness of the portal and tried to catch her breath, lost in the run up from the stables. Her breathing was closer to normal when she opened the connecting door to see Miriam sitting in a chair by her window, reading a book.

'Whatever has happened? You look like you have come across a ghost.'

Emerald's smile was laboured. Hardly a ghost. Asher's lips still burnt into the recesses of her memory and raised the temperature of everything.

Hot. Scorching. Torrid.

She poured herself some water, watching the drips run jagged against the side of the glass before drinking it all.

'You seem better, Aunt.'

'If you could find the cane, Emerald, I'd be better still.' The sentence was finished on a bout of coughing and Emerald's worry grew. After her behaviour today, she was uncertain whether the Duke of Carisbrook would even want her to stay till the end of the week and here was her aunt plagued with illness.

Lord, could things get any worse? She shook her head and made herself concentrate on what Miriam was saying.

'Carisbrook has a map room at the back of the eastern wing. I saw it today when I attempted a walk round the rose garden. Perhaps he has already found the map, and keeps it there.'

Emerald's interest was piqued. 'Near the rose garden you say?'

'Yes. The Wellingham family mausoleum sits further over to one side. The footman I walked with said that the garden has been laid out in memory of the Duchess of Carisbrook.'

'Melanie Wellingham is dead and buried at Falder?'

'She is indeed. The tomb of their son is there too.'

'A son?'

'Stillborn at full term three years before she died.'

Death and loss and waste.

The enormity of Miriam's revelations changed everything. The Duke of Carisbrook had loved his wife. He still loved his wife. The sapphire ring on his finger, the picture in the library and the flower garden, and his self-confessed resistance to being plunged again into the state of holy matrimony—suddenly everything added up, made sense.

She was a small detour in the course of his life. That was all. He was a duke with lands stretching hundreds of miles in every direction and a shipping fleet that plied the world.

He was not for her.

Would never be for her.

She reached into her pocket for the shell she had collected and wished that she could find the map and just go home.

Chapter Seven

He was drunk.

He knew he was by the way the portrait of Melanie that he sat in front of swam in and out of focus. He hated this painting. Hated the sheer memory of it. A brutal reminder of all that he had lost.

He should not have kissed Emma Seaton. Not like that. Not with the raging want in his blood and the sure damned knowledge of duplicity in his head. She was not as she said she was. She was a liar and a would-be thief. She was dangerous to his family. To him. To the world he had spun around himself ever since he had returned home, a slim wedge against chaos. He should kick her out, right now, before the calmer shifts of reason took hold and her turquoise eyes reeled him in like the sirens of Circe, haunting, familiar and undeniably false.

And yet he couldn't. He couldn't. He sighed and

leant his head back against the wall wondering just why it was that he couldn't. Not just the warm willingness of her body or the sharp raw hit of lust that had floored him when her lips had met his. No, there was something else too. Something he had felt unexpectedly as he had held her on the beach against him. Something close and safe and right. Something that took away the cold for ever etched into his very bones and left a question of possibility.

'I thought that I might find you here. And drinking.' The heavy censure in Taris's words jarred his thoughts and Asher closed his eyes against it. Tonight his more usual reserve was lost under the fiery belly of too much whisky.

'When I was with Emma Seaton today…I forgot Melanie. For just one moment…I forgot her.'

He felt the stillness of his brother rather than saw it, but he was strangely relieved by the confession. Saying the words lessened the strength of them. Tonight he needed absolution.

'She is a beautiful woman, Asher, and Melanie has been dead for over three years. Why should you not admire her?'

'Because she's a liar. Because she was here the other night. Right here. Dressed as a boy. And because I think she and Liam Kingston are one and the same.'

'Lucinda's knight in shining armour? The one who bested Stephen Eaton? Lady Emma?'

'She has a tattoo on the soft skin of her right breast.'

'A tattoo?' Intrigue was plain in his brother's question.

'Of a butterfly. Done in blue.'

Taris began to laugh.

'I want her to stay here. At Falder. I want to protect her…'

The laughter abruptly stopped.

'Someone has hurt her,' Asher continued and stood, tripping over a low stool in front of him as he did so and veering towards the wall. Leaning against it, he was pleased to regain his balance. 'And she's frightened. I can see it in her eyes…sometimes… often…and I can hear it in her voice.'

A clock chimed in the next room and Asher counted the hours. Three o'clock. Two more hours till the dawn and the promise of sleep. Tonight it was all he could do to keep from closing his eyes and let slumber overtake him.

But he mustn't.

He knew he mustn't. Not until the dawn when the voices were softer and memory did not cut his equilibrium to the quick.

He slid down the wall, his knees drawn up before him. In defeat. The stubs of his severed fingers rested against his knee and he brought them up into his vision as if seeing them for the first time.

'Sometimes I can feel these fingers…ghost fingers

touching things, feeling things. I used to think they'd gone to the place where Melanie was, a little part of me waiting with her till the rest could follow…and now…I don't want to follow them.' As he leant his head back, his eyes went to the uncurtained window, where he could see only an unbroken darkness and he hated the lack of control he could hear in his voice.

'Melanie would have wanted you to be happy again. Laugh again. Feel again.'

'Would she?' He stroked his finger down the thin crystal stem of his glass and almost laughed. 'I remember once in Scotland when she nearly fell into a raging river and I caught her and pulled her back. She said that if anything ever happened to me, she would be sad for ever. For ever. Such a long time…for ever.'

Taris was quiet. Asher noticed he had removed his glasses and put them into his pocket. Seeing with memory. All that his brother was left with now. Sometimes he hated Beau Sandford with such a passion that it worried him. The smarting scars across his back. Taris's loss of sight. Even in death the pirate haunted him.

'Go to sleep, Taris. I will be all right.'

'I could stay…'

'No.'

He was pleased when his brother left him to his familiar demons.

Emerald strolled back towards Falder after an early morning walk, and caught sight of a light burning low in the little salon off the library as she mounted the front steps. If Asher Wellingham was already up, she would speak with him about yesterday. She should not have kissed him, should not have been alone with him, could not believe what she had done. She, who had always been so circumspect in dealing with the opposite sex. Well, it needed to stop before she did something she knew she would regret and she meant to tell him so right now.

The Duke of Carisbrook was slumped on the floor when she pushed open the door, his back against the wall and an empty bottle beside him. Taris sat asleep in an armchair. Like a sentinel.

Turning back to Asher, she saw that he watched her, the intensity of his gaze startling. He made no move to stand up; with his cravat askew and with the stubble of a twelve-hour beard upon his face, he looked like some dark and dissolute angel.

'I am sorry,' she managed. 'I saw the light from outside and thought I might speak with you. About yesterday.'

'Perhaps another time would be better,' he returned softly, and she was relieved to hear a hint of something akin to humour in his voice.

'You are well?' She could barely just leave it here.

His eyes flicked to the window where the beams of a new day flooded in.

'Very well. Now,' he replied and pushed himself up. Emerald resisted an impulse to help him as he bent over, his hands clamped tightly about his head and holding everything together. She had seen enough hangovers to recognise that this was a bad one.

'Did you sleep at all last night?'

He shook his head, squinting against the light that caught him squarely from this angle.

A new thought struck her. *He never slept.* Her mind ran over the times she had found him up, fully dressed, in the small hours just before the dawn.

After the ball. The first night she had searched Falder. This morning. Each time with a glass in his hand and the look of the damned in his eyes.

'My father had a remedy for too much drink.' Her resolve to confront him faltered under his vulnerability this morning and his eyebrows arched.

'A man of many varied talents, then,' he chided and crossed the room to replace a blanket across his brother that had fallen on to the floor. Taris barely moved as he did so, well wrapped in the arms of Morpheus.

What had they spoken of, Emerald wondered, in the dead of night? What kept them from warmer beds and a more comfortable slumber? Memories? Secrets? Her?

'Could you concoct this remedy for me?'

She was more than surprised by his request. 'I'd need herbs and sugar and milk.'

'We could find those in the kitchen. It's this way.'

He edged his way around her, careful not to touch, and opened the door. She saw he used the solidness of it to retain his balance.

The kitchen was enormous and extremely well appointed. Ten or so people of all genders, sizes and ages scraped, cleaned, cooked and chopped, the smell of a fine luncheon permeating the air. A woman extracted herself from the others, wiping her hands on her apron as she came forward.

'Your Grace?' There was question in her voice. 'I hope all is well with the food…'

'Indeed it is, Mrs Tonner. But Lady Emma would like a few ingredients to make a drink.' He did not say what sort of drink.

'A drink?' Amazement overcame the cook's reserve. 'You wish to cook, my lady?'

'I wish to make a potion with eggs, milk and hyssop. And mandrake root, if you have it.'

A smile lit up Mrs Tonner's face. The secret recipe of Beau's was not just confined to the wilds of Jamaica, Emerald determined, and followed her to a well-stocked pantry where she quickly found what was needed. A smaller maid produced a bowl and whisk and another a large tumbler embossed with Asher Carisbrook's initials.

A.W. Not just his initials, either, but the sum of generations before him. Ashton Wellingham. Ashland Wellingham. Ashborne Wellingham.

Thanking the cook, she set to work, flustered when

she saw that he meant to stay and watch her. The kitchen was as quiet as the dead, though ten sets of ears were fastened on their every movement and word.

'Did you make this often?' he asked as she worked.

Often and often and often.

'No. Only a very few times when a parishioner was in his cups at church. Apart from that…' She let the sentence peter out as a vision of Beau downing the concoction in ever-increasing quantities overcame her.

Her father had been a mean drunk and a series of harlots had taken the brunt of his temper.

Mostly.

She was pleased that Asher was not of that ilk. Indeed, drink seemed to mellow him, make him easier to talk with, more vulnerable.

'Yet you can remember the recipe by heart?'

'It is a simple one, which you have to drink all at once.' She handed the tumbler to him as she finished.

He sniffed it and looked up. 'Is it supposed to smell this way?'

'Yes.' She tried to stop laughter as she registered his incredulity but could not quite. 'Strong liquor requires a strong antidote.'

When he made no move to swallow it she leant across and removed the cup from his hands to take a sip.

'See. Not poisonous. In fact, quite palatable.' She repressed a shiver as the aftertaste hit her and hoped that he had not seen it.

'Palatable?' He questioned when he had finished. 'You call that palatable?' A film of froth coated his upper lip before he licked it away. 'Come, Emma, and I will show you palatable.'

Once outside, he took a turning that she had not seen before that led to a conservatory almost entirely formed by glass, opening out to a wide and formal garden.

'My mother's contribution to the place,' he remarked as he saw her astonishment. 'It is a tradition that the Wellingham wives are always good at something. My grandmother was a horsewoman of great repute and my great-grandmother a musician. It is said at night through the corridors of the west wing that you can still hear the haunting tunes of her pianoforte.' He smiled. 'Ghosts are mandatory in a place like this, though I have never seen one.'

'What was Melanie good at?' The thought became a voiced question and she cursed as she saw his withdrawal.

'My wife was also good at music and good at being a wife,' he said simply and took the head off an orange chrysanthemum at his feet.

'She was beautiful.'

'Yes.'

'Is she the reason you do not sleep?'

He stood perfectly still. God, he seldom spoke of Melanie. And never to anyone save Taris. But here in the light of day, after a night when he hadn't had a moment's sleep, it was suddenly easy. Emma Seaton made it so.

'I was not at home when she died. I was not at home for her funeral. I should have been home.' He was astonished at the well of information he had given her and the depth of his anguish. If he had been by himself, he would have slammed his fist into something hard and finished off another bottle. But he wasn't alone.

'My brother also died when I was not with him. He was three.'

Asher looked up and focused. For the first time since he had met her, he felt as if he was actually hearing about someone in her family who had been real.

'I used to carry him everywhere, you see. I was six when he…went and acted his mother, I suppose. My name was the first one he ever spoke and I taught him songs in the dusk and rocked his hammock. He had a lisp. I remember that more now than his face.'

'How did he die?' She did not answer, though her paleness told him it had not been an easy death. He was trying to work out what lesson he could take from her confidence when she began to speak again.

'How long ago was it that your wife died?'

'Three years.'

'People used to say to me "time softens pain." And I used to think nothing will ever soften this ache. Nothing. But time did. It flattened out the rawness and left only memories. Good memories. Now when I think of James—that was his name—I think of his lisp and his curly blond hair and the thoughts make me smile.'

'I rarely speak of Melanie to anyone.'

'But you should, for it helps. A worry shared is a worry halved. Have you not heard the old adage?'

'Your father again?'

She smiled and in the light of the new day her dimples were as easy to see as the faint holes in her ears. For earrings, he determined, and not just one, either. A whole row of tiny marks pierced both lobes. He imagined jewels sparkling there and was still as a memory shifted and was lost.

Reaching out, he touched the slight indentations and she didn't stop him. Rather she leaned into his embrace.

She was so damnably responsive, he thought. Any slight caress had her heart beating faster and the flush well upon her cheeks. What would it be like to part the moist lips of her womanhood and slip inside? The thought had him stiffening and he pulled away.

Hell. After yesterday's débâcle he was back to acting like some green boy straight out of school. He wondered if she would notice the thickening bulge at the front of his trousers. His much-too-tight trousers, he amended, and readjusted them for the second time in two days.

The sound of his mother's voice made him groan. To be caught in the gardens by a parent with his trousers metaphorically down was something he had not contemplated. It hadn't happened at seventeen, so he had certainly not expected it to happen at thirty-one. Pulling the front of his long jacket closed he watched as Alice Wellingham, the Dowager Duchess of Carisbrook, was wheeled into the gardens by her maid. A quick look at Emma Seaton disorientated him. She was staring straight at him and trying not to smile. Lord, he thought. He was being given the run around by a Catholic chit, who had fed him a potion of ingredients that were causing his eyes to blur with tiredness.

His mother's smile was not helping either. He recognised that look, had seen it before every time some eligible woman had come into the sphere of his notice since the death of his wife, but today for the first time he was unreasonably irritated by it.

'You look terrible, Asher.'

'Good morning, Mother.'

'You look terrible and your servants let it slip that you have not slept at all in a week. And you have finished as many bottles of brandy as you do usually in a month.' Her voice broke. 'You will kill yourself with this behaviour and I hate to think what might happen to Falder and the dukedom.'

'Taris would undoubtedly assume the mantle of responsibility were such an unlikely event to occur.' He was cruel in his response, but he had had this talk before and did not want it in front of Emma Seaton now.

'Unlikely?' His mother was about to say more when her eyes rested on the face of Emerald and he introduced her.

'You are the Countess of Haversham's niece, are you not?'

'I am.'

'Many years ago I had a passing acquaintance with her family. Which branch do you hail from?'

'A distant one, I am afraid.'

Emma was a master at not answering any question about her past, Asher thought, but his mother failed to note the fact.

'She had a brother, Beauvedere. Have you ever come across him?'

'I do not believe so.'

'Then it is well that you haven't—I often wonder what happened to him. He was a striking man with the bluest eyes and a way with the women that was legendary. Ashborne always said he would come to no good…' She began to giggle. 'I am sorry. It is age, I think, this constant referral to times past. Easy to remember what happened thirty years ago and hard to think what it was one did yesterday. Instead of re- galing you with old nonsense, I should be asking if are you being properly looked after here at Falder. Do you like the room you've been given? You are in the yellow room are you not? Do you play whist?'

'Badly.' Emerald looked startled by the quick changes of topic.

'Good. Then I shall set you up as my opponent this evening. Would you mind? My sister usually partners me, but she has gone down to London for the week as my nephew has arrived from the Americas. You will have a lot to catch up on, Asher,' she added, and even as she said the words his heart sank.

Just another person to tell him how he had changed for the worse.

He hoped that his cousin would keep any criticisms to himself and was suddenly as tired by it all as he ever had been.

It was the potency of Emma's remedy combined with a lack of sleep, he determined, and resolved to knock himself out early tonight with a strong brandy. He hoped belatedly that no maid had woken his brother slumbering on the armchair in front of Melanie's portrait. Taris must have come back into the room. He frowned. He had not heard him do so, which in turn suggested that some time around the very early dawn he had, after all, nodded off. The notion cheered him considerably. If he could sleep a little, it would follow that he could also sleep a lot. As his mother's maid wheeled her from the garden, he had another thought.

'Does the potion you made act as a sort of sleeping draught?' He could barely keep his eyes open.

'It does. And quite quickly too.' The laugh she ended the sentence with worried him.

'How quickly?'

When the dizzy whorl hit him he had his answer, then he felt only blackness.

He slept twenty hours straight and awakened just as the sun was rising on the dawn of the following day.

Emma Seaton sat next to him, reading Mary Wollstonecraft, the revolutionary tract criticising the restricted educative norms for women. Even her reading matter worried him.

'You are awake?' she said softly and put down the book. 'I know that I should not be here, but it was my potion and I was worried that perhaps I had wrongly remembered the proportions. I came in to see that you still breathed.'

'Just here?' he asked back and looked around the room for any signs of shifted possessions.

'I would not hurt your family. I like them.'

'But you would hurt me?' He was suddenly still, for today everything seemed clearer. It was him she had bumped into at Jack's ball and him she had targeted at the Bishop's dinner. Talking with George about it the next day, he had discovered that Lady Emma Seaton had intimated to Flora that she was an old friend of his and that she should be pleased to renew the acquaintance.

And when she had fallen against him at the ball he had known her faint to be false.

Lying on his back in bed with almost nothing on, however, he felt it was neither the time nor the place for confrontation. Consequently he turned the subject.

'You could probably make a fortune curing the plight of London's insomniacs with your tonic. The *ton* would take to you like a saviour.'

'How do you feel?'

'Better.'

'You do not sound it.'

'How do I sound?'

'Annoyed.'

'And you could not imagine why?'

'I gave you the gift of sleep.'

'You knocked me out and God knows what you have been up to in the meantime, making free with the things in my house in your quest for…what?' Steely eyes swept across her. 'Is it money? You look as if you might need some.'

Today he was like a bear with a sore head.

'My clothes may not be the latest vogue in London, but I assure you that it is from lack of desire rather than from lack of funds.'

'You would not want a new gown?'

'I know that to you the idea may be a preposterous

one, but not all women have the need to garb themselves in the very latest style. Some—like me, for example—would rather buy books.'

He began to laugh. 'Use my library, then. Feel free to choose something other than Wollstonecraft.'

He looked immeasurably younger with the humour dancing in his eyes and she capitulated. 'When you feel better later on in the day, perhaps we might enjoy a discussion on the relative merits of women's rights.'

'Perhaps,' he murmured and pulled a pillow over his head, ending any possibility of conversation.

Chapter Eight

Emerald walked to the sea early before anyone was about, before the night stars had faded from the sky, before the chamber maids had risen from their beds, and before Miriam would have the notion to miss her and comment. She had searched Falder for hours last night, searched Asher's room and the alcoves off it, searched the kitchens and the salons and the library. Searched the map room that Miriam had spoken of and come away with nothing. Had he thrown the cane away? She shook her head. The jewels on the carved head were too valuable to just get rid of and even the most dull-witted of folk could have determined the worth of the thing. Had he sold it off? Could she ask him somehow of its whereabouts without raising his curiosity and jogging his memory?

The water was cold as she waded into it, but not

the freezing cold she had expected and the temperature took her thoughts on to further possibilities.

Looking around, she wondered if she dared to take off her gown and swim out to the first break of the waves. Behind her the land was silent and grey, a row of tall dark pines sheltering the beach from a cottage that lay half a mile in from where she stood, and the cove was bound at both ends by sharp outcrops of rock. No access there, then. No sudden stranger. No peeping Toms or vagrant passers-by.

She made her mind up in a moment and walked to a large bush at the head of the beach, shrugging off her jacket and her gown and boots. She left her silk gloves on. Out of habit. The slight breeze sent goosebumps across the skin on her forearms and she laughed in sheer and unadulterated joy. Freedom.

Her first true freedom in four months. She rubbed away the tears that started in her eyes and walked straight into the ocean.

Asher saw her from a distance, a lonely Aphrodite with her hair a froth of bright gilt curls upon her head. Nothing was hidden. Nothing. Her long slender legs and arms, her rounded bottom, her waist, her full breasts moving up and down as she turned to look at the shore one last time before diving under. And under. And under…

His heart began to race and he urged his mount on, hitting the beach in a flat-out gallop and pulling off his boots and jacket after he had dismounted. God, where the hell was she?

'Emma.' His voice was wild, angry, desperate, furious, the beat of his heart so loud he thought he might fall over with the power of the blood racing through his veins, thought he might explode with the red-hot fear, thought he might…

She came up fifty yards further out from where he had last seen her and it was her laughter that sent him completely over the edge, a laughter that stopped abruptly as she turned and her eyes caught his own.

'Get out of the water. Now.' He could do nothing to soften his wrath. All he wanted was for her to be safe.

'Go back.' Her voice was breathless, horrified. 'Go away. I do not need any help.' Turquoise eyes searched the shore for any sign of others and her cheeks, despite the cold of the sea, were a burning bright hot red.

He was not swayed at all. 'If you don't come out this second, I'll come in and get you.'

Emerald bobbed down in the water and wondered what to do now, for Asher Wellingham stood directly in a line in front of her clothes. From the look on his face she didn't think he'd be making anything easy for her either.

Already the water had lapped at his trousers and was now just above the point of his knees. Would he keep coming? Would he swim in and drag her out as he threatened?

'All right, then. Turn around.' Her placatory tone was hardly won, and when she saw the white of his teeth gleam in a quick smile she was pressed not to call his bluff and see just who was the stronger swimmer. But where could she then come ashore?

'Turn around.' She repeated the command when he made no move to do so and her trepidation grew as a movement on the high ground behind Asher formed the shape of another man, far away enough to still be safe, but coming closer with each wasted second. Her distraction had Asher turning.

'It's Malcolm Howard, a cottar from the hill.' His barely concealed laughter made her swear and, swimming in on the first wave, she stood up as late as she could manage it. Asher Carisbrook held his bulky jacket out to her, but not before he had had a good eyeful.

'Most gentlemen would have at least averted their faces,' she ground out and pulled her hand away, shrugging into his jacket with the intent of showing as little flesh as possible and pleased when the hem fell below her knees.

'Most ladies would have worn a shift,' he returned, looking over his shoulder and whistling. His large black stallion walked from the bushes at the top of the beach, carefully picking his way across the sand. Glancing across his shoulder, Emerald was surprised to see no sign of the stranger in the distance.

'Malcolm generally calls in at his brother's cottage. It's just behind that hillock,' he added with an edge of humour in his words.

'And you knew that?'

'I did.'

No repentance. No apology. No remorse. But the light in his eyes had changed. Pulling on his boots, he mounted his horse with one quick movement and held out his right hand.

'Come, Emma, I will take you home.'

With sand on her feet and slick with seawater, she was hoisted up before she could argue and the warmth of his body made her start. She leant forward, hot with chagrin and flushed with something else much less definable.

'There is a hay barn in a paddock over the hill. We'll get your clothes and you can change there.'

'With you watching?'

His bark of laughter was contagious and she hid a smile as they rode. Dressed in nothing more than a too-big jacket and miles away from anyone or anywhere, she still felt safe. Asher Wellingham always made her feel safe.

'Where did you learn to swim?'

'In Jamaica.' The petulant silence she had meant to maintain seemed childish and stupid in the face of his humour.

'Sure as hell your father did not teach you.'

'No, it was a servant who showed me.'

'Dressed in more than you are now, I should hope.'

'It was hot and I was a child.'

'And now you are most definitely a woman.'

His free arm skimmed down across the side of her thigh and her breath stopped. 'Are you an innocent, Emma?'

'I beg your pardon?' She could barely believe that he could have asked her such a question.

'An innocent. A woman who has not had the pleasure yet of being with a man. If you are, then I should beg your forgiveness for even suggesting it, but if you are not, then you might entertain the notion of a dalliance that could be of benefit to both of us.'

'A dalliance?'

He pushed forward and she felt the hard ridge of his manhood against the small of her back.

'You want something of me and I want something of you. Badly. Perhaps we could accommodate each other and both come out the happier for it.'

His words tickled her neck and, with the hot flesh of the horse beneath her bottom and Asher Wellingham at her back, Emerald felt like simply leaning back and falling into his dangerous promise. Jamaica had hardly been a world where the passions between a man and a woman were hidden and the morality that hampered just about every social exchange here would have been deemed ludicrous there.

Say yes, her body screamed. No ties. No promises. Just the simple act of union. Here in the barn. Now.

Another voice countered the first one. The sensible voice of a woman who had been around men all her life and knew the easy empty promises they made when the bloodlust consumed them.

He was a duke, for goodness' sake, and his suggestion was that of a man who was used to women saying yes. Such men did not offer more to one whom they suspected of being a thief. She had seen Asher Wellingham in the ballrooms of London, seen the hooded glances of a hundred women with more impeccable credentials than she had. A richer family. A fairer face. Titles of equal standing to his own. And that was before she even considered their shared past.

Her eyes fell on his left hand as she shook her head. She noticed the knuckles whiten around the reins and a small voice inside her wished that he might just reach over and take what he had not been offered, a complete abnegation of any decision on her behalf. But he didn't. The gentleman in him, she mused.

'I have never—' She broke off. Horrified. What had she been going to tell him? That she was a virgin? That she had never lain with any man before? Given her behaviour of late, she was certain he would not have believed her.

'Never?' The golden chips in his eyes darkened. 'I don't usually accost women so blatantly and I—' He halted in mid-sentence as he pulled on the bridle and, dismounting, walked the horse towards a barn perched in the trees.

Accost. Such a harsh word for what he had offered, she thought. And telling. An interpretation of motive? 'I will wait here while you change.' He used the briefest of contact to help her down from the horse.

Formal. Proper. A definitive shift from the suggestion he had just voiced. Clutching her clothes, she scurried into the building, angry at herself for caring.

An easy lay and an easy leave. She remembered her father talking of the women he had bedded and left. Heartened by the memory, she bit back further introspection and finished dressing, tying the laces on her boots with hands that shook. Damn it. Why was it that she became a wanton in the company of Asher Wellingham? She thought of his glance ranging across her naked body and shivered. What had he thought? The butterfly on her breast had been plainly visible, as had the long curling scar across her right thigh. She had seen the surprise on his face when he had offered the jacket.

Surprise, speculation and lust.

Taking a breath, she walked outside. He stood with his back to the barn. Jacketless and shirt open, his dark hair fell across his collar, long from behind and slightly curly, the fabric of his shirt outlining well-defined muscle. Not a sedentary man, she mused. When he turned, she saw in his eyes that which she imagined must be reflected in her own.

Wariness.

'Thank you for your jacket.' Traces of seawater darkened the light brown fabric as he slung it carelessly across the pommel of his saddle.

'You are welcome.'

The English distance in his voice made her wince. In Jamaica, difficulties had always been settled through argument. So eminently practicable, everything said and no chance of ambiguity. Here, problems simmered beneath a more polite façade, the bubbling undercurrent of dispute left unsolved and unspoken; as he offered to help her mount, she wished that he might ask her again to consider this *dalliance* with at least a semblance of love in his eyes.

The very thought made her heart race. 'I shall walk home from here, your Grace, for it is an easy stroll.'

Nothing would make her climb on to his horse again and feel his thighs next to hers and his breath on her neck. Nothing.

He bowed his head slightly and dug his heels into the flanks of his big black stallion, gone before she had the nerve to call him back.

Signalling Azziz with her candle at midnight Emerald joined him on the road that swung between Falder and the sea. He did not look pleased.

'Have you bedded him?'

'Have I what?' Even in the darkness she knew he

must see the mounting blush on her cheeks at his question.

'Bedded him? Toro said he saw you leave the water today in the company of Asher Wellingham. He said you were naked.'

'I'd been for a swim. He found me there.'

'I will kill him.'

Laying her hand upon his sleeve, she pulled him back. 'It was my fault. I should not have gone in without clothes and he did not touch me. He was a gentleman in all of his actions.' She mentioned neither Asher's suggested dalliance nor the barn to him.

'Put a knife to Carisbrook's throat tonight, Emmie, and demand the parchment. Then we can run for the coast and take sail to Jamaica. If we delay our leave much longer, we'll have no money for the passage home.'

The brutal thrust of Azziz's argument worried her. Even a month ago she might have suggested the same thing, but now…

'I'll sell my pearls. That should tide us over for at least a while.'

Azziz shook his head. 'They are the only thing of your mother's you have left. You always said you'd never be parted from them.'

'Please, Azziz, have Toro take the pearls down to London and find the best jeweller in town. You know where they are hidden in Miriam's house. Just give me another few days.'

Another few days. Another caress? Another chance?

She shook her head to rid herself of the image of Asher on the horse behind her and felt the hairs on her arms rise up in memory.

'I could rob a wealthy traveller. It should be enough.'

'No.' Horror swamped her. 'Not in England. Here you are hanged for such an offence. Far better to sell the pearls and buy us some time.'

'If you let me at Carisbrook for an hour—'

'No.'

'His sister, then. Word has it they are close.'

'Leave the family alone. I mean it.'

'Lord, you were always headstrong. Beau had more faults than any one man had a right to, but he was your father and Carisbrook killed him in cold blood.'

'Cold blood? A mid-ocean encounter between two warring ships.'

'You would excuse this English duke?'

She turned away and looked back towards Falder. From here the lights of the house showed bright against the hills behind it. 'My father lived by the sword just as surely as he died by it and before I came here I thought that Asher Wellingham was of the same ilk. But now? I think he is as honourable as you are and I would not see him hurt.' She swallowed as she felt Azziz's large hand come to rest upon her shoulder.

'You like him, don't you, girl?' His voice was soft. 'How do you think he would react if he knew of your Sandford blood?'

'Badly.' Her response was as honest as the question asked.

'And if he exposes you, there will be little that anyone could do to stem the damage. Trust him and you could well be as dead as your father and what will happen, then, to Miriam and Ruby? If you will not think of yourself, at least think of them.'

Emerald shivered. For the very first time in all of her life she had met a man who made her feel like a woman. A man who made her imagine things that she had not before even considered.

Naked beneath his jacket and walking into the barn, a part of her had wanted him to follow her in and take away her virginity. She was twenty-one and she had never bedded a man. It was time. It was beyond time. The throb of lust deep within her loins surprised her and she was pleased when Azziz left his warnings at that and turned towards the line of trees that ran across the eastern ridge and away from Falder.

In the moonlight the garrets and turrets of the house were light against the sky and, skirting the pebble-chip pathways beyond the gardens, she saw a silhouette in the bay window. Stopping, she retraced her steps and crept through the undergrowth directly in line with the uncurtained window.

Asher stood against the glass, looking out. Behind him, hovering in the alcove, was the painted image of his long-dead wife. Watching him. Tying him to a sadness that was all consuming and never ending. She could so often see that wounded look in his eyes, like a man who bled from a gash he could not find and had ceased to notice his own hurt.

Melanie Wellingham, the dead Duchess of Carisbrook.

Everything had to do with her and with his broken hand and his blind brother. And it was all intertwined with Falder, a thousand years of history bearing down hard upon his shoulders. She started forward and stopped. What could she say?

Kiss me. Love me. Let me stay here. Here. For ever. Where the names of your ancestors march through the centuries and the shivers of memory are kind.

Kinder than my own memories. Much kinder.

A ship in the midst of an angry sea and the promise of another storm chasing hard on the heels of the first one. The English ship with the promise of well-laden hulls and Asher Wellingham waiting, sword in hand, on his quarterdeck with two dozen men behind him. An easy target. Slow. Cumbersome. The lightning off the sea silhouetting everything.

She had felt his focus and his expertise, but had still been surprised as he had swung through a swathe of sailors to reach her father. It was the whine of a cannonball that threw him into her path, and into the radius of her blade, though he had laughed as her sword crossed his own. 'You have chosen the wrong pathway, lad. Throw in with me and I will see that you have safe passage back to England—you are too young to be losing your life to the likes of this motley crew.'

Grasping her sword tighter, she had fended him off, though his proficiency was a revelation. He had been playing with her. The realisation had come with a great rush of amazement, given her own ability at swordplay, and she had been pleased to see the amusement harden as she had cut across his left sleeve and drawn blood. If she was going to die, she had wanted it to matter, though his sudden feint had her fighting arm pinioned against the mizzenmast.

'Drop the sword and I will spare you. It's not my way to slaughter innocents.'

His breath had mingled with her own and it was then that their eyes truly caught.

Tight and close.

'Lord, you're a girl.' Amazement narrowed his eyes as he brought his hand across the quivering fullness of her lips. Even now through the gathering years of time Emerald could still feel that caress, still feel the way her body had simply melted into heat.

Unexpectedly sweet. Undeniably woman. In the middle of an ocean, in the middle of a battle, she had run her tongue across the saltiness of his thumb and shock had claimed them both.

She had seen it in the shards of his eyes, the paler ring of brown flaring golden. And she had felt it in the sudden rush of blood beating in her throat, though her father's shout had broken the spell as he advanced upon them, murder in his eyes. In a quick protection she had rammed the hilt of her sword hard across Asher Wellingham's temple and upended him into the sea. A chance at least to cheat death. Ten summers of sailing with Beau had at least taught her that.

'Lord,' she said aloud and banished such memory, running her hands across the knife tucked into her belt.

Right. Wrong.

Good. Bad.

Aboard the *Mariposa* she had been her father's daughter. But here she was no longer sure of anything at all.

'Asher.' She whispered his name and held her fingers up against the warmth of sound.

A home. A family. Responsibilities. Accountability. Unlike her father, the Duke of Carisbrook took these things seriously and she admired him for it, the questionable morality they had lived by in Jamaica less certain here.

Stepping back into the shadows, she cursed her father and headed to the sanctuary of her room.

* * *

Asher paced up and down and remembered the sight of Emma Seaton coming unclothed towards him, the water slick upon her body and the sand marking her feet.

She was the most beautiful woman he had ever seen.

His eyes flicked to the painting of his wife in the small alcove and for the first time he found it difficult to remember her face in life. The exact colour of her eyes, the sharp line beneath the bridge of her nose.

Instead the image of Emma Seaton walking from the water towards him kept replaying in his mind, the butterfly tattoo as surprising as the deep curling scar upon her right thigh. He had enough wounds on his own body to know the mark of a sword when he saw one.

Where had she got it? When had she got it? And why, despite taking everything else off, had she not removed her gloves? What was she hiding there?

He began to smile as he lifted a glass of water to his lips.

Water?

Today even his choice of beverage was different. Emma Seaton made him different. More alive. She made the very air of Falder ring with a vibrancy long missing.

And what might have happened had he followed

her into the barn? He would have taken her hard and fast without a care for who was around or what the consequences might have been. She did that to him with her sun-browned skin and her turquoise eyes. Made him careless and reckless. Brought out the man he used to be. The man who had loved and risked and lost.

Lord. What the hell was happening to him? He had to stop it, for she was dangerous to everything he had made himself believe in.

Rules. Regularity. Carefulness. Control.

In chaos came loss. Of all the men in the world, he should be the best to know it.

He flicked open the casement of his timepiece.

Four o'clock. Outside the wind was mounting and the quarter-moon was high. He glanced down at the atlas in front of him and traced his fingers across the ragged outline of Jamaica. Emma's home. The place where she had been formed. His eyes wandered further west into the shoals of the Yucatan Channel.

His ship had come through the mist there on to the Sandford vessel with remarkable speed and silence and no trick of intent, either, just the cold hard slice of revenge and then an ending. He thought he would have felt more than he did as he had run Beau Sandford through the guts with the sharp point of his sword. But he hadn't. God. After a year of captivity and another year to recover, he should have allowed himself to feel more. He stretched out his right hand

and swore, the stumps of his missing fingers outlined against the light of the lamp. Even now the hate still festered.

Looking at the reflection of himself in the window,

he frowned. He had been so certain of his course in life until lately... Lately, the sharp focus had dimmed and another reality had brightened.

Emma. She was taking up all his waking thoughts and sliding into his dreams. Effortlessly.

And he could not let her with her mystery and secrets. Balling his right fist, he closed his eyes. The only way to protect himself was to never feel again.

Emma Seaton would be at Falder for three more days and then she would be gone. He resolved to spend as many of those as he could well away from her.

Chapter Nine

They tiptoed around one another at breakfast the next morning with polite smiles and bland words.

'Is the food to your satisfaction?'

'Would you mind passing the strawberry jam?'

And beneath it all ran an undercurrent of mounting desperation.

Emerald was glad Taris and Lucy were both at the table.

'I saw Malcolm Howard yesterday at the Red Lion. He said you had been swimming, Asher, down in Charlton Bay.'

'I took Artemis for a jog along the sand. Perhaps it was that he meant.' His voice and eyes gave absolutely nothing away as he reached across the table to help himself to some toast.

Taris changed his tack. 'Do you swim, Emma?'

'She does,' Asher answered for her, brown eyes

flinting a warning, and Lucy, who caught neither the amusement of one brother nor the irritation of the other, jumped into the fray.

'Then you absolutely must teach me, for I have always longed to swim. What do you wear in the water?'

Emerald flushed deep red at the question and bent to cut up the omelette on her plate. 'The temperature of the water in England is a lot colder than that of Jamaica. If I were to venture in here, it would be merely a case of testing the water to the ankles,' she said finally when she had her heartbeat in some sort of check. She did not dare to chance a look at Asher.

Lies were one thing when the recipient had no notion of their falseness or otherwise. But Asher had been there. He had seen her, touched her, run his fingers across the bare skin at her shoulder… The heat in her cheeks did not abate and she took in several breaths to at least try to calm herself.

Damn it. She barely recognised this shrinking violet she had suddenly become and Lucy's puzzled frown only added to her discomfort. Suddenly the day stretching before her seemed indeterminably long. When Asher rose from the table and pushed his chair back, she was glad for it.

'I will be in Rochcliffe till the evening, Taris, and if I stay the night I will send word. Ladies.' His glance barely encompassed her and then he was gone, striding darkly through the dining-room portal. The sun slanting in from a nearby window gave the black of his hair a bluish light and highlighted the hard planes of his face.

She was in her bed by the window by ten o'clock that evening after spending an hour or so in the library with Taris, playing chess. Asher's absence had been a godsend, for under the simple pretext of exploring Falder further she had used the afternoon to search for any sign of her father's cane. And come away with nothing. Lord, she muttered to herself as she lay on her blankets and looked up at the sky, her time here was running out and, if she did not find the map soon, she had little chance of being invited back.

Where could he have hidden it? Where would she have hidden it?

If Falder had been a smaller home, everything would have been immeasurably less difficult, but with its numerous salons and bedchambers and nooks and crannies it was like a labyrinth, much of it joined through a series of inner passageways that defied reason.

Bolstering the pillows behind her back, she plucked her harmonica from beneath them and began to play, the gentle melody relaxing the strain of the day, and the tunes of Jamaica strangely comforting in the colder climes of Fleetness. Azziz had taught her the ways and whys of the instrument ten years ago on the slow watches of the *Mariposa* and ever since she had added songs to her repertoire that she could play by heart. Ruby had often sung along and danced to the music in the room they had shared off the Harbour Road in Kingston Town and the squalor of that time still haunted her: the danger, the lack of money, the dreadful yearning for the sea.

Here at Falder everything was easy and beautiful: the house, the furniture, the food and the people. A little money softened the rawness of life and a lot removed it completely. She smiled at her musings and then tensed as she heard footsteps in the corridor outside her room and a knock.

Tucking her hair back behind her ears and donning a nightrobe left in the wardrobe, she opened the door.

Asher stood there, wind-blown hair and drink-bruised eyes, the shadow of a twelve-hour stubble on his jaw. Carefully she edged the material of the sleeves down across her hands.

'I need to talk to you.'

'Here? Now?'

'It should only take a moment.'

'Very well.' She was not certain whether to invite him in or not. Granted, she knew enough about the social mores in England to also know that asking an unmarried man into your bedroom was unheard of. But did the rules apply when the same man was also the owner of the house? A refusal might look as if she imagined herself as feminine game or as if she suspected his intentions to be less than honourable.

He solved the worry for her by staying on the threshold even as she gestured him to enter.

'No. I should not come in—' He stopped, clearly perturbed.

'Where did you get the tattoo? The butterfly.'

'Jamaica.'

'Is it normal there? Normal for the daughter of a devout father?'

'I think we both know the answer to that question,' she replied.

'I would like to hear it from you.'

'My father was not quite as you may imagine.'

'What exactly was he like, then?' His golden gaze flared in the candlelight.

'He was a man whom life had disappointed.' Pride kept her from saying more, and she was pleased when he changed the subject.

'Taris said that you are a fine chess player. It is not often that he loses. To anyone. Where did you learn?'

'On the—' She stopped, horrified, as she realised what she had been about to say. *On the Mariposa.* Just like that.

'An uncle taught me,' she amended and held her breath as the awkwardness of the moment passed.

'I thought I heard music before, in here?'

'You did.' She brought the harmonica from her pocket and watched a range of emotions play across his face.

Puzzlement. Amusement. Interest.

'My family likes you, Lady Emma. Every time your name is mentioned, Taris and Lucinda sing your praises and it is not often that my brother waxes lyrical about anyone. Especially these days.'

'How did he lose his sight?' She asked the question quietly and was surprised by his sharp expression.

'An accident that should never have happened. If I hadn't been—' He stopped and caught at control, the muscles on the line of his jaw quivering.

'I do not think he blames you, your Grace.'

He smiled at that and moved back. 'No, he doesn't.' Tight words rising from the depths of despair.

'But you blame yourself?'

Suddenly everything was crystal clear. His lack of help for Taris on the road to Thornfield. It was not anger at his affliction that held him back, but guilt. Guilt. The sheer knowledge of it made her insides weaken.

Such a complex man and so masculinely vulnerable. She swallowed back her pity, knowing that at this moment he would not want it, and, as if he could read her mind, he stepped away.

'We are due over at Longacres tomorrow for dinner with the Gravesons. After yesterday, if you would rather cancel, I would quite understand.'

'No, I would like to go.'

'If you could be ready at five, then we would be back before midnight.'

The noise of voices from the stairs that joined this floor to the next had him turning, and, drawing his coat against the draughts of cold in the passageway, he was gone.

She had nothing to wear and two hours to be ready to leave for the Gravesons. Grimacing she pulled the last of her dresses from its hanger. She had never been bothered before about the state of her clothes, but this gown was hardly salubrious wear for any occasion, let alone a dinner date with a duke. She would give anything for a dress that actually fitted her and had a colour in it that was neither pastel nor brown.

And her gloves? The grey silk pair she wore constantly was fraying not only at the wrist but at the base of one thumb now, and the seam was so narrow that she could not reunite the cloth without also altering the fit.

A knock at the door and Lucinda was in the room, her face falling as she glanced at the gown.

'Is this what you were planning to wear tonight? Perhaps I should warn you that Annabelle puts much stock in the dress sense of others.'

'Then she will be sorely disappointed with me, I fear.'

Lucy laughed. 'You do not enjoy fashion?' she asked at length.

'You sound like your brother.'

'Asher asked you about your gowns?'

'He did. And I told him that I would rather buy books.'

'And is that true?'

Emerald's telling hesitation brought Lucinda to her side. 'I knew that of course it would not be true.' She walked across to the wardrobe and firmly shut the door. 'Nothing in there will do, Emma. May I call you that?'

'My friends call me Emmie.'

'Then Emmie it is, and I have just the gown for you. It's in my room and it was one that my cousin left at Falder last year and she is about your size and colouring.'

'She wouldn't mind me using it?'

'No, not at all. She's the least fussy person I know and one of the nicest.'

An hour later Emerald barely recognised herself. She stood in front of a full-length mirror in Lucy's room and stared. This dress was the first one she had ever worn that actually nearly fitted her. Gone were the sagging bodices and the false hems. Gone were the short not-quite-fit-me sleeves and the hideously high or dangerously low necks.

But it was the colour that owed the most to the transformation. Deep midnight blue with a hint of silky grey on its edge, the fabric showed up the line of her body and the gold of her skin. In this she did not look insipid or washed out. In this her eyes were bright and her hair, carefully combed by a maid, was for the first time placed in some semblance of order. Even her ears looked different, for Lucy had found some topaz drops that had been her grandmother's.

'You look wonderful,' she said as she hooked the earrings in place. 'But you have more than one pierced hole?'

Emerald took in breath. 'It is the way in Jamaica.'

'And your gloves? Is it the way there to wear gloves all the time?'

Perfect blue eyes met her own.

'No. That is my choice. I like to wear them.'

'Then you should make it into a fashion statement.' Rattling around in her cupboard, Lucinda came up with some fine white lace elbow-length gloves, looking enquiringly at her when she did not remove her old ones.

There was little else to do but to peel off the grey pair. Quickly. She turned her palms upwards as she pulled the new ones on and took a peek at Asher's sister.

She had seen.

She knew it as soon as she looked.

'I burnt myself once.' It was all that she would admit. She was pleased to see the lace was lined in fine cream silk and that no trace of the reddened scar tissue could be seen. Flame left the sort of mark with its bone-deep ravages that made people turn their eyes away. And her hands had been on fire for all of a minute before she hit the sea.

'I would prefer that you said nothing of my scars to anyone.'

'I promise you I won't.' Lucy made much of folding away the discarded petticoats and chemises before asking quietly, 'Do they hurt?'

'No.'

Her mind ran backwards to a battle in the waters off Jamaica about a year after her first meeting with Asher Wellingham. Azziz had been behind her and Solly Connors out further under the yardarm. Morning fog had engulfed the *Mariposa* and the flash that came from nowhere was strangely magnified by the closeness. She remembered Solly's head flying past her, his body curled around the footrope as if his fingers had a mind of their own, the last ingrained act of survival imprinted in their being. And shouts from below as a fireball whirled up the mast and hit them, the maincourse sheets soggy from the night-time rain sheltering them from the sheer force of it. She had reached out for the shroud and shifted her weight. But her fingers did not grip, could not grip, and she had fallen, fallen, fallen into the ocean.

When she woke up all hell had claimed her.

Thornfield came into view after a good fifteen minutes in the carriage and Emerald was glad to see it. Asher had hardly spoken to her and certainly had not complimented her on the gown or her hair. Chagrin was a strange emotion, she decided, a feminine art form of guilt that she had always despised. But here in the folding darkness of Fleetness Point she found herself pouting at his negligence.

With a sigh she shifted position, bringing the fullness of the skirt out from beneath her. Lucy had told her to do so for the material was heavy silk and liable to crush. In the dusk its silver shimmer was more noticeable, like a living moonbeam come to rest in her dress. She absently shaded her fingers over the lightness and glanced at Asher Wellingham from the corner of her eye.

He sat as far away from her as he could manage, his hands tightly bound on his lap. Tonight he had barely looked at her.

'I need to make a small detour to the harbour, for my draughtsman in London is in need of some plans.'

Irritation dropped away to sheer delight.

'We will go aboard your ship?' She tried to make her voice as indifferent as she could. But it was hard work.

'You can wait in the carriage, if you would rather. I will take just a moment to find the drawings and then we'll be on our way. Annabelle said six and it is not yet half past five, so there is still plenty of time.'

'I would be interested to go aboard.' She could not quite hide the excitement.

'Very well. Though I must warn you it is cramped and difficult to negotiate.'

'Difficult?' She opened her fan and hid a smile.

'I am sure I shall be able to manage, though I should not wish to be a nuisance…'

He did not answer as the carriage veered towards the harbour.

He helped her across the gangplank and the swell and ebb of the sea beneath her feet was like a caress.

Closing her eyes she savoured it, breathed it in.

'Are you all right?' There was urgency in his voice, and for the first time that night he touched her, his hand cupping her elbow as if to hold her up. She swayed into him, her body reacting before her mind warned her away.

'All right?' She was disorientated by sheer longing.

'Seasickness,' he clarified. 'It can sometimes hit quickly.'

'No, I am in good health.' With the greatest of will she broke the link between them and looked around, glad to feel her heart settling down to a more normal pace. 'It's a beautiful ship.' Her fingers reached out to the belayed halyard that led to the main lower topsail, so familiar she could have trimmed the sheet with her eyes closed.

'That's the rope that lets the sail drop. Without that we can't furl it.'

She smiled at his explanation, given to her in such simple terms. 'You have sailed a lot?'

'I used to.'

'But you don't any more?'

'I lost the taste for it,' he returned shortly and bade her follow him down the companionway. 'The chart-room is this way. Mind your step.'

It was the skirt, she thought later. In her haste she forgot to raise it properly and the toe of her shoe caught in the thick folds of silk and simply tipped her up. Asher caught her. Closer this time. The whisper of his breath touched her cheek and his hand fell across the swell of her bottom as he guided her to the master's cabin where they were cocooned in the quiet lap of the ocean, the smell of oil lamps mixing with the stronger scent of teak.

She felt the hard wooden ribs of the hull behind her back and the warm planes of his body at her front, pressing against her, closer. In the half-light only the snowy white of his cravat was plain. Every-thing else was melded into shadow.

'How do you do this?' he asked softly. 'How do you make me want you?' He raised her hand and the wet warmth of his tongue explored the space above the hem of her glove. And left her breathless.

'Asher.' She could barely say his name as her fin-gers threaded through the length of his night-dark hair. She knew exactly what it was he spoke of, this want that defied all rationality and sense and deliv-ered her to a place where nothing else mattered.

Just him. Her. Them.

With lips edged in anger his mouth took hers;

when the hand that rested on her bottom firmed and guided her to the place between his legs, she groaned. It was the residue of yesterday's suggested dalliance, she was to think later and the conjured imaginings that she had dealt with as a result all through the previous night. She could not find it in her to say no, to place her hand on his and call a halt. No, rather she leaned into his embrace, pressed against his solidity as his fingers slid around the edge of her breast.

Here in the dark of the hold of his ship with the gentle sound of water on wood she had no words to stop him. Oh! Love came easy without the stinging drudge of memory, and the girl she had been in Jamaica was the woman who responded here.

Tell me.

Show me.

Take me.

'Emma, I want you.'

Emerald.

For the first time his use of a name not quite her own bothered her. His eyes were dark twin pools of intensity, the brown in them ringed with a harsher colour as he slipped the strap of her low-cut dress from her shoulder and bent his head. Flipping his tongue against her nipple once, he pulled back, watching the skin pucker and crinkle.

'At the dinner with the Bishop of Kingseat you did not wear undergarments and when you bent over...' He stopped, giving her the impression of a man only just holding on to some semblance of control. 'Suffice it to say that I have wanted to touch you here ever since then.' His thumb lightly skimmed the wet coldness of her nipple. 'And kiss you here.' His lips were warm against the small patch of freckles lying in her cleavage. 'I have wanted to know the taste of your sun-warmed skin and find the line where clothes have shielded you. His hand dipped lower. 'Have they, Emma? Shielded you? Here?'

She could not speak. She could only feel as hot drifts of longing assailed her and the rhythm of his breathing changed. Her eyes fell upon his lips. He had beautiful lips. Full and defined. The stubble on his jaw was light as her palm brushed against it and when he tipped her lips to his, the slick shattering passion spun her wild and heat took over.

Away. From everything. She was all woman. Open, alive, free. And he was the sun and the ocean and the warm solid earth.

Again.

For ever. Cast as she was from a storm into the safe harbour of his body. And needing refuge.

The heavy footfall of boots were suddenly heard above them on the deck.

'Hell.' He pulled away and helped her straighten herself, as a man came down the stairs.

'Duke, I thought I heard you...' The words petered out and stopped, uncertainty replacing the earlier hurry. 'I'm sorry.' The newcomer's voice held a strange quiver. Not sorry at all, she determined, but amused.

'This is Peter Drummond, an old friend of mine who is also the ship's captain. Peter, meet Lady Emma Seaton.'

'It is my pleasure,' he said softly, his glance falling to the crushed silk of her skirt. A definite question was in his eyes and the tone in his voice was puzzled.

'You got my note, then?'

'Note?' Asher shook his head.

'To meet here. I thought that was why…'

'I came for the plans to take up to London. Is there a problem?'

'There might be.'

Emerald could tell the man did not wish to say more in front of her, so excusing herself, she walked back up the steps and on to the moonlit deck. The quiet burr of voices from below was a backdrop to the frantic beat of her heart.

What had just happened? Again? If Peter Drummond had not come…?

She could not think of it. Did not want to think of it.

'I am the pirate's daughter,' she whispered to herself.

'The pirate's daughter. The pirate's daughter.'

She remembered the taunts of the children on the dockside at Kingston Town, when the *Mariposa* had come into port, and the slanted glances of their parents.

Her father was a man who used fear to distance himself from everyone. And he had never been honest. Just as she was not being honest. Here.

With Asher.

The realisation made her sick and when he rejoined her she was hard-pressed to smile. He seemed preoccupied and angry and threatening in a way he had not been ten minutes earlier. The evening sun made his hair darker, the tan of his face showing up his teeth and the velvet of his eyes.

He was beautiful.

She admitted this simple fact to herself. And smiled.

They had gone a good mile before he spoke and in a voice that sounded nothing like the one she had last heard him use.

'Who are the men camped in the wood?'

'I am not certain what you mean—' she began, but he interrupted her.

'The men you brought with you from Jamaica. Does that make my query any clearer?'

'Who told you that?'

'Peter Drummond just now and Tony Formison a few days ago. His father owns the ship you came on and he remembers you disembarking with a black man and an Arab, four chests of books and your hair a damn lot longer than it appears to be now.'

'I see.' There was no point in denying it, so she re-grouped her defences and tried to look contrite. 'They are here to see that I am protected.'

'Protected against whom?' He had the answer even as he asked it. She could see the flint of disbelief on his face.

'And if they caught us like now, alone? What would happen then?'

'I suppose they would have to kill you.'

He laughed and then cursed. 'What makes you so certain that they could?'

'You strike me as a man who could easily protect himself, but if there were two of them, then, perhaps—'

He didn't let her finish.

'Who exactly are they?'

'My servants,' she ventured. 'When I left Jamaica for England it would have been dangerous to travel alone. They offered to accompany me to London.'

'And then they offered to follow you up here?'

'Yes.' Even to her ears the explanation sounded implausible.

'And you did not think to ask me to house them at Falder, in the servants' quarters?'

'They like their independence. Once they saw I was safely at your house and that you were a gentle-man—'

He interrupted her. 'How do you contact them?'

'By the signal of a candle at night.' She was honest in her answer, for he looked as if another lie might well incite his anger.

'Through the window of your room?'

'Yes.'

'And should I worry that they may frisk Falder with even more competence than you have?'

Because his summation of the situation was so close to what she had just been thinking she blushed, giving him his answer.

'I see.' He ran his fingers through his hair. Or what was left of his fingers, she amended.

'It is not as you think,' she began.

'Then how is it, Emma? Explain to me exactly how it is.'

'I cannot,' she said simply and turned away. In the shimmering glass her reflection was barely visible, a thin reminder of the person she purported not to be.

'You cannot because the truth is that you are a liar, Lady Emma Seaton. A beautiful liar, but a liar none the less.'

'Yes.' She faced him directly and left it at that. Tonight the untruths just would not come and his kisses still burned on her lips and hands and neck.

Lady Liar.

Pirate's daughter.

There was some sort of symmetry of verse in the expressions and both left her with a completely groundless counter-argument.

She *was* a liar. And *would be* a thief if she could

only find the damn map. Regret swamped her. All she wanted to feel again was the warmth of his lips against her own.

And know again the safety he offered.

She could not remember ever being truly safe. Not since her mother had left and not for a while before then too.

Blood.

And screaming.

The sounds of cold arguments on the warm winds of Jamaica. She tilted her head and tried to catch the glimpse of something elusive. But she couldn't, and when the Gravesons' house came into view she was pleased, for it released her from the close confines of the carriage.

Dinner was horrible.

Oh, granted, Annabelle Graveson had gone to an enormous amount of trouble and was the most gracious of hostesses, just as her son Rodney was the very epitome of excellent manners and careful conversation.

But Asher barely looked at Emerald and when he did she could see only a veneer of distrust in his eyes and a good amount of distance. She missed his banter. She missed his smile. She missed the breathless possibility that he might lean across and touch her and she would feel again the slow rise of passion and the quick burn of excitement.

What was she coming to? She was at dinner, for

goodness' sake, with a widow woman and her son. With an effort she tried to listen to what it was that Rodney was talking to her about.

Guns. She'd never liked them.

'I can now hit a target at thirty feet. Sometimes more. We often hunt in the grounds of Falder.'

'We.'

'Carisbrook and I. He's teaching me.'

'The Duke of Carisbrook is teaching you?'

His eyes swivelled around at the mention of his name.

'Is there a problem with that, Lady Emma?' he asked in his frostiest voice. A voice that implied she thought he could barely hold a gun, let alone shoot it.

'Certainly not.'

'I am pleased to hear it,' he returned and his smile was strained.

Annabelle Graveson seemed oblivious to everything as she leaned forward and placed her hand on Emerald's. On the third finger of her left hand was a ring bearing a diamond the size of a large rock. The house. The jewellery. The clothes she wore. Annabelle Graveson had become a rich woman on the death of her husband.

'I would like to make you a gift of some gowns, Emma. Would you accept that from me?' Her voice quivered.

'Gowns?' She did not umderstand the reason for such an offer.

'For your Season in London.'

'Oh, no, Lady Annabelle.' She went to say more, but could not.

'Is it because I am a stranger to you? I am hoping we may change that.' The fingers on her forearm tightened.

He looked as puzzled as she felt.

'Lady Emma is staying with the Countess of Haversham, Annabelle, and is well looked after.'

'Yes, of course,' she replied, a semblance of calm once again in place. 'Of course she is. When is your birthday, my dear?'

The question was so unexpected it took Emerald by surprise. 'My birthday?'

Annabelle Graveson nodded.

'It's on the third of November.'

Tears filled Annabelle's eyes and she dabbed at them with her handkerchief and waved the attention of her son away. 'No, Rodney,' she said. 'I am quite all right. In fact I have never felt better.' And with that cryptic remark she bent over the pudding she had before her and demolished the lot.

'They are unusual people,' Emerald chanced into the silence as they wended their way home a few hours later. When she got no reply, she amended her observation. 'Nice and unusual, I meant.'

Still no reply. She was not daunted.

'Annabelle seems rather a nervous woman,' she continued.

'Whereas you, on the other hand, are not.'

'I wouldn't say that.'

'Name one thing that you afraid of.'

She was silent and unexpectedly he laughed. 'Thank you, at least, for not lying to me.'

'I did not lie about James.'

'I know.'

She held her breath and looked out of the window. The clouds against the moon reminded her of her little brother's curls as he had lain there asleep while she watched him.

Tonight he seemed close. Perhaps that was because it had been so long since she had spoken to anyone about him. And Asher Wellingham had been a good listener.

What else had he been? A would-be lover, a man whom she could trust and respect and like.

Like? Too tame for what now raced inside her and yet with the ghost of her father hanging so baldly between them nothing else could be possible.

Nothing.

She saw he kneaded his thigh with the fingers on his left hand and chanced the opening.

'Do you have a cane, your Grace?'

'A cane?'

'For your leg. Perhaps if you took your weight off it…'

He stopped rubbing immediately.

'My uncle had a cane once. A fine one, carved in ebony. He had hurt his knee at Waterloo and found the stick to be invaluable.'

God, how many more clues could she safely give him?

One more.

She took in a deep breath and spoke.

'Walking sticks are actually quite a passion of mine. I collect them, you know.'

She did not let the pained look on his face dissuade her.

'I have twenty from all parts of the world.'

'Fascinating.' The tone he used intimated that he found the subject anything but.

'Indeed, your Grace, it is.' She was grateful for the dark and for the movement of the coach. 'If you had any at Falder, I would be pleased to look at them for you to give you some idea of their value.' She felt the thick beat of duplicity in her throat when he did not answer and the look in his eyes was one of singular calculation.

She should not have gambled on his intellect. Already she could see the wheels of his brain turning and so she was not surprised by his next question.

'Would it be a cane by chance that you are looking for at Falder?'

'No.' She met his question directly as the lights of

his home came into view. As the carriage began to slow he lifted her gloved fingers into his.

'What happened to your hands? Are they also a part of the mystery of Emma Seaton?'

'I don't understand.'

'Do you not?' he chided, the soft light in his eyes hard and flat. 'If I looked into the records of the Haversham family, where exactly would you be placed in relation to Miriam?'

Taking a breath, she pulled her hand away and tried to rally. Lord, if he was to do that…

'I am her niece, as I believe you already know.'

'I see,' he returned as the lights of Falder flooded the carriage. All around there now stood servants, waiting. Emerald was pleased when the first footman seemed to take her smile as a signal and moved forward to open the door.

An escape.

Gathering the skirts of her gown, she hurried from the coach. The ruse was up. She knew it. When Asher backtracked into the depths of her family history, he would have his suspicions confirmed that there was no cousin called Liam Kingston. And he would also know that Miriam's only brother was Beauvedere Sandford Louden. It would take him but a moment to work out the rest.

She would have to forgo her searching and be gone from Falder at the first possible opportunity. The map offered riches, but discovery could mean prison. She had failed in her quest and now there was little else to do but return home.

A tight feeling of absolute uncertainty engulfed her.

Ruby and Miriam.

How on earth could she protect them?

Asher roamed the hills above the ocean, cursing the note in his pocket, the note he had found beneath his door when he had returned to his room in the hours after dawn. Emma Seaton was gone.

Back to London.

Back to Jamaica.

Back to God knew where.

The horse beneath him whickered and pranced and he stilled her with a quiet whisper, hating the way his mind kept replaying the feel of Emma's skin beneath his hands.

He wanted her. That much was plain. He wanted her like he had never wanted any woman before. Even with Melanie he had not experienced this white-hot flash of passion, this desperate uneasiness. And the way she responded to him…

'Stop it.' He said the words out loud, surprised by the gut-tearing anger in them. Emma Seaton was a thief and a liar and a threat to his family. He had given her a chance to trust him, after all. More than a chance. If it had been anyone else, she would have been thrown out after the night he had seen her dressed in the lad's clothes in front of his dead wife's picture.

Why had he not, then?

He knew the answer even as he posed the question.

Because he admired her. She was so unlike any other woman who had ever made his acquaintance that she threw him somewhat and he doused down the urge to place his hands around her neck and strangle the truth out of her.

Why would she not trust him?

What had she to hide?

He swore into the gathering wind and turned his horse for home.

Lucinda met him in the front portico and she did not look pleased.

'Emmie is gone.'

'Emmie?' He had not heard her called that before.

'She was my friend. She told me her friends called her Emmie. She said that I could too and now she has gone.'

'Did she tell you why she went?' He could barely keep the irritation from his voice.

'No, she did not have time, though she did leave this note for me.' She handed him a small piece of paper to read.

Miriam and I need to return to London. Thank you for letting me borrow the clothes and jewellery.

'I do not think she went of her own free will, Asher. I think you were cross with her. I think she reminds you of a time when you used to laugh and enjoy life and so you frightened her off somehow…'

'That's enough.' The whiplash of his words shook Lucinda visibly and she turned towards the stairs, but not before snatching her note back.

'She may be gone from Falder, Asher, but you can't forbid me to see her in London, for I like her, even though you are determined not to.'

He watched her as she flounced up the stairs, the letter tightly held in her hand and the promise of rebellion in the staunch set of her shoulders. Life had not burdened her yet, he thought as he made for the library, all her hopes and dreams still intact and possible.

So unlike his own.

Taris sat in the armchair by the window. Today he looked tired, and when he removed his glasses to clean them Asher saw that his right eye was strangely opaque.

'Emma Seaton has gone?' His brother's tone had the same ring to it as Lucinda's. Tired of defending his actions, Asher reached down and took a cigar from a box on the desk near the fireplace. Cutting it, he breathed in deeply before sitting on the leather sofa opposite his brother.

'When Father died he made me promise on his death bed that I should never compromise Falder because a thousand years after our demise this pile of stones and mortar will still be here, and a thousand years past that thousand too. Custody. Tradition. Responsibility. Call it what you will, but I listened.'

'Lord, you actually believe that she would compromise Falder? In what way?'

'Rifling through the silverware at midnight would be one way I could mention.'

'And did she steal anything?'

Asher shook his head. 'Nothing I could determine, but I think there was something specific that she was after and she has not yet found it.'

'Specific. Like what?'

'God knows, for I don't. Money, perhaps. Jewels. The combination lock on my safe had been tampered with.'

'She had the skills to try to break open your safe? Who sent her, do you think?'

'She wouldn't say. I did ask.'

A moment went by as he watched Taris play with the tassel of a burgundy bookmark left on an open copy of Webster's *Duchess of Malfi*.

'She's in trouble, Asher. You said as much yourself.'

'And you think that it concerns me?'

'I can hear it in your voice that you admire her, which leads me to conclude that, if you have any hopes of an heir to enjoy these hallowed halls, now might be the time to take action.'

Asher swore to himself and did not answer. Could not answer. Whatever it was that Emma Seaton inspired in him was irrelevant. Lust? Like? Love?

'You would not think of providing heirs yourself, of course?' His query after a moment or so was cynical.

'Hard to catch a woman when you can barely make out their form.'

'The Caribbean was kind to neither of us, Taris.' He hated the way his brother's face stiffened as the air around them creaked under the dead weight of regret, and the scars on his back smarted under memory as the shifting frames of time and place took him back to the pirates' compound. The jangle of his broken chains in the run between sand and water. The silent ricochet of lead that ripped across Taris's temple and dashed his sight into splinters: a bitter reward for the rescue he had orchestrated. The red of the froth on the waves and aching arms as Asher had dragged them out, out into the greenness of the deep with its blue-edged sky and its uncountable miles of nothingness. Out where the ocean currents were like a river and where letting go of fear was the only way to survive.

And survive they had. Barely. He looked down at his fingers and across at the glazed eyes of his brother.

And knew.

Knew that if he let go of Emma Seaton, even more of him would be lost.

'I will leave for London tomorrow to see how Lady Emma fares.' He frowned as he saw his brother's smile and refilled his glass. With water. 'Don't read too much into the change of plan. It's for peace of mind, that's all.'

'I'll come with you.'

'You haven't been to town in years.'

'Then it's past time I was back there, isn't it?'

'You're doing this for her?'

'I am.'

Asher was astonished at Taris's capitulation. And worried by it too. If the gossip about his sight was not kind, he wondered how it would affect his brother. Another problem, he thought, but one that could be minimised by a careful campaign. It would not be too hard, after all, to mingle in a crowded ballroom, especially if he stayed at Taris's side to smooth any problems.

He was pulled from his reverie as the housekeeper bustled into the room.

'I heard that Lady Emma left, sir, this morning while I was at Thornfield. I wonder if I might have a word.'

'Yes, of course.' Ignoring Taris's obvious interest, he led her out of the library and into his office. The normally ebullient Mrs Wilson seemed almost embarrassed by what it was she next wished to relate to him.

'It's just that I wondered what you wanted me to

do with the bed coverings, your Grace? Miss Emma never used the bed while she was here, and if she is coming back—'

'She what?'

'She did not favour the mattress, your Grace. Nay indeed, she always slept near the balcony with the doors open.' Her face reddened as he frowned. 'Perhaps she liked the fresh air, your Grace, and indeed I have heard it is said to be good for one.'

Another convert to the cause of Emma Seaton, Asher thought. Lucy. Taris. And now Mrs Wilson.

He took a breath and addressed his housekeeper. 'Lady Emma Seaton will not be back.'

'Oh, dear, your Grace. Well, all as I can say is that it's a shame, it is, for a nicer guest we have not had, or a tidier one. And what should I do with all the shells that she collected?'

Asher began to laugh even as he stood.

Five minutes later he took to the stairs leading to Emma's room and opened the wide oak door.

A nest of blankets sat near the French doors, the sheets folded on the bed in a neat pile. And unused, as was the thick felted quilt.

Emma Seaton travelled light and rough, he thought and crossed to the balcony. Two heavy chairs had been moved and placed together to form a platform that one might stand upon. With care he mounted them and before him, through the green fold of a hillock, lay the sea.

The sea.

If he closed his eyes, he could hear it, as she must have done. My God, every single thing he ever found out about her confused him. She was not used to sleeping in a bed and she liked the sea. And the only thing in this room that had been used while she inhabited it was a candle.

A candle used to signal her men in the wood in the very dead of night. A candle used to search his home. He ran his fingers through his hair and wished she were still here.

Near him. Safe. And then he cursed himself for thinking it.

It was late when Asher and Taris and Lucinda arrived back in London, and Jack Henshaw, who had been waiting for them at Carisbrook House, had worrying news.

'The Countess of Haversham is ill and Lady Emma has sent away the doctor and taken full charge of the situation herself. Unusual, but dutiful,' he added and leant forward to his drink. 'Gregory Thomas, the physician, is an acquaintance of mine. He said he saw the Countess last in the company of a burly black man lighting a sweet-smelling fire of oil in a copper basin while the niece pushed hot pins into the side of her aunt's neck. Many are saying it to be witchcraft.'

Asher swore. Lord, if that was the case, Emma

was going to be sore pressed to re-enter the narrow world of society. Clothes a little odd or outdated were one thing, but it was quite another to be accused of practising sorcery. And so blatantly. 'Why the devil would she have done that? Why would she be negligent with her reputation?' The answer came to him immediately.

Because Emma Seaton did not mean to stay in England at all. Because the search of Falder was a means to an end and that end was to be once again ensconced in the place she called home. Jamaica.

When Jack left Taris lingered and Asher could tell that he was disturbed by something, though as his brother began speaking the subject was very different from that which he had expected.

'If you have an Achilles' heel, Asher, it is your love of control.'

'You're speaking of Emma Seaton, I presume?' he bit back. Tonight he was tired.

'She is not like the other women here. She is strong and independent and would not thank you, I think, for seeing to her reputation.'

'You do not think I should help her?' Real anger reverberated in his question.

'I do not think that you should judge her by the standards of society.'

'Because she so obviously is from somewhere else?'

'No. Because she is very much her own person. Like I am mine. Sometimes, even despite my lack of sight, I can feel you watching me and worrying about the next person with too loud a voice who will inadvertently hurt my feelings.' He laughed and softened his tone. 'What will you do, Asher? Fight them all because you feel responsible? Don't you see? I came to the Caribbean to find you on my own accord and Emma Seaton has come to London on her own accord. It is not you who needs to calm the waters to make sure that she fits. She doesn't and she probably doesn't want to either.'

Asher slapped his hand against the wood in the wall. Hard. 'And where will she fit, then? Jamaica has hardly nurtured and protected her.'

Taris laughed. 'Lord, Asher. It's more than a feeling of responsibility for her, isn't it?'

Turning away, he mulled over his brother's last question and was glad when he did not demand an answer, but left the room in that particular way he had of moving around objects.

More than responsibility?

More than friendship?

For a moment Asher imagined Emma Seaton as the Duchess of Carisbrook, immune against all criticism just because of who he was. He could protect her. From everyone.

But would she want him to?

Without a doubt he knew that she wouldn't.

'Lord help me,' he muttered and was wondering what the hell he was going to do when his eyes fell on a cane near the door. Uneasy conjecture caught as he remembered the conversation in the coach on the way home from Longacres. Canes. Questions. The quick flare of interest.

In the corner of a room off the blue salon was a stand set in the wall, hidden behind the thick fold of a velvet curtain. Two canes sat inside it and, as his fingers reached for the black-and-ivory stick studded in jewels, memory turned.

He'd taken this from the *Mariposa* after he'd returned to the Caribbean and killed Sandford. A crutch to aid his damaged leg. Could this be what Emma was after? The stones were valuable after all, and it was a fine piece of carving. Intrigued, he examined it closely and noticed that the handle was not quite round, the ornate twists of wood hiding a catch beneath the lip of ebony stones. Perhaps she had been interested in this particular cane not for its value, but for something else! Something hidden. Swearing, he ran his nail across a ridge and shaved off parings of wax, the sealant hindering the downward motion of the clasp. A dull click and the handle parted company with the body of the wood, a hollowed compartment inside becoming plainly visible.

He smiled at the ridiculous ease of it all as he ironed out a parchment under the light.

A map, he determined. An old map of the Eleutheran inlets and with much more than the gauge of depth shown. A map delineating caves of gold! Contemplation sparked discomfort. What would a woman like Lady Emma Seaton want with such a map and how could she have known about it?

Slipping the parchment into a secret drawer in his desk he sat down to write a note.

The noise came later, much later, as he sat in the darkened library before the embers of a dying fire. A small scratching at first and then a larger bang. Someone was in his office down the hall.

Emma? His heartbeat surged as he moved forward into the passageway that divided the rooms. When the heavy wood of a baton hit him square across his shoulders and sent him to the floor, the parquet was cold beneath his cheek. For a moment he felt winded by shock and disorientated.

'Where's the bloody map?' the larger one of the two men demanded, his accent somewhat similar to Emma's. The lilt of an island cadence. Lord, were these her men, tired of the more gentle persuasion? Dizziness dissipated under the larger threat to his life and, surging forward, he knocked the man nearest to him off his feet. The sharp blade of a knife nicked the flesh of his upper arm, and, swearing, Asher lurched to standing and eyed them both warily, the circling distance between adversaries lessening.

'Who the hell are you?' He looked down at his hand. A red tide of blood dripped from his fingers. The damned blade had got an artery, he thought, suddenly light-headed, though he shook his head to dispel the gathering haze and held his wounded arm tight against his body, balancing as he calculated the seconds left before they rushed him.

They came together and the remembered moves of fighting learned in the hot compound of the Caribbean returned to him. Effortlessly. The sharp clean noise of a broken bone and a knife falling to the floor, to a quick curse of anger as his assailant's heads met.

'Who the hell are you?' he bellowed again as the second thief rose uncertainly up. He had no more energy to fight, though already he could hear the running footsteps of those in the house. Evidently the other man heard it too. He grabbed his accomplice around the shoulders and they crossed to the window and were outside even as he slid to the floor.

Asher looked up as Taris, Lucinda and four servants entered the room. 'Get a doctor,' he said as spurts of his blood rose into the air before him.

He came to in his bed. His sister sat beside him and he could see that she had been weeping. Taris watched him from the window and for a moment the world lightened and his ears hummed. Then it refocused, but strangely. He had never felt so tired in all of his life.

'What happened?' Even words were hard to say.

'You nearly bled to death, Asher, and would have done so had not Lady Emma turned up at the exact same moment that this all happened.' Taris spoke carefully.

'Emma?'

'She arrived just as Lucinda and I came downstairs to see what all the noise was about and she almost certainly and single-handedly saved your life.'

'How?' Nothing made sense.

Lucinda carried on the narrative. 'She stripped off your sleeve with a knife she kept and wound the ties of the curtains tightly around your upper arm and kept it raised. I think she pressed down on the wound as well and when the bleeding had slowed she took the blade to the fire and heated it before searing your flesh. All in the space of a few moments. When Dr MacLaren arrived, everything was over. All he did was to bandage the wound.'

'Is she here?'

'No. She left. Without a word to us. Grabbed the two knives on the floor and left.'

'I want her here.'

'She has gone from the Haversham town house.' Taris walked forward and sat on the bed. 'I had the only servant the place boasted brought here and she intimated that Emma and Miriam were with other friends in London. She had no idea where.'

Asher tried to rise and fell backwards, the pain in

his arm radiating around his whole body and making him feel dizzy.

'Doctor MacLaren said to warn you that if you move too much you will rupture the artery and bleed to death. He also said you were to have this.' Lucy emptied the contents of a sachet of powder into a glass of water and handed it to him.

'To stop it hurting,' she explained as he hesitated, and then smiled as he finished the lot.

'Stand guards around the house, Taris, and if you find Emma keep her here. Safe.' Asher felt the floating dizziness reach out and already the day was fading but he had to be certain his brother had heard. 'It is dangerous here. Everything is dangerous.'

He was pleased when Taris nodded, the tight anger on his face suggesting that the house would be watched over.

It was midnight when he woke again.

Emma sat in lad's clothes at the side of his bed, the tight line of her trousers emphasising the curves of her body. She held an assortment of sharp pins in her hand. Ungloved, he noticed. The searing red of the scars caught his attention, but tonight she did not seem to care.

'Stay still,' she whispered and placed a pin into his skin below the elbow, twirling it this way and that. A small dull pain radiated up into his armpit.

'It will take away any infection,' she explained

when she saw him looking. A dozen other such needles graced his arm and chest, catching the quiet dance of lamplight in their shivering thinness.

He tried to raise his hand to touch her, but he couldn't.

'Why...?' At least his voice still worked. She moved back, the frown on her brow deepening, but he was too tired to try to patch the story together tonight. All he wanted to know was Emma's part in it. He could not quite bring himself to say what he was thinking.

Why did you want me dead?

His eyes flickered uncertainly to the needles.

'They were island men,' she said quietly, anger resonating in every word.

'Are there more of them?'

'Yes.'

'They wanted to kill me.'

She was silent, though he could see the quick flash of temper that stormed through turquoise eyes. The unusual shade was muted tonight. Smoky. Distant.

'I will not let them.'

The absurdity of her vow almost made him laugh. He had no idea of how much time had passed since he had been hurt. One day? Two days? A week? Everything was blurred and difficult and when she bent down he tried to summon up his last reserve of energy.

'Look under the bed, Emma,' he instructed,

pleased when she did not question him, but leant down. 'Is that what they were after?'

A sharp spike of adrenalin raced through Emerald. Her father's ebony cane lay before her. Confused she laid it on the quilt. If Asher did not know of the secret compartment, she could slip the map out once he fell asleep. When she looked at him, however, she knew that the game was up.

'It was easy to open.'

'Open?' She tried to inject a great sense of surprise into the word.

'Move the catch and turn the body of wood to the right.' Said flatly as though he was running out of patience with the whole pretence. With trepidation she did as he instructed.

Nothing was inside save a sheet of paper twisted strangely to stop it from disappearing down into the sharp end of the cane. Removing it, she ironed it flat with the palm of her hand.

If you want what was in here you will need to trust me.

The ornate Carisbrook baronial seal was stamped on to the bottom in red wax and her shock was compounded by the wariness on Asher's face. It was all she could do to stop her voice from shaking.

'Where is the map?'

'I want a promise first.'

She stayed silent, not trusting her voice enough to speak. Where the hell would he have hidden it? Her eyes flashed around his room in a quick survey of possible places.

'Not here,' he continued. 'Falder is the only place I will return it to you and I want your promise to come there with me.

'I cannot—' He didn't let her finish.

'Where are your men?'

'Outside.'

'Bring them in.'

'Now?'

'Now.' The lighter webbing in his eyes was easily seen, giving him a dangerous and predatory look. Not willing to chance a denial, she walked across to the window and lifted a candle, waving it twice.

He noticed the sash had been raised. For her entrance, he supposed. And her exit. Lord, if he felt stronger this would have all been so much easier.

A man came through the window with a knife in his teeth and two pistols tucked into his belt and he was closely followed by a second.

Not servants at all, Asher thought, but pirates. He had had enough dealings with the likes of Beau Sandford to recognise those who scoured out a living on the open oceans. Lord, his ordered and controlled world was tipping up into more chaos by the second and he was angered anew by the silent questioning message that passed between the men and Emma.

Complicity and knowledge. They had seen the cane and it was impossible not to feel the flare of anticipation. Nothing quite made sense and the ache in his head blurred a nagging connection that he knew he should be making.

The burly Arab stationed himself at the door and Asher hoped that his sister would not take it on herself to grace him with one of her midnight visits. Taking a breath, he steeled himself to the task.

'I would like Lady Emma to stay here. With her aunt,' he added when he saw that she was about to argue.

'You what...?'

He ignored the smaller man's outburst completely and carried on in a measured tone. 'She will be chaperoned and protected.'

A slice of steel was the only answer. The knife at his throat pressed in before he could utter another word. He made himself relax.

'No, you will not hurt him.' Emma's voice shook and the knife melted away to be replaced by the angry dark visage of its owner.

'If you cross us, your Grace, the last thing you feel on this earth will be my blade.'

Asher laid back against the pillow. His head throbbed and the steady beat of blood in his ears made the world echo. Why did he not just give them the damn map and get them out of his life once and for all? Let them go back to Jamaica with the hard-won spoils of greed.

He knew the answer as he looked at Emma. Because, like it or not, they were connected somehow. He could almost feel the tie that bound them, and see in the turquoise depths of her eyes the same loneliness that was inside him. He'd felt it from the very first moment of seeing her at Jack's ball. Affinity. Alliance. Knowledge.

And the realisation that her prime motivation for being in England was greed had not bent him from his purpose.

A treasure map!

He noticed she had replaced her gloves before calling in her men. And yet she would show him the angry scars upon her hands. Nothing made sense.

'What did you want us here for?' The man at the door spoke for the first time. 'She could have told us what you have so far.'

'I want you to stand guard on the trip back to Falder. I will pay good clean gold for you to find the safest way back.'

The slur was not unheeded. 'And what do you get in return for all this?'

'The absolution of a debt.'

Emerald started at the words. Had he remembered her from the *Mariposa* or was it the incident after the Henshaw ball that he spoke of? Nothing showed in his face save exhaustion, the tinge of red around his irises giving him the look of someone who had ingested too much bad liquor.

Asher.

He had been as near death as she had seen anyone, the blood from the wound on his arm coursing across the floor in a red river, taking away consciousness and making him clammy. She put the image from her mind and walked to the window, raising her hand against the moon. Her fingers shook when she thought of it. Still.

Lord. The options closed in on her because she also knew enough about medicine to realise that for the next few days at least he should not be moved. And though his offer of a place here was appreciated, she could barely contemplate what his family must think of her.

The absolution of a debt.

The words floated in between the cracks of uneasiness and she felt both the power and the impossibility of them, for when she had torn off his shirt to tend to his wound she saw what she had not before.

Scars. Rows of them cut across his back, ribboned flesh silvered and sliced diagonally. She imagined the pain he must have felt and the sheer raw fury of powerlessness. She turned back to face the room, and when Azziz nodded she let out the breath she had not realised that she had been holding.

They would follow his instructions? They would take orders from a man who lay pale faced in a bed with a quarter of the blood that should have been flowing through his veins and the marks of slavery on his back?

Yes, they would, because, even given his wounds, leadership and authority stamped itself easily into the lines of Asher Wellingham's body and into the cadence of his words. A raw untamed wildness, all the more startling for the setting she had found it in. England. With its manners and protocols and ludicrous comportments.

For a moment she was disorientated with the sheer longing of reaching out and just holding on. He could protect her as he protected his brother and mother and sister. And the tenants on his land at Falder and the servants in all of his homes.

But she was Emerald Sandford and these dreams of safety were not for her. When she got the map, she would take ship for Jamaica, find the treasure and clear the debts that hung over her father's name. And then she would rebuild St Clair.

St Clair. Even the name was hard to say. She remembered crouching in the shadow of the trees with Ruby and watching the place burn, the flames lighting up the night sky for miles around, small pieces of ash floating into her sister's outstretched hand. Ruby had laughed as she had wept, waiting in the glade against the red, red sky; when the morning had finally come, leaving the skeleton of one remaining wall, they had picked through the rubble and salvaged three pots and a half-burned spade. And her jewellery box, slung beneath a beam that had not quite caught fire, a small buffer against impending poverty.

She shook her head and gestured to Azziz and Toro to wait outside. Using the moment of their departure to take the acupuncture needles from his arm, she found the darkness about his eyes worrying.

'A worthy art in the East, Emma, but here in England the pins may be misinterpreted for something else entirely.'

'What?'

'Witchcraft.'

She laughed at the absurdity of it, thinking of Wing-Jin and his patient teachings aboard the *Mariposa*.

'A society without rules is more dangerous then a society with too many. Have you ever heard of the pirate Beau Sandford?'

The colour drained right out of her face. 'He was an acquaintance of my father's.'

'The devout and honourable Reverend?''

'The very religious treat each man as redeemable.'

She could barely utter the words said next. 'It is said that you killed this man?'

She expected him to brag about doing just that. But he didn't, and the pain in his eyes held her rooted to the spot, neither moving nor speaking.

My God, what had she done to him? His words from the night in the gardens at Falder came back to her. *'I was not at home for Melanie's funeral. I should have been home.'*

She had given his statement little notice before,

imagining that perhaps he was on one of his ships plying the coast of foreign lands for cargo. Could there have been a more sinister reason for his absence and for his injuries and for the sleepless midnights when he wandered his library drink in hand and waited for the dawn? She turned to leave.

'No.' Asher's voice was tired, but he fought for consciousness with the same one-tracked determination as he seemed to fight everything else. 'You will stay, Emma. The deal. Promise me that you will.'

'I need to talk to Miriam.'

'No. It is not safe to leave.'

'My aunt will not understand what is happening.'

'Taris will speak with her.'

The lines between his nose and mouth were pronounced. He was exhausted, yet he still fought to have her stay. With him.

'This cannot be proper—' she began, but he broke across her words and smiled.

'Proper? When was anything proper between us?'

When she did not answer he rang the bell on his bedside table. Sweat beaded his upper lip.

'If you are in pain, I could help you.'

'No. Just…want your promise to stay.' His voice shook with exhaustion and his hair was dark and damp against the white of the sheets as he instructed his servant to see her to a room.

Chapter Ten

Emerald slipped through the kitchens into the garden. She had been at Carisbrook House for almost five days now, though she had not seen Asher since the day of her arrival. Her questions as to his state of health had all been answered perfunctorily by the servants, but had included no mention of an invite to see him and so she had stayed away.

Miriam had been installed in the room next to her and the cold her aunt was suffering seemed remarkably better with the ministrations of the Wellingham physician. This morning Emerald had sat reading to her, but now Emerald needed some space, some air and some exercise to temper the quiet edge of waiting.

The gardens, while not as large as those at Falder, were complex and the small sound of a boot scuffed against the shell path had her walking on further and turning a corner. Taris Wellingham sat on a wide marble garden seat, his hat in his lap and his face turned towards the sun.

'Lady Emma,' he said as he registered her presence.

'You knew it was me?' she said before realising the rudeness of such a question.

He smiled. 'Lack of sight heightens the hearing and you walk with a particular gait.' Tilting his head, he continued. 'You walk your world like one who is not at home in England.'

Emerald was still as she considered a response, though he did not seem to require one as he continued talking.

'If you sit with me for a moment, I would like to tell you a little about my brother.'

He waited as she rearranged her skirts and took a place beside him and when he started to talk she heard a reticence. 'Asher thinks that you need…protecting.'

'Does he?' She could barely answer.

'He thinks that you may be in trouble and he is a man who knows his responsibilities and sticks by them. Stability. Trust. Loyalty. All fine qualities, would you not agree?'

'I would.'

'And he is different since he met you, happier, for he has let few others close since his return from the Caribbean.'

Emerald frowned, uncertain now as to where this conversation was leading. Was it a warning?

'He was held captive for a year after the pirate Sandford ambushed his ship off Turks Island. And when a ransom note came to Falder and we finally found out where Asher was, he was full of only one thing—revenge. He came home only to get better to go back again a year later.'

Oh, God. Emerald tried to stop the aching lump of guilt that congealed in her throat from spilling over into her eyes.

This was all her fault.

When she had thrown Asher into the ocean as a means of saving him from the wrath of her father, no one could have foreseen the consequences. And this very minute was one of them.

She had ruined his life. Irrevocably. Undeniably.

'Emma?' His hand covered hers. 'Are you all right?'

'Yes.' She stood and forced a smile on her face. *Judas. Traitor. Liar.*

If she saw Asher now, he would know.

Pleading a headache, she fled to her room and lay down on her blanket near the window, stuffing the fabric in her mouth to stop the sobs that gathered in the back of her throat.

All my fault…all my fault. The litany of guilt was like a mantra. His wife, his scars, Taris's lack of sight and his lost years. Lord, she had done all this to him. Unknowingly. The serpent in the Garden of Eden.

Her.

* * *

She crept down the corridor and across the stairs to the landing on the first floor.

Asher's rooms.

A spike of panic nearly had her turning away from the heavy door, but she made herself stand still until the fear had passed and then pressed on silently. Opening the door, she turned the key in the lock as she shut it behind her. It was dark inside and the glow from a fire in the grate of an adjoining room threw shadows over everything. A quick glance at the moon through the windows gave her a rough timing. Around three o'clock. She stood still until she had her bearings and listened until the scrape of a quill upon parchment drew her attention. He was writing at his desk? Her heart began to thud and the thin cotton shift she wore stuck to the moisture building across her skin. But she would not waver.

'Who's there?' His voice was close, husky, and she could not quite find it in herself to answer.

Emerald.

Beau's daughter.

Judas.

A chair scraped across parquet and then he was in the room, shirt-tails pulled from his trousers and wearing no cravat. Even in the lack of light she could make out the thick wedge of bandage beneath his shirt.

Was it too soon? Six days since the attack.

She placed her arms by her side and made herself relax.

'Emma?' A whisper of disbelief was underscored by soft puzzlement as his eyes came to rest upon her gloveless fingers. And, as if to give himself time, he asked a question.

'What happened?'

'They were burnt.'

'When you were cooking?'

Smiling at his assumption, she knew that she could not give Asher even one more lie. But there was something that she could give him. Something precious.

Herself.

Lifting her hands to the ties at her bodice, she unlaced the ribbon and simply stepped out of her shift, nipples puckering hard in the sudden cold.

'Lord.' Asher breathed in, and the sensual haze in his eyes took the breath from her body in one heavy hit.

'You once suggested a dalliance and I turned you down. I have come to think that was a mistake.'

She cursed the shiver that ran through her words and desperately wondered what was supposed to happen next. The growing thickness of his manhood was plainly seen, though she could not quite bring herself to lean down and open his laces. No, whilst she always swam in the nude and slept in the nude and was rarely hampered by society's penchant for undergarments, the pleasuring of a man was something she had only seen at a distance in the brothels of many a dockside port.

Wetting her lips with her tongue, she tried to remember the less bold moves of the doxies who haunted the drinking houses between Savannah la Mar and Kingston and with precision ran her hand across her stomach and lower, gently swaying her hips in the way Molly's girls did in the Golden Hind, a favourite drinking hole of her father's.

And now what?

A sudden fright consumed her. Would he be gentle? Worse, would he refuse her?

Asher saw the panic in her eyes before she closed them, turquoise bright and shaded by some emotion he could not quite fathom. What game did she play at? Would someone discover them and insist that he do the right thing by her and offer marriage? Marriage? To a woman who posed as a lady, acted the harlot and had the body of an angel. His eyes skimmed across her breasts. Her waist was tiny and the long length of her legs gave her a grace that was…breathtaking. Lord, even at the salons of the select courtesans in London she would be exceptional, the tattoo on her breast and the scar on her thigh adding layers of mystery.

Lady Emma Seaton? Nothing about her quite added up but the sum total of all that she was drove him to the edge of reason.

He felt like locking her up at Falder where no other man would ever touch her again—she was his woman, damn it.

His woman?

The sheer possessiveness of the thought egged him on and he felt his rising lust as a power.

'Come.' He did not move at all, but waited as she walked forward into his arms, his erection hard against her stomach, pressing, eager, ready. When he shrugged out of his shirt, she touched the bandage gently, the pale gilt of her curls whisper soft against his cheek.

'Is it sore?'

Shaking his head, he removed his trousers and reached out to the curve of her waist and then lower.

Emerald felt the first push of his fingers in a place no man had touched before. Careful. Warm. Certain.

So this was it.

This was what she had heard of for ever.

'Asher?' She breathed his name as a quicksilver pain pierced her inside.

She would not stop him.

Payment.

Repayment.

Her repayment.

The guilt torn from her very soul made her still.

'Open for me, sweetheart.' The command was whispered and underlined by a quick movement. And when she did, the shards of gold in his eyes glowed against a darker brown. Triumph, conquest and elation mixed with desire.

The thick-cut pile of an Aubusson carpet beneath her back was warm as he laid her down and opened her thighs, his sex seeking an entrance, finding the pathway.

'I have not—'

He covered her mouth with his own and took away the words, his tongue mimicking the quiet thrust of his hips and her whole world exploded into pain. And then he was still. Desperately still.

'Lord. You're a virgin!' Rising above her, sweat beaded his brow and upper lip, the lines of his face softer now as tenderness stretched across desire. She tried to still him by holding her hands across his back, the firmness of muscle cut by ridged scars.

'Ahh, sweetheart. Why the hell didn't you tell me?'

The message was plain as his hooded glance sharpened, refocused, and she made to move out from underneath him.

'No, Emma. Give it a moment and the pain will pass.' He moved just slightly.

'It hurts.'

'I know. I know.'

He moved again. Forward this time. Deeper as he brought one arm beneath her back and tilted her hips. She felt the very hardness of him against her womb.

Kissing her gently, he nuzzled at her neck and ear.

The cold trail of tongue across her nipple and fire consumed her. Without meaning to, she rocked forward. It was all he was waiting for, the pain less now as another feeling climbed. Higher. Closer.

'Come with me,' he murmured and, pulling her arms above her head with one hand, he turned her, the rhythm different, less known. A pause here. A deeper thrust there. His free hand held her bottom tight and he buried himself in her to the very hilt.

Up and up and up and over, the clenching waves of ecstasy made her jolt. Once, twice, more and more and more.

Spent, she lay lifeless and did not protest as Asher gathered her in his arms and laid her head upon his chest. Lying there in his shelter and listening to his heart while the wind gathered outside and chased clouds across the moon, she wished that time might just stop. Here. Now. For ever.

But the world ran on in the heavy chime of a clock and when his hand dropped she felt again the quick punch of sensuality.

'I still want you.' His words were quiet and the look in his eyes was sensuous, the scent of their lovemaking musky in the air. 'Do you want me? Again?'

When she nodded, he carefully rolled over and bent his elbows to her side to shelter her from his weight. The touch of his thumb against her breast was questioning; as her nipples hardened she pressed into his hand, her breath shallowed and waiting.

She was cold and he warmed her. She was hot and he cooled her. He was of her and she was of him and there seemed no place that they were separate or solitary in the heady secrets of the flesh.

And when he had finished he brought her up into his arms and walked across to his bed, gently laying her down and bringing up the sheets before joining her.

Smoothing back the damp curliness of her hair, he grinned. The golden lights in his eyes were easily seen and he looked younger and happier. 'We will be married as soon as the banns have been read. I swear it.'

Marriage!

God.

As who?

As Emerald Sandford?

She was pleased that he did not notice her confusion or her withdrawal as she lay there, listening to his breathing deepen into sleep.

How long would it be before Asher started to put the pieces together properly? Closing her eyes, she gritted her teeth. She could not tell him. He was an honourable man, a man who took his responsibilities seriously. And here she was, another responsibility, a woman whom he would feel bound to marry just because they had slept together.

Marriage.

In the circles she had mixed in, even the notion

would seem ludicrous. But her father's crowd had never had the sort of moral fibre Asher Wellingham did.

A flare of pleasure warmed her and therein lay the rub, for her steely independence faltered somewhat under the mantle of his care, and if she let herself believe in fairy tales she would only be hurt all the worse later.

The memory of him deep inside her body made her heart race. Lord, but to never again know the sweetness of his kisses and the raw white heat of passion... She slashed at the tears that welled in her eyes and swore.

She was caught between love and lies, frozen into immobility. She, who had always walked her world unfettered and straight, the wind in her hair and the sun on her back and a sharp true blade in her fingers.

And now when her world had skewed and reshaped, she understood how often she had been lonely. Solitary. Isolated. Living in Jamaica under the shadow of her father had allowed no space for frivolity, for girlish pursuits, for love.

Love.

A prickling panic overcame her. Love? Asher had never said it. Not once. Could just lust be enough? Had it ever been enough for Beau?

She rubbed at the ache that was settling at her temples and promised herself honesty.

She was the pirate's daughter and already the

whispers of her difference were starting, just as they had at home in Jamaica. She had never fitted anywhere. Even aboard the *Mariposa*.

Frowning, the slight echo of mistruth startled her. She did fit!

In Asher's arms with the promise of safety in his name and in the strong lines of his body.

Yes, for the first time in all her life she looked neither onwards nor backwards but existed just in the moment, a tiny and fragile reality that offered happiness.

Or hurt?

The ghost of her father hovered near and behind him other spectres lingered, death and pain written across each face.

She would not let them spoil this moment and she shook away memory, laying her arm alongside Asher and feeling his warmth. And then, when he did not stir, she pressed her legs against the long heat of his own and a shiver of delight consumed her.

When she woke again it was morning and the indent of where he had slumbered was still warm. He has only just left, she thought and sat up, running her fingers through her hair to try to straighten it. What should she do next? How many nights of loving constituted absolution? Rising from the rumpled bed, she was pleased to see that a basin with water and a towel had been left on the table. Wetting the flannel, she brought it across her forehead, her face in the mirror showing the struggle of wanting. Wanting to be with him. Wanting to be gone so that he might never know any of it. Today the blue in her eyes was overshadowed by dark, dark green and her hair was a wild array of wayward curls.

Not the face of a duchess.

She could not imagine a portrait of herself above the Carisbrook baronial fireplace to last down through the centuries. The scar that dissected her right eyebrow was reddened and visible and she brought up her finger to touch it. This was the sum of who she was and no amount of wishing it other-wise could preclude her past.

She had just dressed when he returned, and ridicu-lously she blushed. If he noticed, he gave no word of it—for that she was grateful.

'Would you walk with me? We have much to say to each other.' He did not touch her at all as she went past him and kept his distance still as they descended the stairs. Outside in the sun he seemed to relax more as they ambled between the stone walls, the lush green of summer in the leaves of trees that stood as sentinels on each side of the garden.

When he stopped she looked up at him. The brown of his irises was darker today and his hair slicked back as though he had just bathed.

'Who were the men who attacked me?'

So he wanted answers. She hoped that she might

give him at least a version of the truth. 'The Mc-Ilverrays of Kingston Town. They want the map inside the cane. They believe that it should belong to them.'

'And you think it prudent to hold on to a treasure map that might indeed in the end kill you?'

She almost laughed at that, but stopped herself.

'My family has debts.'

His eyes narrowed. 'Tell me how much you owe and I'll place it into an account tomorrow.'

Her mouth fell open. 'No.' She couldn't do it, couldn't escape from here with a fat payment in her pocket after a quick toss in the sheets. That would make her—what? A whore? And every bit as on the game as the ones she had seen peddling their bodies in Jamaica. 'I can't take money from you like that.'

She was unprepared for his laughter. 'And what if you are pregnant?'

She had not even considered that.

'If you are pregnant, the child will be the heir to the Carisbrook fortune. I would not want him, or her, to be brought up on an empty quest for treasure or a hollow prophecy of greed. And Falder would welcome the promise of a child.'

'A child you would risk everything for?'

He shook his head and turned her towards him, peeling away restraint with a quick easiness. 'It is you I am trying to help.'

'Help me, then, by giving me the map.'

'And then watch you disappear?'

She reddened and felt his breath on the soft skin at the top of her ear and her insides twisted in longing. So simply done. So effortlessly won. A throbbing shot of warmth spread as she turned into his lips, groaning when his fingers flicked at her nipples. Even here, in the garden in the full view of the windows along the back end of Carisbrook House, she would let him have her, down on the ground amid the flowers and damn the consequences.

He was hers like no other person had ever been. She felt his familiarity with an ache, and was gasping as he drew back.

'This is not the place to... Come with me.' He led her to a summer house at the very bottom of the garden and stripped off his coat. The shirt he wore beneath was snowy white. After he loosened his breeches he stopped and smiled, the wind lifting his hair away from his throat and throwing a shadow into amber-lit eyes.

He was so beautiful. So masculinely perfect. With care she laid her palm against the rough stubble on his jaw and drew one finger across the fullness of his top lip.

'We could be seen—'

He stopped the words with a quick shake of his head.

'No. Not here.'

Suddenly she did not care. With a slow grace she undid the buttons at her throat, excited as he watched her lift the fullness of her breast above their protection of lawn and lace.

Wanton. Heedless. Immoderate.

She felt his fingers lifting her skirt and the wind on her shins and thighs and bottom as she accepted him with a sigh. Tipping her hips forward to get a deeper thrust his hands anchored her and she bit into the cotton of his sleeve to smother a scream.

'Easy, sweetheart,' he gentled, but she could not be still. The last trace of manners broke and she slid her fingers beneath his shirt and scraped her nails down the raised scars that marked his back. She was wild and free as he rubbed across the nub of hardness in the place where the swollen lips of her womanhood began, and when her head fell back the sunlight was bright upon her face.

She loved him.

'I love you.'

Had she said it? He stilled.

I love you. I love you. I love you.

Not yet, not now, not when he would not want it.

Not when the clenching joy of sex took her over the top of ecstasy and wrenched her on to the dizzy shores of elation.

Asher took her down with him as he collapsed on to the floor of the summer house. What the hell had just happened? He had emptied himself into Emma Seaton with an intensity he had never known possible and in the near-open, where anyone could find them. And with no thought to the consequences. He swore in amazement and kept her head against his shoulder, not wanting her at this moment to see his expression.

I love you. He had heard her say it and the words had melted the cold hard mantle of ice that had coated his heart since he had lost his wife. Since for ever.

Melanie. The soft whisk of an almost-breeze above him made him smile.

'I will have the banns read, Emma, and we can be married next month. At Falder in the chapel.'

When she looked up, tears magnified his face.

'There are things about me that you do not know. Would not like to know.'

'Tell me, then,' he answered and in his words she heard soft amusement. The amusement of a man who would imagine small digressions, little feminine faults. Tiny flaws and imperfections.

Lord, why was this not easier? She knew the answer as soon as she asked it. Because she had fallen in love with Asher Wellingham. And the promise of it was as sweet as it was forbidden. Not just the loss of her virginity now, but the sacrifice of her heart, and she was getting more and more caught up by the second.

Tell him the truth.

Tell him the truth.

A voice chanted in the back of her head, but she could not do it. Could not stand to see what was in his eyes now turn to hatred.

'Growing up in Jamaica was very different from here. The rules were very different. It was looser, less…moral?' She left a question at the end.

'Yet your father was strict?'

'In some things he was.'

And in some other things, like the taking of life, he wasn't.

The image of herself as a ten-year-old, standing on the deck of the *Mariposa* as her father slit the throat of a slave, impinged over illusion. She had never had a chance to become anything other than what she was and for a moment she hated Beau with such a loathing that she was shocked by it.

'After my mother went, there were things that I should have learned…feminine things…that I did not know…do not know still.'

He laughed and moved closer. 'I can see no glaring faults in your upbringing, Emma, and I do not demand a wife who excels in tapestry or singing or the mastery of an instrument. Besides had you been raised here, you almost certainly would not have swum naked from the beach or gone to a bishop's house dressed in little more than a gown. Or come to my room in your night shift and offered me your virginity. I should be thanking your father for the way that he brought you up.'

He leaned across to pluck a bud from the bush next to him and tucked it in behind her right ear. 'In the islands of the Pacific a woman promised to a man wears a bloom here.'

Promised?

Her fingers came up to feel the soft wetness of the petals and she made herself smile.

'You cannot possibly know what it is you are doing, Emerald.' Miriam's voice quivered under the onslaught of anger and the remains of her cough. 'Lord, child, but to bed him? To go ahead and actually fornicate with him… I cannot even contemplate what your parents would have thought of that.'

'I suspect my mother may have understood, given that she was sixteen when she was pregnant with me.' Emerald tried hard to hold on to what was left of her patience, though when her aunt went into another bout of a hacking cough she softened her voice. 'In Jamaica twenty-one would be considered old to be unaware of the pleasures of the flesh.'

'He must marry you, child. Surely he knows his duty as a gentleman…' Shock mixed with utter dismay.

'If I stood before the altar as Emma Seaton, I hardly think the marriage would be legal.'

'So you would have a child outside of wedlock?' Her aunt's old face was pinched.

'I am not certain if there even is a baby.'

'Pretend it, then. You are ruined already.'

'Pardon?' Emerald could not quite comprehend what her aunt meant, though the wily look in her eyes was familiar.

'The Carisbrook name is powerful. Pretend there is a child and marry him. As Emma Seaton if you need to. Who would know? You are young and fit. If a child did not come this month, then with the grace of God it will come in the next one.'

'I could not do that…'

'Oh, pah. Your father took away the future you should have had when he dragged you to sea for his own gains, yet despite every handicap of birth and up-bringing your heart is still in the right place. The Duke of Carisbrook would be lucky to have you as a bride'

'Lucky? A marriage based on lies?'

'Untruth is often the result of need and circumstance; if life has taught you nothing else, it should have at least taught you that.'

Emerald stared at her aunt, seeing clearly for the first time the ghost of her dead father. The change from the nervous and dithery old woman was amazing as, for a second, Beau shone forth in the lines of her face. Beguiling. Charming. Utterly selfish.

'It is wrong…'

'He is as lonely as you are and, if rumour is to be believed, has been since the unfortunate and premature demise of his wife.'

'Which I caused.' Emerald had had enough. She shouted the words, but as she dredged up the courage to explain further Miriam began to laugh. Not softly either.

'Ahh, how the young torment themselves. You think Melanie Wellingham would not have died anyway from a bout of pneumonia after a cold long winter? You think a storm could not have whipped her husband's ship to the ends of this earth and blown him off course to some other death?'

'No. I think that if he had not met my family, he might be at Falder this very moment with a wife and children and a brother who could see. And if I told him the truth I could not bear to see the same thought in his eyes.'

'Because you love him?'

Emerald was silent.

I love you. She had said it to him once.

She was quieter as she answered and a thousand times more resolute. 'If I did as you bade me to, I would have to live all my life in a lie. Like my father did. Always careful, never honest with anyone, for ever looking over my shoulder for the past to catch up.'

Miriam sighed loudly as her hand came from beneath the bedcover. 'It can't have been easy on you, Emmie.' Cold fingers played with the band of lace on her gloves. 'I should have come out…insisted on some contact…for I knew my brother and he was not always such a biddable man to live with.'

Emerald shook her head. *Biddable?*

'*I hate you. I hate you. I hate you.*'

For a moment Emerald was transfixed by the rawness of her voice travelling through time from childhood, and was stunned by the sheer memory of animosity and ill will.

Biddable? She almost laughed at the understatement. No. There could be no happy ending. No small apologies or little mistakes. Lives had been lost and years had been taken; if the scars on her hands and her leg and her face had taught her anything, it was the fact that risk only brought regret. She shook her head and felt her resolve firming. Honesty was a policy that wreaked havoc on the good souls of those who had the misfortune to believe in it, and when she left England at least this way she would leave with her pride.

Asher came to her room after midnight, when the house was quiet. He looked tired and when he reached out she moved away.

A quota of penance? One night of loving for years of pain? It didn't quite seem fair somehow, but her withdrawal was fashioned from kindness. If he hated her, all this would be so much easier. For him.

'Last night was a mistake.' She couldn't even find it in her to be subtle.

'A mistake?'

'I am a lady and I was a virgin. You should not have bedded me.'

She thought she heard humour in his reply. 'Hard to determine experience with your robe pooled around your feet and the look of one well used to the art of lovemaking in your eyes.'

Reverting to character, she turned away and dabbed at her cheeks.

'I was an innocent…'

'To whom I offered marriage.'

'Because you felt guilty?' His silence confirmed all her fears and she was glad that he was not looking straight at her as she continued. 'I would rather not marry out of guilt, your Grace.'

'You think that is what my marriage proposal is?' There was an edge of irritation in his voice.

'Indeed I do. But do not worry yourself on my behalf—I shall be leaving for Jamaica soon to see to some property and I am not certain when it is I might return.'

'So you saved your virginity for some quick and meaningless affair? You expect me to believe that?"

When he came forward she meant to deny him, meant to hold up her head and plead the wrongness of it, but she couldn't. Instead her fingers fitted into his and she laid her head against his chest, feeling the careful touch of his thumb on her bare skin as it traced a line around the wings of her butterfly.

'Did it hurt?'

'No.' She smiled at the ridiculousness of the question in the whole face of what was between them.

'I want you, Emma. Now. Here. Tonight.' A breathless entreaty that set off an aching throb inside and took away denials.

'Just tonight, Asher. After this—' His finger rubbed across her lips and stopped the lies that were forming. And then she forgot everything that she had meant to say as the heat of his body seared into the answering warmth of her own.

She could barely look at him in the morning in the face of what they had shared until the dawn. Lord, even the thought of it drew a blush with the wetness of his seed on her thighs.

His seed. His lips against her and the promise of more in his eyes.

I love you.

She had said it again when her fingers had threaded through his hair and the clenching throb of her sex had made her arch away from the unfamiliar softness of the mattress, and again when he had held her afterwards. Neither of them had slept even as the dawn broke against the windows and flooded the room with the light of day.

A perfect, balanced if-only love to remember when she was old and grey. The one moment to make every other subsequent second bearable.

When he left, she was glad that he went without giving her words that could bind them, badly, into a future.

Chapter Eleven

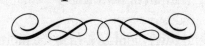

Asher parried with his sword, quickly, against the thrust of Jack's blade and brought the buttoned point to an unprotected throat.

'*Touché.*'

Even his voice sounded stronger and with the sun on his face and the image of Emma entwined around him he felt…unassailable, invulnerable, absolute, all feelings he had not known since…when? It was Emma Seaton's lack of need, her strength of purpose and an underlying will that bent to no one that made him like this.

'More practice, I think, Jack, if an ill man can beat you…'

'Hardly ill. You look better than I've seen you look in a long time.'

Asher turned away as guilt sliced into him. There were days now when he barely remembered the past, days when what had happened was blurrier, less real. All that seemed true now was centred about Emma and her laughing turquoise eyes.

'I'm going back to Falder tomorrow.' He gestured to his arm, freed now from its bandage.

'Because you think they could try again?'

'If they do, I'll be ready this time—no one could surprise me there.' He slashed his blade through the air as if to underline intent.

'I'll see to my affairs and come up and join you before the end of the week.'

'I am not certain as to the safety of it.'

'You think it's that dangerous?'

'I do.'

'It's Emma Seaton, isn't it? All this has happened since she came. And now she's here under your wing? And her aunt, too, I've heard. Take care, Asher, for there are whispers.' A question lay in the air between them.

'Whispers?'

'Some say she is a fortune-hunter who targeted the largest fortune in London with her well-timed faint.'

'And what do you say, Jack?'

'I'd say, if she makes you happy who gives a damn about anyone else; besides, I like her too. She's different.'

After Jack had gone he stood in the gardens at the back of the house and lit a cheroot, pulling on it gratefully after the afternoon of exercise.

He had bedded Emma every night since shortly after the attack, and every night she had told him that she loved him.

My God. *Loved him.* If he had any guts he would have given her the words back. But he couldn't. Not yet. Not until he knew exactly who she was.

He screwed the sapphire ring on his finger around and around and made himself think.

She loved him, but she would not marry him. Why? When they arrived back at Falder, he would get the truth from her for London and the smaller house here hemmed them into properness.

Apart from the night time!

Grinding out the burning end of the cheroot beneath his feet, he wished he could go to her now and smiled as he looked at his timepiece. Four o'clock in the afternoon. For years he had dreaded the dark and now he welcomed it. Just another change she had fashioned in him. Another way she had made him different.

They lay on the covers, the fire in the grate sending flickering shadows across the walls and tingeing Asher's body with the soft glow of orange. His back was to her and her fingers traced the marks that stood up in knotted pearly welts.

She noticed how the skin on his forearm tightened at the contact and chanced a question.

'I saw marks like these once in Jamaica?'

She felt his interest.

'The man who sported them had seemingly lost his mind in a pirates' colony on Turks Island off the Silver Bank Passage. The law never took his ramblings seriously and so nothing was done, but I heard a few years later that the ship of an English lord had levelled the place clean away, blown it from the face of this earth with every last person standing in it, as revenge for what he had suffered there.'

'A fine tale,' he replied evenly.

'Your tale?' she questioned just as smoothly.

'I am a duke of the realm, Emma.'

'You are a man who keeps a blade hidden in the folds of his sleeve. I saw it at the Bishop's party and wondered why you should have a need of it here?'

'I had thought it well concealed.' His voice held the hint of respect. 'And besides…' His finger brushed over the puckered skin on her thigh. 'There are times when the childhood that you profess to does not quite add up. The mark of a sword and an indigo tattoo, flame-scarred hands and an excellence in the Chinese art of acupuncture. Truth be known, your secrets are probably every bit as heady as my own.'

She laughed to ease the tension, feeling his observations permeate the space between them. A hollow sort of sound that had his eyebrows rising.

'I said to you once before that I could protect you—'

Before he could finish she placed her finger across the smooth and full line of his lips.

'And I said to you once that there is nothing that you need to protect me from.'

He rolled on top of her so that she felt the hardening ridge of his manhood against the juncture of her legs.

'All my life I have been around women who have needed…protecting. My mother, Lucy, Melanie. But you…you are different…stronger…'

Their eyes were at a level and the truth was suddenly important.

'I cannot marry you, Asher.'

'Why?'

'Because…because I cannot.'

'And yet you can be my mistress?'

She nodded before she could stop herself.

'Every night you tell me you love me. And sometimes when you sleep you speak in your dreams and you say it again.'

A single tear slipped from her eye and trailed its way down her cheek.

'If you would trust me.' He whispered it into the quiet of the night beneath the swathe of heavy curls under her right ear and she turned away, her fingers skimming across the dark red scar on his forearm. Still healing. A reminder of how fragile life really was and how easily it could be taken away.

If she lost him…

If she caused any of his family harm…

No, she would travel to Falder for the map and then she would be gone. It was the only honourable thing to do.

Chapter Twelve

The birdsong had only just started in the trees beside Carisbrook House when they left London. Robins, sparrows and finches, vying each other for the one perfect note. A quiet refrain, Emerald thought, compared with the ear-splitting cries of the birds back home in Jamaica.

Miriam, Lucy, Taris, Asher and herself sat in the second coach. In the first coach, full of the Wellingham servants, Toro sat on top with the driver. Emerald had seen the outline of the weapon concealed beneath his jacket as she had come down the steps to the street; she guessed that Azziz on their coach would be as well armed. It pleased her that Asher was taking the threat of the McIlverrays seriously and was allowing little chance of attack.

Feeling the warmth of him next to her, she looked across as he pulled the lush and ample furs over her knees. Today he was preoccupied, the brown in his eyes sharper than it usually was and blood from an ill-taken shave seen on his jawline.

'Are you warm enough?' He addressed the query to them all and refrained from catching her eye. She frowned. When he had come to her room last night, he had been slick with heat and want and need, but today the shadow of uncertainty lay between them, unspoken questions and impossible answers. Easier indeed to lose oneself in the promise of flesh, the darkness adding another layer of distance.

Lord, the whispered memories of night were like a shout in this confined space. Looking down, she saw the knuckles of his hand between them whitened to the bone. He felt it too, then? How could he not? She coughed to clear her throat and hoped that he did not hear the racing beat of her heart.

It was colder out of London, and the drizzle from yesterday had turned into a hard beating rain, the windows already fogged up from their breaths.

Emerald tried to see outside across the shoulders of her aunt and wished that she had made certain she was by the window. She had three knives concealed on her person and would have strapped her sword through her belt if she could have. But how? The shape of it could hardly be explained and this way her silent weapons held an element of surprise.

'You seem well recovered, Miriam.' Lucy leaned

forward to speak more on the topic and Emerald used the moment to question Asher.

'How long do you expect us to take till Wickford?' she asked. The town was the first stopover point, a place where the horses could be rested and watered and where there was a fair lunch served.

'Three to four hours in this weather,' he returned. 'More if the front to the west passes over us.' He rubbed at his arm as he spoke, giving her the impression that it was paining him. But she did not dare voice her concern with the others sitting so close.

'I noticed that Azziz and Toro were armed?'

He did look at her then. 'I can protect you, Emma. Do not worry.'

She almost laughed.

Worry.

My God.

She hoped he would not see the quick burst of temper. She had instructed Toro to make certain the inhabitants of the first carriage were safe before returning to help the second carriage should anything go amiss in their travels; although she could see that he did not care for the idea, she was sure that he would do as she had asked. Lord, this was all her fault and she prayed to God that they would need none of it and would journey to the Carisbrook property without mishap.

It was mid-afternoon when she noticed Asher turning in his seat to get a proper view of the land outside. Miriam was asleep, her gentle snores filling the silence of the coach. Taris dozed also and Lucy was reading a book. A romance about pirates, Emerald determined from the title and smiled at the cover.

Visions of the *Mariposa* came to mind, but she shook the memory back, into the folds of time. Here in England the image was unsettling. A few short weeks had given her a taste of what her life could have been like and for just a second she was overcome with the loss of it all.

Asher's hand slapping against the roof shocked her back to reality.

'Riders to the left,' he shouted, 'and they don't look friendly.' When he flipped open the catch of the window, light rain and wind slashed in, but he was already crouched across the seat, prying open the wooden box beneath the feet of his brother.

Three flintlock pistols lay nestled in a leather case and his fingers grasped the one nearest to him.

'Asher?' Taris's voice was flat and Lucy's book slid to the floor as she caught sight of the armoury.

'Get back against the seat. All of you.' He gave little notice to his family's fright as he opened up the door and lent out, his body arching against the force of wind and motion, the violent burst of gunfire loud even against the rushing noise of hooves and wheels and speed.

Lucy began to cry, and Miriam to cough and then the world as they knew it turned over, for the carriage, already hard-pressed in its escape, caught an edge and veered into nothingness, the screams of the women eerie in the slow-motioned silence.

Emerald came to on a bank not far from the carriage, the wheels still spinning against a muted sky. She put her hand to her head to feel the hurt there. Bright blood stained her fingers and she winced as they explored a cut across her temple. Asher was some five hundred yards away from the carriage drawing the riders towards him. She heard him shouting something about the map and urging them to follow him before he disappeared into the undergrowth. Leading the McIlverrays away. From them.

Miriam and Lucy were huddled nearby and Azziz and Taris both out cold against a small embankment. Crawling across to them, she checked their pulses. Fast but steady.

Shots further off had her scrambling up and she grabbed her aunt's arm and entwined it around Lucy's.

'Run to the woods. Don't stop until you are far in and then dig down into the undergrowth and stay still.' When the girl didn't answer, Emerald shook her. 'I'll cover you from behind.' Lucy was sobbing in fright. Miriam said nothing, but the wide horrified stare of her eyes told another story.

Taking Azziz's blade, Emerald began to run, egging the two others on as she did so, the cool greenness of the forest dulling panic, and when a number of shots rang out across the glade she tried to pinpoint movement. Where was Asher now she thought? Where the hell had he gone?

Miriam seemed greatly recovered as she joined them and she instructed her aunt to take Lucinda further into the grove, though Asher's sister took hold of her arm as she finished speaking. 'No. You mustn't go. There is nothing any of us can do. Highwaymen are not to be—' She clapped her fingers to her mouth as a man broke cover not twenty yards from where they stood, the gun at his hip pointed at them, and murder in his eyes.

With absolutely no trace of hesitation Emerald whipped her knife from the soft folds of her boot and sent it rifling through space, the small thud as it connected with the newcomer's head almost ludicrous in proportion to the damage.

Two gawping faces confronted her as she turned, but she had no time for questions. Stripping the second knife from a hidden pocket, she cut the band of her heavy skirt and stepped from it. The thinner petticoat beneath would at least afford her a bit of freedom.

'Get into the forest. Miriam, make sure you don't come out unless you hear me calling. I'll cover your tracks.' Taking a branch from the nearest tree beneath the line of overhang so that it would not be seen, she pushed her aunt in the direction she wanted them to go before erasing the trail of their footsteps. It was all that she could do. Now she must find Asher and help him—if Toro had done as she asked and gone on, Asher would be alone in his battle with the McIlverrays.

'Lord help him,' she whispered under her breath as she circled back, the sum of years of tutelage having her automatically masking sound and her eyes keenly following the track that the single retainer had taken.

Asher felt the sharp sting of sweat obscure his vision and blinked to clear the blurriness. There were a number of men just behind him; as they came into a river valley, one gestured to the right. His heart sank. God knew how many he couldn't see, but, if he let them past, Emma and Taris and Lucy were less then a quarter of a mile back. And helpless. He'd checked Emma's pulse before he'd left her and his fingers had brushed across the gash at her temple. It was deep and his brother and Azziz were completely unconscious. His only help gone.

It was up to him.

Everybody was dependent on him.

Laying his pistol on the grass, he discarded his hat and filled it with damp leaves before jamming it through the sharp point of an oak sapling he'd cut. The shape and form of a head. It was just a little ruse, but it might work.

No. It *had* to work, he corrected himself as he jammed the stick into the earth and circled to the right. He still had time, for the group were talking to one another and laughing.

Easy prey.

He just had to take them off one by one until there was a manageable number. With four flints in his pocket and another two in the barrel he couldn't afford to waste ammunition on a miss. Fitting a polished river stone into his hand his eyes focused.

Closer. Closer. Steady. The stone arced across the sky noiselessly and the chosen man fell hard. One down. He could not think about who else lurked in the deeper woods. The horses stopped and the more urgent sound of voices reached him on the wind. He could see that they scanned the valley for movement; turning, he lobbed another stone into the air to land in a rush of noise on the broad leaves of a sturdy bush.

It was enough. The hat from this distance gave an illusion of movement and the remaining men rushed forward. When he sighted them again, it was from slightly behind.

Perfect.

He brought the gun from his pocket and fired. Another man fell. And then another. Reloading, he sat to wait it out. Three more men left, though a scream of anger echoed through the trees, bringing with it the worrying sound of others.

More of the enemy materialised from the forest and he drew his sword, discarding the pistol in favour of blade as he backed up the embankment with careful steps and on to a ledge of thick brush. If they wanted to take him, he wouldn't make it easy. Here the horses could not follow and with him on foot the odds became more even.

Six men.

He had taken more.

Time slowed and focused. An easy balance and quiet waiting.

'Come on, come on,' he whispered and hoped he could kill a good number of them before they got to him.

Emerald saw him from above first, and even through her sheer terror and from this distance she recognised the style of his swordsmanship. My God, she thought as she scrambled down the incline, no wonder he killed my father, no wonder he cut a swathe through the men on the *Mariposa* like no others before him.

His was not an English style of fighting, but a foreign one. A style learnt not in the polite fencing salons of London, but in the world's godforsaken places, where fair play shattered in the face of sheer and brutal force.

She could barely look away. Already he had downed two men, but the others were circling closer and one held a gun.

They hadn't shot him! Hope blossomed. They wanted him alive as a pathway to the treasure. She shouted as a slice of steel creased the folds of the fabric on his jacket and red blood oozed through.

Asher heard the cry from one side and the flash of white petticoats had him turning.

Emma? With a sword in hand and a dirty bandana wrapped around the bright gilt of her curls? Memory turned, and against the dull grey sky he suddenly remembered what she must always have known.

'You!' He could barely believe it.

The girl from the *Mariposa*. Emma Seaton? He blinked twice just to make sure the image was real. And the turquoise eyes that looked back at him were dark in anguish.

A slash of steel to his right centered his focus and he waited to see whether she would raise her sword against him too. God. Could he kill her? For the first time in all his life he was afraid.

'You'll be wanting the map no doubt, Emerald.' The man nearest to him spoke, gesturing to those beside him to cease for the moment.

Emerald? Asher glanced sideways. Emerald? What sort of a name was that? Fragmented shards of memory clicked into place.

Emerald!

Emerald Sandford?

'The Duke has Beau's map hidden at Falder, Karl. If you kill him, you'll lose it.' Her voice was hard, distant, indifferent, as if the taking of his life was a meagre thing against the possession of what they both sought. In the pale light of a rapidly approaching dusk, the blood at her temple ran dark red, and the pallor of her skin made her look immeasurably older than the twenty-one years he knew her to have.

'You lie.' The older man opposite took up his sword and brought it down, fast. Quick reactions saved the blade from eating into her leg as she parried.

'If I had the map, do you think I'd still be here in England?'

With little effort she pushed his blade back and stood like one without a care in the world.

Like father, like daughter.

How easily they ruined lives. How little they thought of the consequence.

Pure untrammelled rage ripped through Asher.

Melanie. His brother. The aching remains of his right hand and the years they had stolen. Lunging forward, he scattered the circle, another man crumpling under the wicked sharpness of steel and all hell broke loose. In the moment of chaos he felt the small tickling whisper of a voice as Emma edged around behind him.

'Hate me later. I can help you now.'

With a well-timed quickness she plunged her blade through the closest renegade and turned to meet the next one and she fought as if a sword had been born in her hand. He frowned at the thought. Lord, it probably had been. The quick report of a gun close up made him stiffen, the smell of powder acrid in the air. In one movement he pulled his knife from his boot and hurled it before the man could reload, pleased when the blade easily found its target.

He kept her at his back, their paired position creating a circle of safety, the thrust and counter-thrust of the two men left easily beaten back. He heard the rasping of her breath and the quick noise of steel against steel. And then a lightly worded curse. She was tiring. He could see it in the way she held her blade. Parrying no longer, but defending. Why?

Gritting his teeth, he finished the fight. Quickly.

When silence again filtered through the clearing, Emerald found in her the strength to look up. And wished that she had not. Asher was furious and the clamp of his hand hurt the top of her arm. She swayed and would have fallen had he not steadied her. The sting in her side left her breathless and she didn't dare to look down to see the damage. Not yet. Not now.

He was sweating and in the last yellow light of the fading day the fury in his eyes glittered. 'You are the damn pirate's daughter? Beau Sandford's daughter? It was you on the ship…?'

'You have remembered?'

'Damned right I have.'

'I tried to make it up to you. Here and in London. In the bedroom. It was the only way I knew how.'

Even words were hard to say. Beneath the fabric of her jacket she felt the steady drip of blood. She looked down surreptitiously to make certain the white of her petticoat was not stained with red. If she could just be alone, she could remedy it. With the last surge of energy she pulled her arm away.

'My God.' Censure coated his curse. 'You saw our bedding as some sort of a sacrifice?'

'A payment. For my father. For me. We wronged you.'

'Wronged me? Lord, Emerald.' He rolled the name again around on his tongue. 'Emerald. Is that what I should call you now?'

'Some people call me Emmie.'

'But never Emma?' She shook her head as he waited.

'So everything was a lie?' The swollen flesh at the top of his lip creased into a humourless smile, and she refrained in the face of his anger to tell him the whole of it.

A lie?

To lie in the moonlight together and watch the way the light played off the hardened angle of his body. To feel his lips against her own, melding all that had once been into what now was.

Just a lie?

If he felt even a fiftieth of what she did for him, he could never have asked the question. Tears sprung to her eyes.

'Everything.'

One word and it was finished. She almost welcomed it when he turned away, for she could not see the hatred in his beautiful velvet eyes.

Laying her arm hard against her side, she followed him through the forest, pausing at this tree and that one to recatch her breath. He did not wait for her, did not look around to see her progress and for that small anger she was glad. Everything ached and the dizzy rush of blood in her ears was becoming louder. Lord, if the bullet had pierced her stomach… She shook her head, refusing to think about it, and was pleased when she saw Azziz standing against the upturned bulk of the carriage, his fingers rubbing the knot of a gash on the back of his head. Taris stood beside him, looking dazed.

'Where's Lucy and Miriam?' Asher's voice was hard as he looked around the clearing, and Emerald replied as Azziz stayed silent.

'In the woods. I told them to hide there.' She half-turned so that the right side of her body was hidden from him.

'Which way?'

'Over there.' It hurt to even lift her arm and point, the dragging red-hot pain worsened by movement. Let him go and find the others. Let him go soon before she was sick, before the whirling lightness overtook everything.

When he didn't move, she looked up.

'God.' he said roughly. 'My God,' he repeated and stormed towards her. 'What the hell has happened to you?'

His hand was warm against the cold of her own and she curled her fingers into his and held on. Anger she could deal with. Pity undid her. She felt the hot run of tears on her cheeks and hid her head against his jacket.

'Lord, Emma.' He used her old name, a small mistake as he pulled back her coat and his fingers were gentle against the wound, even as the roiling blackness claimed her and she fell into his arms.

Chapter Thirteen

Someone held her down. Hard. Hurting.

'Keep still, Emma!'

Emma! Emma?

Not her name. Nearly her name? Asher's face flew in and out of focus, the dark edges of a room behind, white candles burning on a desk.

Fragments. Memory. Her father mopping the blood from her brow and her mother in a corner. The same candles pushing back midnight.

'I need some more whisky…' The slurred voice of a drunk.

Her mother.

Evangeline.

Little angel.

Murderer.

In the blink of an eye she remembered everything that she had shut out as a six-year-old and, bringing the pillow across her ears, she began to shake. Hard liquor and the sound of screaming. The smell of whisky as a bottle broke. Shards of glass and the boozy face of Mother, close. Too close. Dangerous.

'Mama!' Her voice across the years. Young. Afraid. Unbelieving. She needed to get away. Out of the room. Into the dark of the trees around St Clair. Safety.

'Emerald.' Another voice. Softer. Huskier. Underlined with calm.

Asher was back. Against the shadows, his face impossibly handsome and the smell of drink receding against a different reality.

Falder. They were home.

'Home?' she whispered and watched as uncertainty kindled.

'Azziz and Taris?'

'Azziz is in the room next to this one, nursing three broken ribs and a sizeable lump on the back of his head. Taris escaped remarkably unhurt.'

'How long?' Full sentences were beyond her.

'You've been here for a week. But you have had the fever. It broke this morning.'

'Feel…strange.'

'It's the laudanum to take away pain from the wound in your side.' He stood up and stretched. The dark rings under his eyes were easily seen.

'Stay…please.' Suddenly she was afraid. Her mother crouched in the shadows with her madness and beyond that her father beckoned, tears stream-ing down his cheeks.

'James.' Curly-headed James. She had seen his lifeless body buried in the fertile ground beneath the oak tree at St Clair before her father had calmly read the sermon and sent his wife away. Far from home. Far from them. Far from the grave of a son she had killed.

Emerald swallowed, trying to arrest the moisture that she could feel behind her eyes. Her childhood. The bones of secrets and lies. The product of falsity and hatred. Tears leaked out and fell down her cheeks, warm against a cooling skin.

She had lost them all. And now she was loosing Asher.

'I always loved you…since the *Mariposa*… I thought…I think…you are the most beautiful man I have ever seen.' She took the last of her pride and bur-ied it. At least he would know. Her voice broke and she could not carry on.

Not just repayment, then.

When he said nothing, she turned over and shut him out. Shut them all out.

Just her.

She hated the way her chin wobbled as the strength that she always kept hold of broke into shat-tering sobs, but she could stop nothing.

It was over. Her life here was over and she could not even begin to imagine what she was going to do next.

The clock on the mantel marked the passing of silence as Asher watched her from above, her scar-traced hands linked across the pillow. Ruined hands like his own.

They had both been ruined by circumstance.

The thought knocked the breath from him. He had spent five days listening to her rambling memories of childhood. Memories no one should have, memories fractured by madness and drink and death and dissolved into…what?

Blowing out the candles, he sat in the dark and when her breathing shallowed out he was glad. Looking down at the nightgown her aunt had carefully dressed her in, he noticed things he had not seen before.

The frail thinness of her bones and the way her hair curled beneath the fragile lobes of her ears.

God. Emerald Sandford. He should be furious. More than furious. His mind went back five years to the sea battle off the Turks Island Passage and he remembered other things. The soft feel of her lips against the nub of his thumb, the laughing turquoise eyes, the warmth of the day and the cold of the sea. He frowned. He had drawn back from the fight the moment he knew her to be a girl, and as he had dropped his guard she had retaliated with the hard edge of her sword and flipped him over the side.

Down into the cold of an angry sea where he had caught hold of the barrel she had thrown in after him, the roar of her father's anger loud on the air. Closing his eyes, he remembered other things. The circling sharks and a blood-red boiling sea. Thirty sailors on his ship and ten had survived.

Ten. He swore. Six by the time they had reached the coast and then only himself after a year in the pirates' compound.

Emerald Sandford.

Lord. His eyes ran across her full bottom lip and he laced his fingers together to stop himself from touching.

He wanted to shake her and he wanted to climb in beside her and hold her against the demons of her past. But he couldn't.

'I love you.' How many times had she said it? Would say it? The hollow shaft of memory held him bound by doubt.

As he let himself out of the room, he hated both her fragility and his intransigence.

She had lied, had continued to lie, her motivation based solely on the greed of treasure. Swearing, he walked down the hallway and out on to the balcony, relieved to feel the air on his face. Fresh. Clear. Cold. How long did it take for the sharp prick of vengeance to fade into a lesser ache? A quieter loss?

For ever, he decided, and felt a bone-deep shiver of guilt.

Emerald regained full consciousness just before the morning and lay very still, not wanting to waken the servant who sat dozing in a chair to one side of the bed.

Everything ached, but the mist that had consumed her was lessened.

They knew now. Knew who she was, knew who she had been. Asher. His mother. Taris. Lucinda. Her eyes fell to her hands. Gloveless. Exposed. Like she was. The scars red against the white of the sheet. She didn't even curl them up to hide them but turned her head to the window and watched the first pink blush of dawn on the high clouds outside.

Thus far she was safe. They had not taken her to Newgate. Or sent her to the poorhouse. No, she was still at Falder. In her room.

A portrait of Asher graced the far wall, his eyes watching with velvet gravity and their unexpected dance of gold. Behind him the house was caught in the last rays of a summer sun, the ocean sparkling to his left.

Falder.

As much as she might have liked to, she didn't belong here—she was a dangerous interloper from another world. A harsher world where the price of a life was measured in less than honour and where integrity and tradition were words other people used. *I love you.* She had said it again last night and wished that she hadn't even as the door opened and he walked in.

He had been riding. His clothes were splattered

with dust and when he shut the door behind the departing servant she smiled. His manners were far better than her own. Another difference.

'I think we should talk.'

She nodded and looked directly at him. Beneath the façade of politeness she glimpsed a steely anger, held in check.

'You are Emerald Sandford, are you not?'

She nodded.

'Beau Sandford's daughter?'

Again she nodded.

'Who was it that taught you to fight?'

'My father. Azziz. Toro. Anyone with a bit of time to waste between watches on the *Mariposa*.'

'It was you on the boat, then? The girl who hit me?'

'Yes.'

'Why?'

'If you had stayed aboard, my father would have killed you. There were fifty men from the *Mariposa* and less than a dozen still fighting from the *Caroline*.' She stopped and looked away. 'He always killed those who were left and I thought, since you had given me a chance, that I should return the favour.'

'The favour?' Anger resonated around the room. 'The favour? Better to have lopped my head off then and there than the slow death you sentenced me to.'

'I did not know—'

He didn't let her finish.

'You are a pirate, Emerald.' The name came from his lips as if he did not even like the sound of it. 'You have killed people for your own gain.'

The horror in his words was palpable and, turning her head, she faced him, squarely. The past was the past and she could not change it. 'Believe what you will of me. I came here only for the map.' Her words were flat and she hated the sound of defeat in them, but she had no more to fight with.

'And that is all you want from me? Nothing else?'

Question quivered between them.

I want you to love me. I want you to take me in your arms and hold me safe. For ever.

She almost said it, but at the last second pinched the underside of her left arm to stop herself. When she looked down the red crescent left by her nail on the skin was easily noticeable.

'The map,' she repeated with more conviction this time, 'is all that I want from you.'

He nodded and stood, hands in the pocket of his coat and feet apart, as a sailor might have stood on the deck in a storm. Distant. Lonely. Distracted. 'I have instructed everyone here to keep the secret of your identity. For the moment you are safe. But when you feel better, I would rather that you did not venture outside this room without somebody at your side.'

'Because you feel I might be a risk to your family?' A hollow ache pierced her as he looked up and the blank indifference in his eyes broke her heart.

'I will provide passage to Jamaica for you when you want it. On my ship out of Thornfield.'

She could only nod this time, the thick sadness in her throat rendering speech difficult.

'And if you should need money—'

She stopped him. 'No. Just the map.'

As he turned for the door, the dizzy whorl of relief hit her. Another moment and she would have caught at his hand and begged him for even the scraps of love.

Like. Friendship. Esteem.

Even they might have been enough.

Outside Asher laid his head back against the oak door and took in his breath. Lord, Beau Sandford's daughter. What the hell was he to do with her? She had countered the McIlverray threat with a bravery that had stunned him and had slept with him as a repayment for the hurt done to his family. His teeth ground together as he thought of the hurt he had done to her family.

An equal revenge?

For the first time in days, anger loosened its hold. Perhaps all was not lost. Perhaps in the last threshold of truth something could be salvaged. He imagined Emma…no, Emerald, in satin and silk dancing, candlelight in her hair and the hint of laughter on her lips.

Laughter.

When had she had that in her life? When had she had frivolity or joy or easiness? Not with her mother or Beau. Not since coming to England either, that much was sure.

His eyes flickered to his right hand and he flexed it. Today he felt no movement or sensation in his ghost fingers, another passing reminder of change. Five years since the *Mariposa* had overcome his ship. He did a quick calculation. She must have been, *what*...all of sixteen, perhaps? Younger than Lucinda and expected to fight a man? More than one man? The scars on her hand and face and thigh told him that.

By God, if Sandford was here right now he would kill him again just for the hurt he had done his daughter—she had never stood a chance against the greedy underbelly of that world.

And yet somewhere in the darkness of her upbringing she had discovered and fostered integrity and responsibility. Servants and an aunt she would not abandon and a handful of others to whom she felt allegiance. And when she had seen him at risk she had jumped in to the rescue without a thought for her own well-being.

If it was only the map she truly wanted, why would she do that? Better to let McIlverray do his worst and head by herself for Falder and the map.

I love you.

Perhaps she had truly meant it. Not just atone-ment, but something deeper. More lasting. True. He flattened his fingers out against the wall at his back and tried to take stock of the whole situation, tried to stop the heavy throb in his loins from clouding rea-son.

Emerald sat up in bed and ate the lunch that had been provided for her. She had not seen Asher since yesterday and Miriam had heard that he was in Lon-don on business. She hoped he was safe.

Lucinda and Alice had both visited her that morn-ing and both had looked at her with something akin to wariness.

'You did not tell us of your skill with a knife and sword, Emmie—' Lucinda stopped. She said the name with uncertainty, as if just the mention of it might conjure up the steamy Caribbean underworld. 'Why, when you sent that knife across the clearing and hit that man I could barely believe it—' Again she stopped and her mouth fell into an even greater gape. 'It was you wasn't it, on the dockside with the Earl of Westleigh. It was you, who saved me? You're Liam Kingston?' She blushed profusely. 'I should have known it was you. The gloves. Your height. Lord, it was you all along.'

Emerald could do nothing more than nod, though, as she chanced a look at Asher's mother, she was sur-prised by the gratitude that shone from her eyes.

'You have saved us all from harm, my dear, and I do not know how it is we will ever be able to thank you.'

The thought did cross her mind that such generosity was misplaced, given she had brought the McIlverrays to England in the first place, but she took Alice's offered hand and held it tightly, and the older woman did not pull away or look askance at the scars that blemished the skin beneath her knuckles.

They had seen exactly who it was she was and still they thanked her. For this moment she felt humbled by the generosity of a family who had much reason to hate her. Unbidden tears welled in her eyes. How she wanted Alice and Lucinda and Taris to like her.

Asher's family.

At least then, when she was gone, they would remember her fondly. She dabbed at her eyes and was horrified when still more tears welled. She never cried. Never.

Turning her head into the pillow, she was glad when she heard them leave.

When the last rays of orange were fading from the far-off hills, there was a knock on the door.

This time it was Taris who came into the room. Carefully. She could tell that he was not often here, given the number of times he bumped into things. The table in the middle of the room and the chair near the fireplace. He always stood against the light of the window, she thought, as he stopped there.

'Asher tells me that you blame yourself for this.' His fingers swept up across his eyes and he was still. Waiting. Emerald took a breath. It was rare in England to find people who came straight to the point and she liked him for it.

'If Asher had not met my father—'

He stopped her. 'You do not strike me as a woman who qualifies her life much with "if". If I had not done this....if only I had done that…'

Despite everything she smiled. What was it Taris had said of blindness? Other senses were heightened? Certainly he seemed to have the measure of her and it was easy to be comfortable with him.

'My father was a man who felt that the oceans were his own. Any oceans, but more especially those around the Turks Island Passage. If he had not seen the *Caroline* that day—' She stopped as she saw his lips twitch and rephrased her words. 'Your loss of sight was a direct result of my father's greed.'

'My loss of sight was a direct result of my own need to protect my brother; if it had not happened in the Caribbean, it might have happened somewhere else. On the high mast of an ocean-bound ship or in the slow roll of a carriage on the hills before Falder. Fate, Emerald, or destiny. Call it what you will. I do not blame him and I do not blame you. There is, however, something that you could do for me.'

'Yes?'

'Marry Asher.'

She almost laughed, but stopped herself at the last moment. He was deadly serious. She could see it in every line of his face.

'I think marriage is the last thing that your brother would want from me.'

'You are the only one who can save him.'

'Save him from what?'

'From himself. He blames himself for everything.' He reached down to feel the seat of the chair beside him and lowered himself into it before continuing. 'When Melanie caught a cold, she went to bed with camphor and honey drinks. When it got worse, the doctor was called. And when it got worse still, my mother held her hand while she breathed her last. If Asher had been at Falder, the result would have been exactly the same. He could not have saved her. But a healthy person can die inside just as easily as a sick one and that is what he has done. Ever since.'

Emerald was astonished. She could barely believe what he was saying to her. The power of it! And Taris was close to his brother. Close enough to truly know what drove him, what hurt him, what made him who he was. Could what he said be true? Could she help him in the same way that he had helped her?

'Don't give up on him. Not yet. Can you at least promise me that?'

She took in a breath and nodded because she didn't trust herself enough to speak and then she smiled. He would not see the movement.

'Thank you.'

'You saw me nod?'

'I felt it. In the shift of light.'

'Where is Asher?' she added as he stood to leave.

'He went to London on business. We have a number of ships due out to India.'

Emerald heard frustration in his voice. 'In Jamaica I had dealings with a witch doctor who could heal just about anything—even some loss of sight.'

He laughed, a rich deep sound that resonated around the room. 'You are the very first person to mention my affliction in the same breath as divulging a cure, Emerald. Yes indeed, you should suit our family well.'

And with that he was gone.

Asher spent the next week trying to make sense of everything that had happened, trying to dull the effect that Emerald Sandford had made on him and trying to get his life back into some sort of order.

On the third day in London he found himself in an establishment off Curzon Street; the moment he walked through the front doors, he knew it was a mistake.

Angela Cartwright, a handsome red-haired woman met him as he removed his gloves and hat, the neckline of her gown perilously low. Last time he had been here he had admired her obvious endowments. This time all he could think about were smaller breasts topped with shell-pink nipples and a liberal smattering of freckles.

Emerald.

To be thinking of her in a place like this worried him and he resolved to put her from his mind.

'Why, your Grace, it has been some time since we have seen you here. All of six months, would it not be, Brigitte?'

A beautiful girl, standing against the far wall of the parlour, came forward, her light blue eyes alive with laughter and her brown hair caught in an intricate style at the back of her head before the length of silk tresses fell to her waist.

'Indeed, your Grace. I think you were here last time with your friend Lord Henshaw. Is he well?'

'Very.' Accepting brandy, Asher drank heavily, reasoning that tonight he needed all the fortification he could get.

'Perhaps I could show you the conservatory, your Grace,' she added as she renewed his drink from a crystal decanter. 'It is the latest addition to our household and has been very well received.'

On the edges of her practised French accent lingered the twang of the Covent Garden markets. Normally the contradictions would have amused him, but tonight he was vaguely angered by it, and bothered too by the over-embellished furniture and paintings depicting cherubs in various stages of undress. This place was the most exclusive of all the London brothels, yet it felt cheap in a way that it hadn't before. And the churning dread in his stomach had absolutely nothing to do with anticipation.

In the conservatory, any inhibitions that Brigitte had displayed seemed largely gone and when he felt her fingers suggestively cup his genitals he moved back sharply.

Lord, why was he here?

Why was he not home at Falder with the green hills all about him and the beating ocean in the distance? And Emerald Sandford in his bed, warm and willing and beautiful? Because she was a liar and a cheat and the daughter of Beau Sandford and because everything she had ever told him had been based on her skewed version of the truth.

A room to one end of the structure had been fashioned into a bedchamber, its large four-poster draped in lawn. When Brigitte raised her arms to loosen her hairpins, he marvelled that the sight did not affect him in the least. All he wanted was gold mixed with red and entwined with the lightest of corn.

Emerald.

He made himself come forward and draw a finger against the warm smoothness of Brigitte's skin, trailing his touch along the base of her jaw and down again into the softer places. A swelling bosom and milk-white complexion, the fat abundance of womanhood warm and pliable in his hands as she tipped back her head and groaned.

Emerald. He wanted Emerald. He wanted her joy and her fierce independence. He wanted the feel of her against him as they lay under the full light of a new moon, his ruined fingers curled into hers. Disorientated, he stood back and looked around. Uncertain. Desperate. To leave.

'I am sorry,' he said quietly, jamming a coin into her hand before moving away.

Away from the wrongness of Curzon Street, its inherent loneliness tempered only by rich fine drink and impossible dreams. This was not the way to forget Emerald. This was not the way to claw back a future and find again in his life a place where sheer emptiness did not consume him.

When he was outside he laid his head against the side of the building and thought.

The port beckoned as it always had with its freedom and smell and foreverness. The infinite blue of the waves and a horizon that did not finish. Adventure, new lands, the riches of the colonies spilling into his holds, spices, silks, tea.

As his driver pulled into the curb near him, he walked briskly across and ordered the coach to the docks. His newest sloop was a few weeks away from completion and he would benefit from a good bout of hard work.

Chapter Fourteen

She found the map on her bed after returning from a walk around the kitchen gardens with Alice.

Asher. He was back. He must have waited until he knew her to be gone from this chamber before depositing the parchment. It had been eight days since she had seen him and the exhaustion that had kept her in bed had dissipated into intermittent tiredness, and then disappeared altogether as the wounds at her waist healed into an itchy red.

Unrolling the parchment, her eyes skimmed across the tangents indicated. True west of Powell Point on the tip of the Ship Chan Cay. And a date. 1808. The year after her mother had gone. The year her father had acquired the *Mariposa* and dispensed with his life as a lord.

Tucking the paper into the middle of a book to make certain that the edges were unseen, a new and more worrying thought struck her. Was this Asher Wellingham's final goodbye gesture? Had he not said he would give her the map and provide transport home?

A knock at the door made her jump. The footman outside bowed his head as she caught his eye.

'His Grace requests your company, my lady. He asked me to bring you to him directly.'

Resisting the temptation to go to the mirror and tidy her hair, she pulled at the material in her skirt so that it fell to a more decent length, a slice of pain worrying her side at the movement. Only a scar where the bullet had been extracted, the doctor hurried from London both skilful and competent.

She had been lucky in more ways than one; the McIlverrays were all dead and no longer a threat and the local constabulary was treating the whole incident as highway robbery. Asher with his wide connections had made certain that no trace of scandal ensued. Nothing to touch her. Nothing to hide from.

She smiled as she saw him standing against the open French doors. The gardens behind framed the blackness of his hair, and his clothes were casual, breeches tucked into brown boots and his white shirt open. Her heartbeat began to race as she pushed down the familiar, aching, breathless want for him.

Don't touch him.

Don't let him near.

Don't let him see how much he has hurt me, could still hurt me.

'Good morning, Emerald. You look well.' He made no move to take her hand or come closer. There were no hooded glances or any suggestion of a shared intimacy. Rather he held back, unstintingly correct as he acknowledged her presence.

Today his eyes were the darkest that she had seen them, not even a shimmer of gold visible.

'Thank you for the map.' It was all that she could think of to say. After everything.

Wariness crept into his face. 'You will return to Jamaica to search for its bounty?'

'Yes. It should be easy to read the co-ordinates.'

'How?'

'How?'

'How will you do that?' His question was inflected with a controlled impatience and she was silent. What ship could she use? No one would give her credit in Jamaica and, with the loss of St Clair, she had neither property nor chattels to bargain with. A further lump blocked her throat. He would be rid of her this easily?

'I am not certain.' She made her voice even, indifferent, as though the matter of a vessel in which to travel was but a small and trifling consideration.

'As I said, the *Nautilus* is due for a sea run.'

She could not quite understand what it was he was telling her.

'If you needed passage, I could provide it.' His voice held an iron edge of control as he spoke again.

'Why?'

'Because you were a virgin.' So easily said. So dismissive of emotion.

She marched over until they were face to face. 'I am not pregnant.' The sheer stupidity of her remark made her blush, but his detachment was more hurtful than anything else and she didn't want him to think that he was bound to her by non-existent ties.

'My offer is not conditional on the production of an heir.' She felt the whisper of his breath on her cheek before he moved back, and wanted to reach out and touch the warmth.

This whole conversation was so absurd she suddenly felt tired by it all. The hope. The lack of hope. The see-saw of emotion. The second-guessing as to how he felt. Love me? Love me not? Like the old game she had played as a child with the few other children who were allowed in her company. All she wanted to do was to step forward into his arms and feel their strength around her. Keeping her safe. From everything.

The low wheeling of a gull pulled her attention skywards. Today the weather was fresh, though a bank of clouds sat heavy in the west. There would be rain again later. She was certain of it. Unmindful, she drew her hand across the ache in her side.

'It hurts?'

'Sometimes. Less now than before.'

'I didn't see it happen.'

'It was the pistol. One of the McIlverrays saw my lack of attention and took his chance.'

'You hold your sword like a man does.'

'I was taught by men.'

'And Ruby? Who is Ruby? You spoke of her in your fever dreams.'

'My sister. Beau's daughter by one of the dockside harlots. Her mother abandoned her before her second birthday.'

'Where is she now?'

'In a convent in Jamaica.' Even the saying of it made worry surface. How would her sister be coping in the care of the nuns, for though they were eminently understanding and kind, they were still strangers. 'She is eight and loves music. I taught her to play the harmonica and she tended the gardens at St Clair with some help from me.'

'St Clair is your family house?'

'Was. It was destroyed last summer by the McIlverrays in their search for my father's map.'

'Where have you lived since?'

'On the docks in a room off the Harbour Road until Miriam sent us money for a passage to London.'

'And if the treasure that you seek cannot be found, what then?'

She didn't answer. Couldn't answer. Reaching for

the locket around her neck, she rubbed the gold in a way she had done in all the other difficult moments of her life. A small ritual. A way to be closer to— what? The bauble had come from a time in England when the family had been happy and whole. A time before drink had ripped the heart out of everything.

'I saw Annabelle Graveson in Thornfield and she was asking after your health. She gave me this.' He brought a book from the satchel at his feet and handed it to her.

The burgundy leather that bound the cover was so old it had split across the spine; as she opened the cover, there was a name. Evangeline Montrose. A woodcut of the same design as that of her necklace was etched below it.

One finger reached out to trace the letters as she struggled with the connection.

'My mother's name was Evangeline,' she said finally, feeling the turn of something forbidden shift, and crystallise as Asher spoke.

'And Annabelle's maiden name was Montrose. She said your mother was her cousin.'

Annabelle Montrose. Evangeline Montrose. Cousins. The crest of their family emblazoned on book and locket. The same.

She could barely take the whole idea in. 'You knew?'

'I remembered the locket when I was at Annabelle's last week and saw the design carved upon her crest. Today Annabelle seemed more than upset when she handed the book over.'

'Do you think she is stable?' Emerald asked the question even as she meant not to.

'Stable?' He tilted his head slightly as though trying to catch her meaning.

'In her head. My mother wasn't, you see.' A cold chill of dread seeped into Emerald's blood. Madness? Was it not a family trait? The air around her felt suddenly heavy, the sun that had been out a moment ago lost behind heavy cloud.

June.

Where would she be by July?

And why would the socially conscious Annabelle Graveson risk the exposure of such a damning family skeleton? It didn't make sense. Another darker thought surfaced. Did Annabelle mean to use this as a warning?

After all, she had not given the book directly to her, and Jack Henshaw had said that Asher was the trustee of the Gravesons' affairs. Was it him she was trying to protect?

All this introspection made her head ache. If Asher had looked at her with even a glimmer of want in his eyes, everything would have been so much easier. If he had taken her hand in his own even lightly, she might have clung on and risked it all. But he barely glanced at her, the tapping of his fingers against the side of his thigh giving her the singular impression that he was impatient for her to be gone.

'The *Nautilus* will sail in four days' time, so, if you would like to speak with Annabelle it would need to be arranged soon. I think you could count on her silence as any scandal could by association also affect her reputation and I doubt that she would risk it.'

She nodded, her person relegated now to merely scandal and risk. Someone to be shoved on a boat and sent home before she could do any more damage. Like the remittance men she sometimes saw wandering around the gambling halls of Kingston Town.

For ever outcast.

And conveniently forgotten. Even the thought twisted as pain inside her.

To never see Asher again, to never feel him beside her in the night when the ghosts of memory were strong and only he could quell them. To never walk the green hills of Falder or be a part of a family that had taken her in without question. Unequivocally.

Her chin lifted. She would not grovel—she had Ruby to think of and Miriam. If she could recover even some of the treasure, they would be safer.

'Could I have the use of your ship for a week in Jamaica?'

'To plot the co-ordinates from the map?'

'Yes.' She looked at him directly. One promise and she would be gone.

When he nodded she let go of the breath she had not realised she was holding. 'Peter Drummond is to be trusted, if you should be lucky enough to find anything.'

You. Not us. He did not mean to come with her then? 'Thank you.' She felt her teeth sink into the soft flesh on the inside of her mouth as she bit down to stop herself from saying more and watched as he bent to collect his satchel.

'I shall send a note to Annabelle Graveson within the hour and will let you know of her reply as soon I have it.'

When he walked away, birdsong muffled his footsteps, and she was left to find her own way back to the suite she shared with Miriam.

Her aunt was working on a tapestry and sitting near the window in a sitting room that came directly off her bedchamber.

'Was my mother's name Evangeline Montrose?' The answering shock was plain in her aunt's eyes. 'Annabelle Graveson gave Asher this book.' Opening the cover, she held it on top of Miriam's sewing, digging into the bodice of her gown and extracting the silver locket. 'Her maiden name was also Montrose. They were cousins.'

Miriam placed the sewing on the table beside her, her face white with shock. 'I did not know that. Can she be trusted?' Her voice was strained.

'Not to spread our secret?' She waited until her aunt nodded. 'I should imagine she wants her association with my father known to as few people as possible. For us…I am not sure how much anything matters. We are leaving England on one of the Wellingham ships bound for Jamaica in four days.'

'And Asher Wellingham…'

'Will be pleased to see the back of us I think.'

'I am sorry, Emmie…' But Emerald held out her hand and stopped the sentiment, swallowing back the lump that had formed in her throat before striding through to her own room and shutting the door.

Once inside, she brought her fingers across her mouth and breathed into them heavily, a silent scream of frustration, anger and grief. Grief for the loss of all that was gone. Picking up the book, she traced her finger across the name at the top of the inside cover and held it close to her chest.

When had her mother written this? Where had she written this? Before she had met Beau? After she had gone out to Jamaica?

She had no pictures at all of Evangeline, only the vague recollection of a voice. Standing, she walked to the mirror and looked at her own reflection. Some of her father stared back at her. She had his eyes and chin. She had his height and colour of skin. But her dimples? Where had they come from? And her hair? Beau's hair had been dark and straight, and thin in his last years. Differences.

Chapter Fifteen

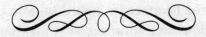

Asher left Falder and visited his jeweller in the centre of London the next morning, even the thought of the gossip that would be rife as a result not swaying his purpose.

He had always lived in the glare of the public eye, his time away giving the tattle-tongues much to conjecture upon; on his return to England as a widower there had been relentless speculation. Speculation that he had used to his advantage—sometimes in the salons of London he could almost feel the sharp taste of fear as others carefully tiptoed around his lost years and his scars.

And his retribution.

Beau Sandford.

It was said that he had run the pirate through the stomach a hundred times just to make sure that he was dead and then sliced off his ears and hands to feed them to the circling sharks below. And laughed as he had done it.

Jack had told him that once after a particularly harrowing dinner party when he was newly returned home, and since then he had restricted his socialising to the houses of friends.

Killing took a part of your soul, no matter how warranted the deed. After he had run Beau Sandford through the heart and watched him drop into the ocean below, he had turned away and fought down bile. And the anger that had consumed him was replaced instead by a kind of shame. Shame for where his life had taken him. Shame because as the Duke of Carisbrook he should have been able to protect his wife and his brother, kept them safe. Kept the English sense of honour and goodness intact. Even the Carisbrook crest reflected that.

An elk with its pointed horns and the rose of England between them, 'Onwards and upwards' printed at its base. Such an English sentiment. Eminently honourable and unwaveringly good. The sum of generations of dukes, their stewardship of the land marred only occasionally by some far-off crisis.

Except for him.

And yet even for him Falder closed around him with its green valleys and woods, with its clear streams and the never-endingness of sea, with its mirrored turrets and carved stone gates.

Falder.

Home.

For the first time he saw that in tradition there was safety and healing and regeneration. The beginnings of another reality. For them all.

For Emerald and Taris and for the ghost of Melanie. And for himself. He smiled and breathed in deeply as Peter Solbourne, his jeweller, met him at the door.

'I was about to send you a message, your Grace. You had mentioned your desire to find a gift for your sister's forthcoming birthday the last time you came to see me and I thought that these just may suit.' He brought forth a burgundy box strangely carved.

E. S. 1801.

The design was interwoven with lines of silver and these in turn were embellished with stones. As the jeweller undid a catch to one side of the box and lifted the lid, Ashe caught his breath. Pearls. Rose-blushed and graded from large to small, the lustre on them attesting to the purity of the shell.

'My God.' He lifted the necklace from its bed of silk and placed a finger against the last roundel. 'Where did you get these?'

'A man brought them in two weeks ago. A most unusual fellow. I have had them certified. They're from the islands around the Caribbean.'

The hair on the back of Asher's neck bristled. 'Did he give a name?'

'No, your Grace, he did not. Oh, he did leave a card

for future reference. The Countess of Haversham's card, actually. I thought it most odd at the time. But he made me promise to let her know who had bought them.'

Asher instantly ceased his questioning. Lord! E. S. *Emma Seaton! Emerald Sandford!* Could these be her pearls? He held them closer.

'How much are they?'

When the jeweller gave him the price, he doubted she would have received even a tenth of the exorbitant amount mentioned.

'I'll take them.'

Solborne looked astonished at the ease of the deal and promptly returned the strand to its bed before handing over the box. 'Is there anything else, your Grace?'

The gleam of interest in the old jeweller's eyes was easily seen. 'I would like to see a selection of your very finest rings. Emeralds. The stone must be an emerald.' He was pleased when Solborne did not query him further.

Twenty minutes later he had made his choice, a narrow gold ring with a large peerless emerald edged in smaller diamonds.

'A fine choice, if I might say so, your Grace, and I am certain that the lady for whom this is destined will be more than pleased.'

'And there is one more thing that you could do for me,' he added just as he was about to leave. 'I want you to make no mention of my purchases. It's a surprise, you see, and I should not want word to get around.'

'Indeed, your Grace. My lips shall be sealed.'

'Good.' Tucking the two boxes into his jacket pocket, he showed himself out and instructed his driver to take him to Madame Berenger's dress shop. He hoped the seamstress would have a selection of ready-made gowns to choose from, for he did not have the time to wait.

Chapter Sixteen

Annabelle Graveson brought a large case of family letters and sketches of Evangeline when she came to Falder and the rather stiff woman who had given them dinner at Longacres all those weeks ago was completely changed. Today she held out her arms to Emerald and held her tightly, tears rolling down pale cheeks and sobs racking her body.

'I have been wanting to do this from the first second of meeting you again, my love,' she said when she had finally collected herself, her fingers entwined about Emerald's as they sat down.

'Again?' She had no memory of this woman in her life at all.

Blowing her nose soundly, Annabelle made an effort to continue. 'When you were five you came back to England and your mother and father brought you and your brother up to Knutsford to our house there.'

Emerald smiled. 'I remember my mother gave me this locket. I remember a house high on a hill overlooking a river and a young boy…'

'Simon. My oldest child. He died of the ague in the Christmas of that same year. And then Evangeline was taken from us the following Easter.'

'She came home to England?'

'She was ill, Emerald. Ill with the depression of spirit, and drink was the only thing that made everything bearable.'

'Because she had killed my brother.'

Annabelle looked shocked. 'Beau told you that?'

'No. I remember it, though. James's broken body and my mother drunk against a wall with blood on her face.'

'He drowned, my dear. He wandered too near the sea and drowned. Evangeline jumped from the rocks into the water to try to save him and she never quite got over it when she could not. Your father sent her back to England to recover.'

'But she did not take me with her.'

'She could not take you. She hardly knew how to care for herself and Beau promised that he would bring you to England within the month. When the storms came early he had to wait and by then it was all too late. Your mother had gone back to her Maker and the first easy spoils of piracy had come Beau's way. There was no going back after that. I often wondered, if she had lived, would things have been different, though. I think her death took the heart from him.'

Emerald sat still and sifted the information through her mind, trying to make some sort of sense of all the recollections. Not a mad drunk woman after all, but a soul-saddened mother who had lost a child. For the first time ever she saw the faint ghost of Evangeline, smiling, beckoning, loving. Evangeline. A woman who had been transplanted into the tropics where the humidity had eaten at both her soul and her sanity. A fragile English rose blighted in the wilder soils of the Caribbean.

Now forgiveness crept in over anger, and an unfamiliar peace chased hard on the heels of a softer acceptance.

James. Beau. Evangeline. A family again in the hereafter. There was a rightness about it that made sense.

The relief was all encompassing.

When Annabelle handed her a small image of her parents, she saw exactly where it was that she had come from. Red-blonde curls and laughing turquoise eyes and dimples. Her mother. Her. Her fingers tightened on the likeness and she was pleased when Annabelle said that she might keep it.

'As family, you know that you would be most welcome to come to Longacres to live with me. With Miriam, of course and your little sister. Asher has told me she is a musical child?'

Emerald wanted to say yes, wanted to hold on to an offer that was both generous and unexpected. But she also knew that to be less than five miles from Falder would be a torture. To see Asher and not be with him, to watch from a distance the milestones in his life. A wife. Children. Grandchildren.

No, she knew absolutely and irrevocably that she could not do it.

'I thank you sincerely for your invitation, but at the moment…' She shook her head, finding it hard to convey in words the depth of her thanks.

'I understand things may be difficult, but, if you should change your mind for any reason, my offer would still stand. You will always be welcome at Longacres.'

When Annabelle had gone Emerald walked across the fields of Falder and towards the water, the breeze on her face cooling and the distant ocean beckoning from afar, a silver thread of ribbon. She mulled over Annabelle's offer and balanced it against the chancy hope of finding treasure. Perhaps she could take up the promise of a home for Miriam and Ruby…

She shook her head. Lord, to leave this place would be a wrench she could hardly bear the thinking of. Tucking her curls behind her ears, she pressed on towards the ocean. The tight squeeze of tears blurred her vision.

They met each other at the stream that bound the

Wellingham land to the west before the road to Rochcliffe. Asher was on the same horse he always rode,
a large black stallion with a streak of wildness in his
blood. Like his owner, she thought, and waited as he
dismounted. She knew he had returned to Falder very
late in the night; she had heard the turn of wheels
across the courtyard cobbles and heard the commotion the incoming vehicle had caused among the myriad servants.

This afternoon a quieter demeanour wreathed him
as he said, 'Annabelle told me that she had talked to
you. She said that she had asked you to stay at Longacres with her, but that you had refused. She was at
pains to understand why.'

'I need to go home to my sister.'

*I need to get as far away from you as possible.
From your eyes laced with gold, from the responsibility that sits so measured on your shoulders, from
the promise of love that could only turn to hate, from
the memory of your hands on my body in the night.*

A quick glance at him made her blush.

'I want to show you something,' he said unexpectedly. 'It's this way.'

The thought flicked through Emerald's mind that
perhaps he had followed her and had waited until she
had come down into this valley. But why would he
do that? He had made it plain that he did not want
her company.

The thickness of trees evened out into farmland as

they went, and ten minutes later a sharp outcrop of rock materialised above them.

'Here.' He beckoned and cut through a wedge of brambles. On the other side there was the mouth of a cave, hidden from view both by the hedges around it and by a large slice of rock that had sheared off from above.

She waited with him without talking for a moment by the entrance so that their eyes became accustomed to the dull light inside. And then she saw what it was that he wanted to show her. The walls on the far side were covered with figures, in red and ash and brown. Scenes of hunting and fighting and family, a thousand years of history hidden among the quiet hills of England.

'Taris and I discovered this place when we were boys. I've never told another person of its existence.'

'But you would tell me? Why?' Nothing made sense.

'When you were sick you told me your secrets. I felt it only fair to tell you some of mine.'

'Do you come here often?' She looked around, guessing the answer even before he gave it. A fur pelt lay on a raised platform constructed of wood in the middle of the room and a stool with a candle on top was beside it.

'After I came home and found Melanie had died, I made a bed down here. It was the only place I could gain a little sleep and at first—' he stopped '—at first it was the only place that I did not hear the voices.'

'Voices?'

'The voices in the compound at night when men were taken to…*hell*.' She could not imagine that she had heard him right until she saw the gleam of moisture in his eyes.

'Were you taken?'

'Yes.'

Anger winded her and then pain, for him, for them, for the truth and lies, and for lives changed by the curious whims of circumstance.

He held his right hand up to the light. The hand that was missing two fingers. 'It was a game to them, the mutilation of bodies, and some men lost a lot more than I did.'

'It is why you do not sleep?'

'Did not sleep. When you were in my bed I slept.'

The power of his words melted away restraint and she moved forward.

'Sleep with me, then. Here.' She did not waver, did not think, did not let the future take anything away from the sheer honesty of this moment, and when his thumb came up to trace the line of her jaw she closed her eyes and just felt.

Felt his hands on her bodice and her skirt. Felt the cold of air and then the warmth of fur. Felt the hard planes of his body and the hot thrust of his manhood. Close. Closer. Inside. Touching her heart. Taking her from the quiet dark confines of this place to heaven and back again and all under the watchful eyes of ancestors drawn in blood.

It was later, much later. Asher had lit a candle and pulled his jacket across them, the folds of wool warm in the chill of the early evening. Silence enveloped them, and timelessness, her cheek soft against the rise and fall of his chest.

'I think I know why you refused Annabelle's invitation when she offered you a home.'

She frowned and leaned back so that she could look at him.

'It's clairvoyancy you have the knack of, then?' She tried to sit up, but he would not let her.

'No, merely sense and reason. I think that you are afraid of staying here.'

His guess was so near the mark she was silent.

'And you are afraid of staying here because you are so much more used to running, from your father, from the law, from your enemies. And the fact that in this little corner of England there could finally be a home for you is tempered with even more risk because you are Emerald Sandford, the pirate's daughter, and you are not prepared to chance it turning sour.'

Restraint broke as she wriggled out from the circle of his arms. 'That's right. I am afraid to stand by and let you see just how hated my family name is, to know just how many people Beau stole from or hurt or killed, because then, in place of what I see in your eyes now, would come something else and I don't want that something else. Not from you, Asher, not when I have had this.' The cold air in the cave against her nakedness made her shiver.

'Then fight them, damn it.'

'No. Don't you see? Don't you know? When life disappointed both my parents, they dissolved into pieces.' She was shouting so loud now that it hurt the soft tissue in the back of her throat. 'Pieces that tore apart reason and left only chaos. I feel that chaos inside me, sometimes, and wonder if I am just the same. What if I stay and ruin you and your family and Annabelle and Miriam…?'

In reply he stood and lifted her up against him, facing her towards a mirror she had not noticed before.

'What do you see?' he asked.

She did not understand.

'Small expressions, the line of your jaw, the colour of your eyes, the way your hair falls down just here, the mark of a knife on your brow.' His finger swept up and pushed back her heavy fringe. 'We are all the sum of what has come before us but we are also the beginning of what will come next. And in the middle stands choice, Emerald. The choice to be exactly who you want to become…here.' His hand fell to the place above her heart and she could feel the beat of her body echoed in his.

'You truly believe that?'

'I do.' The gold in his eyes was strong, intense. 'And it was you who taught me to do so with your courage and conviction. Together we could weather anything.'

'Together?'

'I will come with you to Jamaica to fetch your sister if you will give me a promise.'

She nodded and waited to see what he would say next.

'I want you to promise that you will return to Falder with me.'

'Return?'

'I won't let you go, Emerald. Ever. No matter what.'

The tears in the back of her eyes welled up when he drew her back into the bed beside him for in her acceptance of his lovemaking she knew that she would stay here in England as his mistress. And she had never quite imagined herself in such a role.

Chapter Seventeen

Emerald left England late on the evening tide and, as the land receded against the horizon, Asher's voice broke into her thoughts.

'We will be in Jamaica before next month's end.'

The gathering breeze whipped at his words and the sails above them caught and billowed.

Jamaica? As Asher's mistress? He had never mentioned marriage again, even in the aftermath of last night's lovemaking, and yet being at his side was enough. More than enough.

When he took her hand and led her down to the cabin they would share she followed him gladly, interested as they went in the layout of this ship. There was the galley and surgeon's cabin, to one corner of which was a bench well set out with medical supplies. The *Nautilus* would ride the oceans well, she thought, her lines both gracious and clean and her crew well looked after.

As they came to a heavy door, he stopped.

'Close your eyes.' His voice was husky and full of an anticipation she could not quite understand. When he led her inside she felt the warmth of the air and heard the quiet play of water around the hull. 'Now open them.'

A display of gowns hung in the wardrobe opposite her, shoes and shawls and undergarments in a variety of designs on the large table beside it. Crossing the room she ran a finger down the startling shot-red silk of a beautiful day dress.

'Madame Berenger was sure that they would fit you.'

'You bought these for me?'

He closed the door and came to stand beside her. Swallowing. Almost nervous?

'I thought that you needed them.'

'And she can make gowns without a fitting?'

'I described you. In detail.' His gaze ran across her, lazy, sensual, unhurried, and Emerald's heartbeat faltered. Was this the life of a kept woman, a constant flow of material goods in lieu of the payment for what she imagined would come next?

Suddenly she knew that she couldn't quite do it. Not without honesty anyway.

'I am not certain as to how long we will stay in the Caribbean, but there are some things about me that aren't... aren't...' Her mind scurried through an easier way to say what she needed to and she was glad for his continued silence.

'I am not accepted in any social circles there,' she blurted out, and when Asher stepped forward she stopped him.

'But you lived in the town?'

'We were outcasts.'

The anguish in the words was tangible, even to her. Lord, how she had wanted to be part of something, part of the village or the congregation in the church on the high hill overlooking the sea. Part of the picnics and gatherings at Easter and the joy of May Day celebrations. She had to explain it to him. Before they reached Kingston Town. Before he knew the exact extent of her damaged reputation.

'Even dressed in these, they would still know me.'

'Marry me then, Emerald.' His words were barely whispered, and she had to look up to see that he had indeed spoken.

'Marry you?'

'As the Duchess of Carisbrook, criticism would be far more muted and I have taken the liberty of bringing a parson aboard.' The pad of his thumb wiped the moisture from the soft skin on her cheek. 'I can protect you if you will let me.'

'Why?'

He turned and she saw the muscle in the side of his jaw ripple in tension.

'Because I love you.'

Had she heard him right? The warm strength of hope was like a drug, a heady elixir fed directly into the throbbing jugular at her neck. Could he possibly mean it?

'I've loved you ever since you bent over at the Bishop of Kingseat's party wearing nothing but skin underneath your gown.'

The gold in his eyes was brittle sharp. 'And I have thought about it many a night since.'

Unexpectedly she laughed, the sound fading away as he reached into his pocket to bring out a small box and flipped it open. An emerald ring sat in velvet, its true clear green catching the light from the lamp. Removing it, he caught at her left hand and placed the gold band on the third finger.

'Marry me, Emerald Sandford. Here on the ship. Before we reach Jamaica.'

And suddenly it was easy in the warmth of his embrace as his lips came down across hers to seal the bargain.

She would do it. She would marry him. Now. Today. His eyes were soft with passion and smouldering dark.

"I have something else for you too. Something that you lost in London.'

He leant across to the bureau beside him and brought out a box. Delight claimed her. Her pearls.

'How could you have known that they were mine?' she asked.

'I guessed. The initials. The place of purchase. The fact that Miriam's card was left as surety.'

'Evangeline chose them when I was a baby.'

'And now they are your wedding gift.'

Tears filled her eyes as she carefully laid the necklace in its box and stepped back to her satchel. Lifting out the map, she handed it across to Asher.

'As it is the time for new beginnings I would like to give you this.'

She saw surprise in the lines of his face and the tone in his voice was rough. 'I would waste neither time nor money chasing such a fickle promise.'

'I know.' Relief flooded her as he lifted the parchment and tore it into tiny fragments and when he was finished she let go of the breath she was unaware that she had taken.

It was over. Her old life. It was gone for ever and in the ashes of greed rose a phoenix of love, the bright possibility of a future with Asher replacing uncertainty with joy.

She touched the emerald. Not just any ring, after all, but hers.

'It's beautiful. Where did you get it?'

'I went to London when you began to recover. To a brothel in Curzon Street, a place designed to make men forget their…difficulties. I stayed less than the time it took to finish a brandy before going straight to my jeweller's.'

Emerald began to smile. And when she took his hands in her own she noticed that he was no longer wearing the sapphire on his little finger. She stroked the pale band of skin left beneath it and the ghosts of the past floated between them as he let out his breath.

'When Melanie died I knew, even in the darkest days of grief and guilt, that I would survive it. But if anything were to happen to you, Emerald, I know that I would not…'

She brought her finger across his lips to stop the words and he gathered her close and pulled her down into the softness of kapok, the ocean around them swelling soft and known.

Their world.

'I could stay here for ever,' she whispered.

One eyebrow cocked upward. Hopefully.

'Here in this bed?'

She began to laugh, but amusement faded as he undid the stays on her bodice and pushed the material back.

'You are so very beautiful. Your skin…the tattoo…' He traced around the edges of the mark, a frown across his forehead. 'A butterfly. *Mariposa* in Spanish. I should have guessed. All the time I should have known that it was you. My pirate wife.'

His arms took the weight as he rolled her beneath

him, all humour long gone. 'I will never let you go, Emerald. This is for ever.'

'For ever,' she returned and welcomed the heat of his mouth as it slanted down hard across her own.

Epilogue

December 1823

The cold of winter was kept at bay by a roaring fire in the main hall of Falder.

Ruby sat to one side of Asher and in his lap their eight-month-old son slumbered, his soft breathing making Emerald smile.

'Play us another one, sweetheart,' Asher said as Emerald took the harmonica from her lips. 'It keeps Ashton quiet.'

Curling her fingers around the small instrument, she looked around. Lucinda and Rodney were ensconced in the corner and Miriam and Alice and Annabelle sat further over with tapestries on their knees, Azziz, Toro and Taris laughing behind them.

Her world.

Her world with Asher.

Full. Complete. Perfect.

She fingered the rich satin of her dress and her eyes caught the portrait above the fireplace. The portrait done last month by one of the painters now fashionable in society.

Emerald Wellingham, the Duchess of Carisbrook.

Asher had instructed the artist to draw the *Nautilus* dancing on the ocean, the rolling green hills of Falder behind and the peninsula of Return Home Bay.

And if she looked carefully she could see in the distance the outline of a ship that looked a lot like the *Mariposa,* a man and a woman and a young boy on the quarterdeck holding hands and smiling.

Tradition and the sweet fullness of family. The past bound finally into the present.

With love.

Masquerading Mistress

Prologue

1794
England

His hand brushed the side of her face and he smiled
as she skipped away, the sun in her red-blonde hair. To
take hold of Eloise St Clair was like containing smoke.
She never stopped. Never waited for him to catch her
up or slow her down.

Even here after their tryst in the woods she didn't
tarry, her jacket buttoned and her boots relaced. Maxwell hoped that she felt the same joy as he did in their
lovemaking and the thought worried him. Putting anxiety aside, he reached into his pocket. The trinket lay
against the silk inner lining and he could feel its warmth.

A sign.

That she might say yes.

'Eloise.' He hated the catch he could hear in his voice.

'What is it, Maxim?' Her pet name for him grated against the onslaught of his early manhood.

'I brought you something. Us something,' he amended as she walked back towards him, the hint of gold in his hand catching her attention as no words ever could.

'A present?' Now he had her full regard.

'To keep me close.' Handing over the locket, he watched as she flipped open the catch.

'You drew these of us?'

He nodded. 'It could be like a ring, Elli. Like a betrothal ring, 'til we reach our majority and can be married.'

'Your parents disapprove of me. My father told me he had heard it in church and I am certain that he would not lie.'

A shadow passed over the sun, hiding the blue of the day beneath greyness, leaching out its warmth.

'When we are older nobody can tell us what to do.'

She shook her head; the red-gold curls that spilled out from a flimsy band of velvet reaching almost to the line of her waist. 'Nay, your mother will take you off to London and you will forget me. I am only the Reverend's daughter, after all.'

For the first time since they had met two years ago Maxwell heard vulnerability in her words and, because having the upper hand with Eloise was so unusual, he pressed further an argument that he might otherwise never have used.

'Let's bind ourselves to a troth right now. Here. In the woods today.' He pulled a small knife from his pocket. 'In blood. Yours and mine.'

The spurt of fire in her eyes egged him on. Placing the blade against the skin on his wrist, he ran it clean across the blueness of vein. Blood trickled down the inside of his palm and fell in droplets from his fingers.

He was relieved when she offered him her hand and even more relieved when she did not faint as sharp steel bit in. Mingling blood, he pressed their arms into the shape of a cross. Symbolic. Eternal.

'If my parents do not allow us to marry, we could always elope?'

'You think they would not follow us, Maxwell, would not pull us apart with the influence that they wield?' She used his name, his real name, and the look in her dark eyes was sad. Fey. Knowing.

Unsettled, he pulled back, surprised at the amount of blood that had soaked into the linen of his shirt.

'I will walk you home.'

'No. It's quicker if I go by myself.' A light touch of her thumb on his cheek and she was gone, the ache in his wrist intensifying as he watched her run.

Chapter One

April 1816
Penleven Castle, Cornwall

'She said *what*…?' The Duke of Penborne's shout echoed around the antechamber and Leonard Lindsay stepped back.

'Caroline Anstretton said that she had once been…intimate with you. She did qualify that it was no longer the case, but her tone of voice was such that most people present guessed that she still harboured at least some affection.'

Hearing the words a second time made little difference to the scale of Thornton's anger and, making an effort to temper it, he tried again. This was hardly his cousin's fault, after all, and he was long past the stage of caring enough to shoot the messenger when the news was bad.

'You are telling me this woman said that I was her lover?'

'She did.'

'Is she simple?'

'She definitely does not give that impression.'

'Ugly, then?' He hated to even utter the question given the state of his own face, but he had to know what he was up against.

'She is one of the most beautiful women to have ever graced London. I have heard that said time and time again since she arrived here and I would guess that, even given the enormity of her confession, she would have a hundred takers for her favours were they given half the chance.'

'The chance?'

'The chance to get close to her. Whether anyone is enjoying her favours already is anyone's guess, for she is somewhat…experienced in her pursuit of men.' His voice lowered as he continued in the fashion of one who would hate to be thought of as a gossip, but who, in fact, relished the scandal and prattle of society. 'It is said that she was married briefly to a French general.'

'A busy woman, then.' Thornton's irony was lost on his cousin and, smiling, he brought one hand up across his cheek, the scarred ridge of raised flesh rough against his fingers. Cannon fire had a way of making certain that you never forgot its power, and even two years after the church had been blown up in his face he could still smell the singe of burning flesh, still feel the agony of his melting skin and the blackened weeks of delirium that had followed.

Five months of fighting his way back out of hell. And then a further seven months of seeing that hell reflected in the mirror every time he looked at himself while convalescing in L'Hôpital des Anges in the south-west of France.

He grimaced. He had never been a vain man, but he was not ready to return to society and to all that it entailed.

Not yet.

But when?

Closing his eyes against the thought, he moved towards the window, liking the sound of the wild sea echoing beneath the ramparts of Penleven Castle.

Home.

Safety.

A place where he could hide and lick his wounds and regroup. He had not left it for close on twelve months now, ignoring the whispered rumours that swirled around his name.

Reclusive. Damaged. Solitary.

And now to be thrust back into society because some feather-brained woman had decided to lie about her sexual favours and others had decided to listen…?

Caroline Anstretton. Her face was not difficult for him to imagine. She would have alabaster pale skin and eyes that were threaded in pity.

Lord!

He had come home for peace and quiet and solitude. And to hide.

There. He admitted it to himself as the fragile first beams of spring sunshine slanted across the skin on his left hand. Spring. A new beginning, and all he could feel was the bone-cold chill of winter and the stripped bareness of scars opaque against the slight warmth of sun.

Leonard moved uneasily behind him. Reaching out for the brandy, Thornton imagined, and topping up on courage. His cousin's complexion looked more sallow each time he had seen him of late and he wondered if he was ailing. Perhaps Penleven brought out the worst in him with the lost possibility of any inheritance. He had, after all, been the custodian of the castle for five years when military duty had kept him in Europe. Thorn wondered how he would have felt had the situation been reversed and decided that Leonard's melancholy was probably wholly understandable, for a family stipend of limited means and the necessity to be beholden to the wealthier members of the family could hardly be easy.

With measured care he stood, a cane taking the weight from his left leg.

'I am certain that this whole ridiculous accusation will blow over before the week's end and those who have deigned to take notice of such nonsense will have moved on to the next scandal.' He heard the irritation in his voice and tried to temper it as his cousin looked up.

'If it were not for Excelsior Beaufort-Hughes, indeed it might well do so.'

'Beaufort-Hughes?'

'It seems that he almost won the girl's hand in a game of whist and has been complaining loudly about the fact that a duke of the realm should be openly consorting with a young lady of such…dubiousness in the first place.'

'A young lady?'

'I would put her at no more than twenty.'

'And her family? Where are they?'

'She has a brother. And his reputation is as disreputable as hers. He's a card player.'

A gambler and a liar!

For just a moment he was…curious, an emotion that he had not felt in years, and he savoured the tiny echo of it. Anything was better than the dulling ennui he had been plagued with of late.

But why would the girl lie?

Because she did not expect him to come and refute any untruth. The answer came easily.

'You could return with me, Thornton, to sort the whole thing out. Not good for the Lindsay name, you understand, just to leave it as it is.'

Thornton forced back mirth. The Lindsay name? Lord, if Leonard knew even a half of the things he had done on the continent under the sanctity of country and crown…

He flexed the fingers on his right hand and then drew them back into a fist as he mulled over his cousin's ludicrous notions of manners and protocol. Vague social niceties defining lives lost in far-off lands.

Lillyanna's life.

His life. By degrees.

Of a sudden he was unreasonably tired by the Anstretton girl's nonsense and by his cousin's interpretation of a stain on the name of Lindsay. And to be dragged up to London for such a flimsy reason made everything doubly worse.

And yet, running his fingers across the ache in his thigh, there was something about this whole débâcle that he found…stimulating. A beautiful woman who would lie in front of an assembly of people and expect no redress? A woman with a penchant for theatrics and a family more unusual than his own? Interest blossomed. What possible circumstances could have brought her to this pass?

He smiled.

The spy in him was not so easily dismissed, after all, and the puzzle of Caroline Anstretton beckoned with a jarring unrightness.

No more than twenty and ruined.

Beautiful. Deceitful.

And desperate. He wondered where that thought had come from even as he imagined the personal effort required for a stay in London. Lord, the memory of the last time he had ventured up to the city was still raw in his mind. The stares and the sympathy, the artfully disguised condolences of those who had known him before his accident and the hypocrisy of whispered truths as he passed them by. *'He used to be... He once was... I remember when...'*

One week, he told himself even against his better judgement.

One week in the city and then he would return home.

She should not have said it.

Should not have dragged the name of a man lauded for his very solitude into the sticky equation of survival.

But she had had no option.

The Earl of Marling, Excelsior Beaufort-Hughes, was as old as he was obnoxious, and, as she had held the lace hanky to her nose, she had said it. To everyone at the house party of Lady Belinda Forsythe.

'Thornton Lindsay, the Duke of Penborne, was my lover once and after him there is no way on earth that I could ever deign to sleep with you.'

Caroline still remembered the silence after her utterance, the shocked gasp of her audience and the hatred of her aged would-be suitor as he thrust her brother's gambling chit forward and again demanded redress.

Redress in the form of Caroline's body.

It was the lateness of the hour that had saved them

as those full in their cups had drifted off to the next social engagement, leaving Thomas and her to sort out
the whole sorry affair.

Sorted! Lord. That had been over a week ago and
now the Duke of Penborne was due at the Wilfreds'
ball at any moment. Her heart began to hammer. As the
most famous recluse of his time he could hardly be
overjoyed by her false proclamation. Lady Dorothy
Hayes, an elderly woman of some notoriety, was standing next to her and spoke the words she was sure everyone else in the room was thinking.

'Lindsay has barely left Cornwall since returning
wounded from the Continent. He was a captain in the
army under Wellington, you understand.' She paused
for effect before continuing. 'An intelligence officer,
if the rumours are to be believed, and there are many
who say he lost his heart in the role. The Heartless
Duke: a man with neither the inclination nor the desire
to keep company with others.'

Sweat pooled in the hollow between Caroline's
breasts as the buzz of conversation became louder. She
had never enjoyed the good will of the society doy-
ennes since arriving in London; solid women with the
weight of manners and propriety on their shoulders and
with husbands who wielded influence in court. And
yet, conversely, she had never been quite as isolated
as she found herself now. A self-confessed harlot and
one abided only because of the intrigue of scandal. She

stood now in the shadows of a netherworld, a darker
corner of society where card sharks and pimps lingered
around the bright glitter of respectability, garnering the
crumbs of small outcries and using them to their own
advantage.

A fallen woman.

Shoved away from properness by circumstance.

She shook away introspection and thought she
might be ill as the line of people parted and a tall figure with his cloak collar raised high around his face
limped forward. It should take Lindsay about six seconds to name her a liar for the gathering silence all
around was more telling than any whispered gossip.

She could barely see his face between the folds of
material and his arm weighed heavily on an ebony
cane as he came to her side. Pushing back the cloth,
he ignored the collective gasp of shock, indifference
in his gait as he made an easy bow in front of her. His
left cheek was crossed with raised scars and he wore
a leather patch on the eye above. The buttons on his
jacket caught the light from the candelabra above and
sent a blade of lustre across the floor, its edges stained
in rainbow.

'I have it on good authority that you are Caroline Anstretton?' A sharp hint of question filled his words and
when she met his glance she almost recoiled, one dark
gold eye imprinted with such startling and brittle indifference. 'And I understand that you and I share a history.'

His gaze moved across her in a desultory fashion, taking in the over-made face, she guessed, before his glance fell to her hands. She stopped wringing her kerchief immediately and tried to salvage the situation.

'You may not remember me?' The sound of pleading made her voice high and wobbly so she tried again, taking no notice of the titter of the women around her. 'Of course you must be extremely busy…'

'I doubt, madam, that I would ever forget you.'

With his glance running suggestively over her body, Caroline batted her eyelashes and dredged up the last of her acting skills. 'I can see that you fun with me, Your Grace.'

Her teeth worried her upper lip now in sheer desperation and she was pleased for the length of the wig she wore, its bundling red curls hiding a growing shame.

Anything to shelter behind. This whole charade was a lot harder to perform in front of a man whose face espoused a keen intelligence and a hint of some other emotion she could not quite fathom. Her heart began to pound as the voices around her became louder and people moved back. *Please help me, God,* she thought to herself and took a deep breath of air. *Help me, help me, help me.*

Unexpectedly his one visible eye caught hers, sharp irritation overlaid by perplexity.

'Was I a good lover?'

The question was said in the tone of one who did

not give a damn for the reply and in that second Caroline understood two things: he had absolutely no care for what society thought of him and he was far more dangerous than any man she had ever met.

Her bravado faltered, Excelsior Beaufort-Hughes's toothless grin suddenly less frightening than the steely stare of the man opposite her.

She felt strange, dislocated and uncertain. What manner of man would leave himself so open to insult and be amused by it?

Slowly she rallied. All of London knew her to be the fallen and discarded mistress of the Duke of Penborne. And worse. But this war-weary soldier-Duke had a home here. A place. And with the scars of battle drawn upon him, she knew without a doubt that he must have suffered.

'You were the most competent lover I have ever had the pleasure of being with.' She said the words carefully, so that even those far from them could, in the silence, hear the statement.

And for the first time she saw a glimmer of amusement.

'How old are you?'

The question was unexpected.

'Twenty.'

'Old enough to know, then, that she who plays carelessly with fire must expect to be burned by it.'

He looked around at the pressing crowd, disdain in

his eye and distance, though in the tightening of his lips she sensed a quieter anger, a deliberation that gave her the singular impression of not being quite as detached as others might have thought him. Many had dropped their gaze from his and shuffled nervously.

He had once been beautiful. So beautiful that she had heard many a whispered confidence of hopeful girls.

She wished that he might lower his collar so she could see the true extent of his damage. But he stood there with his ruined face and his ebony cane and by the sheer and brutal force of his personality he dared the room not to comment on the changes upon him that war had wrought.

Such a victory she thought, and admiration surfaced.

'Perhaps we could come to an arrangement.'

'Pardon?' His suggestion puzzled her.

'You seem to be between...protectors and I find myself interested in being reacquainted with your bounteous charms. Where is your brother?' He was still, waiting, danger harnessed only by the thread of circumstance.

'I am not certain that you quite understand the situation, Your Grace...' she began, but the sentiment died in her throat as Thomas pushed through the gathering crowd from the direction of a gaming room.

'You are the brother?' Thornton Lindsay's voice was barely civil and Tosh looked as nervous as she was.

He nodded and flushed.

'Your sister has told the world that she and I were

once…close,' he enunciated carefully. 'I thought perhaps we could be so again.'

'No.' The pulse in her brother's throat raced.

'No?' A languid humour replaced anger as his right hand reached out to the lace on Caroline's bodice and traced the line of her bosom.

A challenge. Pure and simple.

And when Tosh came forward it took the Duke of Penborne less than five seconds to lay him out cold on the parquet floor. No thrown punches either, just a twist of his hands against the pulse in his neck and Thomas lay still.

Silence blanketed the large salon as he bent to retrieve his cane. 'When he wakes up, send him to my apartments. I shall be happy to give him a chit for any damage he may have incurred.' He pulled a card from his pocket as he spoke. 'Here is my direction. I shall expect you both tomorrow at two in the afternoon.'

And then he was gone, a solitary figure making his way slowly down the marbled staircase.

Bested. They had been bested by a master at the game and so, so easily. She looked neither left nor right as she helped Thomas up and they departed.

'I do not think Penborne is quite the man we thought him to be, Tosh.' Caroline dipped the cloth into cold water and brought it to the bump on his head, gained when he fell at the Duke's hand.

'And what sort of a man was that?'

'A man who would do anything to avoid a public scandal. A man who would stay in his castle in Cornwall and ignore the issues of society.'

Her brother rolled up from his place on the sofa, the dimples in his cheeks easily seen. 'Well, then, if you had not baited Excelsior Beaufort-Hughes in the first place, none of this other fracas would have been necessary. My hand was full and his was the next throw. I could have beaten him easily if you had just been patient.'

'Patient? You had already lost your winnings for the last week. And the fellow next to you had a full flush.'

Thomas paled. 'He could not have. I held three aces.'

'But not the ace of hearts. It was left in the cards that you opted to pass. If I had not knocked the table as I stood and proclaimed Lindsay as my lover, I might well be ensconced this minute in the Marling country estate and there would be little that you or the law could have done to change it.'

'God help me,' Thomas whispered and his eyes met hers. Dark blue orbs mixed with grey. The perfect rogue. Her beloved twin brother.

'Well, we cannot stay here any longer, Caro. With the Duke a damn pugilist we'd better be gone from here by the morning. Though perhaps we should take him up on his offer of money.'

Nodding, Caroline kissed him on his forehead and declared his injuries healed. 'After which, we will leave for Bath. Helena Alexander has asked us down for her soirée with the promise of a few nights' accommodation attached. She is a pretty girl, Thomas, and kind with it—I have seen how she looks at you.'

Crossing to the mirror, she loosened the pins that held her wig in place and shook it free. Her own cornblonde hair was plastered to her scalp, the heat of the day apparent. Leaning over, she ruffled her fingers through the roots and almost instantly the curls began to reassert themselves. The heavy rouge she wore looked incongruous against the short elfin cut and she smiled.

'I like England. I like everything about it. It feels like…home.'

'Pity it's no longer ours, then.' Her brother walked to the sideboard and poured a large brandy. Caroline frowned. He had been drinking too much lately and she could hear more and more a note of desperation in the tone of his voice.

Ever since the death of their mother.

Ever since they had fled Paris, penniless and hunted.

'There are other ways to deal with our problems, Tosh.'

His eyes flashed. Real anger evident. 'How, Caroline?' He seldom called her by her full name and she knew now that his patience was stretched, the dark streaks of dye in his hair making him look tired.

'We could hit Lindsay for a large amount. He is rumoured to be as rich as Croesus. With money we could change identities, leave London and begin anew somewhere else.'

'He knocked me down in a minute flat. I can hardly heavy-hand him into giving more than he wants to.'

'Let me do it, then. Let me go to see him.'

'You?'

She heard laughter in his tone and smiled. 'I can be awfully persuasive.'

'I am not sure. He seems…menacing.'

'But I cannot imagine that he would hurt a woman.'

When her brother hesitated she knew that she had him, and, looking back at the mirror, she saw a shining anticipation in her dark blue eyes.

She wanted to see Thornton Lindsay again. Wanted to understand better what made him so…beguiling. Even scarred and hurt he had a strength that was undefinable and a power that made others look ordinary. Masculinity and distance and the sculptured fineness of what was left of his face made him more attractive again.

She would wear her light blue dress with the half-boots that added a few inches to her height. And for extra measure she would carry a rock in her reticule. If he became difficult, she would need something to contain him.

His quick subduing of her brother came to mind as a warning and she pushed the thought back.

One chance. One meeting. Destiny tore apart common sense and she began to imagine things that she had long thought dormant inside of her.

And then just as quickly dismissed them.

Chapter Two

She should not have come.

She knew it the moment the Duke of Penborne shepherded her into his library and closed the heavy door behind her.

Today he was dressed entirely in black and the pantaloons he wore harked more of the country than the city in both cut and style. With his cape removed she saw that his dark hair was long, tied at the nape with a sliver of leather, neither carefully attended nor fussily arranged.

Uncertainly she clutched her reticule in front of her, the light from the window falling on to the scars of his face and adding mystery to an arrant and blatant dangerousness.

What was she doing here? she asked herself, as courage faltered. What stupidity had overcome her to make her even think that she could outsmart this man? God help me, she cursed beneath her breath and felt a rising dread, but she had brought the charade thus far and had to finish the thing off. Even a small amount of money would bolster a flagging purse. Carefully she removed her coat, the thick wool a shield to her daintier charms.

Tossing her head, she reverted to character and brought her hand to her throat, thrusting out her bosom, and pleased when his eye wandered to that part of her anatomy.

'My brother is very cross with me. And I know that you are too.' A breathless voice. Little girl innocent. So easy to accomplish. She leant over slightly so that the neckline of her day dress sagged open. 'He sent me here today to collect the chit that you so kindly offered us.'

If looks could kill, Caroline thought she might well be lying at his feet, and in truth the ridiculousness of the whole situation was beginning to hit home.

She had lied and he had exposed her. A hasty retreat might have been a better policy, yet in the face of their lack of finance even that was not a viable option.

'How much?' His words were clipped and as he leaned forward to take her hand she could not quite understand what it was that he meant.

'How much?' This time her voice sounded exactly like her own.

'How much are you paid for your services? With men?'

Shaken, she tried to disengage her hand, but he would not let her. She wondered if he felt the quick spark of shock as he touched her, jolting her into a breathless bewilderment. 'Oh,' she managed, 'I am not cheaply bought, Your Grace.'

'No?' The base of his first finger pressed down on her wrist, the blue vein marking the accelerated beat of blood. 'Is there a discount for the second time around?'

'You fun with me, sir. There was no first.'

'A pity you didn't relate that fact to the many interested ears of the *ton*.'

Uncertainty swamped her. 'I thought that you would not wish me to, for I had named you as the best of lovers by then and could not in all good faith take that sentiment back.'

'Why not?'

'Because it would have hurt you. Hurt your reputation.'

He dropped her hand and reached for the decanter of brandy on the table beside him, pouring out a liberal amount.

'Know that my reputation is the last thing I would worry about.'

'Then we have another thing in common, Your Grace.' She punctuated the unimportance of it all with a vacuous wave and rearranged her bounteous curls, but he ignored the sentiment and changed the subject completely.

'Where are your family, your people?'

'Thomas is my family,' she countered and accepted the brandy that he held out to her. The fluted glass was beautiful, she thought, as she raised it to her lips and drank, the warmth of the liquor bolstering confidence. It was not usual for a lady to drink brandy, especially at this time of day, but Caroline was not a conventional woman.

'Your parents?'

'Dead.'

'Your husband?'

'Killed.'

'And so your brother tries to make ends meet by plying the card tables and you try to help him by sleeping with whoever takes your interest?'

'He does and I do.' Fluttering her eyelashes, she pushed down a rising nervousness. A string of probing questions was the last thing she wanted, and she needed for him to see her as the shallow and flirtatious opportunist she portrayed.

'A rather uncertain profession, I should imagine, and dangerous. You seem young for it?'

'Young in years, but old in life.' She had read that line in a book once and had always wanted to use it. But it did not have quite the desired effect on Thornton Lindsay. Instead of being impressed, he laughed. Loudly.

'Why did you choose me as your would-be lover?'

Colouring, Caroline decided on honesty.

'I knew you to be a...recluse, a man who would not come to London to refute a small untruth. However, had I known of your injuries, I would have most certainly chosen another.'

'Because you feel sorry for me?' His deep voice sharpened, irritation easily audible.

'Sorry for you? I doubt you would allow that, Your Grace.'

He laughed again.

'How long have you been a courtesan?'

'Long enough.'

The gold in his one good eye darkened. Considerably.

'I will pay you fifty guineas to stay the night with me.' The words seemed dragged from his throat as if he could not quite control his voice and she looked up, startled.

'Fifty guineas?'

More money than she had ever held in all her life. Enough money to make a new start somewhere else. Excitement churned.

'Fifty guineas.' She repeated the figure just to make certain that she had heard rightly. And in that second Caroline saw the answer to their problems.

One night of shame in exchange for a new chance.

No more scampering from town to town with the law on their heels and a weighty dollop of guilt on their shoulders.

'It cannot be tonight.'

His amber eye slanted in question.

'I am busy tonight,' she added and the meaning of her words flared in his face.

'Tomorrow night, then. Here. At six o'clock.'

Shoving his hands in his pockets he stood very, very still. When she nodded she could have sworn she saw relief.

'I shall expect you then, Miss Anstretton.'

Without waiting for her reply, he helped her into her coat and opened the door. A footman outside came forward and ushered her though to the hallway. When she turned to bid him goodbye, the library door was firmly shut.

Thornton replaced the lid on the brandy decanter and looked out on to the dreary day as he listened to the sounds of her carriage departing.

Why had he offered her such a bounty when, for an eighth of the price, he could have repaired to Venus's and used a girl with almost as much charm as that of Caroline Anstretton?

Almost.

It was in the touch of her fingers against his. And in the uncertainty of her eyes, the sooty lashes so long that when she looked down they rested on her cheeks. And her strange sense of honour.

She was a cheat and a liar and God knew what else. The reticule she carried had strained at the handles indicating something much heavier than just a handkerchief inside and the boots she wore were at least half a size too small.

She was making everything up.

He could feel it in every word she uttered. Questions! He smiled and turned to refill his glass.

His intelligence days were over and still they did not let him just be. Everyone was suspect; even a beautiful harlot who had made sure that her breasts had fallen easily into his line of vision and had accepted an assignation with very little pressure for tomorrow night.

Lord.

Tomorrow night and it had been years since he had had a woman.

The thought worried him.

'Lillyanna.' The softness of her name seemed like a travesty in the light of what he was about to do.

And yet in the remains of sorrow something else had suddenly budded and he could not just give it up.

Caroline Anstretton, with her rouged cheeks and breathless voice, had touched a part of him he had long thought of as dead.

A chance.

A chance to feel again?

Even at fifty guineas the exchange was cheap.

He called in his butler and instructed him to give the servants the next night off.

And then he pulled his pistol from a drawer and began to meticulously clean it.

Caroline laid her head against the padded cushioning of the coach she had rented. And breathed.

In and out.

Deeply.

Her hand shook as she pushed her red ringlets back against the lie of her shoulders and when she glanced outside she barely saw anything at all.

She had sold herself.

Sold herself to the first and highest bidder.

Sold herself for the price of freedom.

Sold herself to save her brother from spiralling downwards.

The brandy that had warmed her before now lay in a cold hard thickness at the bottom of her stomach and she shuffled on the seat. Her second-hand boots hurt her feet and the rock had begun to unravel the dainty stitches of silk on the bottom seam of her bag.

Unravelling.

Everything.

She could still be safe. She could simply not turn up tomorrow and leave London with her brother.

To go where? And with what? To Bath for a few days and when that welcome was up...?

Thornton Lindsay's money would afford them a passage out of London and the hope of the rent on a house until they could climb back upon their feet. She could sell portraits and her brother could work on the land. He had always liked the thought of growing his own food and fishing. Perhaps they could live by the sea.

Vegetables, a few chickens and the chance of a small boat. Caroline pictured a cottage, sitting high above a bay. Security. For a while.

All for the price of her virginity.

Lord. Her eyes flew open.

Her virginity?

Would he know?

Was it possible for a man not to know?

Her mother had said there would be blood and pain.

And if Tosh should ever find out? Taking a deep breath, she tried to devise a plan that would throw her brother off her trail.

Suzette.

Her friend had asked her to come and stay last week and Tosh had overheard the conversation.

Without waiting for another moment she ordered the driver to Clapham and asked him to wait whilst she ran just one simple errand.

What her brother did not know would not hurt him and his morals were ones that quite simply were no longer tenable. Not for her, set as she was outside of ever marrying well, her reputation tangled in disapproving threads of gossip.

One night and they could be on a carriage going west with a goodly sum of money in their pockets. And a new life.

A reasonable exchange.

If she could just get through tomorrow night.

Chapter Three

Caroline dressed carefully, her white muslin frock buttoned down the back and cinched up high just under her breasts. Today she had also worn a thick pelisse, the velvet coat knee-length and fur trimmed.

More for him to peel off, the voice in her head whispered as she turned to look at herself in the mirror.

A tasty sacrifice.

The rouge only highlighted the paleness of her face.

'Are you completely certain that this is the best of ideas, Caro? What if the Duke of Penborne tries to get you into his bed?'

She smiled. Wanly. 'He will not, Suzette. 'Tis just a dinner at his friend's house and a late concert.'

'Very late, if you ask me, seeing as you say you won't be home till the morning. Are you certain there is nothing you are not quite telling me, *chérie*?'

It was on the tip of her tongue to confess it all, but Caroline knew that, if she did that, there would be no way she could leave here with the certainty that her brother would not turn up at Lindsay House in the night and demand redress.

A duel.

At dawn and the Duke an accomplished shot by all accounts, even given the extent of his injuries.

No, she was the only one who could get them out of the mess they now found themselves in. Consequently she smiled and said nothing as she tied up her bonnet and stuffed her reticule with a hanky and a comb.

Two things for the night. She could not risk the inclusion of her nightgown in case Suzette saw it.

Massaging her right temple, she hoped that the pain would not worsen. Migraine or not, she was going through with this…business proposition. And if she could only half-see Thornton Lindsay, then all the better for it.

He opened the door himself when she knocked and straight away she could tell that he had been drinking. She could smell it on his breath when he reached forward and took her pelisse, the warmth of his fingers brushing her arms in a certain way.

When he closed the door behind her she felt as if she had strayed into a dream, as if she had passed through the threshold of good sense into some sort of unimaginable mistake.

'I thought that you would not come.'

'I am a woman of my word, Your Grace, and fifty guineas is a lot of money to turn down.'

'Indeed.'

His answer was closely whispered and tonight the scars on his face seemed less…frightening. The eye-patch he wore was made of soft leather, giving her the impression of the blinding of the falcons in centuries past that she had read about.

A falcon. That was exactly what he reminded her of.

Alert. Dangerous. Vigilant. When his right hand reached out and touched her cheek she jumped back, her teeth biting into the soft inside of her mouth.

'You seem a little ruffled.'

'I had a late evening last night and I have a head-ache—'

He stopped her simply by placing the first finger of his right hand across her lips.

'As this assignment is affording you a large sum of money, I would appreciate you keep your mind upon the moment.'

Nodding, she met his eyes and frowned. No brutal lording glance stared back. Nay, today she saw only lust.

Such a simple word for what was next to happen.

'I hope you have ways of avoiding conception? A child is the last thing I would want from this union.'

'I have, Your Grace.' She fumbled for words and hated the aching fear at the back of her throat. What exactly did that mean? What were the ways that women ensured no child should come from a union?

'And you are cognisant of the fact that it is a whole night I have paid for.'

More than once? Many times? How many times? *Bought and sold.*

The throbbing awareness she felt in her lower region surprised her. Lord. While her mind rebelled at such a life-changing act, her body melted into acquiescence. More than melted. She felt the heat as a blaze of pain, delved into the very marrow of her bones. And he had barely touched her…yet.

Her eyes went to the clock on the mantel. A quarter past six. Her innocence quivered beneath the heavier passing of time.

Still early.

Would he rip off her clothes and throw her on to the ottoman and have his way with her? She could not imagine how any of it would begin. When her breathing quickened, she felt the hard beat of blood in her throat and the thinner line of alarm in her stomach.

Thornton leant back against the wall and watched Caroline Anstretton eye up his ottoman. He knew apprehension when he saw it and hers was every bit as visible as that shining in the faces of the young and green boys he had so often consigned to battle.

But she was a courtesan and by all accounts a damn experienced one. And he was paying her well.

The light frock she wore disguised none of her abundant charms. Tightly draped about her body, it looked almost too…small, the generous curves easily seen, the swell of her breasts as visible as the wares in a shop window.

Her trading commodities.

The thought made him harden. He could take her whenever he wanted to and however he wanted to. After years of self-imposed celibacy, that realisation was a potent aphrodisiac.

He was glad that she had chosen white. It suited her. Suited his intentions. Virginal white to stave off the demons that raged inside him, aching for release.

Stepping forward, he cupped her elbow and pulled her closer. Here in the nearly dusk before the beeswax candles were lit, the shadows of late day masked their faces, any money paid for services mellowed beneath a kinder promise.

He could almost believe that she was Lillyanna resurrected from the dead. Warm. Alive. Laughing.

No. He could not have her like that and be healed.

He had to know that it was Caroline Anstretton. Vapid. Careless. For sale.

His fingers unbuttoned the cloth at her back and he

was glad that she did not pull away or question. And her curves beneath the petticoat and chemise were enchanting.

'I want to see you.'

'Here, Your Grace?' She looked around the parlour and towards the door.

'I have dismissed my servants for the evening. They will not return until well into the morrow.'

She smiled, tremulously, and Thornton understood just exactly why it was said that she was the most beautiful woman to have ever come to London.

It was nothing to do with the red of her hair or the curls softly rounding her waist. Nothing to do with the alabaster skin strangely plied with a heavy layer of rouge. No, it was her eyes, the dark blueness of them studded in sparkle and dimples deeply etched into each cheek even when she did not smile.

'Would you possibly have some rum? I'd like it neat.' Her voice was low and beckoning.

Rum and neat! The drink of sailors and harlots and people who had little left to lose.

'Of course.' Stepping back, he poured her a double shot. She drank it quickly, draining even the few drops at the bottom of the glass before putting down her reticule and removing the bracelet at her wrist.

'I should not like to misplace this when we…if we…' Stopping, she laid the jewellery carefully on top of her bag, a dark flush of redness standing out on her cheeks.

'A bauble from an admirer, perhaps?' He did not know why he had asked that question given his blanket prohibition of the same subject a few moments prior, but he could not help himself. He was glad when she simply shook her head and turned to face him.

'Should I take my underclothes off?'

A blunt unpolished frankness that had him guessing that she had perhaps not been in this game as long as she had said. He frowned, the fright in her eyes making him soften his approach.

'I think we might eat first.'

Her laughter surprised him. A throaty laugh, the first real glimmer of the woman who was not a whore; because of it he ran his finger along the line of her jaw, tracing his way on to the smooth skin of her bottom lip.

Warm, wet, hot.

Like the rest of her?

The thick throb of desire almost unnerved him and he made himself slow down. The whole evening lay before them, after all, and he wanted to savour every damn moment of it.

Food! They would eat first? Relief rushed through Caroline, almost making her dizzy, and the rum compounded the whole effect. She rarely drank, apart from the occasional unconventional brandy, not even wine. But tonight with the thought of what she was about to do before her she could have picked up the whole bottle and emptied the contents down her throat. She was glad for the light silk shawl that he draped across her shoulders.

The table in the next room was set with numerous candles and a fine supper. Pheasant and salmon, scallops of chicken and turbot, apricot tartlets and a compôte of apple. Fluted glasses completed the laying, the whole effect embellished by a large bowl of flowers sitting squarely in the middle of the cloth.

Thornton Lindsay pulled out a chair for her and was careful in his assistance. When he sat, the light caught his eye, amber velvet, and beneath the scars she could see again so easily the man he had once been.

Still was!

His frock coat was a dark, dark brown and he wore this over a charcoal waistcoat. And at his neck sat a simple white cravat. No pretence to the highest of fashion and it suited him, ornamentation and foppery a far cry from the interest of an officer who had caught the King's attention and favour after his bravery in Europe.

She longed to ask him about it all, about the battles and the intelligence work he was rumoured to have been so good at, but she stopped herself.

One night.

Anonymity.

And if she asked him questions, then he might ask them back of her. And she could not tell him anything. Nothing real, at least, for as a master of intelligence, she was certain that with only the least amount of information he could put together a whole tableau of possibility.

Consequently she lifted one fluted side plate and held the workmanship before a candle.

'Sèvres, is it not? I have always loved their designs.'

He did not answer.

'Once I went to a ball and the whole of the dinner set was embellished with white swans and I thought to myself, what if someone drops one, what if they should slip and...'

'Why did you need to name me as your lover?'

He broke into her diatribe, effortlessly, and his long fingers entwined round the crystal stem of his glass. One nail was blackened, she noticed, and the scars so evident on his other hand were harder to see on this one.

But still there, running up into the cuff of his snowy white shirt. The signet ring he wore was engraved with a crest that portrayed a knight's helm surrounded by roundlets. And half of his little finger was missing altogether.

'It was a mistake.' Frantically she plastered a smile on her lips and dropped her glance. What he could see on her face would not be reflected in her eyes and to make this whole charade work she needed him to believe in her story. 'My brother had thought he could best his opponent in a card game and when his coins ran out he bet me instead. Or my hand in marriage, rather. I remembered your name and used it.'

'And do you often partake in such…pranks?'

Gritting her teeth, she frowned and for just a second bleakness filled her. Filled her to the very ends of her toes. And she swallowed. Hard.

'Promise me you will return to England. Promise me, Caroline. On your honour.' Her mother's voice as she lay dying on the edge of the winter of 1813. *'It is not safe here for you. Guy can be…'* She had stopped and tears had rolled down her cheeks.

A bully? A pervert? An intimidating oppressive tyrant. She had been seventeen and no match for him. Until Tosh had saved her!

Shaking her head at the memory, she steeled herself to her set task.

'I am a woman of the night, Your Grace.' Licking her lips, she helped herself to a goodly proportion of the turbot in a lobster sauce.

'Delicious,' she proclaimed after trying a little piece, the fish sticking in her throat like cardboard.

Anything to get your mind off me and on to the food, her subconscious screamed.

But he did not eat, did not even pick at the grapes on a plate next to his elbow. Rather he watched her. Closely.

'I have heard it said that you lived in Paris?'

She took her time before nodding. 'I spent some time there a few years ago?'

Beat. Beat. Beat. Her heart in her ears and danger.

In consternation she reached for the wine glass, clumsily, and it toppled over and over and over, the red staining white linen and blossoming like a pool of blood, almost transparent at the edges.

He was not a man to be trifled with. Even from here she could see his brain ticking over, a plethora of facts evident in the keen perception of his one uncovered eye.

Suddenly she just wanted the whole thing to be over. Completed. The money in hand. Finished.

Fifty guineas of freedom.

With care she pushed her arms in close against her sides, the shawl falling away and the flesh of her breasts swelling markedly.

When his gaze thickened, she knew that she had him.

Thornton put down his wine glass and stood. Any thought of food flew out of the window as the bounty of her womanhood was so carelessly offered. Giving her his hand, he pulled her up.

She smelt of roses and softness, and her hair tickled the side of his cheek.

It had been so long since he had had a woman. So long since he had touched another person with…care.

He ran his finger down the length of her bare arm and slipped the material on her chemise lower. Her nipple stood proud in the cold and he forced up her eyes to his to make sure that she knew where it was he was looking.

'I want you. Now.'

When she nodded he simply bent his head and suckled, the taste of sweetness and the brighter echo of a time in his life when everything had been easy and innocent. A time when he had not known how to break a man's neck or leave a family in tatters simply because politics demanded tough choices and he was the only one left alive to make them.

Lillyanna.

He shook away memory.

Caroline. The soft easy abundance of her charms and the husky cadence of her voice. Alive. Real. Here. When he looked up again, the heavy languid burn of sex showed in the shadows of her eyes and in the pull of her hand against his.

And when she traced the outline of her lips with the tip of her tongue he leant forward.

To take.

Apprehension exited Caroline's body in a single second to be replaced by liquid silver longing, and delight. It was not hurt he had paid for after all.

She felt his tongue lave the surface of her breast and the sharp sting of pressure when he nipped her. Not hard. Not hard enough. Her fingers threaded through the darkness of his hair, drawing him in closer, pressing outwards, filling his mouth and her body, and making them one. An unbidden groan. Hers. More it said, *and more*.

And when he shifted focus to lifting the thin muslin petticoat she opened her legs further and invited him in. Needing, craving, everything. With her head tipped back and her neck stretched tight against the raw desperateness of want, she felt as if she was floating. Weightless. Waiting. His fingers weaving a magic that she had never believed could be possible.

'Now?'

Had he heard her?

No more hesitation.

When he led her into the parlour again she did as he bid and lay down on the thick rug, watching as he removed his jacket and waistcoat. The clock against the mantel chimed seven and the day outside deepened into night. One night.

This night. The money on the table beside her bag.

Fifty shining guineas.

Payment.

Her hand reached into the material beneath his shirt as he lay across her. Scars and knotted skin. The essence of him. Strength and steel. Tempered with gentleness. The soap he used left an elusive scent and when she caressed his chest, as he had done to hers, she heard him take in breath and was pleased. The corded knots of muscle in his throat stilled and the heavy beat of his heart quickened. And further down she felt the hardening of his sex laid long against her stomach. Ready.

More than ready.

His finger slipped inside her, testing. She was tight, moist.

When her knees fell open she heard the rent of lawn. Exposed. Bare. The swell of her stomach white with moonlight.

Waiting to be taken.

The thought egged her on, made her hips buck up into his hands, asking for something she knew nothing about.

Then he was in her, stopping, retreating, before the hilt of his manhood slipped home into the warm darkness of her very being.

'God, you are so tight.'

Thornton tried to stay still, tried to stop the wrenching waves of climax that beached themselves in the very act of caution. And then he was lost. Lost to this world as he spilled his seed into her. Without protection. Without anything. On and on and on until the red blazing lust was sated and he had no more breath to even lift himself off her. Covering. Her white against his brown, spread against the night. The musky smell of what was between them filling the air. Finished. Satisfied. Undone. The slash of her red full lips smudged against the moment.

Tears? He felt them warm against his chest. And felt them again in the uneven gait of her breathing.

Instantly he lifted himself away from her, feeling for the tinderbox.

'No.' She stopped him with her hand. 'Just the moonlight.'

'If I hurt you…'

'You did not.'

She sat up and tried to bring the fabric of her petti-coat together. 'I brought no other clothes with me…'

The clock chimed the half-hour. Loudly. Surprising them both.

'Will it be safe?' His question. As if now that they had been joined he could read her mind.

'I think it will be so.'

The expletive told her that her answer was not the one he was after. When his hand stilled she knew what he was about to say and stopped him.

'No, I shall not be with child. A woman of my per-suasion has other ways of making certain.'

Other ways? For fifty guineas she would find a way—she did not want irritation to change his mind about the amount.

His fingers tightened around her upper arm; bring-ing her on to his lap, he tilted her hips and claimed her breasts.

One night. All night. The clouds and the moon and the darkness rolled into one and the clenching want made her shake, made her sweat, made her say his name in the wildness of passion.

'Thornton?'

Just as a question.

And then she could say nothing.

* * *

Much later he took her upstairs to his bedroom, the quiet light of candles suiting his purpose of truly seeing her body as he stripped off her chemise and petticoat and waited for her to wake up.

Two o'clock. Four hours before daybreak and the end of a bargain.

Too soon. He willed the hours to travel more slowly and bent to wake her.

The touch of a finger against her cheek, a gentle finger, his finger. Her hand came up to cup his, and he saw a crescent-shaped scar on her thumb as she pushed forward.

Kiss me, she longed to ask.

For he had not kissed her once.

Not even when she had taken his face and brought it up to her own.

The truth hit her suddenly. Men did not kiss courtesans. She had heard that bit of news from her brother when he had returned home from an evening with his wilder friends.

Did not kiss.

Did not kiss.

She was surprised by the loss she felt at this knowledge.

The wallpaper in the room also surprised her. They were no longer in the parlour. This room was larger, more elaborate. The softness of mattress beneath her and above the canopied bed, draped in burgundy velvet held open by tassels of multi-coloured silk. A full-length mirror to one side of the bed caught the flame of candles burning on silver plinths.

Turning, she caught him looking at her, and was astonished to see that he had removed his eye patch. No scars were visible.

With care she traced her finger across his brow and, heartened by his smile, asked her question.

'I thought there must be some disfigurement?'

'No.' He returned gently. 'It just gets tired sometimes.'

'What happened?'

'I was not careful enough.'

Catching her hand, he brought her forefinger into his mouth when she went to say more. Sucking. Warm.

'No past, all right. Just now. Just tonight.'

She understood and, emboldened by his words, wrapped her leg around his, pleased when he rolled on top of her. Her breasts were squeezed beneath the heaviness of his body and he caught at her hands, dragging a long silk tassel to bind her wrists to the bed-head and tying off the knot with his mouth. And one arm came beneath her hips, raising them and pressing open her legs.

'This time I will watch you,' he said simply, and trailed his fingers up the insides of her thighs, up and up to the fullness of them, touching a place high within her, a place where the thin pain of delight blossomed and grew, the throb of the nearly-there elusive until the bolster of his arm beneath her tightened and the clenching contractions tugged at reason. She called his name loud, loud, loud in the night, slicked in the smell of him, tight-close bound, the movement of his fingers beginning again even as the last orgasms were fading.

Heaven.

She never wanted to leave this room, his magic had woven her fear and need into something else indescribable.

Love?

The word came unbidden and she squashed it back, the fifty guineas decrying such a promise.

And then she forgot to think altogether.

She sat on the bed after eight in the morning and rolled up her stockings, every part of her body vibrating with a languid heat as he watched her from across the room.

She wanted another night. Another thousand nights!

Her stockings, dress and pelisse were all she had left, her underclothes balled in a broken ruin.

He had mentioned no further contact. He had not asked her for anything.

Just this night.

No past.

No future.

Finished.

Filled.

Banished.

When he buttoned her coat about her she was silent. When he told her he had hailed a carriage to the door to take her home she did not look at him. And when he pushed the money into her hands she did not thank him.

The coach ride home to Suzette's was like a dream and Caroline was glad to find the house empty when she let herself in.

Once inside, she peeled off her clothes and washed. Washed the scent of him from her body and the feel of him from her limbs. Placed lavender oil where pure masculine strength had left the marks of loving and massaged attar of roses through her hair, now bereft of the wig.

Much later she sat bound in a bath cloth before a mirror and allowed herself to truly look into the depths of her eyes.

Enchantment sparkled.

And disbelief.

And nowhere lingered shame or reproach.

Unexpected. Freeing.

She had been brought into the delights of womanhood by a master, and regretted none of it.

When the tears came they were not filled with sorrow for what she had done. No, they were filled with the secret aching anguish of knowing that such a night would never happen again, and that any knowledge of another man would be tempered by this one unattainable perfection—Thornton Lindsay.

Even now his golden eyes watched her in memory, etched in sadness and hurt, lust measured only in the hours of payment.

Balling her fists, she pushed away the sweet promise of impossibility and began to dress for her journey home.

Chapter Four

'So you are telling me that the Duke of Penborne gave you fifty guineas just like that. I don't believe you.'

Tosh was as furious as Caroline had ever seen him and she struggled to find words to placate the anger. She had never lied successfully to his face and wasn't about to start now.

'Well, it wasn't quite like that.'

'You bedded him, didn't you? You tupped the bastard for money.'

'No, I slept with him because every single part of my body wanted to know what it would be like to make love to Thornton Lindsay and for the first time ever I felt…I felt whole.' Swiping away the gathering tears from her face, she kept going. 'It wasn't dirty or rough or hurting, it was just…beautiful.'

'Lord.' Her brother's anger foundered the second he

saw her tears and he moved forward, his arms coming around her and holding her close. 'Lord,' he repeated. 'So where exactly does this leave us now?'

'With a passage from London and the means to survive for at least another year if we are very careful.'

'I wasn't talking about our future, Caro. I was thinking more about yours and Lindsay's.'

'There is no future. He made that clear.'

'And if you are with child?'

She was silent.

'I see. And if you meet him again?'

'I won't. The money will allow us passage to wherever we want to go, Tosh. A leeway for a while at least…'

Shaking his head he sat down on the chair. Dazed.

'At what cost, Caroline?'

'At the cost of twelve hours of pure delight, Thomas.'

Puzzlement etched his features, and also a good measure of relief. 'Then you do not wish for me to call on him?'

'And say what? Insist that he marry me and challenge him to a duel when he refuses. He is said to be one of the finest shots in all of England, even given his injuries, and what indeed would you be fighting for? My reputation?' She shook her head. 'My God, that disappeared the moment we left Paris. No, far better to take the money and simply disappear. Become other people and start again.'

'So you are not…hurt in any way because of this?'

Disquiet surfaced at her brother's perception.

'He gave no mention of seeing me again. He wanted no further contact.' A single tear slipped down her cheek and she wiped it away with the back of her hand.

'If we went to his town house together, Caro, and told him a part of our story…'

'Which part? The part about murdering our mother's lover and being in disguise ever since?'

'I was thinking more about the part where he should take some responsibility for what he has done. You are not a courtesan and he used you as one. If he knew who you truly were, then perhaps he would—'

She didn't let him finish.

'I never want him to know that. Never.'

'Why?'

'Because if he offered marriage under duress….'

'You like him, damn it. You do. I can see it in your eyes and hear it in your words.'

Caroline turned away. She had had enough of supposition and wanted to be far away from London, far away from Thornton Lindsay, far away from the temptation of just turning up on his doorstep again and offering him another night.

And another one.

She was pleased when Thomas brought out their battered old map of England and laid it on the table between them.

'Your turn to pick a place this time, Caro.'

She simply closed her eyes and laid her finger on

the paper and when she opened them the name of Mortehoe was easily read.

On the coast, near Barnstaple, the gentle shores of the Bristol Channel lapping at its feet. A new beginning. And this time she resolved to be a widow. A very prim and proper widow who would make it clear from the beginning that the husband she had lost was her very first and definitely very last love.

Thornton held the remains of her petticoat in his hands, the delicate white lawn somehow symptomatic of Caroline Anstretton, though flecks of blood made him pause. Had he hurt her somehow, or was it his own, a result of her nails as they had raked hard down his back in the final act of taking?

She had been nothing at all as he had expected. An experienced courtesan with all the wiles of a virgin? He laughed. She had been married once and had had her fair share of lovers. Perhaps acting the *ingénue* was the way that she had thought he had wanted her to play it, and fifty guineas was a lot of money in anyone's book.

The gold bracelet on the floor caught him by surprise. She had forgotten it after being so careful to remove it in the first place. He lifted it up and in the light of the day an inscription showed on the middle band.

Paris 1807—TStC.

A bracelet fashioned not in England, but in France? He held the delicate chain in the middle of his palm and looked more closely at it. The emeralds encrusted in the middle were all fake and the metal was thin, brittle and cheap. Almost the jewellery a child might treasure and a strange thing for a courtesan to value so highly?

Perhaps she was down on her luck. Perhaps that was why she had named him as her lover in the first place.

Questions.

Puzzles.

And an indefinable interest.

She had got to him with her strange mix of innocence and naïve righteousness, and when he had felt the soft touch of her lips on his cheek he had almost been undone.

Almost.

Placing the bracelet on the table and his hands in his pockets, he closed his eyes and listened to the sounds outside. A passing carriage, the wind in the trees, the sounds of birds on the shrubs by the front windows, the footsteps of pedestrians going about their business.

For so long the sounds of life around him had been measured, deciphered, collated, interpreted; the smallest of noises a warning against an enemy that had never slept. And suddenly, now, today, this second, he felt unreasonably tired by it all.

He wanted a normal life, a real life, a life that included sitting in a room without his back to the wall and a well-weighted blade in the deep pockets of his jacket. A life without the brutal aching regret of war and the suffocating fear of loneliness that had consumed him since coming home. A life with a woman to warm his bed and his nights, a woman to make him laugh again and feel again and touch his ruined cheek with the same care as Caroline Anstretton had.

A wife?

Perhaps that was what he needed! A happy sunny-natured girl who was as open-minded as he was closed and who had never once in all of her life knowingly told a lie.

Not a paragon.

He did not want that, but virtue had its own ease and was a cosy companion when the demons raging inside of him threatened to take over. After all, he was wealthy and passably young, and the half of his face that he had left was not unpleasant.

She would not be Lillyanna. He knew that. But Caroline Anstretton had shown him something that he would have never thought possible even as recently as last night.

The feel of soft skin against his hand, the warmth of her against his back, the smell of roses and woman. His blood had risen, easily, hard grief softened beneath the promise of the forgotten, and coursing through his body like a river in winter after the rains, all the banks washed away under the onslaught of an unexpected and startling thawing.

Even now in broad daylight he could still feel the sharp echoes of his body's response, and he smiled.

If he offered her the position of his mistress whilst he searched for the new Duchess of Penborne, he could kill two birds with one stone. His lust and her need for money, and a companionship that would be beneficial to the both of them.

Taking a fresh sheet of paper from his armoire, he dipped his quill in ink. A careful offer, quartered in the temporary. She was a courtesan and he was a duke. It was, quite honestly, all that she could expect.

At three in the afternoon when the doorbell rang, Thornton sat up and listened with interest as he made out the voice of his visitor.

Caroline Anstretton. Here in person to answer the generous terms of his offer? It took all his resolve to make himself stay in his seat behind his desk and wait.

She was wearing a heavy wool jacket over a yellow gown and her hat sat across carefully arranged red curls. In her hand he saw his letter, her fingers clutching the sheet in a way that made him cautious.

'Your Grace.' She curtsied and waited till his man departed and the look in her eyes was disconcerting. Knowing. Flaunting.

Something had changed. He could feel it in the air between them and in the space of silence that last night would have been filled with anticipation. Today a wooden awkwardness replaced ease and her fingers shook as she deposited his note on the table.

'I think perhaps you may have got the wrong impression of me last night.'

'Impression?' He frowned when she did not quite look at him.

'I am not a woman who could possibly…ever…be with just one man. Not like that, you understand.' Gesturing to his letter, she continued. 'The position you offer of mistress, whilst flattering and indeed very generous in its terms, is rather a restricting sort of arrangement. For me.'

'You are saying you would want more,' he returned, the hint of anger in his voice annoying him.

'Well, Your Grace, I am young…and many say I am the most beautiful woman to have come to London in…years and years.' She turned to the mirror above the mantel and moved her head this way and that.

Admiring herself!

'Perhaps it is in the line of my jaw or the colour of my eyes or the way my nose tilts just here.'

Puzzlement gave way to plain distaste.

'Why, I have already had an offer for my hand in marriage, from a lord, no less, and the family is not at all daunted by my reputation. But my brother thinks I should wait a while and hope for better.' When she giggled, the brittle vacuous sound rankled.

She was vain and stupid.

He had not expected that.

'It's not that I don't like you, you understand. Last

night was wonderful, it's just—' He didn't let her finish.

'It's just that you would rather be a duchess than a mistress.'

'Exactly.' Her blue eyes widened and she shook her abundant red curls, hopefully he thought, as he made himself smile.

'I shall remember your offer, Miss Anstretton. But as I am returning to Cornwall tomorrow, I shall decline it.'

'Oh.' She made a lot of ironing out the folds of her skirt, the yellow of the fabric bright against the paleness of the skin on her hand. All her nails were short.

Flipping open a drawer, he extricated her bracelet. 'You left this here last night and, as it seemed important, I would like to return it to you.'

Sharp relief filled her eyes as she fastened the catch around her wrist, testing it by shaking her hand.

'Thank you.' For the first time today a small shiver of what had been between them last night returned and her bottom lip quivered. If she had looked at him then, he might have reached out, requesting explanation, but her quick movement away demanded silence. When she raised the reticule from the seat where she had flung it on first entering the room, he knew that he had lost her.

'I have a fitting for a new gown in half an hour. Madame Celeste has chosen it for me and I shall wear it first to the Forsythe ball in Kent in a month. Perhaps if you return unexpectedly from your home in the country, you could look me up and be my partner. For old times' sake.'

When he did not answer she held out her hand, giving Thornton no option but to take it. The coldness of her fingers was startling. Yesterday she had been like a living flame. He dropped it immediately.

'I do not like to dance.'

Her eyes flicked to his left leg as she answered, 'No, of course not, I am sorry…'

Embarrassment and pity were written across her face and all he wanted was for her to go.

But she did not. Not until she had leaned forward and touched his left cheek, softly, her thumb running on across his bottom lip.

And then she was gone, the lingering scent of her perfume all that was left in the silence.

'Lord.' Thornton filled his brandy glass and downed the contents in one shot, the touch of her hand still burning.

'Lord,' he repeated and leant back against the wall. His instincts about people were usually well honed and seldom wrong, but Caroline Anstretton confused him.

A conceited harlot or a brilliant actress—there was something in her story that did not quite add up. Something in the way she had clung to him last night, an edge of unsullied innocence in her lovemaking.

She would not be a mistress and yet she would be

a wife! Even *his* wife, should he up the stakes and offer her his hand. He smiled, for something in him even wanted to throw caution to the wind and take a chance, take a punt on last night's loving returning again, and take her with him to Penleven. To safety.

But he could not quite do it.

Not till he knew a lot more about her, about them, the brother and sister who had come to London out of nowhere and created such a storm.

His head began to ache against the complexity of it all and he poured himself a large glass of water. London and its business bore down upon him in a way the countryside around Penleven never did, making him remember things he would far rather have forgotten.

Lilly there with him in the happy times before she had died at Orthez, in the south-west of France, blown into pieces during the last defensive campaign of Napoleon. His regiment had been assigned to the town and when the French four-pounders had battered their position they had taken refuge in a small stone church that, in retrospect, had made an easy target. Twenty men and Lilly, and very few of them had come out alive. Just another assignment that had ended her life and changed his and nothing had been the same since.

Hating the alarm that was beginning to pool across his forehead and the numbness that was overtaking his hands, he pressed his thumbs against his temple. Memories were closer here. All encompassing. And the injuries that had left him temporarily blinded still bore down upon his health two years later.

'Lillyanna,' he called as she came towards him, her skirt billowing blue and laughter in her eyes.

'Lillyanna,' he shouted as the roof caved in. Red rolling pain and slow, slow movement. And fabric floating downwards, all that was left of joy and goodness.

And when the shaking started he let go of the wall and felt himself fall, hard against the floor, sweat-slicked and hot, the sins of his past weighing against his chest and denying him breath.

The light made him open his eyes. Bright. Too bright. Holding up his hand, he tried to shield his face from it.

His butler Henry was in the room. And his secretary James. Their faces an exact copy of each other's.

'How long this time?'

'Twelve hours, Your Grace.'

He shut his eyes. Twelve hours? Last time it had been only a few. An improvement or a decline? He liked the land of limbo that he had been consigned to, forgetful drowsiness and the absence of memory, but if he did not return…?

'Is there water?' His words sounded thick, skewered.

Henry poured him a glass from a jug on the bedside table, lifting his head. One sip and then two. A sheen of perspiration and nausea. He winced and tried to concentrate on what James was saying.

'François de Gennes was here this morning and left word that he will return again on the morrow. In the afternoon.'

The name hit Thornton with an ache.

Lillyanna's brother. He had had no contact at all with François in three years, but knew instinctively what he was after.

Names.

The claws of intelligence sharpened against the futility of an oath sworn when he was twenty. Sometimes it seemed like a lifetime ago, a green boy with the naïve hope burning in his heart of making the world a better place.

Better for whom?

Not for himself.

Not for Lillyanna.

Not for the people he had killed, slung into unmarked graves on the edge of a conflict few of them truly understood.

And now François was here? In London.

Thornton wanted to be home—home with the noise of the sea against Lizard Point and the lonely call of gulls as they wheeled above the cliffs before heading seawards.

Sanctuary.

Sparkling blue eyes distracted his musings and he wondered again what Caroline Anstretton was doing at this exact moment.

Flirting, probably. Or angling for the hand of a titled peer who had no notion of the deceit that underlined such beauty, her ivory skin hot as she leaned towards him.

Shaking his head, he finished off a glass of water.

'Leave her to it,' he whispered beneath his breath, angry that she should even be taking up a moment more of his time.

François returned the next morning. His hair was a shade lighter and the lines around his eyes had deepened and Thornton noticed a long weal of raised skin along the line of his knuckles.

François caught him looking and smiled.

'The peace of the past year has not been as easy as I hoped. You, on the other hand, seem much recovered. Lilly would be pleased.'

The mention of his sister made Thornton frown. Connections and favours. He waited to see what was to come next, resolutely ignoring his headache.

'I have recently come into the possession of a note written to Lillyanna the day before she was killed. It was unsigned.' Reaching into his jacket pocket he extracted an envelope. 'If you took a look, I thought you perhaps might recollect…something, anything.'

Reluctantly Thornton took the letter. As he glanced at the handwriting, he stiffened in shock.

'Adele Halstead wrote this. I recognise the handwriting.'

'Wroxham's wife?'

'She was one of our sleepers in the Peninsular Campaign. I saw her correspondence many times.'

'Did her husband know?'

'I am not sure. I only found out her identity by mistake when the carrier let it slip he had come from the "Mistress of Wroxham".'

Thorn read the gist of the message and anger crystallised.

A specific warning. Why had Lilly not taken the caution to heart and stayed away from the little town outside Orthez? Why had she not, at least, warned him? And how was it that Adele Halstead should have been cognisant of any French army movements in the first place? A growing sense of betrayal made him wary. 'I think it might be wise to pay a visit to the Halsteads.'

Folding the paper, he carefully gave it back and did not question the look of relief in his old friend's eyes.

Chapter Five

There was no moon, not even a sign of one hanging on the horizon as they tethered their horses in front of the Wroxham town house.

Ten o'clock. He hoped that Adele Halstead would be at home as he had received no reply to the note sent earlier in the day, requesting a meeting.

François slid in against him and looked up at the rain filled sky. 'The weather is turning, Thorn. Do you think they will have company?'

'I am not certain.' He pulled a knife from his belt and tucked it into the folds of his sleeve. Out of sight. François looked perturbed.

'She is a woman. You would not kill her…'

'It is 1816, Franc, and peace is upon us.'

'Uneasily.'

Thorn laughed and knocked on the door, surprised

when a rather weary-looking butler answered almost immediately. 'Can I help you, sir? Sirs,' he amended as he caught sight of François.

Thornton pulled a card from his pocket and handed it over to the man. 'We have come to see Lady Adele.'

The man frowned. 'I am sorry, Your Grace, but she and her husband left this morning for her sister's house in Kent and shall not be returning 'til the morrow. I would be happy, however, to forward your card into her hands when she returns.'

'I see.' He moved back, feeling a vague sense of unease, the shadows of trees in the mounting wind jogging memories of other nights in other towns. Something was not quite right. He felt it in the air as he looked around and saw a shadowy figure signalling from the roofline in a brief slant of moonlight.

Ordering François to stay outside, Thornton charged up to the door again and rapped hard. When the same servant answered he pushed him aside and strode in.

'I think you have intruders in the house. What are the rooms facing the street on the second storey?'

'My mistress's rooms, sir.' The tiredness had vanished and he looked relieved when Thorn bade him to remain at the bottom of the staircase. Civilians were more trouble than they were worth in times of struggle and this servant was decidedly frail.

A fire was dying back in the grate of the chamber as

he slipped inside and stopped, waiting for his eyes to acclimatise to an even darker space. The smell of the town house seeped in around him, damp, old and unkempt.

A tabby cat slumbered on the chair, its pupils gleaming in the small light of the embers and a clock boomed the hour of ten loudly from further out.

On instinct he checked his own timepiece. Ten past. Running slow. Everything about this place seemed lost in time.

Every chamber he checked was empty. He determined this quickly, though a noise outside one window made him pause. A soft scrape of boots against the slate of the roof and a heavier bang before silence reigned again. But not for long!

A head poked around the window frame and then a leg hooked across the sill with some skill as the interloper gained traction. A lad with a hat tucked low across his head.

Thornton waited as the newcomer came further into the room, tripping on the upturned corner of a thick Aubusson rug.

'Damn. Damn. Damn.' A distinct whispered curse before a hand-held candle lightened the room. In the beam he picked out a dirty face, teeth worrying the bottom lip in a peculiarly feminine movement.

Removing a drawer, the interloper emptied the contents across the coverlet of the bed, turning out the second and third drawers when the first proved fruitless.

Thornton knew the exact second that he found what it was he sought. A whistle distracted him after a few seconds had passed.

Someone else was close. He watched as the lad walked to the window and waved his candle three times before blowing it out.

A signal.

Of success?

Stepping into the pale light, Thornton crossed the room and the lad turned in fright.

'If you make a sound, I will kill you. Understand?'

A short nod and then stillness.

It was difficult to make out any features, though the shaking of his bottom lip was clearly visible.

A newly commissioned thief. A green and timid pilferer with neither weapon nor sense.

'Keep still and raise your arms.' His firm command brought on a rush of words.

'I'm not here to hurt anyone, guv, it's just some money I need to help me mum and the little ones.'

A young voice, tremulous, rough and familiar, even given the thick cockney accent. He frowned, for the accent did not quite ring true, the lilt at the end of each sentence and intonation somehow…unEnglish. Memory of other times flooded back, for his wanderings on the continent had brought him into contact with many a man wanting to hide his true identity and choosing to speak instead with the voice of another.

Like this one did.

'How old are you, lad?'

'Thirteen, sir. I be fourteen next month.'

'Old enough to know the insides of a jail, then?'

'Please, sir, I'd never hurt no one, and me mum's hungry and me dad is gone—'

'Enough.'

'I'm all that she's got left, guv…'

The voice petered out as Thorn frowned.

A slight scent had caught his attention. Roses. Not the usual odour that one associated with young boys. Caroline Anstretton had smelled exactly the same the other night as he had stripped off her dress.

Shaking his head, he wondered if the tryst had driven sense from it. Lord, all he could think of was the softness of her skin and the feel of her body beneath his. Even here in the bedchamber of an enemy and in the company of a thief? With more force than he meant to, he pushed the lad down on to the side of the bed and lifted the candle. His tinder was dry and it took less than two seconds for the flame to take. Light made the room bigger and he saw that the youth was shaking, tightly drawn-in lips the only thing genuinely determined in a grubby visage.

'What was it you were wanting here?'

When the boy did not answer him, he emptied the right-hand pocket of his trousers in one short movement and took in a breath.

Not gold or jewels at all but a locket, a bauble worth only a fraction of nearly every other thing in the room.

He revised his opinion of the youth being a thief. Nay, there was another motive, he was sure; flicking the locket open, he had his answer.

Thomas Anstretton's face was younger and happier, but the mouth and eyes were exactly the same.

And before he even looked at the other side he knew the sister's face would grace it.

'Who the hell are you?'

Danger spiralled. He was too old and jaded to believe in the coincidence of chance.

The lad rose from the bed and tried to snatch back the locket; as he did so the chain of a familiar bracelet appeared from beneath the folds of a too-big shirt.

Lord.

Suddenly Thornton knew exactly who this was. Knew it to the very marrow of his bones. Neither a lad nor a cockney, but a courtesan and a liar.

Ripping off the hat, he was surprised again. No long red tresses tumbled down to her waist. Instead, unruly short blonde curls sprouted, curls threaded in gold and wheat and white honey, the deep sparkling blue of her eyes highlighted by the colour.

'You.'

Nothing made sense. Secrets beneath secrets and the first glimmer of something more sinister.

Adele Halstead, Lillyanna and the Anstretton twins

tangled in a web of deceit and subterfuge. No simple burglary this, but a carefully targeted hit.

'I can explain if you would just let me…'

'Please do.' His civility was barely measured.

'The locket is ours. Lady Wroxham stole it from my mother. You can ask her. This is not a theft.' Her sentences were cut short by fear and breathlessness.

'And why should she want it?'

'She hates us. Hates who we are.'

Suddenly it all made sense. 'Because you are Halstead's mistress?'

This time he was certain of the emotion shining forth in her eyes. Pain and hurt and perplexity.

'You think I would sleep with him?'

'He is an earl,' he reminded her. 'I thought you were angling up the ranks of the peerage. And Wroxham is well moneyed.'

'He already has a wife.' Her argument cut through logic, but as he went to say more a noise from behind made him turn and the dull thud of something crossed his temple. Stars blossomed as he made one last flailing attempt to grab his assailant before the world lost shape.

A sharp curse and the soft feel of her fingers against his face, then all he knew was darkness.

Caroline watched Thomas replace the pistol in the belt of his trousers and bent to feel for a pulse at Thornton Lindsay's throat.

'You hit him too hard, damn it,' she growled, though the steady beat reassured her. As relief surged she stroked back a wayward curl that had crossed his forehead.

How much did he know about them?

Straightening out his fingers, she collected the locket, the thin white scars that covered his hands taking her back to another time, a time when he had run them across the naked skin between her thighs, searching, wanting.

A pure bolt of passion tripped across the core of her being, startling her with its intensity.

Why would he be here in Adele Halstead's room, knife in hand and the look of the haunted in his eyes? Had he still some connection with her through his intelligence work? She knew the answer as soon as she formulated it.

Lillyanna de Gennes.

The woman who had died in the church outside Orthez.

Shock intertwined with horror.

Lillyanna. Running. Towards Thornton Lindsay and his group of soldiers.

She began to shake as the possibility of exposure became real. His scars. His involvement in espionage.

They had heard later as they had crossed into Spain that one British soldier pulled from the wreckage of the chapel had called out the name of his lover.

Lillyanna.

The world began to close in on her though she was

shaken back to reality by her brother's whisper, filled
with worry.

'We need to go, Caro, before he awakens and there
is less than ten hours to catch the early coach to Bristol.'

'I know.' She did not want to stand and go, to leave
him like this, not conscious, vulnerable, the darkness
of deceit hanging across the room like a pall.

But there was nothing else to do.

Pushing her forefinger to her lips, she transferred the
kiss to his. *'J'espère vous revoir bientôt,'* she whispered
before stepping from the room behind her brother and
out into the night. *I look forward to seeing you again.*

'I don't think you should be drinking.'

Thornton smiled and took another swig of the
brandy from his flask as he looked up at François.

His head still swam and the realisation of Caroline
Anstretton's deception made the throbbing worse.

Lord, he had been one of Wellington's masters of
intelligence during the Peninsular Campaign and here
he was, being duped by a girl whose persona changed
every time he met her. And changed markedly.

Who the hell was she and where was she now?

'Who hit you?' François's hands were steady as he
checked the gash on the back of his head. Fire consumed agony as he pressed down on the wound. All
around them stood a ring of the Wroxham servants,
eyes wide open at such an unexpected happening.

'I don't know.' Lifting up his flask, Thorn clung to the cold of it. Why was he lying? Why would he even think to protect her?

He knew everything about Caroline Anstretton that she was not. Not a thief. Not a redhead. Not English.

If she kept up this subterfuge, she would soon run into the hands of someone who would hurt her. Badly.

But how could he find her? Where could he look? The systems of intelligence that had at one time surrounded him were no longer in place. He felt in his jacket and was not surprised to find the locket missing.

Tilting his head, he tried to remember the intricate design on the outside of the casing. It had been dark and he had glanced at the bauble for only a second. Concentrating, he went backwards. The smell, the light, the shapes and sounds. Think. Remember. Basic rules of espionage surfaced as he searched for a pathway and the same silent awareness that had kept him in such good stead for six long winters in France surfaced.

Little clues. Reminders. The feel of her skin against his and the smell of roses.

There is less than eight hours to catch the early coach to Bristol. Hearing was always the last of the senses to dim.

Grappling for his timepiece, he saw that it was almost eleven.

'Get the horses, Franc.'

Ignoring the headache and the protests of his friend,

Thornton pulled himself up, stopping for a moment as the dizzy whirl of pain made him feel ill. He had to find out exactly who Caroline Anstretton was and understand the strange connection that kept throwing her up into his life.

In his experience, chance always led to trouble and the presence of Adele Halstead worried him even more.

The answer lay in the bauble, he was sure of it, not in its worth, which was negligible, or in the likenesses of the Anstretton twins inside, but in the reason it was hidden in the first place.

Caro saw him from a distance. He sat on his horse with a companion beside him, both watching the steady stream of patrons stepping up to the Bristol coach. Pulling into the shadows of a side street, she gestured for Thomas to wait, her brother seeing them a second after she had. 'Damn, I thought I hit him hard enough to keep him out of action for at least a week.' His voice was filled with an undercurrent of respect. 'And how the hell could he have known we would be here?'

'I think we spoke of these plans when he was unconscious.'

'And he heard? Perhaps the things they say of him are true after all.'

Both turned back to look at him. The morning mist was rising as Lindsay drew his collar up against the cold, and, with his eyepatch and soldier's hat, those around gave him a wide leeway. A constant reminder of difference, Caroline thought, and hoped futilely that he would not notice, would not see the way onlookers glanced away from the spectre of such horrific injuries. Still, with the promise of leaving London close, her spirits rose. She had the locket and fifty guineas burning in her pocket. She had Tosh beside her and felt light without the heavy red wig of Caroline Anstretton.

A new beginning.

Another direction.

She hoped Thornton Lindsay's head would not be too sore. She hoped the man who rode with him was a friend. She tried not to notice the way his left hand threaded through the soft skin at his temple, massaging away pain. He was a duke of the realm, after all. His servants would see to his every need once he returned home. A bath, a good meal, and the prospect one day soon of a wife to warm his bed. A wife. Any wife? A girl of spotless name and rank and the truth of heart that he deserved after all his years of service.

She hated the stinging smart of tears in her eyes as she watched the coach doors shut without them on board and the driver call the horses on.

Now he would go too. For ever lost to her.

When the two men turned away she strained to see the last of them, as they disappeared into the thickening fog.

'The next coach leaves at one,' Tosh informed her as they backtracked with their one suitcase and entered a nearby tavern. The smell of food made her mouth water and the itchy wool of her nun's habit stretched full about her face. An easy disguise. She thought her brother suited his priestly robes and determined to tell him so as a group in one corner disbanded and made way for them to sit down.

God's people travelled well, she mused, when the tavern master refused payment for both bread and water.

Fingering the locket in her pocket, she smiled, the light of the fire catching the gold of the cross at her neck, reflecting beams across her brother's face. Tosh. Her saviour. Flesh-and-blood warmth, born from the sameness.

Tears blurred vision and she wiped her eyes against the generous cloth of her sleeve. Together they could hold the world at bay. And would. With a growing fervency she bent to a heartfelt prayer of thanks.

'You look rather changed from when I saw you last, Fox.'

Fox. The name he had used in the shady corners of the world where it paid to tell nobody your business.

'I cannot say, either, if the change is for the better or for the worse—I have always loved a damaged man, Your Grace.'

Following Adele Halstead into the salon, Thornton saw that she had lost none of her lithe beauty since he had last seen her, though her hair, once black, was now lightly silvered.

'I also have been told that it is you I have to thank for chasing off some intruders from my house. My servants were full of your bravery, though it seems they may have got the better of the exchange.'

'I am not the man that I used to be.' He tried to keep the irony light.

'Oh, I very much doubt that. Rumour has it that you are in London to discourage the advances of a…lover, and a woman of some notoriety, I am told.' She laughed. 'All of London is agog with the details of your meeting.'

Ignoring the banter, Thornton pulled the letter François had given him from his pocket and handed it over.

'This came into my hands two days ago and I recognised it as your writing.'

Puzzlement showed in Adele's face and then comprehension as she read the note. 'Lillyanna de Gennes?'

'Why did she not take heed of your warning?'

'I asked myself the same question at the time. As for my cousin, I would have thought her to have had a greater sense of self-preservation.'

'Yet you did not warn me.'

'You would never have believed me—though I had heard that there might be a problem, I did not know the details, and superstition in the field in the heat of the moment can be interpreted as a weakness. You could be a heartless bastard when anyone made a mistake,

Thorn, and you had the ear of Wellington. I am surprised that Lilly did not confide my uneasiness to you.'

He broke into her diatribe. 'Enough. I am not here for excuses.'

'What are you here for, then?'

He held up the note. 'Was it you who set the trap?'

She shook her head and bitter anger burned in the back of Thornton's throat, the scars on his left cheek throbbing with the memory of everything, trust cast away in a barrage of cannon fire.

His life.

Her life.

The lives of fifteen of his soldiers.

Treason and loyalty, two sides of the same coin. France and England. War and peace. And a betrayal that was unexpected.

'I think you are lying.'

'Do you?' A calculated question. 'You always were so...honourable; if truth be known, it is a fault in the end, for no one else can quite live up to the standards you expect of them, not even Lilly. Besides, she had lost her own parents in the war to the British at the Battle of Maida and sometimes old loyalties rise up to stamp out new ones.'

A searing jolt of anger made his world blur, though he was careful not to let her see his fury. 'Lillyanna did not know about the French cannons stationed on the hill above the town.'

'You are certain of that?' The slur was distinct, though her laughter that held softer pity confused him. 'Perhaps Lilly did not warn you because then you would have known she was playing both sides off against the other.'

'As you were?'

'I am married to an English earl, Your Grace. Solid aristocracy and the wealth of generations. Why should I do anything to threaten that? Besides, I only ever dabbled in the game of espionage, and after this incident I returned to England cured of any need to pursue a career in it.' Pouring herself another cup of tea, she changed the subject altogether. 'Word has it that this beautiful widow, who swears you were once her lover, is from Paris? And a twin? I should have liked to have met her.'

He felt the slow turn of a familiar distrust as her interest and instinct took over. 'They left London two days ago on the Edinburgh coach and were hoping to spend some time with relatives. I doubt if I will ever see them again.'

'You know a lot about their movements?'

'That's my vocation. To find out as much about people as I possibly can.'

The silence between them lengthened and it was Adele who broke first.

'Well, then, let me test you. Did you happen to see the faces of the intruders the other night?'

'No. I was hit from behind as I entered your chamber. What was taken?'

'A purse of gold, some pearls and a fob watch.'

'Then you were lucky it was not more, for I counted at least three men in the shadows.'

For a moment Thornton saw uncertainty taint the arrogance in Adele's eyes.

'Did your husband return with you from Kent?'

'Yes. But he is ill in bed. A stomach upset from something he has eaten, I am told.'

'When he is better, I would like to talk to him.'

'I think it would be far better for us to just part company for good. My husband would not wish to be harried by the less salutary times in my life.'

'Because he has no idea that his wife was such a traitor?'

In reply she picked up a small bell from the table beside her and a footman came hurrying in.

'Yes, madame?'

'Could you show the Duke of Penborne out, please? He was just leaving.'

Thornton drew himself up from the chair that he sat in. 'Always a pleasure to speak with you, Lady Adele, and please do give my regards to your family.' He almost laughed at the cold hard line of her mouth as he found his cane and left.

In the carriage Thornton mulled over the conversation. Was she lying about the locket to protect her husband or herself? He had seen duplicity in the quick beat at her throat and the beaded sweat on her forehead when he had mentioned Wroxham and Adele Halstead did not want anyone to know the details of what had been taken in the robbery? Why should that be?

Clues that led nowhere. Ties that bound people without conceivable bonds. A note that gave a warning completely ignored. A locket stolen and then re-stolen. A war, whose tentacles reached into the present with echoes of betrayal. Words beneath words and the aching reminder of loss.

His fingers tightened on the carved ebony handle of his cane as loneliness welled unbidden. He had no one. London with all of its people accentuated that truth as Cornwall never had.

All he wanted to do was to go home.

But first he would interrogate the driver and the inn servants and try to match up Caroline and Thomas Anstretton with any new form of disguise they might have donned.

Chapter Six

August 1817

Readjusting the mask on her face, Caroline turned back to the ballroom, her silk dress catching the light of candles, the material shimmering gold.

Excitement coursed through her. It had been all of sixteen months since she had left London with her heart on her sleeve and the fifty guineas safely in her reticule. And in those months her life had taken a different twist again, the girl she had been submerged into the woman she had become. Wiser. More careful. And meticulous in her dealings with the opposite sex.

Her fingers checked the bun she wore and she tucked in the errant blonde curls that had escaped their confines during a dance with an elderly relative of the Hilvertons.

After leaving London, she had imagined she would never grace a ballroom again, never feel the promise of youth and exuberance, never mingle with the local gentry with even a modicum of propriety. But she had, and a good deal of that fortune was due to Gwenneth Hilverton, the daughter-in-law of the Earl of Hilverton and the wife of the heir to this house and land and fortune. She had met Gwenneth by chance at a soirée in Bristol and been offered the chance of a cottage in return for portraits of her children.

Smiling, she crossed the room to stand by Gwenneth's side, warm fingers curling around her own in welcome.

'You look beautiful tonight, Caroline. The dress fits you as well as I thought it would.'

'And you are certain that you have worn it before. It looks too…new.'

'I wore it once when I was as thin as you are but that was some time ago. Malcolm keeps telling me to stop eating so much, though goodness knows I have tried.'

The mention of Gwenneth's husband brought a cloud over the euphoria of the evening and Caroline looked around furtively to make certain that the young Lord Hilverton was nowhere near. She had endured many a clandestine pinch on the bottom since she had come to this place, but had refrained from complaint simply because of the hurt it would bring to Gwenneth.

Her disguise as the prim widow ensured most men were happy to keep their distance. The spectacles probably helped, as did the rather stiff countenance she had now perfected, but Malcolm Hilverton was the one man who seemed attracted to her austerity.

Sometimes she wondered what Gwenneth had seen in him to make her accept his proposal in the first place. Rich in her own right, she had not needed to place her hand in that of a man who would scorn her at every available opportunity and treat her as a woman with very little of importance to say.

Caroline shook her head. Tonight she would not let problems impinge on excitement. She would enjoy the evening behind the safety of her mask and before midnight she would make very sure that she slipped away home through the little path to the cottage on the other side of the glade.

And become the Widow Weatherby again. Respectable. Proper. Reputable. The woman who lived quietly with her brother, making a living from fashioning portraits for the very well-to-do.

An irreproachable paragon, the likeness of a husband framed on the dining-room wall, a young husband lost off the coast of Plymouth in a storm that had overturned his boat.

Sometimes, with the sea winds soft off the Bristol Estuary and Alexander in her arms, she could almost believe the fabrication herself. And yet it was in those moments that the memory of Thornton Lindsay was strongest.

That awful scene in his library.

Vain. Selfish. Stupid.

The pain of deceit in his amber eye as Tosh had struck him in the darkened Halstead room. Falling. Again. The scars on his face white against moonlight.

No. No. No.

Safety depended on anonymity. And distance. And she had sold her soul to make certain that her brother should stay safe.

Shaking her head, she put her mind to enjoying the last hours of the evening, pulling Gwenneth towards the supper room where the lines of hungry guests were finally abating, pleased that the mask she had constructed hid her countenance.

'I am not certain that I should eat quite yet, Caroline. We have guests from London here tonight, and Malcolm says I must make an effort to draw them into conversation, but they look rather…menacing, so I have managed to avoid them all thus far. Particularly the taller man…' She petered out, pointing to a group on the other side of the room.

Alarming. Dark haired. Formidable.

Caroline's breath congealed in her throat. Thornton Lindsay stood dressed all in black, the ruined side of his face wreathed in a half-mask and a beautiful woman draped provocatively across his arm.

If Gwenneth had not held her up, she might have fallen; indeed, even as it was, she tipped forward, a whirling lightness unbalancing reality, her pulse in her temples beating so loud she thought everyone must hear it, must know it, must see that here, right here in this room, ten yards away, was a man whom she had once known…intimately. Bought and sold in lust.

Fear enveloped her and then a curious calm as he looked up, his eyes exactly as she remembered them, caution threaded with intelligence.

She made herself smile, made herself stand straighter, made herself breathe as he approached them, a whisper of a frown on his forehead.

'Lady Hilverton.' He held out one gloved hand, and the sound of his voice filled the cold draughty corridors of Caroline's heart and the pit of her stomach where the butterflies collided against exposure.

Could he know her? Would he remember? She did not dare to risk looking up in case he watched her and was pleased when Malcolm Hilverton pushed in between them, his face ruddy and his eyes full of self-importance. 'It is a great honour to have you here, Your Grace. I hope we can persuade you to stay on for at least a few days. Perhaps you would like to come riding tomorrow and partake in a picnic lunch with us down by the rocks of Morte Bay.'

'Perhaps.' His reply was abrupt and Malcolm, covering the awkwardness of the moment, pulled Caroline forward, his hand tarrying on the crook of her elbow for longer than she would have preferred.

'I would like to introduce you to Mrs Weatherby. She has lived on the estate for more than a year now with her brother and baby son.'

Alex!

His amber eyes the mirror image of his father's and his hair the exact same shade of midnight black.

No future.

No contact.

No place for a woman such as her amidst the *ton* and a family that could trace their ancestry back for generations.

And no place for a bastard heir, either...

Glancing up, she saw his eyes upon her, questioning and unsettled, the unevenness of skin beneath the bottom edge of mask familiar. Dangerous. Risky. His visage toughened by a life that had allowed him little ease and a reputation that always kept others at bay.

'I understand you are here visiting your property, Your Grace,' Malcolm spoke in the tone of one with the full confidence of the other and even when one dark eyebrow tweaked upwards he continued unabashed. 'I could offer my services to familiarise you with local knowledge...'

'I have someone to help in that.'

Thornton Lindsay did not mince words or soften the message and the young woman standing beside him wound his arms through her own and tilted her head proprietarily, the ivory sheen of her skin making her look as if she were barely old enough to even be up so late.

Suddenly Caroline felt as if she were one hundred and one, lumped in now with the older matrons. A woman who was over the hill at twenty-two, placed as she was outside the boundary of any true and lasting relationship by a past that would crucify her in any and every salon of repute.

Looking up, she caught the full flare of the Duke of Penborne's gaze on her, abstruse and probing, and the room began to tilt.

Could he see her through the mask? Did he know? Had he remembered?

She ground her teeth together in pure fright. Let them move on, let them pass; let them return to wherever they had materialised from tonight. Far away from here and from her. Far away from memory and regret and the aching true knowledge of want.

Want—to take his hand in her own and never let go. Want—to lie down on the thick rug in his town house and feel things that she never had before and never would again.

Again.

Alexander!

The consequences were even greater this time and she could not afford the risk of anything.

Malcolm, true to form, was making the most of the moment, and his ridiculous comments were consolidated with his next outburst.

'I had heard that you have a team of fine horses with you, Duke. Word has it they are of Arabian stock you had especially brought over to England.'

In Lindsay's glance Caroline detected a glimmer of surprise, though he answered with a semblance of polite distance.

'If you would care to look them over, you would be welcome. We will be remaining at Millington for the rest of the week.'

Six more days? Caroline pulled her mask more snugly against her cheek and frowned as she saw the Duke watching her fingers in a way that worried her.

Horses and houses. Heirlooms passed from one generation to the next. She and Tosh had missed out on such traditions and now Alex was going to do the same. Guilt sliced through reason and she turned away, ignoring Gwenneth's surprised query as she strode towards the door, tears seeping down inside her mask.

She had to get home, away from the lights and music and the whirling pressure of what could have been.

She had to get away from the dangerous Duke of Penborne.

She gathered herself together out in the silence of the cottage garden, the unfairness of everything diminished somewhat under a sky of twinkling stars. A beautiful night, summer in the air and the strains of Mozart far off in the distance.

Opening the front door, she found Tosh reading a book, Alexander slumbering across his lap, his cherubic cheeks reddened by a cough he had developed over the past few days. She had never felt so glad to see them both, her anchors against the world.

'You look…worried.' Tosh carefully disengaged the sleeping baby and stood.

'Thornton Lindsay was at the ball.'

'Lord. Did he know you?'

She shook her head. 'I hardly spoke and the mask…'

'How long is he here for?'

'I am not sure. He actually owns one of the neighbouring estates.'

'We can find somewhere else to go.'

Love engulfed her. And sadness. For the first time in a long while she felt they had the chance to make something of their lives. Yet here her brother was, prepared to just up and leave.

She shook her head as his fingers curled up into hers. So familiar. So known.

'He has appointed a new manager for the farm and shall be here only fleetingly. Gwenneth introduced me as Mrs Weatherby.'

'You had your mask on?'

'I did, and I am certain that you cannot see my eyes

through the feathers?' She held it in front of her face and was pleased when he shook his head.

'Even I would be hard pressed to know that it was you.'

Instantly she relaxed and crossed back to the sofa to perch beside Alexander. 'Then I think I am still safe.' Her fingers pushed back a strand of darkness and her son shifted in his sleep, the faint warmth of his breath tickling the top of Caroline's thumb. 'But to be certain I think we should both stay in tomorrow. Malcolm made mention of a riding expedition and a picnic at Morte Bay. And if Lindsay should see us together...'

'I'm due in Exeter for the next few days to help Johnathon Wells at a cattle sale. Perhaps you could come with me.'

She shook her head. 'No, there is a portrait I have to finish and Alexander is grizzly. Besides, the Duke looked more than enamoured with his beautiful travelling companion.'

Tosh looked up sharply and Caroline held out her hand to stop him saying anything. She could see in the perplexity of his glance a raft of questions and did not feel at this moment up to answering even one of them.

Carefully she bent to lift Alex in her arms, his warm body moulding into her own.

Alexander Thornton Weatherby. In the moments of joy after his birth she had chosen the name of his father to also be his. A reminder and a keepsake.

She had known she was pregnant within three weeks of leaving London, a tiredness sweeping over her every movement and an utter sadness that she hadn't lost until the moment she delivered her son. When she had held him in her arms and felt the first tug on her breast, the inexplicable vagaries of her world had been healed, and her transient nomadic life had come to an end.

She had argued with herself as to whether she should contact Thornton Lindsay with her news. But the letter she had received after their night together had dissuaded her completely, his offer telling her exactly just where his heart lay. He did not want her for a wife. He did not even offer her a residence. Nay, he wanted a temporary liaison, a provisional and interim union whilst he looked elsewhere for a life-long partner.

A wife.

But not her!

Far better then for all concerned just to leave everything as it was. A chance meeting that would not be repeated. The beginning of a new life that contained none of the what-ifs of the old one.

She dashed away the tears with the back of her hand and went to settle Alexander, her world suddenly on the edge of teetering into chaos and negating everything she had so carefully built around herself over the past months.

Well, she would not let it. She would make certain

that he did not know her, and would keep her ear to the ground so that she should discover the movements of the Millington party well before they could inadvertently come across one another again.

As she sang a night-time song to her son, tears scalded down her cheeks and her heart was heavy.

Thornton Lindsay.

Here.

Not even half a mile from where she sat.

Seeing the same moon.

Breathing the same air.

She chastised herself soundly for her silliness and tucked the blankets firmly about her son.

Thornton stood against the window and looked out across the dark valleys of this part of England. Civilised, rolling, manicured. None of the wildness of Cornwall with its untamed beaches and windswept coves, where long breakers eroded sandstone into jagged ramparts.

He felt stymied and caught, and he wondered about the turning his life had taken. He seemed to have lost something…inexplicable. Lord, he was twenty-eight and his conscious and calculated decision to take a wife wasn't turning out in quite the way that it should.

He muttered beneath his breath as he remembered another night, in London, the fifty guineas small payment for the hours that had followed.

The Weatherby widow had in some way reminded him of Caroline Anstretton. Strong. Unusual. Something in the turn of her head and the upward line of her lips.

He wished he could have removed her mask and seen her eyes.

Lifting a full glass of brandy, he remembered other things. The shape of her nails and the crescent scar at the base of her thumb as she had held her mask in place. White honeyed hair slightly curly.

And a baby son!

His mind began calculating back the months and came up with an answer that had his blood boiling.

It had to be Caroline Anstetton and—she was a mother.

And in that one simple moment of clarity he was glad that she was not standing there before him with her deceit and her vanity and her cold-hearted calculation.

Because he wondered if he could have stopped himself from placing his fingers around her beautiful throat.

Chapter Seven

Caroline dressed carefully, the thick glasses she had brought from London jammed hard over her nose, and leaving her to wonder if she should contemplate removing them. Already they gave her the beginnings of a headache and the bun stretched against her nape was uncomfortably tight.

Still she needed bread and some meat; at this early hour of the morning she was almost certain she would go unnoticed.

Anna, a girl from the village, had come to watch Alex whilst Caroline ran her errands and she was glad not to have to take her fretting son anywhere. Thomas had left even before she awoke, on his way to the cattle sales in Exeter, and she knew he wouldn't be home until the day after tomorrow at the earliest. If she made a stew today it would keep, and whilst it cooked she would try to work on the portrait she was completing of Gwenneth's youngest child.

A busy life, she thought, as she wandered down the path towards Campton. And safe. She would not let anything happen to compromise it.

This morning the sky was blue and the sun warm, a beautiful day with the promise of a hotter afternoon in the air. Her second summer at Campton. Would there be a third and fourth? She hoped so with all her heart and imagined Alex growing up here.

A satisfying life. A life bound not by what they could get, but by what they could give.

So different from her own upbringing, the halls of the Château du Malmaison on the outskirts of Paris filled with priceless baubles, and Guy de Lerin prowling around every corner. Nay, she would not think of him on such a day, for his lingering shadow of doubt and guilt dulled everything.

Campton was bustling with people as the market settled down for the morning's trading. Caroline glanced around quickly, making certain that no tall dark-haired stranger lurked amongst the crowd, her heartbeat quietening when everything seemed as it always was, though as she passed by the high fence to the left of the Selman's shop someone blocked her path.

Thornton Lindsay.

He had been waiting for her!

She could see it in his eye, dark flints of certainty unveiling deception.

The trickling dread became a torrent and dizziness swept across her. When he touched her arm, the heat from his hand sent a shock wave down into the very depths of her stomach and then darkness swallowed her.

She came to on a bed in an alcove at the back of the shop, and her glasses were gone.

Staying perfectly still she listened to the voices of those about her to try to determine safety.

'She has always seemed such a strong girl. I can't think why she should swoon like this.' Kathleen Selman's voice was as puzzled as her husband's.

'Should we send for her brother?'

'No, he is in Exeter, but someone has gone for the midwife. She will know what it is that ails her.'

'Perhaps another child?' Kevin Selman questioned, refraining from further speculation as the shocked gasp of Mrs Selman quietened him.

A child. A widow? Caroline's indignation gathered. She had spent the past sixteen months living on the moral high ground and still they could say this of her.

Where was Thornton Lindsay? As she struggled to get some sense of him, the tingling in her neck told her that he was close.

Opening her eyes just a little, she stared straight into his furious face.

And in his hand he held her glasses.

A heavy stain of blood rose up her cheeks and tears pooled. She was ruined. Exposed.

Waiting for him to say her name, she was surprised when he did not. Rather he handed her back her spectacles and stood, rigid anger in every line of his body.

Ignoring the pleas from Mrs Selman to stay lying down, she replaced her spectacles. Shakily. Not looking at him.

One word and chaos would claim her.

The very thought of it had her caught like a moth in flame. Nowhere to go.

Kathleen Selman bundled forward with a cold flannel and pushed the wet rag against her forehead.

'This should make you feel better, though I'm not quite so certain you should be standing.'

Caroline was pleased for the cloth that shaded her. Anything to hide behind. Even for a moment.

'It's an odd thing for a young lady to come over quite so dizzy, I'd be a-thinking, though perhaps the broken nights with young Alex—'

'It was the ball. I must have eaten something.' It was rude to break in over the woman's concerns but she wanted no mention of her son.

'I will escort you home.'

His voice, and one that brooked no argument.

'Oh, you do not have to do that, Your Grace, for I am almost recovered…'

'Bring around my carriage.' Thornton Lindsay signalled to his servant by the door as he laid his hand under her elbow. She felt the pressure of his fingers biting into her skin, and, short of making a scene, she had no option but to accompany him.

If she could get him by himself and plead her case, perhaps he might simply disappear. Leave. Responsibility happily relinquished in the face of opposition.

When he spoke as the carriage moved off, however, she knew that nothing would be easy.

'I want to see my child.'

'Your child?'

'Our child,' he amended. His knuckles were white. 'Alexander Thornton Weatherby?'

She swallowed back both bile and fear.

'How did you know…?'

'My purse is a hefty one and any information has a price.'

'I am the Widow Weatherby here. Prim. Proper. Eminently moral. Did you also discover that?'

His lips twitched. 'What happened to your husband?'

'He died.'

'How?'

'He drowned.'

'Very convenient of him.'

She did not look around.

'I want to see Alexander.'

'Why?'

'Because he is my son.'

'No. Alex is the son of a man who drowned off the south coast.'

'Whose name was Thornton?' His fingers bit into her flesh. 'Come now, Caroline. Play it fair. Alexander was conceived on the night of the fifteenth of April 1816 and for the payment of fifty guineas. His mother was a well-known harlot who was remarkably un-skilled in the ways of *amour*.' He smiled at her sharp intake of breath. 'He is mine.'

Fright claimed her and the insides of her stomach began to clench as her breath shallowed, the burning pain of want betraying her sense of honour. When his thumb came up against the outline of a hardening nip-ple, shocking against the sunlight slanting in through the window, she gasped.

'The driver….'

'Will not stop until I tell him to.'

Anger consumed her. 'You think I am that easy? You think that you can come back into my life after sixteen months and expect…expect…. Again? Just like that? Here? No. I will not do it.'

'Ahh, but I think that you will. Is this your cottage?' He banged his cane upon the roof. Twice. And the car-riage halted.

Absolute panic replaced everything when she looked outside, her small house with its profusion of creeping roses achingly familiar. Completely unprotected.

'Yes.'

'And our son is inside?'

Terror kept her mute.

'I will be here for a week and before those seven days have passed I would hope you could see sense and give me the truth of at least your name. Do you understand me?'

When he opened the door and she climbed down he did not wait for her answer, but tipped his hat and moved on, the hollow sound of her heartbeat muting the heavy hooves of the horses.

And then she ran. Into the cottage, past Anna busy in the kitchen and into the room where her son still slumbered, the small whiffs of his breath immeasurably reassuring.

'Alex.' If she lost him, she would die. Her son. His eyes opened suddenly, amber dark and beautiful.

'Mine.' The word was whispered beneath her breath, across her fear, over the beat of her heart and between the grasp of her shaking hands as she held him close.

He tried to wriggle from her grip.

'I love you, Alexander. You will always be mine.'

When he snuggled in she knew the exact moment that he fell fast asleep.

From the carriage, Thornton watched Caroline run from him, again, watched the sensuous tilt of her hips and the swish of her homespun gown. And his fingers tightened against his thigh as he stopped himself from following her.

She was furious, but he had no choice. A gentle reason and a well-hewn logic would have been preferable, but he could see the fear in her eyes over outright distrust. Better to seek out a solution when she had calmed down and then gain the access he wanted to his son.

Lord. His son? Were women always destined to deceive him? Adele Halstead's accusations about Lilly's betrayal that he could not quite dismiss, and now the Weatherby widow with her ridiculous denials of his fatherhood.

He could leave. He could return to Penleven right this moment. Keep driving and never look back.

But then what? A child would grow in the world without a father, a child with his name and his blood. A child that he had never seen or touched or known.

He slapped his hands hard against the door of the carriage and tried to think.

Caroline met him again the next day at a luncheon Gwenneth had arranged in the beautiful gardens at Hilverton. Tosh was still away in Exeter and Alexander had been carefully left at home.

This time she was prepared. Glad to see him even, her ire so raised as to almost welcome another encounter with the Duke of Penborne, though today in the company of these people he looked anything but comfortable, the collar of his jacket pulled well up over his jaw.

Distance, wealth and power enveloped him and the arresting menace of his scarred face was shamefully fascinating.

Fawning, simpering, flirting women stood nearby: the Raymond sisters, the Furnesses. Even Gwenneth seemed swayed. Ice coated Caroline's veins and she plastered civility tightly across her demeanour. Sixteen months ago she was certain Thornton Lindsay would have never attended such an occasion and she wondered just what had changed to make him come.

'Your Grace.'

When he tipped his head and watched her there was a stinging tension in the hard line of his jaw and in his one uncovered eye she could see a vigilant, guarded anger.

'I trust you are feeling better today, Mrs Weatherby.'

At least he had remembered her name.

'Much, thank you, Your Grace.' She accepted a glass of punch and tried to look as nonchalant as she was able.

'I hear your brother is in Exeter.'

'He is. Yes, Your Grace, but when he is away I always have a local girl who sleeps over.' She needed to make it plain that she was hardly alone.

'Anna?' The surprised question in Gwenneth's voice grated as she joined in the conversation. 'I thought you said you enjoyed your own—' She stopped as the true message of the lie hit her and Caroline had to give her full marks for the way she dredged up another topic and ran with that one. 'How is the portrait of Megan coming along? Why, I was saying to Malcolm just the other day how much I adore the one you did of young Jack.'

'You are an artist?'

For the first time since meeting him Caroline heard surprise in the Duke of Penborne's voice.

'I dabble with a paintbrush and charcoal to help pay the rent. Gwenneth is kind in her patronage.'

'She has made portraits of both my sons and of my mother-in-law. They hang in the main hall if you are interested in seeing them, Your Grace.' Gwenneth's eyes positively shone with support and even as Thornton began to speak Caroline knew exactly what he was about to propose.

'Would you consider taking on a commission from me? I would pay well.'

There was a titter of voices all around as the others overheard his suggestion. Envy combined with a good deal of shock. Today in the sunlight the markings on the left side of his face were well evident, his cheekbone dented in by a mass of lesions.

If the painting he spoke of was to be a portrait of him, she knew that he would never hang it in any one of his houses. No, it was time he sought. Long unadulterated spaces of it! Her heart raced because she knew that if she refused him outright there would be questions.

Already she could see a frown on Gwenneth's brow at her tardiness.

'Of course, I shall be delighted to.' She tried to insert some enthusiasm into the acceptance.

'Would tomorrow suit, then? I could send over my carriage to fetch you after lunch.'

With no other recourse left she nodded her thanks, turning towards the table where an expansive array of food was set and helping herself to a plate. With her mouth full at least she would be excused from any conversation.

She was the Widow Weatherby. Pious. Circumspect. Grateful. And any hint of something else would raise a suspicion she could ill afford.

Tucking her blonde hair up under an ugly cap, she admonished herself for even thinking that she could play the Duke of Penborne at his own game. He had been a soldier and a spy. The kind that hung like a ghost in the trouble spots of the world, coaxing intelligence from the population with whom he mixed. He wanted answers from her, and an explanation of the different circumstances under which she now lived. The virtuous widow was a long way, after all, from the woman he had once known briefly but intimately in London, and a longer way still from the thief he had disturbed in the night-dark rooms of the Wroxhams' town house.

Questions. She could see in his eyes that which had been reflected in countless acquaintances across the years.

Who are you?

I am a murderer. I am a liar. I am a survivor. The smaller whisper from inside her was stark. Unremittingly honest. Desperately powerful.

Subduing her horror, she turned to one of the Furness girls standing nearby and made herself contribute to a conversation about the new season's fashion, even as a trickle of sweat made its way down between the heat of her breasts.

Thornton watched Caroline as she chatted with another young woman. Today she looked tired, the violet rings beneath her eyes giving her a bruised and fragile countenance.

He would not let guilt rise. After all, she had hidden their child away from him and, as yet, refused to acknowledge his fatherhood.

The Widow Weatherby had changed her name and her profession, and ended up here in the Bristol estuaries, painting portraits for the aristocracy.

He had to smile—Caroline Anstretton never ceased to confound him.

Yet where was it they went from here? He knew almost nothing about her and the thought worried him.

If he could get her alone tomorrow even for a few

hours under the guise of a portrait sitting, perhaps he could find out who she was, where she was from, who her family were and what it was she believed in.

He hated the necessity of being here and of accepting an invitation to a party of women with little else on their minds save the snaring of a rich husband. But he was caught by Caroline's indifference and by time, which allowed him only a few days in this corner of England. Lord, if he could have walked away this minute with her on his arm he would have, but she was doing her level best to stay well out of his proximity. Even so, he felt her eyes upon him, though when he turned she made much of appearing distracted by those closest to her.

His left eye throbbed with the beginnings of a tic that came when he was tired. All he wanted was to be alone with Caroline. All he wanted was to feel again the warmth of her skin against his own and the heady smell of roses.

A child.

His child.

Their child.

Together.

As the sun slanted down on to corn-blonde curls he felt his world turn into place.

Simple.

Easy.

He closed his eyes momentarily against the very

ache of it and tried to appear interested in the lesson on local history that the well-meaning pastor of the village was regaling him with.

And when he looked around again five moments later, she was gone.

Chapter Eight

'Is there a particular angle or feeling you would wish me to capture?'

'I think we both know that you did not come here to draw my portrait, Mrs Weatherby.'

Caroline's heart sank. She had been at Millington for less than two minutes and already the tone of this meeting was disintegrating.

Squaring her shoulders, she put down her painting satchel and took in breath. 'I hope you do not believe that I have come to…' *Bed you, sleep with you, do what we did in London.*

She could not quite say it and so changed tack. 'I am more than certain that you would not insist on intimacy if a woman was saying no. Which I most definitely am, Your Grace. Saying no. To anything.'

'I see.' The light in his amber eyes was not as

menacing as she might have imagined after such a confession. Indeed, he looked almost amused.

'Why am I here, then?' Suddenly she had had enough, this exhausting charade sweeping away politeness.

He took a moment before he answered, but the gist of his message was anything but hesitant. 'I want to know who you are. I want to know something, anything, about the mother of my only child. And I want to see him. I want to see Alexander.'

'I do not think that would be such a good idea.'

'Do you not?' Absolute stillness followed the question.

'No. I think it would be better if you simply believed my story and left.'

'Which story? None of the versions you have regaled me with so far quite add up.'

'I needed money in London. You offered it.'

'From all accounts there were many others in society who were offering a lot more.'

'I did not want marriage.'

'Ahh.' He walked right up to her, his face not six inches from her own. 'And therein lies my dilemma, Miss Anstretton. A beautiful woman who, for all intents and purposes, has no past?'

Fear kept Caroline silent. What could he find out after all? It had been a few years since they left Paris by way of many other cities and countries. Still, there was something about the Duke of Penborne that made her believe he could uncover any secret, and with Alexander between them she knew she would need to be wary. And conciliatory.

'You afford me a more mysterious and enigmatic background than I in truth do have, Your Grace. I am simply a woman who has encountered some hardships in life and is trying to keep her head above the murky water of debt. The silly vacuous girl you encountered all those months ago has long since gone and, should I have been faced with the same problems now as I was then, I would have certainly taken a different course in solving them.'

'I see. And you are what…twenty-two now?'

'Next birthday I shall be twenty-three.' She was cautious in her reply.

Anger shifted across his face. Bitter and distant, the whiteness of his scarred cheek opaque against the light in this room. Her heartbeat raced as the quicksilver pangs of desire rolled in her stomach. Upwards.

Always.

If she could just reach out and touch him. To see. To see if what had happened before could happen again.

But she couldn't. Because if he stepped back, what was left of her heart would surely break.

'I departed from London because I knew that if Thomas had met you he would have challenged you to a duel and he has not half the skill at weaponry that you are rumoured to have.'

'You think I would have killed him?'

She shrugged her shoulders and tried to lower her voice. 'I think that you might have hurt him in the dead of some night when you had both had one too many brandies. And I could not take the chance.'

'So you ran?'

'Yes.'

'Why here?'

'We closed our eyes and placed a finger on the map.'

He smiled, dangerously, the gold in his eyes brittle sharp.

'How much would you charge for a portrait of yourself, completed here, at Millington, for as many afternoons as it took?'

'A picture of me? I do not know why you should want—'

He didn't let her finish. 'I would also like a portrait of my son. That you may fashion at your own leisure.'

'I am not certain—'

'The portrait, or meeting him in person, Caroline. Your choice.' His voice was hard, the softness of compromise completely gone, and all the fight left her body.

'As you wish.'

'I have had a table brought in, and a mirror.' His glance flicked to the satchel she held that contained all her equipment. The alcove he led her to was filled with light, two chairs standing at right angles to each other and an empty easel between them.

He would stay and watch? The thought unnerved her but she could not afford to lose the commission.

With care she sorted out her paints and charcoal, laying a cloth down so as to keep her canvas clean.

Blank. White. The gesso on the frame waiting for colour and shape. Her shape. She had not painted her likeness before and hesitated as her eyes met his in the mirror.

'How would you like me to stand?'

'Straight on.' His hand rested beneath her elbow and when he did not let her go she took in a breath and held it.

Kiss me, she longed to ask. Take me again. Here in the light of your house and without payment. The latent ache in her belly strengthened as she felt her nipples pucker, hard against his nearness.

But she could not say it, could not take again in lust what she had done so earlier in greed. Twenty-two and a mother. The responsibilities in life had her pulling away as she took up the charcoal and drew the first lines of her face, hoping that he did not notice the way her hand shook.

Thornton watched her, the smallness of her fingers bruised with smudges of old paint and her nails as short as he had seen on a woman.

Like her hair.

It was tucked into a bun but stray tendrils were escaping. And she still wore her gold bracelet, the fake glass emeralds dulled by age.

'If I looked up the Anstretton family lineage, where should I find your names?'

'Nowhere.'

Her glance met his head on.

'Because Anstretton is as false as Weatherby?'

'Yes.' She did not elaborate.

'Does the reason for such secrecy lie in the inscription on your bracelet, by any chance?'

Her face paled so alarmingly he thought she might faint. An answer.

Paris 1807—TStC.

He would work on the clues later and see in which direction they would take him.

'I should be pleased if within the time you take to complete this portrait you could entrust me with the truth of at least your name.'

When she nodded, the bleakness of her expression told him that she acquiesced only because he had demanded it and told him also that she had absolutely no intention at all of letting him close.

'You may be interested to know that Adele Halstead claimed a string of pearls, a fob watch and a purse of gold were the only things taken from her house the night you stole the locket.'

'You saw her?' Fear gave her query a breathless huskiness.

'In London, a few days after I found you in her rooms. I thought it prudent not to mention the fact of your visit, though I did wonder as to why she might have lied about the items taken.' He watched her blue eyes darken. 'If you would trust me, I may be able to help you—'

She stopped him by breaking over his offer with a breathless laugh.

'There is nothing you could help me with, Your Grace.'

Thornton recognised in her the same stubbornness he often saw in himself and he smiled.

'Were your parents also skilled as thespians?'

'You have been too long the spy, Your Grace,' she said sweetly with a touch of humour.

'And you have been too long on the run, Mrs... Weatherby.' Admiration drove a wedge of respect into his answer as he deliberately left a pause before her name. ''Tis in my mind that Adele Halstead kept the trinket for a reason, hidden in a drawer of her room.'

The bottom of her chin began to shake and she held her hand up against it. In the folds of her fingers Thorn could see the too-quick beat of the pulse at her neck. But he could also see the woman he had known in London, breathtakingly beautiful and frightened, and it was this vulnerability more than anything that made him stop.

'I will expect you tomorrow, at exactly the same time and we will continue our discussion.'

When he bowed and left, Caroline stood very still. In this sun-bleached room above the stairs with the light streaming in, tears drenched her eyes.

Worthiness. Intelligence. Acumen.

Replacing one canvas with another, she began to draw. From memory. The lines of his face bold against the pureness of light. Exposing everything in the way that she saw it.

Beautiful.

Honourable.

Tarnished by the glory of war rather than by the agony of it. Scars that lay in bravery and valour and in the unflinching courage of conviction.

She had heard the rumours.

And seen the man.

Complex. Layered. Tortured.

If you trust me, I may be able to help you.

If their crime had not been so heinous, she almost believed that he could have. But no one could change what had happened. Even him.

An hour later the first lines of the portrait were complete and, tucking Thornton Lindsay's likeness beneath her own, she tidied her working space and left the house without once looking back.

She lay in bed that night and hated the hot tears that scalded down her cheeks, running with all the pent-up fury of her life so far.

One chance.

This chance.

If he left, she would not see him again. Ever.

The memory of the afternoon was close in the careful rendition of her face, fire in her eyes watching. Him.

Even in her rough charcoal sketch she had drawn the lines of a woman who wanted.

Would he see it too? She was certain that he must.

But why would he want this picture of her?

Why would he pay for a portrait that could mean nothing to him? That he could never hang?

A small flurry of hope fluttered before she pressed it back.

Today had been surprising.

Instead of argument there had been a kind of exultant truce, a reckless familiarity, a *détente* that was as heady as the slow burning want in her stomach. He had barely touched her; indeed, he had stood back as she had fashioned the first lines of the portrait, silent in his consideration of her drawing. And yet every pore of her body had been cognisant of the fact that their breath mingled and the warmth of his skin touched the coldness of her own.

She remembered her mother's tales about the court of Josephine de Beauharnais in the heady time before General Bonaparte had dispensed with her services. The days when her mother had laughed and danced, sheltered by Josephine's friendship at the Château du Malmaison.

'The good Lord in his wisdom provides one soul-mate for each man and woman, Caroline,' her mother had told her just before she had died, the light and airy flightiness that had been so much a part of her person-ality dimmed by the nearness of an impending eternity. 'Josephine found hers in Napoleon, a man whom the whole world feared. Be wary in your search, my daughter, and do not squander such a chance as care-lessly as I did.'

The shadows in the room grew, pulling Caroline backwards to a corridor overlooking the gardens, the shadow of plane trees long against the true green sweep of lawn and the first crocuses pushing their way up through the frozen earth.

Cold hands across her breast as she was arched downwards to the floor, Aubusson carpet and parquet.

And Thomas, furious, the bust of marble in his hand heavy and the look on Guy de Lerin's face puzzled.

Just another tryst with a young girl who would one day be more willing. An easy conquest. A meaning-less dalliance to lighten the load of dark winter days and inclement weather.

Too late he had understood the extent of Caroline's resistance and the special bonding of twins.

They had slid him into the cupboard above the small landing on the second floor, his hat covering the rising bruises, his coat soaking up the blood from his nose, his face a deathly white. Broken. Badly. It would not matter. Hell had no need for beauty and his outer appearance mirrored his inner soul.

They had barely looked backwards after they fled, making their way south across the countryside where they had come across Adele Halstead on the outskirts of Orthez. Lord, she probably had their mother's locket in her luggage even then, stolen in the last moments of Eloise's life after pretending such an interest in her dying days.

But why? Why should she do such a thing?

Caroline's heart began to race as she thought about what happened next and, skipping across the danger, she remembered running into the Pyrenees mountains of Spain, two young lads of fortune. The first of their disguises.

How many had there been since? Shaking her head, she refused to even contemplate such a question.

Hiding.

For ever.

A single tear fell against the back of her hand and she watched it slide down between the gully of her fingers, a trail of coldness against the warmth of skin. And the wedding ring that sat there seemed to mock her, call her a liar, remind her that she would never have the luxury of intimacy with anyone.

Imitation and falsity were the calling cards of

those who had broken the cardinal rules of humanity. And murder sat at the very top of the list of the Ten Commandments.

Thou shalt not kill.

The face of Guy de Lerin seemed to gloat from a netherworld, a battered spectre demanding redress. Caroline wondered if the image would ever fade, the bright red blood on his forehead mingling with shocked and disbelieving leaf-green eyes.

The knock came much later.

Her eyes slid across to the cot of her sleeping son and she clenched the material of her skirts into her fingers, caught in an immobile frozen uncertainty.

'Mrs Weatherby. Are you in?'

Johnathon Wells. Tosh's friend.

Hurrying to the door, she unbolted the locks, apologising for her tardiness, and instantly alarmed by the worried look on his face.

Thomas? Where was he? She could feel the beat of her heart in her throat as an ache.

'Your brother did not meet me at the arranged place today, ma'am, and neither did he accompany me home. The last I saw him was in the evening of yesterday enjoying a tipple in the Dog and Cart Tavern on Dilworth Street.'

'My God.' The very worst had happened. The fear that she had been burdened with since running from the Château du Malmaison, realised. Clutching at the lintel on the side of the door, she tried to steady herself, tried to listen to just what it was that Johnathon Wells was saying to her, tried not to let the vision of Tosh with his neck sliced open consume her.

'He did not return home to the lodgings last night and his bag is still there with the landlady. I left it with a message to say I had returned to Campton and that you would be worried.'

'Thank you.' The words stuck in her throat, making her swallow as she tried in the midst of fear to find a way out.

'Could I call someone for you, Mrs Weatherby? You look ill.'

'No.' She made herself smile. 'I am certain there will be a reason.'

The furrow on his brow told her he didn't believe her, but manners had him bidding her a good day and turning down the path.

Inside again, Caroline re-bolted the door and took three deep breaths. Panic made her hands shake and she closed her mouth tight to stop the scream of hysteria that threatened.

Alexander was in the next room and Tosh needed someone who would not go to pieces. Someone who would think and plan and do. The de Lerin family had taken him. She was certain of it. They had discovered where they were and come for retribution.

The Dog and Cart Tavern on Dilworth Street. A
starting point at least.

She could not go as herself, that much was clear,
and she would need to take the handgun that Tosh kept
in the bottom drawer of his desk. It was a duelling pistol finished in walnut and engraved with gold inlays,
the richness of the scrolled barrel recalling the heady
days of Paris.

She smiled to herself as she wrapped the firearm in
soft chamois. Her brother had taught her to shoot with
it and she still remembered clearly the basic details of
the loading mechanism. If anyone had hurt Tosh, she
would have no compunction whatsoever about shoot-
ing them.

Thornton tethered his horse against the fence in
front of the Weatherbys' small cottage. Caroline had
not come in the carriage that afternoon to work on her
portrait and he was concerned.

He could tell nobody was at home even before he
knocked on the door, and was about to leave when a
young woman came up the path behind him.

'Caroline Weatherby has gone, Your Grace,' she
said shyly and blushed a bright red.

'Gone where?'

'To Exeter. Alexander, her son, is up at the big house
with Lady Hilverton, Your Grace.'

'And her brother?'

'That's the strange part, sir. He didn't come home with Johnathon Wells and I think Mrs Weatherby was very worried about him.'

'How long is she expecting to be away?'

'A good few days, I'd be thinking. The bag she took was hardly small and she asked Lady Hilverton the directions for Dilworth Street before she left. Down by the river it is and not a place I'd have thought she would have favoured. But cheap, maybe. She did ask me to water her garden if it was dry, though, and that's why I'm here.'

Thornton looked around. A window at the back of the house remained unfastened.

A quick exit, he surmised, Alexander sequestered at Hilverton Hall and the maid despatched to watch over the house.

Bidding the girl good day, he untied his horse's reins from the palings at the front gate and swung upon the back of the animal.

Dilworth Street. My God. He had been to Exeter a number of times in his youth and knew the area even if Caroline did not. He tried to determine just how fast he could get there.

Chapter Nine

It was late, almost ten-thirty when Thorn arrived at the Dog and Cart Tavern, the last of the watering holes on this side of the street, and the sound of earnest drinking was spilling out into the night. Bidding his men to wait with the carriage on a road opposite the establishment, he pulled up his collar and stepped inside, his fingers curled around the handgun primed and ready in his pocket.

A number of people stood in a large group to his right, though as he tuned into their conversation he felt no threat at all.

Further away a series of harlots worked the room, their costumes garish in the brightened light and, on a plinth to one end, a group of men were drinking themselves stupid. Instantly his hackles rose.

One of the whores moved towards them with a large

tray of ale and when a man fondled her ample breasts she swatted his hand away playfully, egging on re-joinders from those next to him.

Something about her seemed familiar and when she turned and her profile was silhouetted against the light, a growl of pure disbelief sounded in Thornton's throat.

Caroline Anstretton/Weatherby!

Her cheeks were whitened with an almost theatrical make up and she wore large silver hoops in both ears.

What the hell was she doing here, dressed like that?

No longer thin, the padding in her harlot's gown portrayed her as a buxom and easy girl, with the ac-cent of the docks in her words to boot.

'Ye'd be wantin' a warm night in a cosy bed, I sup-pose, sir? How many of you could I favour?'

Laughter built as she pulled one man's head into the charms of her bosom, though when he reached out to touch what she offered she moved back. Quickly.

'It's payment I'd be wantin', sir, and me room's not far.'

The long tresses of her black wig stuck to the thick pan make-up on her face and her tongue circled red-rouged lips in a singularly sensual movement.

Thornton felt a thickening want and looked away.

Lord, what was she making him become? The same leer of sexuality on his face was reflected in those of the group as they looked her over.

An easy charmer. Already one man stood adjusting

the line of his trousers as his hand reached into his pocket for coinage. 'What's a night worth, me darlin'?'

Dark blue eyes flashed uncertainly.

'The price of a drink first, if ye don't mind. I've a thirst for cognac.'

As she sat down the outline of a small pistol was just visible below her left-hand sleeve. So she had come prepared, but how well could she use the weapon? Thornton watched as she made much of topping up even quarter-empty glasses.

Information. That was what she was trying to gather. Information about her brother and his movements. He wondered why she had singled out this lot of patrons given there were several other groups that seemed more…lawless. Perhaps it was simply the position of the table, placed as it was on a higher level than the rest of the tavern and facing the door.

He was pleased she had not seen him, though as he turned away a gaudily dressed older woman laid her hand across his arm.

'Is there a girl who has taken your fancy, guv'na? We have rooms upstairs.'

An idea formed as he looked at his timepiece.

'The black-haired whore. How much?'

Desperation began to assail Caroline as the night wound down into the minutes after midnight.

She had recognised nobody. She had heard neither

a thick French accent nor seen a face with the lines of the de Lerin family stamped upon it and no whisper of any information about Thomas had surfaced. The coinage she had slipped the older woman for the chance to work the room had also been wasted.

Even now as the tavern master began to wipe down the tables and sweep the floor, no last customers tarried, lingering either inside or out in an effort at communication.

What should she do?

Call the constabulary?

Tears washed her eyes and fear licked at the lining of her stomach.

Thomas.

Where are you?

Shutting her eyes, she tried to imagine him in these surroundings. She had heard of this particular gift of twins many a time, but had never felt it herself. Perhaps in such dire circumstances....

The tug at her shoulder had her up and off the seat in a second, though she relaxed as she saw it was the older woman in charge of the girls here.

'There is a gentleman who would like to speak with you upstairs.'

'Gentleman?'

She handed over two gold coins. 'We like to keep it clean here, you understand. No funny business.'

Disorientation assailed Caroline. Had she been recognised even in this disguise? Her head began to ache with the dilemma.

Was this merely a harmless sexual proposition or was it the work of a well-thought-out plan, for, alone and sequestered in an upstairs salon, she would be vulnerable. Yet if it were the de Lerins and she did not take up the opportunity to meet with them, what might happen to her brother?

Would they kill him?

She was caught and the clock was ticking away a chance.

Carefully she stood, accepting the money from the woman.

'Could you tell me a little about what he looks like?'

'He's wealthy, dearie. What else does a girl in your position need to know?'

'I am not certain how safe…'

'We'll look after you, don't worry. Any problems and you just need scream, Harry here can see to anyone.' A large man materialised out of the darkness behind her, a velvet cloak draped around his shoulders and a cap of sorts perched on his balding head. Indeed he did look as if he might deal with anybody and for the first time that evening Caroline relaxed. If she saw it was one of the de Lerin men, she would scream before he even had the time to cross the floor towards her and when Harry had done his worst she could then grill him with her own questions.

And if it were a stranger just there to gather a whore for the evening, she would turn and leave straight away. Her gun was in her sleeve, after all, and she knew how to use it.

'Very well.' Pulling down her wig more firmly, she followed the woman upstairs and took a deep breath before she stepped into the room.

It was darker than she had expected inside, a fire glowing dull against the far wall and not a single lantern lit. Before her eyes could even acclimatise to the dimness, a hand reached out from behind, cutting the circulation from her throat and bringing her body full against his, the gun she held clattering to the floor. Useless.

'Ooooolp,' she tried to shout as she stamped down upon the instep of her assailant's boot, and was rewarded with a harsh whisper against her cheek.

'I would strongly advise ye to keep very quiet.'

Her heart almost stopped in fright. Would he hurt her? Or worse?

Cursing, she tried her hardest to draw breath. His fingers smelt of soap, as if in the moment before she had come into the room he had washed his hands.

At least he was clean!

Such a ridiculous thought had her shaking her head even as his other fingers made free with her body, trailing over her breasts and pulling at the fragile lace that covered her cleavage.

Within a second his hand lay inside, thumb effortlessly stroking her nipple into hardness. Horrified, she
stiffened, striking out with her hands, trying to loosen
his hold as he spoke again.

'Gold coins and the middle of the night. How seriously can I take a refusal, lassie, dressed as ye are.'

Scottish. He was Scottish. With renewed fervour she
banged her elbow against the wall behind, the sound
surprisingly loud. Surely Harry would come. Surely
someone must hear.

Five seconds went by and then ten. No knock at the
door, no footsteps down the corridor. Nothing but the
aching silence of the house closing around her with a
growing and terrible certainty.

She should never have come here, should not have
risked herself as carelessly as she had, the plan formulated on the way to Exeter ridiculous now in its clumsy
execution.

He would rape her and she would be truly ruined.

For ever.

Struggling, she tried to force his hand from her
mouth. Perhaps if she reasoned with him, offered him
money....

Unexpectedly his tongue caressed the skin at her
neck, a single trail of feeling.

Warm.

Soft.

A tangible echo in her mind of another night!

She stilled, waiting, disorientated by familiarity as his palm pushed inwards against her stomach. Lord. When his fingers trailed down further her eyes widened.

She really was a whore. Like her mother.

One sob and she was free, panting in her deliverance, not a single thought running through her mind save the despair of what she had become. Easy. Loose. Wanton.

'St…st…stay away. This is not right.' She could not find it in herself to even scream.

His shadow loomed in the dimness, and an expletive filled the room as he turned her back easily against him, wig entwined in a tangled web of blackness.

'Enough, Caroline.' The desultory tone bereft of accent surprised her and in that second she saw just exactly who her assailant was.

Thornton Lindsay, deep shadows bruising his one good eye.

'You.' Her palm slapped hard against the uneven skin on his left cheek and in reply he came in closer.

'Aye, and 'tis my view, Mrs Weatherby, that any woman who risks her life, as you just have, deserves at least a fright.'

Shame kept her still.

He had seen. He had known. Her pretended piety was a damning contradiction to the truth of her nature.

Fury roiled through her at the thought, though as she kicked out long fingers closed across her knee, warning her to stop.

She hated him. She did. She hated the way he could, with merely a single touch, make her body dissolve into a desperate sensual longing.

Again.

Like before.

Sweat beaded her forehead and dampened the place between her breasts as his hand on her knee travelled higher, teasing, provoking, the tantalising feel of pressure sending shivers into her very core.

'You planned all this,' she threw at him, hating the tears that ran down her face as delayed fear had her shaking, the torn chemise hiding little against his gaze when the fire caught and momentarily blazed bright.

'Hardly, madam. If I had not been here—' His voice was hoarse, but she did not let him finish.

'I would now be in my room along the road.'

'With one of the drunken patrons who was eyeing up your movements and more than interested in your bounteous charms.' He plucked out the layers of padding and for the first time she felt the hard heat of him against her skin; the air, already charged between them, became red hot.

'I prefer slimmer women, with long lithe legs, and a bust that needs no enhancing.' Drawing out the contraption that she had tied to her chest, he hurled it into the corner with the other accoutrements. 'A harlot. And paid for. Ahhh, Caroline, but it seems we have been in this place before.' His hips pushed in against hers, testing the waters, seeking what it was between them, sensuality vibrating with an ache. And when his fingers tipped her face up to his own, forcing her to look at him, she simply went to pieces.

Gold carnality shone forth in his eye. Lust and want completely unhidden in a man who normally guarded every nuance of his expression.

'I want you.' His whisper held more than a hint of desperation, words melting into feeling as he lifted her skirt, the night air cold against her thin petticoat. Ripping it off her with one twist, the lawn pooled at her ankles.

Surrender.

Anger.

The heady joy of coupling.

No one emotion, no single explanation.

Only feeling.

Only him.

His fingers opened the throbbing thickness between her legs and, lifting her up on to the hilt of his sex, he plunged in without hesitation.

Tight. Wet. Yielding. Filling her with heat.

Punching into the question of what lay between them with an uncompromising certainty. Taking her. Completely. No arguments. Now.

She cried out. Not in pain. And he laughed. The sweat on his brow as beaded as that on her own, the scent of their bodies slick, moistened and pungent.

Heaven.

She was there.

Again.

Her toes curled in loose leather shoes and her breath broke as his did, waves of wonder rolling across them, and the rough wall behind.

Release. Relief. Deliverance.

Even her lungs forgot how to breathe as she arched backwards, his groans in rhythm with her own.

Another noise, loud and urgent, and furious shouting as the heavy banging at the door finally registered.

Thornton thrust her away, off him, even as she fought to stay, a veil of languid unconcern between her and the world. Still.

With quick hands he flipped her skirt down and grabbed his jacket from a nearby chair to cover her shoulders.

And then the door was agape. Flung open. Malcolm Hilverton stumbling inwards, Gwenneth and Tosh at his back.

Tosh?

Silence. Punctuated only by her friend's plaintive and sobbing cry.

'Oh, my God, Caroline. What have you done?' The furrow on her brow denoted horror and grief. 'I hope that you realise you are now completely and utterly ruined.'

Ruined!

Thornton pushed Caroline behind him and stepped forward. To explain. What?

With her black wig hanging to one side, red lip paint smeared across her cheek and her clothing torn, she did indeed look...ruined.

By him.

Utterly.

'It is not as you might think—' he began before his explanation was cut short, Caroline's lost brother hurling himself from the door against him and pushing him off balance. Both he and the boy crashed to the floor and Thornton felt the sharp cut of broken glass pierce his arm.

Lifting away, he turned to fend off Malcolm Hilverton, who had come to aid Thomas Anstretton, his rotund paunchiness easily dealt with. A single right-hander to the ears and he was quiet, though in the interim Anstretton had collected himself and fronted another attack.

The boy was certainly brawnier than he had been in London, the country air making short work of a card player's softness, and it was several moments before he felt like he was getting the better of the situation, Caroline's screams to not hurt her brother grinding at his sense of honour.

Thorn's arm streamed with blood and she was barely taking the time to notice. Why, even as her brother came in to attack him again she had the thick end of a broom pushed down hard, and his hands opened under reflex as he staggered against the remaining intact chair in the room, regrouping.

Her twin's nose bled profusely as the boy slid down the wall, red staining both the floor and Caroline's skirts as she bent over him, cuddling close. With her wig discarded, the shade of their hair was exactly the same in this light.

Whispering.

Shaking.

No one else existed in that room. Certainly he did not, the steady drip of blood from his fingers unnoticed. Lifting his elbow, he jammed it into the bony ridge of his right hip to stop the flow and tried to make sense of tonight.

Love.

Hate.

Loss.

Henry had come to stand at the door, awaiting instruction.

'I think it would be better if you left.' Gwenneth Hilverton's voice from the side of the room where she crouched over her groggy husband.

Caroline said nothing.

The sound of running feet outside. The local constabulary, he supposed, and cursed roundly.

If he were found here, scandal would ensue, his name grand enough for the cheap broadsheets to be more than interested in a story. And by association Caroline would also be tarnished. Nationally.

'There is an exit out the back, Your Grace.' Henry gestured to a door to one end of the passageway, and a dizzy tiredness forced Thornton to follow.

Within a moment they were in the side street and then he was ensconced in his coach, thick woollen blankets laid against a gathering coldness.

'Stay awake, sir.' The worried voice of Henry pierced a receding reality as the conveyance turned into the inn, the red light of the carriage lamp dancing strangely in a gathering wind.

Chapter Ten

'You cannot stay at Hilverton.' Gwenneth wept over the words quietly. 'Malcolm is not a person who could ever condone such…looseness and these are his lands.'

'Of course.' Caroline handed a handkerchief into Gwenneth's shaking fingers and tried to console her.

'I told him I would refuse to acknowledge the gravity of what happened in Exeter should he feel the need to repeat it to…anyone at all, and he threw a passage from the Psalms at me… "Who shall ascend into the hill of our Lord? He that hath clean hands and a pure heart."' Watery eyes raised up to her own. 'What was I to say to that, I ask you. He is a devout man…' She began sobbing again, this time without even an attempt at quietness. 'He said that he would honour my wants so long as you left. By the end of this week.'

Caroline's spirits fell. Three days. And the weather

unseasonably wet and cold! She could not even imagine where to begin, where to go and this time with a child in tow.

'Malcolm told me to say that your brother still has a place here if he should want it; after all, it is not his fault that you…that you…'

The accusation of immorality sat in her eyes, and in the quivering distaste upon her lips. 'Surely you must know that Thornton Lindsay would never marry you. He is a duke, for goodness' sake, and you met him for the first time less than a week ago?' Her voice strengthened considerably. 'For the life of me, I cannot comprehend the reasoning that should make you behave in such a manner and so…out of character, Caroline.'

'I am certain you cannot.'

Angry grey eyes lifted to her own before she pocketed the handkerchief and stood. 'This will be goodbye, I am afraid, as I shan't be requiring the finished portrait of my Megan under the circumstances. I would, however, like to give you this. It is saved from my own pin money, you understand, and money that my husband has no notion of. I want you to use it for Alexander. For his education.'

A heavy purse clunked down on the table before them.

Friendship. It was never black and white, Caroline mused, and the greys sometimes had the propensity to break your heart.

She swallowed before she spoke.

'I will never forget you.'

For the first time a small smile blossomed around tightened and disapproving lips. 'And I am certain that I could say exactly the same.'

When the door closed Thomas came forward from the side room where he had watched the conversation, undetected.

'She is a fine woman.'

'And a generous one.' Her fingers felt the number of coins in the leather.

'Pity you cannot tell her the truth, then.'

'Which is?'

'That you love Thornton Lindsay, the Duke of Penborne. That you have loved him since your first tryst in London when he fathered your only child.'

'A monogamous whore, then. But a whore none the less. Did you not hear her recited passage from the Bible?'

'I tried not to.'

For the first time in days Caroline actually laughed; the sadness she had been etched with since Lindsay had deserted her in Exeter relegated for a moment to some place distant.

Where had he gone? Back to Penleven, she suspected, to lick his wounds and brood upon a woman who lacked both principles and sense.

Even now she blushed at the memory of her wantonness.

Twenty-two and she had known the pleasures of the flesh only twice. If the reality had not been so tragic, it could have almost been funny.

But at least Thomas was safe. She put her hand into his, liking the feeling of closeness.

He had had absolutely no idea as to who had abducted him, but had escaped from the small cottage he had been incarcerated in after two days of isolation.

The perpetrators had not come back, and, after crouching in the undergrowth for half a morning to see if they might materialise, he had returned to Campton to find the Earl of Hilverton and his wife about to leave for Exeter.

'If only you had come back to Exeter on your own to find me,' she said softly and her brother looked at her, surprised.

'No one would have known about us then.'

'I think we would have had to leave anyway, Caro. The de Lerins,' he clarified when she looked up, confused. 'They have obviously found out where we live.'

'Why did they not kill you then or at least haul you up before the judiciary? Why just leave you there? Why take such a chance on escape? And no note of intent either.'

'Perhaps someone scared them off?'

'Who?'

'I don't know.' Tosh rubbed his nose and grimaced.

Both his eyes were now swollen and the skin across his cheeks was a violent yellow green.

'Does it hurt?'

'Not as badly as before.'

'I could get you a cold compress.'

'No, don't fuss.'

Sensing irritation, she left it at that and folded a pile of damp washing to lay out by the fire.

For the first time since she was young, life had ceased to delight her, the charade of being somebody she wasn't becoming increasingly intolerable.

To leave Campton with its green rolling hills and soft brambled lanes was distressing. To never walk the path again between this house and the big one or experience the kindness of those who knew her here.

Belonging.

Something she had never had before.

A place.

A home, with Alex raised not in the midst of strangers but with friends, raised exactly in the fashion that she herself had never been.

It was her fault. All her fault.

Wicked lust spoiled everything.

'No!'

Such an easy word to say and Thornton Lindsay would have listened had she had the backbone to say it. But she hadn't. Her own fulfilment had been paramount over everything, Alexander's happiness, Tosh's future, Gwenneth's friendship.

She had sacrificed all for an out-of-control libido.

She was ashamed. Deeply. The predicament they found themselves in again was all her fault. And her brother's magnanimous lack of accusation was not helping either.

'If we travelled towards the east, it might be safer.' Tosh was already laying out the map and tracing a path of travel with his finger.

'I've always thought Norwich might be a town that would be worth the visiting. It's out of the way of the regular London traffic and far enough into the countryside to be a long way from anywhere.'

Tears blurred her eyes. 'I don't know if I can do this any more…start again—'

She could tell he was losing patience with her when he butted in. 'What other option is there, then, Caroline?'

She thought of Alexander and shook her head. 'None.'

'Then let's get packing. If we can be ready to leave tomorrow, it will be better for everyone, and if I see Hilverton sniffing around here and looking at you like he was doing on the journey home, then I'll bloody well punch his head in. A devout man, my arse.'

Caroline smiled, her brother's humour dispersing the true ache of regret.

'Anna could keep all the bigger things. She is getting married in the middle of next year and could do with some furniture.'

'And Johnathon can have our books. He reads, you know, even given his lack of education, and would appreciate them.'

The dissemination of their lives.

Again.

Rising from her chair, she walked into her bedroom on hearing the small waking sounds of her son. And her heart fell further when she saw that with every day he began to look more and more like his father.

Thornton frowned as he read the letter that had arrived in the morning post.

The insignia of the Earl of Ross was vaguely familiar; slitting the flap open with his paper knife, he began to read. His shout brought his secretary into the room at full tilt.

'Is there a problem, Your Grace?'

'Do you know anything at all about the Earl of Ross and his daughter?'

James reddened considerably, giving Thornton his answer.

'The Earl wrote while you were ill, sir, demanding an immediate answer. When I asked you for a reply to his letter regarding a visit to Penleven with his family and daughter you gave me reason to think that the idea was a good one.'

'How?'

'How what, Your Grace?'

'How did I give you this…reason?'

'You did nothing to make me think that the visit of a woman known for her virtue and piety would be counteractive to your own good well being.'

'I was unconscious.'

'I beg to differ, Your Grace. At one point you seemed much recovered and it was then that I broached the subject.'

'I see.'

'I have heard much about this particular lady, you understand, and the thing that strikes me above all else is her ability to make others happy. She has an easy nature and is seldom at odds with anybody.'

'A sterling attribute, indeed.' His tone decried that he thought anything but. 'She will be visiting us early next week as her family are travelling through these parts and it seems we have been chosen as a…convenient stopover.'

'Then I will inform the housekeeper of the dates, sir, if you could supply me with the numbers.'

'Very well.'

He handed over the letter, though as his secretary walked to the door he stopped him.

'And, James…'

'Yes, sir?'

'I would prefer to hand out these sort of invitations myself in future.' Thornton heard the anger in his voice but could not, for the life of him, soften his chastisement. After all, he was now stuck with a visitation he did not want and a father who was probably expecting a lot more than he was going to get.

'Very good, Your Grace.'

There was a low-tone whispering outside even as the door shut.

Henry, he presumed, and no doubt in on the scam. If they were less like family he would have had no compunction in dismissing them on the spot, but James's family had served the Lindsays since time immemorial, and the clumsy attempt at matchmaking would have been done with the best of intentions.

Thornton's arm hurt, his eyes ached, and the memory of Caroline wrapped protectively around her twin brother in the room in Exeter infuriated him.

Five days ago he had never wanted to see her again. And yet now he knew that he could not just leave things as they were. He wanted to understand what it was that kept her so firmly in his mind, the feel of her body against his soft and pliant, her midnight blue eyes locked into his own.

When he lifted the second letter from the pile he frowned. Gwenneth Hilverton's letter was full of eloquence, describing Caroline Weatherby's current position in every detail, the village gossip, the local priest's sermon, shopkeepers withholding their goods and their upcoming departure from a home that they had known for well over a year.

And blaming him in that peculiarly careful way that well brought-up women had of expressing opinion.

Anger surfaced as Thornton balanced leaving things exactly as they were against the odds that the child could actually be his. Lord. Could he leave Caroline to the mercy of circumstance when his part in all of this had been every bit as culpable as her own? More, perhaps, given the cold calculation of their meeting. And if she was the mother of his child… Had he actually ever doubted it?

'James.'

His secretary came back, wariness in his eyes and a hint of sullenness.

'I want you to organise a coach to Campton and bring Mrs Weatherby, her son and brother back to Penleven.'

He could give them shelter for at least a while. He had had dealings with what it was like to be an outcast before, and if others thought that she was now easy game…

'And, James…'

'Yes, Your Grace?'

'Make certain that you don't take no for an answer.'

Caroline heaved the last of her few clothes into an old trunk and folded Alex's blankets and bedding across the top. In their past sixteen months they had acquired ten times as much as they ever had before and she was at a loss as to what now to get rid of and what to take.

The toys and books others had gifted to Alexander were ones that he would grow to cherish and love and her new gardening tools could certainly be used in the next house. Her paints were also too valuable to just give away and she hoped that perhaps she could continue bringing in money with her portraits.

Wiping her hand across her brow, she tightened the mob cap around her head and bent to the task of sorting, smiling at Alexander next to her as he reached out for a doll Gwenneth had brought him only two weeks prior.

A soldier boy doll, his knitted jacket scarlet red. What had Thornton Lindsay worn, she wondered, as he had crossed Europe under orders from the King? She had heard stories of intelligence officers being summarily executed by the enemy when caught out of uniform and incognito. A dangerous life of extremes. He still wore secrecy and distance like a cloak and she found herself imagining how difficult it must be to just come back…and fit in.

Tosh's shout had her standing and her eyes were caught by the sight of a coach rounding the corner and coming to rest outside their gate. A coach with an insignia.

Endure forte was written in gold and red across the helm of a knight in armour.

The Lindsay coat of arms! Her heart raced as fear, hope and dismay coursed through her, and Alex, reacting to her alarm, began to howl. She would not

go out there! She would not meet the Duke of Penborne dressed like this, looking like this. Her hand
snatched the cap from her head and she straightened
her skirts, angry at herself for even thinking such con-
siderations important, and watching as Tosh spoke
with a small dark-haired servant who had alighted
from the coach.

Perhaps Lindsay had not come at all. The windows
were dressed in thick velour, sheltering prying eyes
from any inside inhabitants, and she could detect no
twitching of the curtains.

When Tosh turned to come inside she tried to read
the expression on his face.

'You have no idea what has just happened, Caro,'
he began even before he had crossed through the door's
lintel. 'The Duke has invited us to stay at Penleven and
his man said he would be in severe difficulty should he
not be able to persuade us to accompany him back.'

'I do not know... Is he there?'

'Lindsay? No. I didn't see him, at least.' He stopped
to peer out of the window and began to shake his head.
'I doubt he would just hide inside, do you?'

'Go out and see.'

Tosh's answering frown was heavy. 'We have little
money, Caroline, a small baby and lots of luggage.
Outside lies a means of transport, two men to help us
lift our possessions and the chance to reach the south
coast without parting with a penny.'

'You're saying you think we should accept the offer but get out before we reach his lands?'

He drew his hand through his hair and swore. 'I no longer know what to think, Caro. At Exeter I tried to kill Lindsay for what he had done to you, but I can see in your eyes that things aren't as simple as they would appear.'

'He is Alexander's father, Tosh.'

'He is also the man who will never marry you, Caro.'

'But if I just leave…without knowing…without trying…'

He began to laugh. 'The Lord moves in mysterious ways. "O my God I trust in thee; let me not be ashamed, let not mine enemies triumph over me." I looked up Malcolm's quote and found it was from Psalms 24. Mine is Psalms 25. Perhaps there is a message in it. I, for one, think we should see just where this invitation takes us.'

He smiled as she reached out and took his hand. Penleven. She imagined the castle repelling a thousand years of enemies. Lord, once they were inside such a place they need never fear anyone again, save for the lord who owned it, walking his corridors in isolation and reclusion. Why would he want her there? Them there? A worm of promise turned and she quickly stamped it down—she could not afford the luxury of groundless hope around a man like Thornton Lindsay.

And survive.

Chapter Eleven

They had been on the road now for hours and the storm that whipped at the coach as it travelled towards Penleven showed no signs at all of letting up.

Trapped within a velvet cocoon that was transporting them ever closer towards a man who had ruined her. The thunder outside made her jump as she looked across at her brother, fast asleep on his side of the seat, the bruises faded now to a light lemon colour and strange against the gilt blond of his hair. Tears pricked at the back of her eyes. For him. For her. For Alex tucked up in his little basket at her feet. A small family with no home and no past, hurtling through a rainswept dusk to no future.

A movement outside made her turn to the window. Wiping the condensation from the glass, she saw a lone rider, effortless in his movements and hair loose in the gathering wind. Wild. Dangerous.

Thornton Lindsay. She knew it was him even before the flash of lightning lit up his face, runnels of water on the hard planes of his scarred cheek.

And yet the carriage did not slow, did not stop, did not veer at all from its course as the darkness swallowed him up, lost in the tempest.

Had she imagined him there, her mind playing tricks on what she would have wanted to happen?

Placing her fingers upon her throat, she felt the moisture from the glass trickle down the valley between her breasts and, sensing a shiver up her spine, she closed her eyes and slept.

They arrived at the castle well into the night and an icy blast from the north filled her cloak as they stepped from the coach.

Everything was cold. Her feet, her hands, her face. Wrapping Alexander close, she tried to infuse into him what little heat she still had as she looked around.

Penleven stood against a cloud-whipped sky, a fortress on the edge of the sea itself, she thought, the voice of waves high pitched as they beached themselves against cliffs.

Penleven.

Alexander's lost heritage. She wondered again as to why they had been asked here and came up with no answers.

'Welcome to Cornwall, ma'am.' The man she had

seen from the cottage window at Campton was beside her, soaked despite a heavy oilskin coat and hat, and the driver behind him made her look twice.

Twins.

She was certain they were twins. Her heart warmed and she laid her hand upon his arm.

'Thank you. I hope you will now both have the chance to get dry.'

Surprise laced his eyes. 'We will, ma'am. Now if you'd go with the housekeeper, she will see you inside to your rooms and out of this weather.'

A line of servants held large umbrellas over the disembarking party, the rain softer now and easing. Caroline folded a blanket across the head of Alex and watched as Tosh lifted his basket.

Where was Thornton Lindsay? she wondered, glancing down the manicured driveway to make certain that no single rider trailed in, but only the rain slanted across the track, the leaves of trees blown in eddies of wind, dark against the light of the moon.

Plastering a careful smile upon her lips, she followed the housekeeper and the lesser servants inside. Perhaps he would not come at all. Perhaps he truly did not care. Exeter after all had taught her that, for the Duke had disappeared the moment after their lovemaking and had made no contact in person since. Eight days ago now. And almost nine. She hated the way her mind could calculate exactly what her soul did not want to know, hated the fact that sorrow could take such a hold of joy and wrench the very gladness from her bones.

An old woman dressed in black stood in the portico, her hair severely tied back and a look that was hardly happy in small dark eyes.

'So ye'd be the woman my grandson has been telling me of.' The accent of Scotland was well imbued into her words. 'And this is the child?'

Before Caroline could stop her, the woman pushed back the blanket and bony fingers caressed the side of her son's chubby cheek. 'A bonny wee lad to be sure, but a Lindsay?' There was a strong sense of challenge at the end of her question, and a decided crusty impatience. 'I am the Duchess of Penborne and Thorn asked me here to act as a chaperon whilst you are visiting.'

Thornton's grandmother!

Feeling it appropriate, Caroline curtsied and introduced her brother. 'It is very good to meet you, Your Grace, and we thank you for your hospitality.'

'Do you indeed, Mrs Weatherby? Penborne Castle must be a far cry from your cottage in Campton.'

The question was said in such a way that Caroline was at pains as to know how to answer it. Was the old woman implying a lack of breeding, or, worse, was she hinting that she felt their presence here smacked of gold digging? Uncertain, she merely smiled.

Thomas, however, seemed completely unaware of

any tension and jumped into the growing gap of silence. 'I have always wanted to visit Scotland, Your Grace, and see the places spoken of in the poems of Robbie Burns. "Let other poets raise a fracas, 'Bout vines an' wines…an' stories wrack us…"'

'From Rabbie's "Scotch Drink", I'd wager?' The old Duchess waited till he nodded before continuing, her curiosity overcoming frostiness. 'Did ye learn that as a wee bairn?'

'No. I learned that on a card table in Antwerp. The Scottish fellow I was playing found his concentration much improved when reciting a good dollop of poetry. And the strange thing was that I did too after I beat him.'

'You were a card player?'

'And a good one, too.'

When Thornton Lindsay's grandmother laughed, Caroline saw, for the first time, the ghost of a woman who must have once been breathtakingly beautiful. Perhaps she had judged her too hastily, she thought. There was little time to dwell upon any of it, however, as the housekeeper shepherded them through to the first floor and to their adjoining rooms, leaving them with the promise of a hot meal delivered on a tray as soon as their luggage had been seen to.

Her room was decorated in cream and white and the bed was the largest she had ever seen. Even the state-rooms at Malmaison had not been as impressive or as comfortable. A roaring fire blazed in a grate that stretched across an entire wall and, to one side by the window, a sofa and two chairs were placed before a generous oaken table.

She laid Alexander down on the bed, bolstering pillows around him so that he would not fall, and placed her bag on a wooden chest. A knock at the door had her turning and the housekeeper entered, pushing a cot with two wheels at one end.

'We thought that you might need this, ma'am. It was the Duke's when he was a little baby and his father's before then. There are more blankets should you want them.'

'I am sure that this will be perfect.' Her fingers ran across the wool of the covers, and the lawn of tiny embroidered sheets. Thornton Lindsay had slept here as a baby. The fact intrigued and delighted her, though as she shut the door behind the departing housekeeper she wondered who the 'we' she spoke of was. The Duchess or the Duke himself? Lifting Alexander up, she removed the top layer of his clothing and placed him carefully in the cot, smiling as he reached out to the colourful embroidery along the side.

'Do you like it, darling?' she crooned and bent to kiss him on the cheek just as her brother came into her room.

'They seem well prepared for a baby,' he commented and sat down in one of the armchairs by the fire.

'It was Thornton Lindsay's.'

'Lord.'

His sigh was so heartfelt that Caroline frowned.

'I hope that the Duke understands that you are not the fair game you were in London. If he beds you and expects to—'

'We have had this talk before, Tosh.'

'And will do so again, Caroline.'

'Thornton Lindsay is Alexander's father and you promised me you would not say anything at all about what has happened before, that you would let me deal with this situation as I saw fit.'

'I hope that was not a rash promise.' His winsome smile defused the tension and he shrugged his shoulders and leant back. 'I wonder where Lindsay is? Perhaps he is away?'

Caroline thought of the dark shadow-rider chasing rain and wind and carriage and shook her head.

'He is here.' Her spirits sank even as she said it, for she could feel that he was, in the soft recesses of her own heart.

A noise awakened her, barely the whisper of a footprint in her room. Staying perfectly still to gauge the threat, she saw Thornton Lindsay standing next to the cot, his hands drawn tight across the wooden rails, moonlight from the opened curtains falling across him.

He did not touch, did not reach out, did not lay even a finger against the shape that was his son, but in the lack of movement Caroline saw something that was far more all consuming and passionate. His face burned with desperation and want and the muscles along the line of his cheek were taut with longing.

For his child.

For Alexander.

For family.

She knew exactly how it was he was feeling because in the first moment of his life when Alexander had been placed into her waiting arms she had felt it too.

A parent.

A place in the world measured neither in wealth nor knowledge nor position, but simply by love.

When a single tear fell from her cheek into the softness of the pillow, he turned.

'You are awake?'

Caroline saw how he stepped back from the cot and brought his hands behind him, saw the mask of indifference fall like a shutter over amber eyes. She barely knew how to answer and the fact that she wore only a very thin nightgown made it even more difficult again. She could not sit up, could not meet his glance as she would have liked to, head on and direct.

'Was it you on the horse?'

A ridiculous question and no way to begin any sort of conversation, but then this whole situation was absurd.

He made no answer as he changed the subject altogether.

'He looks like me. What colour are his eyes?'

'A lighter shade of your own.'

'I see.' He nodded his head and drew one hand through his hair. In worry. In bafflement. In the sheer and huge responsibility of offspring. Caroline knew that feeling too and hurried into an explanation.

'I never knew who my own father was…' She stopped and tried to rein in a surprising anger. 'I am glad it will not be the same for Alexander.'

'And you are certain that he is mine?'

The words cut her to the quick, but she kept her face perfectly impassive.

'You said yourself that he looks like—'

He gave no credence to her argument, but interrupted easily. 'If I were to claim this baby as my own, how many other men might come forward to challenge me on the fact?'

Caroline felt the hard punch of betrayal wind her. He had not asked her to Penleven for a truce or a tryst. He had not asked her here to be his mistress, or for even a milder version of friendship. He had brought her here to determine whether this child was indeed his son.

Fright made her shake.

If he were to ascertain such a thing, how far was he likely to go to make sure that Alex stayed in Cornwall?

Any length!

For the first time since being in the company of Thornton Lindsay she felt fear. Bone-deep fear. The kind that kept her mute and clammy.

And his anger-laced eyes were leached by wariness.

'I see.' He turned away and then turned back. 'I asked you once before for the truth of your name, Caroline. Are you now ready to give it to me? For this child's sake?'

'I do not understand…'

'Disguises have a way of tearing the heart out of honesty. If he is mine and you do not allow him the protection of my title, how in the hell are you going to shield him? What happens when he is ten or twenty? When he has children of his own? Anstretton. Weatherby. Lindsay. The son of a widow or a harlot or a Duke?' His eyes settled on the bracelet on the small table next to her bed. 'Or a French woman with the surname of "St C"?'

She froze. Her bracelet. He had worked this out from a tiny inscription in gold? This time she could allow no question.

Thomas's safety or Alexander's?

A choice.

Give her son a home and her brother would die.

No choice at all.

She sat up and made certain that the sheets of the bed fell to her lap and was pleased when the dark glow of the fire danced in beguiling shadows across the full roundness of her breasts. Distraction. With the Duke as an adversary she needed all the help that she could muster.

'The child is not yours.'

'You are lying.'

'We will leave Penleven in the morning.'

'No.'

'You cannot stop us.'

'But I think that I can. Which sane person would question where this baby would be better placed? Penleven and stability, or a number of different addresses and masquerades? Do I need to go on?'

'No.'

'I thought not.'

He smiled and moved away. 'I would be seen as a father, Caroline, who is trying to protect his only child. What manner of man would allow his progeny to become a gypsy?' The amber in his eyes danced bright. Bitterly gold.

'And me? What will happen to me?'

He walked across to the bed and traced the line of one areola in a cold and dispassionate manner. 'You have bounteous charms that I am more than prepared to bargain for; a liaison will at least give you the opportunity to be close to Alexander.'

'And Thomas?'

'I could do with another manager.'

'I see.'

And she did. Saw just how neatly he had tied her up to a position she had previously refused, made her morals ludicrous and pointless things with the neck of her son and her twin brother at stake.

The Heartless Duke.

She remembered his *nom de plume* and tears flooded into her eyes.

'For how long?'

'When I find a wife, you will be installed in a house in the village.'

'And forgotten?'

For the first time he smiled. 'I am not certain that it would ever be possible to forget you.'

When his hand fell lower to cup her breast she looked up. Fully dressed with his hair falling across the whiteness of a snowy cravat, his harnessed sexuality was completely evident. She felt the heat of want blush her cheek. Saw it too in his face, the muscles of his jaw grinding tense.

'It is not a fight I want, Caroline.'

'Then let me go.'

'I can't…'

His voice broke on the admission and he laid back the sheets, carefully looking at her. She felt the cold rush of air and the warmer touch of his fingers. Lower. Lower. And when he stood a few minutes later to remove his clothes she merely opened her arms and waited.

* * *

When she awoke he was gone. And the shadows that wreathed the room were heavy.

Like her heart!

She was a mistress: a woman who could be taken whenever and wherever her protector should demand it. A fallen woman like her mother, existing on the crumbs of rich men for survival. Her hand wandered to the wetness between her legs. She had not even taken precaution against conception! Another child.

'When I find a wife, you will be installed in a house in the village.'

Her hand came up to her mouth and she felt the hot tears of self-loathing spill across it, a noise from the cradle opposite keeping her cries silent.

She was trapped, here at Penleven, caught in a role of her own making.

Her mind began to spin as she thought back. Back to the heady days of Malmaison when Napoleon had rejected Josephine for another. With stealth and wit Madame de Beauharnais had stalked him, bringing the general back into the shelter of her arms, indiscretions and alliances forgotten under the onslaught of what was truly theirs.

Could she do the same?

How far apart were the emotions of lust and love? Thornton was judicious in his movements, vigilant with his words and his time. He had not stayed in bed after they had made love, had not tarried to be woken in the morning with her beside him and had, even in the final heat of lovemaking, held some part of himself back, some important part. And that was the part of him that she so desperately needed.

What could she use to bring him to a point of no return?

She wiped her tear-wet hands against the sheet on the bed and rose to look out of the window, the moonlight bright now on the lands around the castle. Her ears picked up the sound of her brother snoring in the next room and of her son in his beautiful new cot as he turned to find comfort.

At least they were safe behind the ramparts of Penleven, well fed and warm and with a gap of time that offered them shelter should she do what was expected of her.

Thornton walked to the cliffs, walked to the very edge of the world before the land fell away into the boiling white cauldron of sea and was lost into nothingness.

The child is not yours. We will leave Penleven in the morning.

Not his, when he could see the mark of his father on the small white face and his father and his father's father, stamped with the particular features of a thousand years of Lindsay lineage.

Not his!

Not his?

Caroline Anstretton/Weatherby made him furious, made him careless, made the familiar dulling ennui vanish into either a fathomless lust or an unending wrath.

He could not believe how he let her bait him, how he rose to the lure of her breasts in the firelight like a green and untried boy, all brawn and no brain.

Stooping to pick up a rock by his feet, he threw it with his full force out into the darkness of sky. God. He had even threatened her whilst demanding his rights as her lover in exactly the same sentence.

Was he stupid?

She made him so.

She did not trust him, that much was certain—and to be honest, how was it possible for him to even be thinking of trusting her?

He should let them all go: her and her brother and the son with the eyes in a lighter shade than his own. He should take a wife and start a family that was truly his, and far from the deceit, chaos and illusion that Caroline Anstretton seemed for ever fond of. He should toss her out of Penleven with a hefty purse and forget her.

And yet here he was, blackmailing her into staying, and following the carriage on a wild and rainy night from the north coast to the south just to make certain that she did not get out, did not disappear.

He smiled at himself and turned the signet ring that he wore on his little finger around and around.

Circles.

Life came in circles when you thought about it.

Lost. Found. Happy. Sad. Lonely.

Content.

The small bud of it warmed his heart and blossomed into an almost ache.

He could not lose her.

Not again.

Not even when she looked him straight in the eyes and denied the child was his. Not even when the tears that filled her eyes magnified dark blue orbs of hate.

His mistress. Caroline.

For now, at least, that would just have to be enough.

Chapter Twelve

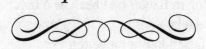

Breakfast was set out in a downstairs salon, the sideboard filled with as much food as they usually consumed in a whole week at Campton. She marvelled at the waste of it all and smiled as Tosh sat beside her, his plate filled with every conceivable thing on offer.

'You are not eating, Caro?'

Sipping her tea, she tried to push down nervousness, a noise startling her as the Duke entered the room.

'Good morning. Welcome to my castle. I hope you are both comfortable.'

Today the stubble on his chin was dark and he wore his patch. And in his eye, when it caught her own, there was something akin to guilt.

'If there is anything you should require, you just need to ask my housekeeper. Whatever you need shall be provided.'

When Tosh stood she held her breath. Last time he had seen the Duke of Penborne he had been trying to knock his head off and the situation here seemed slightly ludicrous. Good manners had her brother holding out his hand and Caroline was pleased when Thornton took it. She did not need the extra worry of retaliation for perceived wrong and in all honesty that awful scene in Exeter had been as much her doing as it had the Duke's.

'Your nose looks a lot better.'

'I could say the same of your arm, Your Grace.'

The air between the men bristled with unsaid accusations, an uneasy truce brought about by circumstance.

With real consternation she pushed back her own seat and stood. 'It would be most appreciated if you could find my brother a position on one of your farms, Your Grace. A good position.'

Tosh turned to look at her in utter disbelief.

But Caroline merely smiled. Two could play at the game the Duke had set out and she had fulfilled her part of the bargain more than amply last night.

She lifted her chin and looked him straight in the eye, and as the moment lengthened the Duke of Penborne dismissed his servants to a further distance with a quick gesture.

'How is it you know Adele Halstead? I would prefer the…truth.' He left a slight gap between the words, giving the question an edge of danger.

No mincing words, then! No careful circling around honesty.

'We met her in Paris. She lived there for a time when our mother was still alive.' Not completely a lie.

'Your mother?'

'Eloise St Clair.'

There was a silence. Caroline could almost see the way Thornton Lindsay was putting together the fragmented facts into a cohesive whole. And knew the second that the name of her mother truly registered.

'The infamous daughter of the Reverend who ran off alone to Europe?' An unexpected humour laced his words. 'Lord, she was your mother?'

He waited as she nodded.

'I see.'

'She was not as people in England said that she was.' Caroline hated the anger she could hear in her voice and for the second time that day she bit her tongue hard, wondering what it was in him that made her want to explain.

'No?'

'No. She was a woman who found the strictures of life difficult.'

'How old were you when she died?'

'Seventeen. We were seventeen.'

'And had you always lived in France?'

Looking across at Thomas, she shook her head. 'We lived in other places too.'

'With her?'

'Not always.'

'But together?'

'Yes.'

'And your father?'

Silence.

'Are you interested in farm management, Thomas?'

The quick change in subject had Caroline reeling. A few short questions and the Duke of Penborne had found out more about their lives than anyone ever had before. Their loneliness. Their uncertainty. Their togetherness. Their lack of family. And now he would offer her brother the chance of work that could see him self-sufficient and eminently respectable? She watched the slow blush of excitement tinge Tosh's cheeks.

'I am, Your Grace.'

'Then perhaps you could accompany me on the rounds of Penleven later today and we could talk.'

'I would very much like that.'

'If you have finished breakfast, my secretary could show you the boundaries of the estate on a map in the library.'

When he was gone, Caroline took a breath. Left alone, the familiar pull was stronger, like magnets straining against opposite poles. She stepped back a little. Embarrassed. Breathless. Almost nervous.

'Thank you for helping my brother, Your Grace.'

'One promise for another, Caroline. Is it Weatherby

or Anstretton I should be placing on any legal contract with him?'

'St Clair would be more correct. Though I would prefer to be known here as Mrs Weatherby.'

His eye brushed across the inscription on her bracelet. 'I shall be taking a short drive around the hills of Penleven in an hour. Would you and Alexander like to accompany me?'

He did not touch her, did not move forward, did not in any way allude to the sensuality of last night, and yet in his eye she saw the burning promise of what was always between them.

Heat. Fierce and incandescent. Unstoppable. The throbbing want of him unbalancing her anger, replacing the risk of it all with hope. Hope of making things different.

When she nodded he turned and left and she realised that he had eaten nothing and that the large plates of eggs and bacon and toast had remained untouched.

She had dressed carefully in a dark brown coat and matching dress, a froth of lace at the collar and a cameo of her mother's pinned on top of it.

Alexander cooed on her lap as the coach trotted out of Penleven, his eyelashes dark against rosy cheeks and his hands grasping at the gold catch on the door.

A happy family going on a jaunt into town? How appearances could fool. Three people. A mistress, a

man who was in the process of acquiring a proper wife
and his unwanted bastard son.

Pushing down ire, she tried to rally, but today, with
last night's sleepless worry pulling at her, she found
that she just could not.

Thornton, on the other hand, was in the best of
moods as he pointed out a river and the local hills and
a cave that he had sheltered in with his brother when
he was younger.

'You have a brother?' She had seen no sign of any
family save the old grandmother.

'He died young of scarlet fever. My mother and father caught it too and passed away a few days after him.'

'Who cared for you?'

'I was at Eton.'

'And at term's end?'

'I stayed there.'

Challenge was plainly scrawled across his face
when she looked up. The scarring on his left cheek in
this light was easily seen, the skin pulling at the edge
of his eye in a way that she had not noticed before. Perhaps that was why he wore the patch. She longed to
ask him about the explosion in the church, but did not
dare to because of the questions that he might ask her
back. When the carriage jolted she felt the length of
his arm against her own and moved away quickly,
tense in her reaction to such a tiny contact.

Stupid. Stupid. Stupid. She chided herself firmly,

making herself relax and smile. Her teeth gritted to-gether as she did so, the muscles in her cheek protest-ing the staunchness.

'I would not think to send a small child far away to school even if it was the vogue to do so.' Here was a chance to install some of her philosophies of upbring-ing at least.

'Neither would I.'

'I would hope a nanny could be employed at first and then a tutor. One that was not harsh and one that I liked.'

'You do not believe in discipline?'

'Punishments benefit no one. Were you punished as a child?'

He pushed open the window next to him by releas-ing the leather catch. His hair moved in the wind and he deftly tied it back with a strap of leather he wore around his wrist. 'Eton was a school where retribution and penalty were art forms, and I was a worthy recipi-ent, having no parents to ever complain about the bruising.'

'Why did you not live with your grandmother, then, after…?' She petered out.

'Morag had problems of her own at that time and could not also deal with mine. It is only more recently that she moved from Edinburgh to Plymouth. There…' He pointed as if he were tired of the personal nature of the conversation, and rapped on the top of the roof of the coach with his cane. 'This is what I wanted to show you.'

Sorrow consumed her and enlightenment. His childhood had been even lonelier than her own, a small abandoned boy who had grown up to be a man trusting nobody, patterns moulded in youth hard to shake in adulthood.

When the carriage slowed, he jumped out first and turned to help her.

'Could you take Alex?' she asked as she collected her reticule and lifted her skirts.

Uncertainty crossed into his eyes. 'I have not held a baby before—' His words stopped as she deposited Alexander into his arms and Caroline tried to hide a smile as he reached up to play with the Duke's snowy white cravat.

In the sunlight and close, the colour of their hair was exactly the same. Black night dark and slightly curly, almost touching as he leant downwards.

The spark of interest had taken. Alike. Alight. The flame of love would come whether he wanted it to or not. Already she saw how her tiny son watched him. When Thornton scratched his head Alex did the same, his nearly-words soft in the afternoon breeze.

'He speaks?'

'A few baby sounds that I recognise.'

'And walks.'

She smiled. 'He is only seven months. But he can sit now unaided.'

Information. She could see Thornton Lindsay storing it, remembering it, wanting to know what every father has since the very beginning of time.

Alex resisted as she tried to take him back, clinging on to his father with a surprising fervency, and when Thornton's hand came up telling her to leave him, she did.

'The place I want to show you is just here. My father built it for my mother.'

The cottage was beautiful, smothered in vines, a porch running the full length of the front and French doors placed to allow easy access from any point.

Walking up the small number of steps and on to the terrace, Caroline could see why the house had been positioned exactly where it was. A vista of hills and valleys and sea lay before her and far in the distance, through a stand of trees, Penleven jutted tall, the last bastion of human existence before the land fell into the sea below.

This cottage was all that the castle was not. Quiet. Calm. Peaceful. Simple.

A retreat.

'I can see why your mother would have loved it. Did she come here often?'

'Not as often as my father may have liked.' A peculiar tone lay in his words, giving Caroline the idea that there was more to this place than he was saying. When they went inside she saw what it was that he had not told her.

The house was just one single room with the biggest bed she had ever seen square in the middle. Draped in netting and heaped in pillows, she understood exactly his reason for bringing her here.

A love nest.

A mistress's lair.

Anger made her lash out. 'Do I have the right to ask you how often you plan to bed me, then? Now? This afternoon? This evening?'

'I will bed you when I want to, Caroline St Clair. Whenever and wherever I want to.'

Unexpectedly tears sprang. 'This may be a game to you…'

'A game. Ahh, but you have played me, sweetheart, as a master might. Your names. Disguises. Charades. This person. That person. Every time I have met you, you are completely different from the time before. And you tell me I am the one playing false.'

Sweetheart. He had called her sweetheart. It did not sound like a term he would often use and it had slipped out unconsciously. A beginning. Hope. Suddenly the world seemed like a brighter place to Caroline, a happier place, a place where perhaps in the unfolding scheme of things she might find sanctuary. With him.

The thought hit her hard, making her turn away to hide what she could so plainly feel in her eyes, on her face.

'Have you brought many others here?'

He did not answer.

'A wife might take exception to a mistress living so close.'

Still he said nothing.

'There is also the possibility to consider, I suppose, of other children conceived.'

'Enough, Caroline.' He took her hand and pulled her up close against him, the warmth of his body startling through the thickness of cloth. And for a moment she stood still, her son and her lover making a circle around happiness, their breaths against her skin offering the promise of something more. Something treasured. The sun was on their heads and the scattering clouds ran fast against the sea winds straight off the continent.

Home.

Safety.

An echo of something precious. When her fingers tightened against the breadth of his forearm he instantly pulled back.

'I think we should go.' The tone of his voice was reserved and formal as he shepherded her out and closed the doors behind them. Shut. Sealed. Secured against intrusion. Against the feeling of what had just been.

When Alexander began crying in earnest, she was

glad, for she knew that the Duke of Penborne would not stay in their company for long.

He could not.

She was the daughter of a woman who had fled England in a scandal and one who had no notion of whom or where her father was. She owned nothing save a ruined reputation and a past that could never be told. She was like the perpetually unwelcomed wedding guest that Samuel Taylor Coleridge had spoken of in his poem about an ancient mariner: 'Alone, alone, all, all alone.'

With one child conceived out of wedlock, she could claim the pretence of widowhood. What if she were to fall pregnant again? And again? How long would it be before Tosh challenged Thornton over her honour? And lost?

Soon. Now, if he only knew.

Another secret.

This time from her twin brother, the last person in the world whom she would deceive. And if one of these men killed the other, how could she bear any of it?

She shook her head firmly and resolved to make certain of holding her confidences close. Perhaps if she encouraged Thornton to install her brother at Millington for a while, she could sort out what to say? The very thought of separation made her stomach sick, but to keep Tosh safe she would be prepared to do anything.

Anything.

Even lie with a man night after night in the hope that love might blossom, and smile as if she did not nurse even a care in the world when she met him the next morning.

Thornton sat in his library, watching the dying moments of a candle flicker in front of him.

Three o'clock.

All he wanted to do was to take Caroline St Clair into his arms and lose himself in her very warmth.

Lord. He worried about the way she was reeling him in. Her smile. Her voice. Her easy laughter and unexpected tears. Always there had been a part of him that had remained…his…in any relationship. Even with Lilly there had been a distance, a place where he observed and calculated, where his heart did not quite follow into the deep watches of night. He had maintained a coldness that with Caroline he could feel the first thawing of.

A few days she had been at Penleven and he was desperate to be with her as soon as the darkness fell, as soon as the candles were lit, the ache of his want standing proud even here in the library. All he yearned to do was to take her. Quickly. To spill his seed. Without caution. Heedless. Deliberate. So unlike him! Desperate.

Dangerous.

Relax your guard and chaos would follow. How often in his life had he learned that lesson? When he had shown her the cottage on the estate it had been in his mind to tell her that this was where he had thought she could live. But he had not. Why not? Why had he not laid down the ground rules of a relationship that could never be…sustainable?

He swore and sighed.

Because he could not hurt her. Because in the depths of her midnight blue eyes he saw a vulnerability that broke the resolution of his intent and made him want to…cherish her, make things easier for her, to take the worries of the world from her face and provide a sanctuary.

Lord, the very idea of such altruism concerning a mistress made him smile and he was laughing at his own questionable reasoning when a letter to one side of his desk attracted his attention. The Earl of Ross would be arriving tomorrow with his family. And his daughter. He groaned and threw the letter into the fire where it caught immediately and went up in a welter of flame. Why the hell had he let himself be talked into this proposition? Why had he not followed his initial instinct and cancelled the visit completely?

He did not want a wife.

He wanted Caroline.

He did not want a happy guileless girl.

He wanted Caroline. Full-fleshed and mysterious. Complex. Sensual. The mother of his child. Children. More than one? He wanted to see her belly swollen with his seed, her full breasts round and ripe. He had missed out on that once and would not again.

His mistress.

To take.

Throwing back a stiff brandy, he cursed at the power she was exerting over him and resolved to take a step back. In sheer self-protection.

The sound of voices made Caroline tense. Laughter. Gossip. Children. When she rounded the corner of the blue salon, she saw the place filled with people, a beautiful girl on the sofa next to the Duke of Penborne.

Thomas was watching them from a chair at one end of the room and it was to his side that she went. There had been no talk of visitors, no preparation that a whole family was to descend on Penleven. She tipped her head when the men stood at her arrival, glad when she could sit down as Tosh vacated the armchair and stood behind her.

'The Earl of Ross and his daughter Jennifer will be with us for a few days, Mrs Weatherby.'

When all the gawping faces turned her way she was at a loss as to what to say about her own presence here, although the Duke solved the problem for her.

'Caroline and her brother are old acquaintances. They arrived earlier this week from London with my grandmother.'

'And a long journey it is too, Mrs Weatherby.' The

Earl of Ross was a large red-faced man with a generous nose. His poor looks, however, had not been
passed at all to his daughter, an amber-tressed beauty
with lightly freckled luminous skin. 'Have you visited
Cornwall often before?'

When the Duke said yes and she said no, there was
a small moment of tension. Sitting back, Caroline let
Thornton extricate her from the difficulty, for it was
his lie after all.

The eyes of the young woman next to him were
fixed on his face, on his cheek, on his ruined cheek,
the slight frown marring her beautiful countenance
suggesting that she had had no prior knowledge of any
injury and was rather disconcerted by the discovery.

Did she not realise how rude she was being, how
very tactless?

'Will you be staying in this part of the country for
long, Lady Jennifer?' Perhaps a question could distract
her from such an inconsiderate observance.

Vacuous eyes raked across her own. 'We will be in
these climes for a fortnight with my cousins and I love
Cornwall.'

Her father chuckled as he turned to the Duke of Penborne. 'We always remark on her interest, Your Grace.
Every year we do the same. Some predestined fate, according to her aunt, who has the reputation of being
something of a seer.'

'Indeed.'

There was barely a note of interest in Thornton Lindsay's voice as he gestured to the butler to proceed with the tea, though it did not seem to put the Earl of Ross off his stride at all.

'Jennifer is also a prodigiously good piano player and I see you have a particularly fine piano, Your Grace?'

The question quivered in the air, and for a moment Caroline thought that the Duke would ignore the implication altogether.

'Please feel free to give us a tune, Lady Jennifer,' he finally said and Lady Ross clapped her hands and leaned forward.

'Oh, do, Jenny. Do play us something, dear.'

Jennifer's smaller sisters and brothers looked anything but happy when she rose and made much of adjusting her skirts and sitting at the piano. Her nails were so long that they almost raked the wood above the black and white keys, the ease of her position and life evident in the soft milky whiteness of her hands. Looking surreptitiously down at her own, Caroline frowned at the contrast. Short nails with the pigment of paint still residing in some of them and calluses on her first fingers where she had scrubbed Alex's clothes clean last week in boiling hot water.

She buried her fingers into her cotton skirt, angry at herself for even thinking such things important and resolving to enjoy herself.

The music that followed was like nothing Caroline had ever heard, though she was hardly an expert in anything musical. When she looked across at her brother she almost laughed at his face, which showed amazement crossed with an effort not to grimace. Thornton Lindsay sat implacably still, no expression at all giving any indication of his true feelings. Like the master spy he had been, she thought, and watched him. When his eyes caught hers they were carefully bland before he looked away. She wondered what he would have seen in her own.

The final flourish of Jennifer's rendition of a Mozart tune was greeted with loud claps from her mother and father and more polite accolades from Thornton and Thomas and herself.

Jennifer's father slapped his hands on his thighs as he stood more than proudly. 'She is our delight and joy, this young woman. Whoever marries her will be the luckiest fellow alive.'

His daughter beamed, the smile an exact copy of her mother's, and sat down even closer to the Duke of Penborne. Success had buoyed her confidence and she smacked his arm playfully as he said how interesting he had found her interpretation of the Mozart classic. Her parents watched the couple on the sofa with an ever-increasing felicity.

'Do you ride, Lady Jennifer?' Tosh's question was phrased more in politeness than in any true interest.

'I do, sir. My father taught me when I was young and we go to our country seat in Kent every summer.'

'She rides a horse as well as she plays the piano,' her father put in and his wife's laughter trilled around the room.

'Quite an accomplishment, then.' Something akin to abhorrence was just audible in Thornton Lindsay's voice, and when a message came for him he made much of the contents and excused himself summarily from the room.

The Ross girl sat pouting on the empty sofa, sullen pique written all over her. Her mother, trying to placate her, leaned over to pat her hand, but she flung it away and stood.

'I want to go back to my room now. I am tired.'

In less than five seconds the whole salon was emptied and Tosh and Caroline sat across from each other in a state of sheer disbelief.

'I would not wish her on my worst enemy,' her brother said when he had had time to recover his voice.

And they both began to laugh.

Alexander was fretful that evening, two new teeth cutting their way through swollen gums. As Caroline pondered a remedy for such a thing there was a knock on the door and the Duchess of Penborne walked in.

'I heard the child crying from outside on my way to bed. Are ye fine with him?'

'Thank you, yes.' She curtsied and waited until the older woman sat. 'Can I get you something, Your Grace?'

'Och, nay. 'Tis just that I heard the boy—'

An angry scream from Alex made her start and she was surprised when the old lady leant over and with strong hands plucked him out of her grasp.

'It's cold he'd be needing. The end of a bone against ice or a green twig from the oak tree. To bite on, you mind. It brings the teeth through quicker.'

Swollen gums clamped on an ancient finger and she smiled with an unhidden delight. 'It's been so long since I had a bairn on my lap, so long since the sound of children has rung through the halls of this place. I did not realise I missed it so.'

'Was Thornton an easy child?'

'He was always striving towards the next baby milestone, I recall. The first baby on the estate to walk by nine months, the fastest runner in the area before he went off to school. After that I did not see him so much.'

Why?

Why did you not bring your grandchild home and let each other heal your broken hearts? Why did you leave a child at a punitive and distant school and never find the time to claim him? Caroline longed to ask the questions. But she did not because already the old lady was standing and handing back her grizzly son.

'I will talk to the housekeeper tomorrow and have

her bring ye something cold to soothe his gums. She is a competent woman with potions and well able to be trusted.'

'Thank you.' Cradling Alex, Caroline watched the old woman leave her room, feeling a small pleasure in the tone of their conversation. At least there could be a politeness between them, and she imagined she could learn much about the younger Thornton Lindsay from his grandmother, should she gain her confidence.

The Duke came before the clock had even struck ten fifteen. Earlier than usual and not alone.

'There is something I wish to speak to you about. The maid here will watch over Alexander while you are gone.'

The young woman curtsied. 'I have six brothers, ma'am.' Her voice and smile were both kind. 'I promise you I will watch him well.'

As the woman settled herself, Caroline had little choice but to accompany the Duke as he left the room.

He led her down the corridor and up a flight of steep stairs to a chamber at the top of the tower. It was a library, the shelves of books around the room reaching to the ceiling, and subsisting of a substantial catalogue from what she could see at first glance.

'Why am I here, Your Grace?' Suddenly she was wary. Had he had enough of her already?

'We need to talk, Caroline. And I would prefer you

call me by my given name. Thornton. Thorn if you should favour it.'

'Yes, sir…Thornton,' she amended when he looked at her sternly.

'I need your help.'

Of all the things she thought that he might have said, this was the very last of them. She stayed mute. Waiting.

'The Ross girl is proving annoyingly persistent and I hoped you might be able to be a foil.'

'A foil?' She could not quite keep amazement from her voice. Or her relief.

'An interested party, if you wish. A woman who would show some affection for me.'

'To deter Miss Ross?'

'Exactly.'

'I would have thought your personage enough to frighten even the most brave of young girls.'

'This one is proving surprisingly resilient and her parents' presence in the equation is not helping either. I should not wish to be trapped into a marriage I don't desire.' He pulled down a full bottle of brandy from a shelf behind him and, turning over two crystal glasses on a tray, poured out a generous measure in each. 'I found Miss Ross in my bedroom just before dinner. She said she had made the wrong turning and had come in by mistake. If my valet had not been with me…'

'You may have been attending your own wedding on the morrow?'

'I knew you would understand.'

She looked up sharply, a tone in his words that she did not quite fathom, the glint of amber surprisingly light.

Thornton smiled and finished his drink. Lord, her serious little face nearly undid him and the way she was now pacing up and down his library in thought made him want to snatch her to his side.

After a moment she turned back towards him, her mind seemingly made up. 'If I stayed near you and made certain that you were never alone in her company, would that help?'

'It would.' He tried his hardest to keep his words grave.

'My brother would not condone this, of course?'

'He won't know. He is due to leave for Holston after breakfast to look over some cattle.'

Nodding, Caroline chewed at a nail on her left hand. When Thornton looked closer, he saw each fingernail was indeed very short. She bit her nails. Often. The fact intrigued him.

'Did you have any plans in mind for the morrow?'

'I have promised the Ross party a ride around Penleven.'

'All of them?'

'Not the small children.'

'Well, with everyone there you should be safe?'

Thornton almost laughed, but stopped himself, liking the way Caroline counselled him. He had seen the way she had watched Jennifer Ross observe the scars on his face in the salon this afternoon and had tried to distract her from her rudeness. Did she think his feelings would be hurt somehow by such an exchange? Lord, he had spent over five years amongst men and women who would have had no compunction in murdering him were he to give them even half the chance and the last three ignoring the fascinated glances of well-meaning English folk when they comprehended the changes in his countenance.

Almost ten long years on the very edge of humanity and yet he was unsettled by the way Caroline now looked at him, concern on her face.

And care.

The Ross girl was of no threat to him whatsoever, but she did represent a way of keeping Caroline by his side and attentive within the company of others. And he needed her there! Beside him. Close.

He did not at this moment question the logic behind this deduction.

'You will promise not to allude in any way to the fact that I am your mistress?'

'I will.'

'Very well.' She held out her hand and he took it, warm and small in his, the gold bracelet catching the light of a candle, the warmth between them startling and distinct. 'Though if Jennifer Ross asks me questions about you it might be difficult, for we barely know each other.'

'I would beg to differ, Caroline,' he returned, suggestively raking his eyes across her body, and damping the smile that came as she snatched back her hand.

When she reddened dramatically, he tried to check his teasing. Lord, she had travelled Europe, carving a livelihood out of deceit, and yet she blushed in front of him like this? How the hell had she managed that? A slight uneasiness assailed him. Even when he thought he had the measure of her he did not.

He capitulated. 'What is it about me that you would like to know?'

'How did you become an intelligence officer under Wellington?'

'After Oxford I was at a loose end. Leonard had come back to stay at Penleven and was doing a good job of running the place and I was bored with country life. After expressing an interest in the army I sort of fell into it. At first I was a captain in Spain with Paget's Reserve Division and then I was seconded to Wellington as an intelligence officer.'

'And why did you stop?'

One hand scraped across the ridges of his left cheek. 'Part of the job of being a spy is to have the ability to blend in. After this I found that was difficult.'

All humour fled. 'Do you miss it?'

'At the time I cursed my bad luck, but returning to Cornwall was like a balm after all the years of uncertainty.'

'A balm.' She echoed his words.

She knew that feeling exactly. The hills had embraced her and the wild valleys had called her name. Her, an intruder with little claim to its beauty and a lifetime of homelessness. How must have he felt as heir of Penleven, with the march of his ancestors in the very bones of the earth and a solitude that protected completely?

'"Life marks the passage of our days." A woman in Paris told me that once not even a month after her husband had had his head blown off by cannon fire in the high hills of Corunna.'

'A brave acceptance. I was not quite so…acquiescent.'

'Of your scars?'

'They were the easiest things to bear,' he said quietly and moved back. Standing against the shelves of books in the half-light of his library, she drew in her breath.

'I have heard talk of a woman. Lillyanna?'

Real anger now masked his eyes and for the first time Caroline saw raw pain beneath the façade.

'There is always talk. The trick is to determine what is worth listening to.'

'And what isn't?' She knew he didn't wish for any further conversation, but whilst she had the chance she kept at it. 'I did not wish to pry…'

The clock behind suddenly boomed out the hour of eleven, startling them both.

Thorn placed his glass on the table. 'Stay with me.'

His finger ran down the line of her jaw. 'Stay with me tonight, Caroline, and the maid will sit with Alex.'

'If Tosh found me with you and challenged you, would you fight him? If he got hurt because…'

'He won't.'

'You would promise?' She kept on at him because suddenly it was vitally important to her that she had his word.

'I promise.'

Breathing out, she felt her worry lighten even as she hated the red flush that marched across her cheeks and his answering lazy smile.

'If anyone else were to know…'

He circled behind and caught out at her hand, bringing the sensitive skin on the inside of her wrist up to the warmth of his mouth and holding it there.

Measuring the beat of her heart.

Pacing the moment in quiet.

And the amber strike of his velvet eyes up close was startling. Alive. Challenging.

'I think your last explanation to a packed court as to my sexual prowess was more damaging to your reputation than being my mistress could ever be.'

The thought made her grimace. 'I can never go back.'

'Oh, I don't know. London is notorious for its forgetfulness of scandal and yours, as a married woman, is not in the same league as the brutal deflowering of an innocent.'

Her pulse raced as she took in his words. A deflowered innocent. Her.

The hand that held her wrist brushed higher across the line of her bosom, cupping the round firmness and pulling at the lace overlay. And, further down, his leg came between hers, riding her loins on the rock of his thighs.

Hard. Meaningful. She shuddered as he took a husky intake of breath. And shuddered again as his thumb stroked her nipple into a proud rigidity. Her groan came involuntarily from the very depths of her stomach, an instinctual uncontrolled reflex of want. Primal. Elementary. Her head arched back, breath shallow against the knowledge of what his hands so easily could do to her body as fluid acquiescence overcame resistance.

Anywhere. Any time. Take me.

She no longer had the will to stop him. No longer the means to hold him at a distance, no matter how little she would receive in return.

An unequal giving. And she could not care. All she wanted was his hands on her body and his mouth at her breast and the final joining of flesh against flesh. Wet. Hot. Warm and melding. Release.

Love me, Thorn. Just me.

Please.

A single tear traced its way down her cheek and he stilled, his hands dropping away and an expression on his face that she had not seen there before.

'I promise I will not hurt you.'

Ambivalent hesitancy.

In a man who never faltered the emotion was more than surprising and when he moved back she let him, as much for her own well being as his. She had shown him too much of herself, and the ground beneath them had shifted somehow.

'But you do hurt me, Thornton, by keeping me here as your mistress.'

He frowned and pulled away, breaking contact. Now they were some place that words could not define, a watershed where decisions were needed to go forward. Or back.

But not tonight.

Not so soon.

Not when the feel of him bruised her with passion even as restraint was scrawled undisputedly on his face. The implacable distance that was his badge was back, lodged against sensuality in a hard band of need.

'I should really go. Alexander may have woken.' Shaky ground had the propensity to crumble at your feet after all and she had to be wary. For everyone's sake.

When he nodded she turned before he saw her disappointment. He would not come to her tonight. She knew it.

Thornton Lindsay, Wellington's most famous intelligence officer, needed to be in control, needed to fashion his existence in exactly the way he would want it.

Tonight that had not happened. Tonight she had pierced a little place in the armour that held the world at bay.

The beginning of a true relationship?

She must take one step at a time, her brother protected by his promise and her son shielded by his name.

Like a phoenix, from the old rose the new. Better. Stronger. Real.

The banked fire in her room warmed her after the coldness of the passageway and she crossed to the cot beside her bed. Alex was fast asleep, as was the maid who watched over him. Gently tugging the woman's arm, she hushed away apologies and bade her find her own bed to sleep.

And then she sat in the wingchair by the fire and watched the sparks fasten themselves to the sooty back base of the grate.

Soldiers. Armies. Flaring. Dying. Small worlds within bigger ones, the flames of a piece of half-burnt wood catching and throwing orange shadows across everything. Outside the south-west wind howled against the castle, blowing straight in from the sea, and further afield, if she listened carefully, she could make out the sound of the waves hitting the land, long beaching rollers from the channel and beyond.

Home. Here. In the folds of Cornwall. In a countryside that had known peace for so long it was careless in its defences.

So different from Paris.

Her breath shallowed as she raised her hand up to the light from the fire, opening her fingers to warmth. Tears banked in her eyes for the goodness of this place, for the solid timelessness of it, for the durability of a castle built when the family name was young and for the love and laughter it must have known between then and now.

Permanence. She had not known how desperately she had wanted this until coming here. Coming home.

To Thornton Lindsay.

Chapter Thirteen

The ride across Penleven land was exhilarating. Seated on a horse that Thornton had chosen for her, Caroline felt a sense of freedom that she had never experienced before.

Shaking her head, she chased behind the Duke, his huge black horse exactly like the one she had seen from the carriage window on that first rain-filled night. The thought made her smile. It had been him then, racing against the wind and shepherding them towards his home. Why would he have done that if he truly did not care?

As they came to the top of a hill Thornton called a rest and waited for the Ross family to catch them up. Jennifer came first, her mouth slack with exhaustion and her face an unbecoming blotchy red. Her parents were only a few seconds behind her and all looked hopeful that this might indeed be the very end of the excursion.

'It's a beautiful land you live in, Lindsay.' The Earl of Ross's wife nodded diligently behind him as her husband gave the compliment. 'Our lands are, of course, as expansive, but this place has the sea beside it and there is something about the mix of green and blue.'

Jennifer pulled her mount over beside the big black and trilled with laughter as she slipped in the saddle, her arm grabbing at the Duke's in the process. 'The trail is rather testing, Your Grace. Perhaps I could ride home with you.'

Caroline had heard enough.

'Oh, do not give up on the joy of riding, Lady Jennifer. I did so once when I fell off my pony as a youngster and it took me all of three years to gather the nerve to again mount a horse. No. No. You must let me lend you some assistance, and follow my lead. Would that be all right with you, Thorn?' she added and gave him a beaming and intimate smile. 'I remember when I was a novice all those years ago and you allowed me to ride beside you when I was afraid.'

The use of his Christian name did not go unnoticed. 'You have known each other for a long time, then?' Lady Ross's voice was cold, the edge of displeasure at Caroline's meddling plainly audible.

'Oh, for ever.' The laugh that accompanied the words rang across the glade below them, and when she caught the eye of the Duke of Penborne upon her, she smiled. Broadly. 'When we were younger we made a pact that one day we would marry each other and live happily ever after.'

'Your own marriage, of course, put an end to that.' Thornton's voice held an air of humour.

'Still, I live in hope,' she returned boldly and met his stare.

And in that moment on top of the hill under the sun of a blue, blue Cornish day, something turned inside Caroline's chest. Something real and true and infinitely surprising.

She wanted it all to be true. His regard. His love. The sense of history that only real lovers ever had between them, keeping the world at bay, away, away, caught in each other's eyes and breathless.

Hating the sheer and utter impossibility of her life, she turned. She wanted to love him and she wanted him to love her back, for real, her earlier optimism dimming under the realisation that all this could only ever be a dream. For her.

Jennifer Ross was the sort of woman that he would marry. Connected, moneyed, and with an impeccable background, her parents melding the wealth of the Ross estate with that of Penleven.

Still, she had been asked to create an impression today and she was never one to back down from a promise, so when the others dismounted from their steeds to admire the view she stayed on hers, pleased when the Duke came over to her.

'Can I help you?'

'Indeed you can.'

Placing his hands about her waist, he lifted her down. She felt the full front of his body against hers and even when her feet touched the ground he did not let her go. The beat of his heart was slow and steady and she wondered what he might be making of her own accelerated pulse. Lord, he was a spy after all and damn clever and the heat in her face and neck must be a tell-tale sign of things being not quite as they ought.

Caroline frowned. The art of assuming the next character had always been easy in her life, but here the transition of status was unremittingly difficult.

'I am beginning to believe your ruse, Mrs Weatherby,' he whispered in her ear. 'Keep it up and we will have the Rosses gone in the morning.'

The lightness in his words was just what she needed. Laying one hand on his arm, she made herself stay still, giving the impression, she hoped, of a woman who was vying for more than Jennifer Ross was ever going to get.

'When are you planning to return to London, Mrs Weatherby?'

'I usually stay about a month, Lady Ross, and it was only last week we arrived back in this part of the country. Fortuitous, I thought, to coincide with your own visit, for otherwise I might not have met you at all.'

The weak smile she got in return was the result, Caroline suspected, of a woman who did not forget her manners even in the most trying of circumstances. Certainly, to a mother armed with the possibility of marrying off an eldest daughter to one of the richest Dukes in the land, her presence here must be more than galling.

'And your own family? Do you visit them?'

'Oh, no. My parents both died some years ago and it is just my brother and me left now.'

'And a child. We had word from a servant you have a child.'

Damn. Caroline had hoped to keep Alexander right out of this and she was therefore pleased when Thornton broke in on top of the conversation.

'There.' He pointed in the distance. 'If you look to your right, far in the distance is one of the fastest schooners you will ever see in the Channel. She's the *Sea Witch* and she plies the oceans between London and the Americas.'

Three pairs of eyes followed his finger and Caroline marvelled at the ability of a man who, even under duress, could conjure up a small and unnoticed thing as an excuse to change the subject completely. She supposed it came from his training, this careful observation of everything and anything around him, nothing unexpected or unforeseen. Even now he was turning the little party towards a low-lying peninsula and describing the beauty of the place that he named Lizard Point. And the mention of Alexander was completely forgotten.

They finally reached home a good two hours later and Caroline was exhausted from both the riding and the pretence. All she wanted was to sit on the chair in her room overlooking the sea, with Alex on her lap. She wondered how long it would be before Tosh came back as well, her slight uneasiness at any prolonged absence still very real after Exeter.

But the Duke of Penborne seemed to have other plans and as the Ross family retired to prepare for dinner he asked her to walk with him for just a few moments in the formal gardens at the back of the castle.

Tugging off his patch, he placed it in his pocket. She noticed that when they were alone now he very seldom wore it, preferring instead to squint his left eye if the light was harsh. His jacket, the collar of which was usually raised in company, was also dispensed with.

It pleased her, this lack of defence, and she smiled.

'Thank you for your help today, Caroline. I think Miss Ross may well be thinking any relationship with me a lost cause after your theatrics.'

'Your grandmother, of course, may be sorely disappointed. I think she would welcome the sound of more children in the castle.'

He laughed, but Caroline was not swayed from asking her next question.

'Why did Morag stay so far away from you when your parents died?'

He shrugged his shoulders in a peculiarly vulnerable movement and turned to the window. 'Because it was me who brought the illness of scarlet fever home to Penleven. From Eton. All of my family were dead and I survived. I think Morag knew that if she saw me then she would betray what it was that she felt.'

'Which was?'

'My father was her only child. She wished that it had been me lying dead on the chapel slab and not him.'

Shock and compassion overwhelmed her. 'How old were you?'

'Eight.'

Lord. No wonder he had left England at twenty and not returned for years. No wonder he was distant and solitary and dangerous. Life had taught him not to trust in anything or anyone. She weighed up carefully her reply.

'Alexander is not yet one. If he were to take ill and infect someone you loved and they then passed away, would you hate him?'

He looked surprised at her question. 'No. I would give my own life so that his should be saved.'

'And would have your father not have felt exactly the same?'

'Yes.'

'Well, there's your answer then.'

Running his hand through his hair, he turned towards her. 'I hadn't thought of it in quite that way before.'

'Because you were not a parent before.'

'Am I, Caroline? Am I Alexander's father?'

'You are.'

His fingers tightened around her own. 'My grandmother never stops telling me how like me he is.'

Another thought suddenly struck Caroline. 'Do you and your grandmother often share time at Penleven?'

He shook his head. 'No, we have not been close. In the past few years she has made Plymouth her home.'

'Did you ask her here because of me? Because of how it would look if there was no chaperon?'

'I did.'

Warmth and delight filled her.

'That's the nicest thing anyone has ever done for me in a long while and I thank you for it.' Taking his hand in hers, she raised it to her lips, tracing the edges of his knuckles with her tongue.

It was such a new experience to feel safe with someone else apart from Tosh that she savoured the feeling, Penleven bathed in the soft light of dusk and the flowers wildly prolific behind his shoulders. The noise of footsteps had him pulling away, his hands dropping to his side as he greeted one of the many gardeners, and their intimacy was lost.

* * *

He did not come to her that night either, though Caroline waited for him, the ring of a clock somewhere in the deep recesses of the house finally telling her that the hour was too late. Perhaps he had left the castle to go to Holston or somewhere even further afield. Perhaps there was another woman, like the woman she'd seen him with at the Hilvertons', a less complicated woman, a woman who did not cry when he held her or think of impossible endings to a relationship steeped in inequality.

She could not think this, would not think this. Her fingers pulled through her mass of curls, bed messy and wild, the silken nightgown she had worn tonight clinging to her skin in a taunting way.

He did not come, will not come.

'No.' The single word was strangely comforting and she lay very still, listening to the tree branch against her window and the whispering of servants doing their final evening rounds.

Her former life seemed far away. She wondered if Penleven would have for ever ruined her with its luxury and easiness. Warmth. Food. Safety.

Penleven had a community of people whom she was beginning to care for and like, and her brother was looking happier than he had done in years.

She stretched, the silk sheets just another luxury. Tomorrow she would get her painting satchel out again and start to draw, a tableau of the castle and its inhabitants. And a memory of everything when she left.

Thornton heard the sound of laughing coming from the kitchen the next afternoon as he returned from a ride around the estate.

Usually the castle was a bustling place as servants got on with their cleaning and duties, but today Penleven was strangely empty, Henry missing from his station at the front door and James from the study where he usually waited to greet him after a ride.

He stopped and frowned as the sound of his housekeeper's voice boomed in delight. What on earth was happening? With determination he strode towards the kitchen and swung open the door.

James and Henry stood next to each other, sheaths of wheat artfully threaded through the lapels of their jackets and Caroline St Clair in front of them with her hair jammed beneath a lad's hat to stop the curls from falling into her eyes. A canvas set up before her was filled with rough outlines of almost everybody in that kitchen, the housekeeper in an apron, the small maid Polly holding a basket of lemons, two other serving girls behind her and the almost completed silhouettes of Henry and James prominently in the foreground. Marvelling at how she had with just a few lines caught the essence of everybody, Thornton saw Alexander in his cradle, the kitchen cat curled in the empty space on the floor beside him.

Penleven was being changed in front of his eyes, its quiet efficiency undermined by an onslaught of laughter and art and for the very first time since he had limped home from Europe he felt…out of place here. Too serious. Old, even.

Caroline looked up. 'Would you like to be in the picture, Your Grace?' she asked, a hint of amusement taking the sting out of the formal use of his name. 'This is just the drawing, but I plan to make it into a larger canvas and bequeath it to you all here at Penleven when I leave.'

'Leave? Indeed, Mrs Weatherby, without your presence here everybody might still be busy doing the jobs that I am paying them all for.' His impatience was belittling, but, with the fervour of a person who knew that they fought a losing battle, he kept going. 'My horse is outside, Henry, waiting to be brushed down. Get the stable lad on to it.'

'Of course, Your Grace.' Both twins hurried past him, but not before taking a quick look at the likenesses of themselves in Caroline's picture.

The other staff returned to their duties and even the cat woke up, removing itself from the warm softness beside Alexander's cot.

Caroline just looked at him, her charcoal still poised. 'I seem to have lost my models. Will you pose for me?' He had to smile at the sheer temerity of her question before shaking his head.

'I am still waiting for my portrait of Alexander.'

He mentioned nothing about the one that he wanted of her and saw the hurt in her face when she registered the fact.

Today he could not be kind. He had missed her these last nights, missed her warmth and her smiles and the particular way she had of holding on to him when she fell asleep after making love, her fingers entwined about his as if by their very grasp she might keep him there with her until the morning.

Tired of his poor humour, he turned away and walked out into the gardens, annoyed at seeing the Rosses already there, enjoying the sunshine. The Earl disengaged himself from the family party and came his way.

'If this is a good time, I would like to have a word with you.'

Thornton's heart sank because, in the face of the man opposite, he saw the beginnings of a conversation that he did not want at all. A discussion on the varying merits of his daughter.

Shepherding the Earl into the formal garden, he was relieved to see that his wife and children were only a little further off in the distance enjoying the fountain in one corner of the display. Perhaps he could make this relatively quick after all.

'Jennifer is coming up to a marriageable age and she seems to have a *tendre* for you, Your Grace.'

'*Tendre?*' Even the word was ridiculous.

'Feelings. She has feelings for you that she finds quite strong. As her father I thought it only right to approach you to see whether there would be any way in which you could reciprocate these feelings.'

Thornton was pleased by the question as it gave him such an easy out. 'I am afraid my feelings are placed elsewhere, sir.'

'I see.'

Donald Ross looked crestfallen and disgruntled, a dangerous combination in a man with a daughter who was spoilt rotten.

'I suppose it is Mrs Weatherby who holds your affections?' His tone implied it would be easier giving Jennifer the bad news were he to be more specific than vague.

'Indeed it is, though I had not thought myself so transparent.'

'Not you, sir,' he replied quickly. 'Her. My wife has the knack of seeing a woman in love and she tells me Caroline Weatherby certainly shows all the signs.' He carried on as Thornton frowned. 'And a damn fine-looking woman she is, I have to say.'

Distracted, he nodded and greeted the Ross family as they joined him.

A woman in love?

Lord. Could that be possible?

Jennifer Ross looked at her father hopefully and when he shook his head she burst into noisy tears and ran in the opposite direction. Her mother trailed her with the nursemaids behind, the other children hanging on to their skirts. When Ross shrugged his shoulders, Thornton felt a strange sense of empathy for him. He was a father, after all, who was only trying to do his best.

Would he not be the same should he have a daughter? The very thought made him bid Ross goodbye and head for the house. He needed to apologise to Caroline for his boorish behaviour in the kitchen not half an hour earlier.

She was in her room painting, though when she saw him she quickly covered the canvas.

Alexander watched her from his place on the bed, the cat from the kitchen cuddled down by his feet.

'You do not wish me to see it?'

'It isn't finished. I never show unfinished works to anyone.' She barely looked at him.

'What of the picture in the kitchen.'

'That was only a drawing. A quick drawing.' With care she put her paintbrush down on a palette. Still looking away, the blonde in her hair caught the light of the sun, the indent of deep dimples in her cheek. *A damn fine-looking woman.* Ross's words came back to him as he sat down on the bed next to his son.

'The Ross family will be leaving in the morning. I have just had an interesting conversation with Donald Ross.'

'You have?'

'He seems to think that his wife has extraordinary powers.'

A frown marred her brow as she turned towards him, obviously interested.

'He says that she is able to distinguish a woman in love.'

'Her daughter?'

'You.'

Anger darkened her eyes and brightened her face. 'I have never heard of such a gift.'

'Is she right?'

'I am a mistress, Your Grace. One who will go to "a cottage in the village" when you tire of me. I have not the luxury of falling in love.'

'So she is wrong?'

She looked him straight in the eyes and answered, 'She is wrong.'

When he left, Caroline merely turned back to her canvas, removing the cover hiding the painted amber eyes of Thornton Lindsay.

'Damn you,' she whispered beneath her breath, smiling to reassure Alex as he looked up at the sound. 'And damn the stupid and interfering Margaret Ross for imagining herself a seer in the art of love.'

With care she added the last touches to the portrait, shadowing the background to illuminate the face and dabbing at the canvas in an attempt to create the illusion of depth. The earthy tones of the painting were exactly right for capturing Thornton Lindsay's dark golden eyes, and the muted light cast from the window behind him seemed to accentuate the roughness on his cheek.

One finger reached out and traced the lines that crossed the left side of his face. Today in the kitchen she had felt anger within him. And isolation. He did it to himself, this way he had of standing aside from people, of keeping up his guard, of being the lord of a place even in a sunny kitchen that had smelled of pies and oranges.

Thornton Lindsay. Thorn. Even his name was prickly.

And yet when he turned away she had also felt a certain hesitation, even longing.

Sighing, she massaged the tightness at her temples.

What had Margaret Ross seen? Crossing to the mirror, she searched her face.

Anguish lingered in the depths of her eyes. A woman who would never be a wife. A mistress who had been a virgin.

And one of the few people in the world who knew exactly what had happened to Lillyanna de Gennes.

Adele Halstead had been standing at her back and the girl before her, Tosh further away beside another group of unknown Frenchmen.

'If you go down that hill you will die, Lilly. You are French and your parents would be looking down from the hereafter with pain in their eyes in the knowing that Thornton Lindsay has consigned hundreds of good

*French folk to their deaths. Why do you not under-
stand that?'*

*Hatred of anything British was easily heard in her
voice and Caroline watched as the trajectory of her gun
had lowered to the vivid scarlet red of the British soldier's back one hundred yards from them.*

Thorn. Walking without a limp.

*She had not known him then. Had not understood
the anguish in Lillyanna's voice or her quick decision
to run to him, placing her body in the line of fire. Protecting. Shielding.*

*Adele had sworn soundly and in the eyes of her
mother's friend Caroline had seen something…wrong.
Something dreadful. Some awful knowledge of what
was going to happen before it did.*

'Come back, damn you, Lilly. Come back.'

*The girl did not turn once, her long blue skirt bil-
lowing in a freshening wind before she entered the
church where the other English soldiers sheltered.*

*One minute and then two. Even the birds seemed to
stop singing and listen as the rolling clouds hid the sun
and the world exploded.*

*Horses. The sound of cannon fire. Screaming. They
had run, she and Tosh, whilst the air uncoiled around
them, run for the shelter of the forest where it was still
possible to hide, stopping finally under an oak tree, the
harsh and ragged wheeze of their breath the only
sound filling the moss filled glade.*

'She threw her life away,' Tosh had said finally.

'For him.' Caroline had returned and saw firsthand the power of a love that was prepared to sacrifice everything.

'Everything,' she said quietly to the woman reflected in the Penborne mirror five long years later. And knew, had she been in Lilly's shoes, that she would have done exactly the same to save him!

Thornton hit the bottle in the library and drank more than he had in a long, long time, the gathering hours of wayward thought settling on the one thing in his life that he knew was good.

Caroline.

She did not love him. She had said so to his face. Donald Ross had been wrong.

Upending the glass of brandy, he liked the feel of forgetfulness as it ran down his throat, melding the ghosts of the past into faceless nothings, the fierce strength of their presence softer in the amber glow of brandy. Diluted into calm.

Quiet.

Only shadows of what had been.

Carefully he pushed up out of his chair, hand against the wall to steady balance as he walked to the window.

Night, almost.

Another night.

And then another one.

And all he wanted was Caroline St Clair with him,

around him, next to him, warm against his back and protecting against the nightmares that had him up after midnight pacing the floor.

The explosion as Lilly had kissed him, her body full against his own and waiting. No warning except the rapid beat of her heart and a certain knowledge he could remember in her grey-green eyes. Not quite honest. Hiding fear. Anger made him shake, the sweat on his forehead beading in a familiar tremor and, cocking his head, he breathed in and out, willing away panic.

Memories of another time hovered on the edge of his awareness, a long ago time when he was young and happy and Penborne had held the easy echo of joy. Before Eton. Before Europe. Before his skin had been shredded by the shrapnel of molten lead.

And Caroline. A light amongst the darkness, a flame in the ashes of what his life had become. Protecting him, from everyone.

He placed the bottle that he held on the table. Melancholy was a shady drinking companion and today he could barely stand himself sober, let alone stone-damn-bitter drunk.

Caroline had been painting. He tried to remember the glimpse of canvas that he had seen before she had covered it up. Another secret.

He was not even surprised.

'Lady of secrets,' he whispered and liked the sound

of it, shades of Lancelot and the court of Arthur and the haunting beauty of Guinevere. Could she ever love him?

Damaged beyond repair. His face. His heart. His trust. His honour. And only Caroline could mend him.

She had to love him, because if she didn't he would be lost. Adrift. Irrecoverable.

She heard the door handle turn, slowly, carefully and the curse that followed the noise of the hinge.

Thornton.

He was here, in her room, leaning against the portal and finding his bearings, swaying drunk.

She could smell the brandy even from this distance, and see the tremor in his hands as he lifted them to the candle still burning bright on the mantelpiece.

His portrait lay covered and she knew the exact moment that he lifted the canvas, for his breath was drawn in.

'Why are you here?' Whispered.

'To…apologise.'

'For…?'

'Everything.'

She could only smile. 'Everything is a lot to apologise for.'

He came closer and sat down on the bed, bringing one finger to his lips as Alexander stirred.

'Shhhh…'

He placed the candle on the table, watching it for a

moment as it wavered and then caught again, strong in the breathless silence of night. Not careless of fire and flame. An ingrained learning.

His eyes turned to her own, intense and measured, his teeth white against the darkness as he spoke.

'I wanted…the Ross woman's…words to be true.' Slurred in a voice not quite his own. Given in confidence, quietly.

Hunger flared and caught. The unevenness of his skin in relief against the candle-glow, shadows of pain thrown into ridged cold grey.

'There are things that I have done…bad things… that you could not like and England needed done. But with you…I feel whole…good…and when she said it, the Ross woman…when she said the words, I wondered…hoped…' Question ripped uncertainty wide open on his face and in the depths of his eyes was just a little piece of the agony of war.

His war.

He had been positioned between armies and intelligence, balancing the local needs of one kingdom in danger of invasion against another whose Emperor ran rampant across all of Europe.

She sensed that he did not quite know what it was he was saying and so she chanced it. Chanced the words that he might not remember come the morning, but needed now.

'I love you.'

Simple.

Joy. His laughter broken as his mouth came down, nothing held back in the lips that slanted across her own. Seeking.

'Love me, sweetheart.'

'I do.'

She made no quiet response, no gentle ladylike carefulness. Opening her mouth, she revelled in the feeling of his tongue against her own, close, close and closer, his fingers threading through her hair, twisting her hard against him, breath erratic in the force of passion. Time stopped.

Still.

Suspended between a languid intense stab of wonder, her whole body vibrated against the connection of her soul against his.

Their first kiss!

Wildness released her from restraint. More. She wanted more, no longer careful but barbaric, frenzied, free. In the violence of their need for each other, the glass of water on the table knocked to the floor, breaking into a hundred shards, sharp and glistening, like her heart, never to be put back together, but scattered and dispersed by a feeling she had no sway over. And still he took her, hard, hard pressed as if he might never let her go.

Pain and ecstasy, close, entwined. The feel of his tongue against her own and the harsher nip of teeth.

She bit him back and he swore. Fighting. Truth. The sharp pain of love unravelling everything.

'Lord,' he said when they finally drew apart and the world slid back into a recognisable shape.

'Lord,' he repeated as he slumped down on the bed, his eyes glazed in wonderment as the sleep that tore at equilibrium claimed him, slaked by confession, hope, relief. And brandy.

He awoke with a headache that would have made mockery of any hangover cure. And he awoke in his own bed, the blankets pulled about him and his shoes removed.

Even the curtains had been drawn.

James? Henry? No. The recollection of Caroline was distinct. And a painting. Of him? Honest. Open. Not quite him.

Moving his head, he groaned, placing his neck against the pillow and gradually regathering his balance.

He'd been in the library amongst the memories of Europe and the brandy that made it all distant.

Hadn't he?

A candle. Dancing against the gilt bright of blonde hair.

I love you.

She'd said it. He was sure.

Had he said it back to her?

Lies, deception and guile were the touchstones of his life so far. And suddenly he just wanted it all to stop.

I love you.

No trace of deceit in that.

None either in her dark blue eyes as he had tipped up her face to his.

'God, help me,' he prayed for the first time in a long time, the spirit of the celestial infinitely reassuring, reminding him that he was not alone.

When Henry came in with a glass of something he had concocted to help a headache, Thornton took it gladly.

'Where is Mrs Weatherby this morning?'

'She was just here with her son, asking after you.'

'My son,' he corrected and saw the flare of interest in the eyes of his butler.

'And the Rosses left just after dawn. There is a letter of thanks on your desk, Your Grace.' He crossed to the window to pull the curtains.

Thornton smiled. The Rosses gone, his headache going and the lingering sound of Caroline St Clair's voice on his mind.

I love you.

'Could you find Mrs Weatherby and ask her to come and see me.'

'Here, sir?'

'Here, Henry.'

* * *

She came ten minutes later. And alone.

'I hope your head is not too sore this morning.' There was a tone in her voice that was foreign, shy, and a wave of protectiveness engulfed him, throwing him off balance. On the right sleeve of her blue gown was a dab of rich red paint. Jarring memory.

'You made a picture of me.'

'It is not quite finished…'

'I liked it.'

She smiled then and the sunshine that had been hidden behind cloud all morning broke through, illuminating her hair blonde gold. Like an angel. His angel.

For the first time in her company he felt…nervous? Like a young boy in the attendance of a girl.

'I remembered other things too.'

She looked up, but did not speak, and he faltered. Unsure. 'I broke something.'

'A glass. It is of no importance.'

'And if I said anything at all that was offensive, then I am sorry.'

'You did not.'

'I was a paragon?'

'Of restraint.'

Both of them began to smile. A shared joy. Another first. Laughing with a woman in his bedroom on a bright morning, the promise of anything possible.

He saw how the fingers on her right hand kept fingering the gold bracelet on her left.

'Thomas gave you that, didn't he?'

She nodded. 'When I was twelve, and we had returned to Paris. I had been ill, you see, and he had been worried.'

'How ill?'

He was surprised when she paled.

'It was not Eloise's fault, you understand, or Thomas's.'

'How ill?'

'I got shot.'

'The scar near your left hip?'

'It was an accident. We were hungry.'

'Hungry?' Now he had lost her again.

'We lived in a cottage for six months on the north coast whilst Eloise journeyed west.'

'With her lover?'

She did not answer that question, but in her eyes Thorn could glean the truth. 'As children we had little idea of money and what she had left us was spent. Thomas shot a rabbit and I was cleaning the gun when it went off.'

'Who else was with you?'

She looked him straight in the eye and the fear he saw there nearly broke his heart.

'No one.'

Lord. The thought of it had him sitting up, the sunshine gone from his day. 'How long were you ill for?'

'A long time.'

Two children left on their own to survive. The bracelet a gift of the fact that they had.

Still were. Together. He thanked Thomas St Clair beneath his breath and resolved to have a talk with him that very evening. With care he reached out and took her hand, all form of teasing about last night gone.

'I will protect you,' he said and meant it. Not linked with lust or need or want. Her short nails made him smile. And he smiled again as her fingers curled in around his own.

'Where was Alex born?'

Suddenly he wanted to know everything about her. About them.

'At Hilverton. Thomas helped and the Campton midwife.'

'I wish I had been there.' His words surprised him.

'You were in spirit, Thorn. I kept on screaming your name.'

'Hating me?' There was amusement in his tone.

'Until Alexander was born. After that I could only ever thank you.'

Thank. Not love.

He was astonished as to the depth of his need to hear the words she had said last night.

I love you.

To his face when he was not drunk. For him to answer. Now.

'Who brought me back to my room?'

'Me.'

'Alone?'

'You took directions well.'

'And you tucked me in? I am sorry for the need—I don't usually drink as much.'

'You have given me protection, Thorn. Sometimes it is good for one's soul to reciprocate the offer.'

'Protection,' he murmured, leaning against the cushions at the back of his bed, a new resolution forming.

'I was engaged to be married once. Did you know that?' He frowned at the way quiet anger was oddly juxtaposed against his need to tell her. All of it. His life that had been, and still was, secrets stored in the deep places of regret, secrets that had eaten at him for too many years.

When she did not answer he carried on. 'I thought I knew Lilly. I thought that I knew who she was until she followed me into a church in Orthez and blew us all up.'

Caroline blanched. Paper white. Her bottom lip shaking in fright.

'I am sorry if this distresses you.'

She shook her head and in her eyes there was suddenly something that made him stop. Cognisance. Knowledge. No mellow sorry this, but complicity. His mind began to reel with theories. Oh, Lord, that she should betray him, too. He felt sweat prickle beneath the light cotton of the sheets and a hollow ache of sorrow.

'She did it because she loved you.' Caroline said the words quietly.

'Pardon?'

'Tosh and I were there with Adele Halstead. She had a gun on your back and I think she would have shot you if Lillyanna had not walked towards you in the line of its fire. I don't think she had any idea about what would happen either, for from where we sat we could not see the horses with the cannons.'

'You were there?'

She held up her hands against his fury. 'It is not as you think it was. Adele said that she would take us back with her to England when we came across her outside Orthez. Our mother had died, you see, and the offer was…enticing. An easy travel in a wealthy woman's carriage or a dangerous trek alone across the mountains into Spain. We were just in the wrong place at the wrong time, two seventeen-year-olds wrapped in the fabric of revenge and intelligence unknowingly, and when we did understand what was happening, we ran.'

'Lord. You are telling me…'

'I think that Lillyanna was set up. I don't think she knew anything at all about Adele Halstead's true plans, but she loved you enough to risk her life. And lose.'

Thornton brought one hand across his eyes, shading utter hurt and relief. He was glad for the fact that she kept on talking.

'If I were to have a guess, I would say that Lillyanna

was expendable. Adele Halstead did shout out to her to stop, but she just kept on going towards you.'

The clock in the room marked the passing of silence. One moment and then two.

'Thank you for telling me this.'

Caroline nodded her head. Thorn's voice held an edge of tiredness and exhaustion. A bottled-up ache. An old wound. With the legacy of the brandy and the new knowledge of Lillyanna's sacrifice, he probably needed some time and space to assimilate the truth.

Not betrayal.

Only love.

'In the bureau behind you, in the third drawer down, there is a picture wrapped in green velvet. Could you possibly get it for me?'

Crossing the room, she did as he bid, resisting the urge to unwrap the material from the image as she handed it to him.

'Is this what you are after?'

He held it for a moment as if taking a breath, as if finding the courage for what he was about to do next.

'I just wanted to be certain...' he began '...certain that it was Lillyanna that you saw.'

The fabric fell away from the face of a woman he had once loved.

Caroline nodded. 'It was her.'

'I am glad that it is so.'

'You had the portrait commissioned.'

'No. Her brother left it for me after she was killed. Sometimes it has been a curse.'

'Because you cannot move on…?' She knew too well about the ties that the dead wrapped around one.

'Not that,' he returned quickly. 'Just that there were always questions, uncertainties about what had happened at the church. About betrayal.'

'And now they are answered?'

He smiled.

'And now they are answered.'

Chapter Fourteen

Thornton was standing by the window looking across at the evening sea when Thomas knocked on the door of his library.

'Your servant said you needed to see me, sir.'

'I think you and I need to talk.' Caroline's brother's eyes were guarded, his position on the edge of the sofa neither relaxed nor still as his fingers drummed, exposing nervousness. At that moment Thorn felt immeasurably older than the young man opposite as he took breath and paced before him.

'I would like to ask you for your sister's hand in marriage.'

The spluttering told him Thomas St Clair was clearly astonished by the words.

'You have asked Caro already?'

'No. Good manners insist that I talk to you first.'

Thornton hesitated before continuing, mulling over the nickname that had been used. 'As her only relative I thought it was right that you should know of my intentions.'

'Caroline is in no position to marry you—the St Clair name was sullied by my mother when she ran away with—'

'What else?' He dismissed the argument with barely a thought.

'Our days in London would be remembered and you would be the subject of much gossip.'

'I have been that for all my years now, and it has never concerned me before. Besides, your disguises would protect you from memory. Even I could barely recognise Caroline without the red wig.'

'And as the Weatherby widow?'

'I am certain that we could live with that. Pious. Moral. Virtuous. Until she met me and threw it all away. What person in the world would not forgive her that were I to marry her?'

Silence greeted his statement and Thornton turned to the window and tried to catch his breath. He was suddenly aware that there was more and he did not want to know it, did not want knowledge and fact to distort what he felt now, ruining the memory of their kiss, or of her kindness.

It was Caroline whom he needed to hear this secret from. Not her brother. He wanted to see her eyes as she said it and understand her part in whatever had transpired.

'If your sister would like to talk with me, I will be here for the next few hours. I also give you leave to discuss the topic that I have raised.'

'Very well.' Thomas held out his hand, grasping Thornton's own in a surprisingly strong grip. 'If I could have chosen a brother-in-law, it would have been you.' Sincerity shone from his face, but at the edge of that was guilt. *If I could have...* Past. Finished. When he got up to leave, Thorn did not try to stop him.

Caroline walked across the hills as fast and as far as she could, the wind splaying her hair and the tears spilling down her face.

He wanted to marry her.

He wanted to protect her.

And he had waited for her in the library as she had cowered in bed, not even trusting herself to get out of it lest she just kept walking into his arms.

And killed Thomas in the process.

So she had stayed away and locked her door. And late into the night when the candle had burned away to nothing he had knocked. Twice.

And then left.

Her heart thumped in her chest and her throat, the landscape blurred and empty. The cliffs she now marched along were endless, chalky soil, crumbling down into nothing but sea. Endless ocean and endless sky. Catching the hem of her skirt with the heel of her boot, she turned to a slight sound on the air.

A whistle of wind. She felt something close and strange before the world turned over. And her last thought before she fell was of Thornton Lindsay's proposal.

'Where the hell is your sister?' Thornton demanded of Thomas as he stormed into the room. 'She has been gone since this morning and Alexander is fretful.'

Thomas came to his feet. 'She didn't return for lunch?' Consternation laced his question.

'No one has seen her since she went out for a walk after breakfast and it is now almost three o'clock.'

'And last night? Did you speak about things last night, Your Grace?'

'No.' A single clipped word and silence

'She would never stay away from Alexander this long unless…'

'Unless?'

'Something was wrong.'

'Lord.' Thornton had the bell in his hand and was ringing it even as he strode from the room. More servants joined him as he stormed through the house, stopping only when he reached the front lobby. His cousin Leonard had also arrived unexpectedly that morning from London and had been the first to offer up his help, and his presence here was welcomed. Another body to help in the search for Caroline, and one who knew well the layout of the house and its lands.

'Mrs Weatherby is missing, Leonard. She has not been seen since this morning around eleven o'clock and it is unlike her to be away so long.'

'Could she have gone into the village?'

Thornton looked back at Thomas, who shook his head. 'No. But I will send a servant to make certain.'

He took the middle of the floor and began to speak loudly to all who were gathered.

'Everyone else can leave their duties and follow me. I will assign you places to look. If she has fallen…?' He made himself stop. 'When you find her, send someone back here.'

Within ten minutes the room was emptied. Only his grandmother sat on the sofa, her ancient crepe-lined hands wringing back and forth against a wet handkerchief.

'She did not go into the village, Thorn. She was upset—' she began and took a breath to begin again. 'Upset when she left, for I caught her in the corridor. Just a short walk, she said, to clear her head, but her eyes were red and I could see she had been crying.'

'Did you see which way she went?'

'No, because I went into Alexander directly after speaking with her.'

'Then you saw what she was wearing?'

'Her red cloak with a dark blue velvet dress.'

Red. A colour easily seen from a distance or from the top of one of the high cliffs that bordered Penleven. Thornton made himself stop. She was missing, but she could be anywhere. Asleep in the library, perhaps, or in the gardens. As he strode through the front door, a steadily pouring rain changed his mind.

The barn, then, or the covered gazebo? Or the small cottage overlooking the sea. All these places would be searched. And he would find her!

'I could look in the fields behind here.' Leonard walked beside him, a building sweat on his brow and a glazed emptiness in his eyes. Lord, was he truly ill? Thornton could see his cousin wanted to tell him something, but he had no time for the problem as he ran to saddle his horse.

Cantering along the line of the cliff above Lizard Point, Thornton searched the deep fissures of land carved into rock. And saw nothing.

Dismounting, he tethered his horse before climbing down on to a ledge below the grass level.

'Caroline.' His voice was taken with the wind and returned to him as an echo. 'Caroline.' Loud. Futile. Hollow.

Climbing down further, he inched between the narrow ledges and called again. Still nothing. Thomas's voice sounded in the distance further down the coast.

And away to his left up by the line of trees that led to the high fields more people ran.

Looking. Looking.

I love you.

'God, please help me find her.' His words, soft against the harsher panic.

He wanted to shout it like he was shouting her name, just in case…

In case what?

He shook his head and made himself think. He was a man who had tracked the enemy from Paris to Madrid and had seldom missed his target. He had been looking for Caroline foolishly, with his heart.

Now he needed to begin to use his head.

It was well after dark when he returned, the moon barely visible and the rain setting in.

Candles blazed at every window. Like a beacon he thought. Like a lighthouse. *Here I am. Come home.*

Thomas met him even before he had halted his steed.

'Any sign?'

'No.'

The look on her brother's face was the same as he knew would be on his own and he turned away so his heart did not beat quite so loud and so the tightness in his throat should again allow him breath.

'I will find her, Thomas. I promise you.'

Morag stood at the head of the stairs with his child

and, shrugging off his wet jacket, he took the steps two at a time.

Alexander. In his arms. Close. Closer. The smell of baby and mother and hope all wrapped into one and the wet warmth of recent tears staining his shirtfront.

His child.

Their child.

Needing both mother and father. And afraid.

When he felt his grandmother's arm around his shoulders, he closed his eyes and prayed.

He didn't sleep. He lay with Alexander cuddled in against him and listened to the weather. Rain and wind and cold. And Caroline out there. Somewhere. Hurt.

It was three o'clock and only two hours before the dawn, two hours before he could begin his search again. The tiny fingers of his son closed around his own, and when he looked down, wide-open eyes watched him back, a tremulous smile wreathing his face.

'I will bring her home today.'

And he would. He promised himself even as he refused to give any credence at all to the niggling doubt of it.

Wet. Her face and arms and dress were all soaking wet. Caroline tried to stop the shaking and roll up on to her knees, but nothing seemed to be working and the darkness all around her was complete.

Drifting. Blurred. Pain. She let her head fall back and then she knew nothing.

Thornton's hands were bloodied as he scrambled up the cliff from the rocks. He had waded around from the beach and the barnacles had scratched him badly although the pain was hardly felt because he had caught a movement further up the cliff. Red cloth fluttering on the brambles.

She was here somewhere. He knew it. His heart pitched a huge jolt of relief when he saw only the ledges of rocks far below. No broken body. No trace of clothes or hair or blood.

'Caroline.' His voice wavered on the wind and he tried again. And again.

No response.

Climbing higher, he hauled himself up on to a narrow ledge, a few stray tussocks growing in the crack of rock and puddles of water in a fissure at the back. And then he saw her crumpled against the cliff not twenty yards from where he stood.

He could not even shout out as fear congealed words and robbed him of breath. Crawling across, he clung to the ledge, trying to find a foothold in the narrow space. Then he was there, beside her. As he lifted her into his arms she groaned, still alive at least. Tapping her cheek, he was relieved by her effort to sit up, the first movement he had seen her make.

'Easy,' he whispered, as a shower of small rubble was kicked up by her feet and flung through the air to crash fifty feet below on to jagged rocks. His hands searched Caroline's arms and legs and body for injury, finding the stickiness of blood pooling behind her left ear and running down her back. Lifting away her hair, pink from rain and blood, he cursed as he saw the scour line of a bullet where it had grazed her scalp. Another quarter of an inch…! He would not think of it.

The nearness of the escape winded him as he wrapped his arms tightly about her and held her, infusing his warmth into her coldness in an effort to stop the shaking.

'Caroline?' he tried again, swallowing as he willed her strength. 'Caroline. Can you hear me?'

She opened her eyes, the whites scrawled with redness. 'My head hurts.' Her fingers curled around his and she held on tight. 'And I fell. There was a sound… like a whip?'

'Can you sit up?' He did not want to scare her, so said nothing about the bullet. He needed to get her off the ledge and home and already the dark clouds forming above them threatened more rain.

'I think so.' She winced as he helped her and held both her hands to the side of her head. 'It hurts.'

'I know.'

'Where is Alexander?'

'With Morag at Penborne.'

'And Tosh?'

'Looking for you. Everyone is looking for you.'

'But I knew you would find me. I knew it would be you who would come…' Large tears welled and fell down her face, relief and shock mixed together and she saw the blood from her head on shaking fingers. 'If I don't survive…' She stopped and swallowed.

'You are not dying, Caroline.'

'I'm not?' She wiped her damp tears with her jacket sleeve and sniffed. Loudly. And explored her scalp further.

'It's only a scratch.'

His anger heartened her. 'You call this a scratch?' Now that she was sitting up, she had her skirts raised as she searched for other injuries, turning her legs this way and that to make certain that everything moved. When she was reassured that nothing seemed wrong, her hand returned to her face.

'What of this?' Her first finger ran over a sizeable lump on her forehead. 'Do my eyes look normal?' Widening her eyes and turning towards the light at an angle, she looked to him for reassurance.

Without meaning to Thornton began to laugh, the tension of the last twenty-four hours suddenly taking its toll.

'Damn it, Caroline. You never ever do what I expect you to.'

She was still.

'I saw a man once in Paris with a bump just like this fall right over and just stop breathing and another time—'

'Enough.' He pulled her hand away just as the clouds burst and a deluge poured down across them. Removing his jacket, Thornton slung it across her shoulders, helping her to thread her arms through the sleeves and buttoning up the front when she had done so.

'We need to get down from here,' he shouted across the noise of rain, pointing upwards to where a large section of soil seemed to be peeling off from the bank, threatening to fall across them and knock them off their tenuous perch.

She nodded, her already pale face whitening further as she stood. Thornton kept a firm hold on her arm as she took a few deep breaths and tried to calm her panic.

Bringing her behind his back, he instructed her to place her arms around his neck.

'Don't let go whatever happens.'

'I won't.'

'Good.'

He took one step out into space and heard a strangled scream of fear.

Caroline clutched Thornton tighter. If they died, at least it would be together, here, on the rocks beside the sea at Penleven. She felt his heartbeat loud against her fingers, no quiet even pulse either, but a hammering hard quickness, belying his calm exterior and his easy reassurance.

She could barely believe that he would be able to find a track down from this impossible position. But he seemed to, inch by inch. Foot by foot. The muscles on his arms bulged against resistance and the corded veins in his neck were a raised black blue.

'Nearly there,' he said softly as he rested for a second, laying his forehead against rock and taking deep breaths.

'I could try to walk by myself—'

'No.' The word was barked sharp and she did not argue. Besides, looking at the descent he was taking, she knew she had no hope of managing it herself.

A bunch of brambles here. A rock that became a handhold there. Sheer guts and brute strength and a belief in himself that she found beguiling. When a trunk of old tree crumbled beneath his grip, she heard him curse and waited for the fall, but he clutched on to a thorny shrub nearby, the blood from prickles running down his hands and across the rolled-up sleeves of his shirt.

And then they were down, the last steps to the pancake rocks below, easy in their execution.

Tears welled in her eyes as she clung to him, true shock now setting in given their relative safety.

He had saved her.

He had risked his own life to save hers.

She smelled the sea and freedom. And love.

In his actions.

In his body.

It was in the strength and largeness of him, in the valour and bravery and fearless challenge of what he had done. No words yet, but something more.

Love.

Translucent in the pale light of morning, hanging on the edge of death and shimmering wordless in the very act of sacrifice.

When his lips came down across her own, she leaned in and the world around them simply disappeared.

Chapter Fifteen

Caroline woke up the next morning and stretched. Everything ached. Her neck, her head, her legs—even the tips of her fingers where she had dug them into the soil to make certain in the night that she would not slip off the ledge into nothingness.

Thornton had not stayed with her, for the drink that the housekeeper had plied her with on her return had contained some sort of sleeping potion and this morning she felt a strange sense of disquiet. He had seemed angry with her. For slipping across the embankment, perhaps, and putting them in danger? She wished he would come and see her, for the clock on the mantel gave the time as well past eleven.

It was almost twelve when the door opened and he appeared, carrying flowers from the gardens at Penleven.

'My grandmother thought you would like these,' he said as he laid down the vase on her bedside table. 'She picked them with Alex this morning and sends her love.'

'And Thomas. Where is he?' Suddenly she felt the same dread that she had after his disappearance in Exeter.

There was a second of silence.

'He left for Plymouth this morning.'

'What?' Sitting up, she pushed the bed covers from her legs, her whole world skewered into fear. 'Why? Why has he gone there?'

'He said something of a man he needed to see. I did offer him a coach and driver, but he was adamant in his refusal. He took a horse from the stables and left after dawn.'

Panic claimed her. Lord. She suddenly knew why he had gone. Thomas thought that the de Lerins had something to do with her fall, that was why.

A fall? Her fingers went to the space behind her ear. 'I didn't just fall, did I?'

'No. You were shot at.'

'And Tosh knows this?

'He does.'

Everything fell into place. His anger. His disappearance. Her brother was going to France to find the de Lerins and give himself up so that something like this would never happen again. He was going to make certain that she was protected. She knew it to the marrow of her bones.

Her heart raced. Could she ask Thornton Lindsay for assistance? He was a man with contacts and skill and the father of her child. Would the connection between them be enough to make him break the law entirely and help?

And then what?

Face the de Lerins virtually alone? She knew how honourable he was. If Tosh was to be incarcerated for the killing of a man with no principles, she was certain Thorn might well take the whole affair in his own hands and do away with those left who still threatened them.

Horror consumed her. *Don't give him the chance to do so,* a small voice churned inside. *He has already given more than anyone should be asked for his country and for his King. Make him stay. Make him safe. For Alexander's sake and for mine.*

Utter calm claimed her and she sat down, lying back and placing her hand upon her forehead.

'I feel ill…' she just managed, trying to make her voice shake and her tone plaintive.

'I'll fetch the doctor?'

'No. It's just that I can't help remembering…everything…the fall…' Closing her eyes to shut out probing amber eyes, she groaned. 'Perhaps if I slept I'll feel stronger…' The warmth of his fingers scored the back of her hand. A last touch? A final goodbye that he did not know he was making? She resisted the urge to turn her palm over and hold on as a lump formed in the back of her throat.

'I shall return in an hour or so and see how you fare. Is there anything at all that I could get you?'

'Just…need…to sleep.'

As soon as Thornton withdrew from the room she stood, pleased that the woman who had been sitting with her did not return. Alone. At least for the time it would take to escape from Penleven and follow her brother.

Thorn found the letter pinned to Alexander's cot less than three hours later.

> Please can you look after Alex, Thorn. He likes to be cuddled in the morning and sung to at night, and when he goes to sleep he needs his red woollen blanket next to him.
>
> Don't follow me.
>
> With love. Caroline.

His howl of anger brought his grandmother into the room and, when she had finished reading the note, her voice was steady.

'You will need to fetch them both back, Thornton, for we cannot do without them. I made a mistake in not coming to you all those years ago because my heart was broken. Don't you make the same one with Caroline.'

'You will stay here, then?'

'For as long as you need me. I am sure that Leonard would be glad to stay as company.'

He liked the feel of her hand on his arm. Family. It always came back simply to that.

Grandmother to grandson. Father to son.

And Caroline. If he lost her, he knew that nothing would ever be right again.

Plymouth was bustling with people and he scoured the streets and taverns for the only two that he wanted.

They had to be here somewhere—the first ship to France was not departing till the morning tide and there had been no sailing at all across the Channel since the very early hours.

Where would they have gone? He kept his eyes peeled for a white filly and her sable sister, both steeds missing from Penleven. Eight o'clock now. He had been here since six and the churning worry of not being able to find them in time was growing. Had Thomas lied about his point of departure? Were they in some other port town, finding a way across the Channel? His mind skipped across the possibilities. Lord, it could be any of a number of villages along this part of the coast.

Raucous cheers from a nearby watering hole drew

him inside. Thomas was keeping a roomful of people entertained by reciting the more lewd poems of Robbie Burns as he played cards. His sister, dressed as a youth, stood behind him, guarding his back.

Hardly ill. Barely recognisable. His blood boiled with the evidence of her brazen lies and the fear, that had been his companion from Penleven to Plymouth, crystallised into something else entirely.

Rage. Savage and powerful.

Duped one time too many by a consummate deceiver.

He wasn't even cautious in the way he sat at the table, ignoring the St Clairs altogether as he asked for the hand to be dealt.

Twenty minutes later, when he had amassed a sizeable part of the winnings, Caroline settled at the side of her brother. Unexpectedly she too asked to be dealt in, her face as bland as hell. He couldn't remember ever playing another person who gave so little away and when she won the first play he was not surprised. Just another secret that she had kept from him. Just another skill that a conwoman might need as she wreaked havoc in the lives of lesser men before moving on. Caring for no one.

She did not sew or knit or darn.

She did not sing or play an instrument.

She was not interested in the planning of a menu or the setting out of a favoured garden.

Not these woman's pursuits, the soft gentle accomplishments of a well brought-up lady.

No. Caroline played cards as well as any sharp he had ever met and was able to take on the persona of another with an astounding ease. Here, with her hair tied back in a queue she was…more than believable. It was in the way she swiped her sleeve against her nose as she sniffed and took an easy swallow of brandy in the glass before her, before calling this hand.

A challenge.

He met it.

Laying down three kings and an ace.

Her three aces and the joker trumped his easily and when the onlookers dispersed as she gathered her winnings he stood, tired by the pretence of it all.

'I have a room in the coaching inn around the corner. If you are not there within half an hour, I will have you both arrested as horse thieves. Do you understand?'

'Yes.'

When he walked out, he hoped that they knew the game was up.

They arrived at the inn within fifteen minutes. Caroline had reverted to the costume of a woman again, her cloak draped across her shoulders and inviting more than a little attention.

She looked beautiful. Scared. Lost.

All around the entrance hall men stared at her.

'Alexander?'

'Is fine. Morag has taken it on herself to look after him until I am back.' He refrained from including her in the equation.

Shepherding them up the steps and into his room, he was glad for the fire that had been lit in the hearth and the bread and wine laid out on the table.

'Have you eaten?'

'Not for a while.'

Thomas's voice was wary. Resigned.

'Then help yourself.'

Neither twin did so.

'How is your head, Caroline?' He had seen the twinge of pain on her face when she had inadvertently brushed the cloak against her neck as she had slipped it off in the mounting warmth of this room.

'It is fine, thank you.' Polite. Formal. Infinitely distant.

'I presume you have acquired a passage to France?'

'We have, Your Grace.' Thomas's turn now. 'On the *White Swan*. She leaves on the morning tide.'

'Why?'

Silence.

'Is it because you are chasing the person who shot at Caroline?'

Silence again.

'And is that person the same one who took you hostage in Exeter?'

He was close. He could feel it and see it in the thin pulse at Thomas's throat. Markedly faster.

Caroline was better at hiding everything! She stood, looking straight at him, a hint of anger in the tip-tilt of her chin. Wishing him away.

Nothing made sense. But then it never had with the Anstrettons. Or Weatherbys. Or St Clairs, he corrected himself. Accomplished liars with myriad identities.

'It seems to me that we are at an impasse, then.' Crossing his legs, he leant back, pouring himself a generous drink as he waited. He had had enough practice with the emotions of guilt and deceit to know that it took very little to induce an outpouring once you had uncovered the true root of its cause.

With a flourish he extracted his timepiece, a quarter to nine. If he had anything on his side, it was time.

Caroline felt dizzy and she laid her hand against the side of the sofa to keep her balance. Today dressed in his riding clothes and sitting in this beautiful room, Thornton Lindsay looked…at home. Just as he had in the gaming room in Plymouth, his ease at playing cards amidst the company of people he usually avoided startling.

He was a chameleon, adapting to what life threw at him with an astonishing ease, the scars on his face the only sign of a time when things had gone astray. And he was clever. Already she could see his mind assessing their destination and their reason for flight.

He was a King's man, a soldier, versed in the arts of war. Right and wrong would hang in shades of black and white with such a man and a life like hers with no strict codes of conduct or discipline would be wholly foreign to him.

Her mother had flitted from person to person and from place to place, a gypsy and loose, any restrictive morality sacrificed to her own personal needs and tailored to want.

Any want!

Guy was one such case in point. Beautiful and deadly, like some giant exotic reptile crawling through their lives, he had invited comment and interest. How their mother had loved being the centre of attention after so many years of being on the outer circle of everything.

For once she was envied! She would not leave him because a hundred other women wanted him, no matter what he did! That was the way of people with no moral fibre. They became trapped by their ineptness and greed and buried by their inability to ever quite do anything right.

They had been fourteen when their mother had met him, in the autumn of 1809. Eloise had gone to a ball with one lover and come back with another, her red dress exposing ample charms. They had seen her from their hiding place beneath the stairs when she had returned, seen her laughter and her thrall, seen the danger on his face and the way he did not quite meet her eyes, seen the marks on her neck where he had pressed too hard.

Lord!

Her life.

Their life.

No wonder it had come to this!

Angry shame consumed her.

'There is nothing at all you can help us with, Your Grace. It would be far better if you were to return to Penleven and forget us altogether.'

His eyebrows rose up as he considered her statement.

'And our son. Should he also forget you altogether?'

'No.' Her voice shook. 'When we can come back, we will—'

Thomas stood suddenly and interrupted her. 'I think it is time for the truth, Caro, for if Alexander should suffer…'

She knew the look in her brother's eyes. Familial duty. It had been there before in all their moments of need.

'I murdered a man, Your Grace. I am returning to France to confess it.' Flat. Categorical. 'I planned on leaving Caroline behind, but she has insisted on coming too.'

Caroline felt her world spin and stop. Pulling her brother's arm hard, she turned him around. 'He does not know what he is saying. It was not him.' She shouted the words. Loud. Too loud. She saw confusion on Thornton's face and resignation on Tosh's as he continued.

'I hit him hard on the back of the head with a marble statue until he fell. Until he did not breathe.'

Stop. Stop. Stop. Desperately she laughed, hearing an unbecoming edge of hysteria on the edge of it. 'He does not know what he is saying. It is the wine, perhaps, or—'

'Why?'

One simple question. She could barely look at the Duke. But it had to be answered because otherwise her brother would be completely lost and damned, held solely accountable for an act that had saved her.

'He almost raped me.' There. It was out. Said. Raw in the sunlight of this room. Unreal amidst the polished furniture and fine velvets. 'At Malmaison one Sunday afternoon when prayers had finished…'

The events of that day were engraved in her memory, never to be forgotten. She hated the way her breathing quickened and the damp heat of shame beaded beneath her clothing.

'How old were you when this happened?'

'Seventeen.'

'Hell.' He stood and walked towards the window. 'Hell,' he repeated.

'He had tried before.' Pulling back the sleeve of Thomas's shirt, she pointed to a wide band of wrinkled skin. 'He had hurt us before. Many times!' Her breath

came in strange gulps and she swallowed to contain absolute panic.

'You think this was your fault?' Thornton Lindsay
seemed even more dangerous than usual. 'You were
forced into an act of self-defence against some loathsome lowlife and have been on the run ever since. And
you think to explain your actions to me? To apologise?'

Caroline blinked. Was he implying...? Did he
mean...? She could not quite understand his message.

'Why the hell would you even think of going back?'

Tears blurred her vision.

'Guy de Lerin's family have kidnapped Thomas
and shot at me. If Alexander were to get in the way by
mistake...'

She didn't finish.

'What was the name you mentioned?' Interest flared
in Thornton's eyes.

'Pardon.'

'The name of the man you think you killed. What
was his name?'

'Guy de Lerin.'

'Guy de Lerin? A man with dark brown hair, a
moustache and a mark on his lip, just here.'

Both Caroline and Thomas nodded.

'He is dead, but *you* didn't kill him. Guy de Lerin
worked for General Soult in France, and his throat
was slit after accosting the daughter of a Spanish land-
owner a few days before I met up with Adele Halstead

in Orthez. I know it was him because I received his sabretache and its contents from a local who was more than unhappy with the pretensions of Napoleon and his troops.'

'My God.' Tosh sat down heavily on the sofa, trying to ingest such a revelation. 'My God. I didn't kill him?' Tears welled in his eyes and Caroline sat down next to her brother, taking his hand in her own.

'You are sure that it was him?'

'I never forget a name or a face and good intelligence was only ever about memory.'

An altered truth. Dead, but not by their hands.

'This changes everything.' Caroline framed her statement in the way of one who could not quite take in the changing of circumstance.

'It certainly does, though there is one small problem.'

Both looked over at Thornton as he spoke.

'Somebody out there is still trying to kill you.'

They travelled back to Penleven with hired horses pulling the coach to give the horses they had ridden to Plymouth a rest.

In the aftermath of their revelation there was a strange silence between them.

Trust. Distrust. Honesty. Dishonesty. Their confession had left them feeling uncertain and Thornton Lindsay wasn't making any of it easier as he sat opposite them and looked out of the window.

Catching Thomas's glance, Caroline saw the same puzzlement on his face that she was certain must be on her own.

Laying her head back against the cushioned seat, she momentarily closed her eyes, exhausted, with hope and worry, and from the sheer and utter weight of her love for the man opposite.

If Tosh hadn't been sitting next to her, she would have risked rejection and moved across to sit next to him, but with her brother here and the very real chance of a rebuff, she stayed where she was.

The Duke's hands were still scratched from his search for her on the cliffs, and the mark on his forehead where a rock had hit him was red raw and raised. And today in the inn in Plymouth when he had guided her through the lobby with his arm against the small of her back, she had felt that familiar bolt of warmth. Safe. Protected. Cherished.

'Do you still have the locket that you retrieved from the Halstead house?'

She frowned even as Thomas nodded.

'I wonder if I might look at it?'

'You think it holds a clue?'

'It's something from your past and the attacks did not begin until after you had taken the trinket.'

'You think it is Adele Halstead?'

He did not answer.

Caroline tried to fit all that she knew of her mother's

friend into some sort of a pattern, her head still reeling from the fact that they were now free to be whoever they wanted to be.

No longer murderers.

No longer running from the law.

Caroline and Thomas St Clair.

The tight knot of uncertainty dissipated. Whatever happened from now on could be faced because Thomas's life was no longer suspended in the fear of recognition and accusation.

'Was there anyone in Campton that you were at odds with?'

She shook her head at the same time as Thomas did.

'What about in London? Did you tread on anyone's toes unduly?'

'Excelsior Beaufort-Hughes, perhaps? He felt he should have been allowed Caroline's hand in marriage. And I played a number of card games and won. Some of those I faced may not have been happy with the losing, though I never cheated. Could it be someone there?'

'At the moment I am as much in the dark as you about motive.'

'But you think they will try again?'

'At Penleven you will both be safe.' He barely looked at them as he said it and Caroline felt the full force of the weight of his duty settle around them.

Just that. Just duty.

With a half-smile she nodded her gratitude and turned away, hating the tears that sprang to her eyes and the aching regret in her heart.

Chapter Sixteen

Caroline pulled the wrapper more firmly around her shoulders as she climbed the stairs to Thornton Lindsay's room. It was late. Almost two o'clock, and the noise of the servants had stopped some time ago, the house wreathed now in silence. She clutched the locket in her palm, glad she could use it as an excuse to come to his room if all else failed.

Slipping inside the door, she took a breath and was surprised by the sound of his voice.

'Who's there?'

He was not asleep. The light of a small lamp bathed an adjoining room; when she walked a few steps more she saw him sitting at a desk, a pen in one hand and a glass in another. A fire burned dully in the grate and on the wall in front of him was a picture of a beautiful woman. The artist in her was instantly interested in the lines, colour and strength of the work.

'My mother had it done,' he commented as he saw her looking. 'As a gift to my father just before she died.' He buttoned up his shirt where it gaped open across his chest as he saw her looking. 'Why are you here?'

'I have the locket of my mother's that you asked for.' She placed the trinket in a small silver dish on one end of his sideboard. 'And I wanted to say thank you for coming to find us and for bringing us here to Penleven with you.'

'This is the third time I have brought you home, Caroline. Will you be staying or is there another charade that is yet to play out?'

Removing himself from her proximity, he walked to the table, lifting a large brandy glass and emptying the contents. He looked wary.

'I thought I knew you. But every moment I know you less. And I am not certain that I can survive more lies.'

'You think that of me?'

'This morning you were a woman who lay back against her pillow and feigned illness before stealing a horse from my stable and chasing her brother over half the county. Today dressed as a lad you were a card sharp, and tonight, in nothing save a smattering of lace and silk, a siren comes to my room when the house is quiet.' He shook his head and faced her directly. 'Who am I to believe is you? This person, that person? I spent years on the continent watching my back and trying to determine the truth amongst myriad lies. And all I want now is honesty. Can you give that to me, Caroline, for if we are to have any chance at giving Alexander a family, there needs to at least be trust between us.'

Trust.

Not love!

'If you would prefer that I leave…'

'No. I would not prefer that.'

The clock on the mantel ticked loud, marking the seconds of silence between them. Awkward. Heavy. She wished she had not worn this nightdress, its inherent thin silliness so suggestive of what she sought, and of what he refused. Embarrassment swamped her, the red bloom of blood a tell-tale sign of shame.

'There is one more thing that I think you should know.'

He turned towards her. Warily.

'My mother always said that our father was from the English aristocracy, though she would never mention any name.'

'Why not?'

'She had washed her hands of England, I think, and did not want us going back to be laughed at, or criticised. Besides,' she added beneath her breath, 'Mama was not a woman who limited herself to be the exclusive property of just one man.' The bleakness of the truth fell between them again. A mother who was a trollop and a father who could have been anyone.

Unexpectedly Thornton began to smile.

'Could you promise me, Caroline, that there will be no more secrets between us?'

'I could.' Her voice shook.

'I asked your brother for your hand in marriage. Did he tell you that?'

She nodded, hating the hope that was beginning to bloom inside her.

'And yet you locked your door and didn't answer it.'

'I thought if you knew about de Lerin, you might follow us and kill him yourself. I was trying to protect you.'

'So you are saying…?'

She took a breath and risked it. Risked everything.

'I love you, Thornton. I've always loved you since the first moment of meeting you at the ball in London with your collar up and your one eye daring the world to comment.'

'Comprehensive!'

She frowned. It was not the answer that she was wanting back. Not at all.

'I love you, but I can only marry you if you love me back.'

He began to laugh.

'Do you truly not know how I feel, Caroline?'

She shook her head and in response he brought her

hand to his mouth, his tongue laving a singular thin pain of passion that grew from her groin and blossomed. Quicksilver heat!

'I have loved you since that first night when you came in your white gown and healed me. I had not been with a woman for more than two years…'

'And I had not been with any man before.'

Lord! Suddenly he knew exactly what it was she was saying. The succession of lovers and husbands was as much of a cover as everything else in her life and she had been a virgin when he had paid her fifty guineas and forced her into his bed! Another secret! And with this one, guilt racked the very fibre of his being.

It had only ever been her and Thomas against a world that had labelled them as outcasts because of their very lack of alternative. And he had used her as his mistress.

'You were a virgin?'

'Yes.'

Everything made sense. Her fear. Her tightness. The blood he had seen on her ripped petticoat as he had stuffed it into the fire.

He could barely breathe with the fineness of such an unexpected gift.

'I love you, sweetheart. Nay, don't cry! 'Tis my heart I am offering you and that's the truth of it.'

'I don't know if I deserve it. There are things that I have done…'

'As the Duchess of Penborne, no one could touch you, I swear it.'

'And Thomas?'

'Will have a tongue of land nearby on the coast and build a house of his own.'

Tears streamed down her face.

'You would do that for me? For us?' Tracing the line of scarring up his cheek, she leaned in, kissing the hurt away, her tongue careful in its passage, a quiet touching. 'I like it how you do not wear your patch with me or pull your collar up high. When I first met you, I thought your eyes were like those of a falcon.'

'Blinded?'

She laughed. 'No, amber and dangerous.'

'And predatory?' He began to peel back her thin wrapper, his brows rising when he determined how little she had on underneath.

Caroline stood completely still, waiting as the clothes pooled at her feet. In the candlelight with his eyes upon her she felt beautiful. Loved. Cherished. Sensuous.

She laughed as he lifted her up into his arms and brought her to his bed. In a moment he had joined her, his clothes also discarded on the floor.

Heat engulfed her and the throb of want drummed heavily, like it had right from that very first time in London. And when his hand came between her legs to open them, she arched into his touch and welcomed him in.

* * *

It was dark when she next awoke, the candles blown out and the light beat of rain steady against the window. When she moved she knew that Thornton was not next to her. Confused, she sat up and saw him, leaning against the wall by the fireplace and smoking a cheroot, its small red ember easily seen in the night.

'You cannot sleep?'

He flicked the smoke into the fire and stretched. 'Did your mother ever tell you anything else about your father?'

Of all the questions he could have asked, this was the last one that she expected, and she tensed further when she saw the locket and a small knife in his hand.

'Once at Malmaison, she told me that she believed God provided a soulmate for everyone and that she had squandered her chance.'

'And you were born in…'

'1796.'

'In France?'

'Yes.'

He pushed away from the wall and came towards her, a smile replacing the frown that had been there.

'Eloise St Clair arrived in France in the winter of 1795 according to the information I have gathered from the shipping lists. Do you know if your mother had known Adele Halstead for long before she died?'

'No. She came to Paris when Mama was ill. They spent a lot of time together talking, and I think she helped my mother come to terms…with everything. That was one of the reasons we did not denounce her when we found the locket and other jewellery missing.'

'And when you came to London you tried to get these things back?'

'Only the locket. Mama was always careful to take it with her, you see. It was the only possession that she truly treasured.'

The tone of his voice made her hesitate. 'You think Adele Halstead could have something to do with…' She did not finish because in the fog of uncertainty another thought suddenly congealed. 'You think that she knows something about who our father is?'

'More than something. I think she came to Paris knowing exactly who your father was.'

'Because…?' She could no longer follow any of his reasoning.

'Because it is my guess that your father is her husband, Maxwell Halstead, the Earl of Wroxham.'

He placed the small portraits of herself and her brother before her. Caroline saw that they had been carefully removed from the locket, their edges still curled from many years of placement.

Silence settled between them and she waited as he lifted the lamp and opened the trinket to the light so that she could more properly look inside.

Her mother's much younger face stared out of the roundness, and the other held the portrait of a boy.

'The man is Wroxham. Do you know the woman?'

'It is my mother. They were beneath our likenesses all of this time?'

He nodded and history fell into place.

Her fingers entwined around his. 'When did you know?'

'Nothing is ever truly coincidental, Caroline. And Adele Halstead is not a woman to be trusted. Did your mother know she was married to Wroxham?'

'I am not certain. I never heard her speak of her life in England and she did not use the name Wroxham or Halstead in Paris. She called herself Madame de Chabaneix. It was only by chance that we saw her here in London as Lady Wroxham in the gardens at Kew, though we were careful not to let her see us.'

'From my information Wroxham married her in Spain in 1801. He had bought a commission as an officer there and she was already "helping" England with intelligence about the French.'

'Do you think he knows? About her?'

'I am sure that he does not, though the better question would be what was the relationship between your mother and the Earl.'

'Eloise always said that she had loved him.'

'How old was your mother when she had you?'

For a moment Caroline counted back the years. 'Nineteen, I think.'

'Under age for a marriage then in the church, though there was always Gretna Green.'

'You think they could have eloped?'

He shrugged his shoulders and stood up straight. 'If he had married your mother, Adele Halstead would have strong motive to be rid of you.'

The truth crystallised with a stinging clarity. 'Because Thomas would be the heir to the earldom? My God. He needs to be told about this.'

'If he is, it will probably be dangerous. The bullet missed your brain by less than a quarter of an inch. I think it is safe to say that whoever shot at you wanted you dead, and Thomas is inclined to rush into things.'

'Whoever? You don't think it was her? Adele Halstead knows how to handle a gun.'

'Yet she has been nowhere near Penleven in the past month. I have had her followed since the locket incident and there has been nothing in her movements to arouse suspicion.'

'And Tosh? Why wasn't he killed in Exeter?'

'I am not sure.' His eyes flared in interest as she brought his hand up to cup the full softness of her breast. 'But I will find out.'

'Tomorrow. Think on it tomorrow, Thorn, for I need you now.'

Her simple invitation was quickly taken up as he gathered her body to his own in the bed.

'You are telling me that you think we are the off-spring of the Earl of Wroxham?' Lifting the locket to the light, Thomas peered inside. 'So what happens now?'

'As I see it, we have two choices. You could stay here at Penleven—'

'Where we have already been attacked once.' Her brother's impatience was easily heard. He had been incredulous when Thornton had told him of his theory about their father and the meeting here in the library this morning had tilted him from disbelief to anger.

'Now that we have identified the risk, it will be easier to protect you.'

'To stay inside, you mean. To be guarded and hidden—'

'My grandson only means to keep ye both safe.' Morag Lindsay got up from her place near the fire, the pain on her face reflecting old bones that no longer moved as they once had.

'Safety at what cost? For how long would we be prisoners?'

'I think you are overreacting, Tosh…' Caroline tried to distil her brother's anger and Thornton overrode them both.

'Your brother makes a fair point, and this brings me to plan number two. If we played Adele Halstead at her own game, we might indeed have more luck. Morag will introduce you into London society as the children of one of her great friends and she will make certain that the Earl and his wife are included in the dinner party.'

'I don't understand.'

'Wear the locket around your neck and see if the Earl has any sort of reaction. Often attack is a better policy than being defensive.'

Morag began to laugh, slapping her hands against her leg and cackling gleefully. 'Ahh, Thornton. You are getting more and more like your father.'

'Thank you.'

Caroline wondered if he should have taken such a statement as a compliment, but with the possibility of Thomas finding his place in the world she did not wish to express even the slightest notion of doubt.

Besides, she knew that they were playing this game according to the rules of a master. Thornton looked neither worried nor perturbed by the situation, and his confidence in coming out with a result by following this course was beginning to find favour with her.

'We can open the family house in Mayfair,' Morag was saying. 'Leonard could come too, and of course we must visit a modiste and have some clothes made up for you both. And a hairdresser and a dance master.'

Lord. Caroline caught Tosh's eyes as the old lady

continued to rattle off a long list of helpers, and when he smiled back the most extraordinary thought hit her.

We were born to this! This extravagance and excess. After so many years of penny pinching and being careful the notion was bittersweet.

Chapter Seventeen

Caroline was dressed in the most ornate gown she had ever seen. It was of blue silk because, according to Morag Lindsay, 'she was too old to wear white'. The buttons down the back were fashioned from pearls, and at her neck she wore her mother's locket.

She made herself stay still as she waited for the woman sent out from the London modiste to finish pinning the last alterations. After the woman had done so, Caroline was flustered to hear Thornton's voice downstairs. They had spent every night together since coming to London, but he seldom came to his grandmother's town house in the daytime in an observance of society rules and she wondered why he should be here now.

A maid brought in a note and gave it to her and she read it quickly. He wished to meet her as soon as she was able in the salon downstairs. With care she tried to hurry the highly strung French seamstress, but it was a good half an hour before she was finally able to join Thornton.

He was alone, standing against the window looking out, his patch across his left eye and his collar drawn up. And in that singular moment Caroline understood what it must have cost him to be here, amidst the tittle-tattle of society and the gossip that he hated.

'I am sorry to be such a long time.'

He took her hand in his and drew her against him, close, the slight pressure of his fingers a silent communication between them.

Together. Just them.

'I wish we could go home.'

'So do I.' The tone in his voice worried her and she looked up.

'Is there a problem?'

'I am not certain,' he answered and drew away, shutting the door that was open behind them. 'I went to see the Halsteads yesterday and whilst Adele is undoubtedly devious, age and position have definitely mellowed her.'

'Perhaps she is resigned to the fact that she cannot change things, that the truth will come out.'

'Or perhaps it was not she who shot at you on the cliffs at Penleven.'

Caroline felt her eyes widen. 'Who else could it have been? Who else is there?'

Anger sparked in his eye at her question, but there was also a puzzled dawning, a realisation that was crystallising even as she watched him.

'My grandmother has Alex in the garden, Caroline. Could you ask her to your room on the pretence of some information you are seeking and stay there until I come for you.'

When she nodded he looked relieved, the prickling sense of danger slightly diminished.

'Give me an hour and I promise that I will tell you everything. And keep to your room with the door locked until you hear my voice.'

And with that he was gone.

Morag grumbled all the way from the garden to Caroline's room, the stick she used to help her get around punctuating the conversation as they climbed the stairs. The town house had never seemed as big as it did today and Caroline was pleased when the last steps were reached, for Thornton's whole attitude had made her wary, his deductions about Adele's innocence leaving them wide open to danger.

'I am not quite…as agile as I once was…if you could just give me a moment.'

Her rasping breathing pierced the silence and, holding her son very closely, Caroline wished with all her might that the old lady would hurry. She resisted the impulse to take up her hand and drag her along because she did not want to frighten her and had no real idea as to how she could explain the rush.

Thornton's cousin's shadow fell across them just as they came to the beginning of the last corridor.

'Why, Leonard,' Morag said, as she turned to rest against the solid wall behind her, 'you gave me quite a fright—we were not expecting you back until the evening.'

In the dull light Caroline could see a glistening sweat on Thorn's cousin's upper lip, and his eyes were unusually dilated, a smell not unlike sugar permeating the air. A familiar scent!

Was he ill? Had he been hurt somehow? A darker thought crossed the others when he did not answer, but continued to observe them.

Opium. Guy de Lerin had been a proponent of the drug and she knew now where she had smelt that particular sweet pungent aroma before. She moved in front of Morag and pushed Alex into her arms. Lord, and look what opium had made him do!

'I need to speak with Leonard for just a moment, Your Grace. Could you take Alex to my room and wait for me there?'

The old lady looked surprised at the request, but relief blossomed in Caroline as the woman did as she had been asked and shuffled off. Ten minutes since Caroline had seen Thornton. How long would it take him to realise his cousin was back, for she was suddenly certain that Leonard Lindsay was dangerous? Plastering a smile across her face, she gaily began to talk.

'I am so glad to have this opportunity of finding you alone, Leonard, for I wish to have a surprise party for your grandmother's birthday in another month and I was hoping that you could attend. I had thought something along the lines of a small soirée here, though, of course, if you think she might prefer a celebration at Penborne, I could keep that in mind.' She hoped such ramblings had given Morag the time she needed to reach her room, but did not dare to turn around and check.

He looked puzzled.

'I know you are a busy man and there are a lot of other social occasions on in London, but perhaps…' She made a point of looking past him, clapping her hands suddenly over her mouth. 'A spider, there behind you. A huge spider.'

When he looked around, she ran by, pushing him off balance. But he did not follow her and in that second Caroline knew that she had made a fatal mistake.

Alexander. It was Alex whom he wanted.

Horror consumed fear.

'Thorn,' she shouted and began to retrace her steps, screaming a warning to Morag as she came through the door to see what all the commotion was about.

Thorn's grandmother fell like a puppet pulled on

some unseen string, back and down, crumpled still, Alexander's cries from behind her.

And then everything went black.

Caroline came to in a carriage, a sturdy rope around her wrists. Two men she did not know sat opposite her, and in the arms of the one with a ring in his ear Alexander lay sleeping. Her heart, already racing fast, began to race faster and fear consumed her, tightness constricting her breath, and her cheekbone was throbbing.

'Why are you doing this?' She barely recognised her voice.

Neither answered.

'I will give you double what you are being paid. Triple if you just take us home.'

Lord. Her eyes flicked to the other man, hoping to see some humanity in his face, some humanity that she could appeal to. But his visage looked as uncompromising as his cohort's.

'If we took you home, lovie, no doubt we'd be seeing the bars of a prison for a long time to come.'

'Then let me down at the next town and I promise that you will be amply rewarded. I give you my word that it will be so.'

Both laughed. 'The payment for depositing you in a brothel in Gloucester is payment enough and no strings attached.'

She blanched.

'And my son?'

'An orphanage will take him.'

He leaned over and ran his thumb across the downy skin on Alexander's cheek and horror crawled down Caroline's spine.

These men were mad. She was in a carriage with her son heading towards God knows where with two men who were mad.

'If it were me, I would think about taking my chances on a generous payment from the Duke of Penborne. He would reward you amply were you to bring us home and I promise you no questions would be asked about your involvement in any of this.'

'The man who gave us the gold said this is what you would say. He said you were only the Duke's mistress and that he would never marry you. He said that you held no sway at all over the purse strings of the Lindsay fortune and that Thornton Lindsay was tiring of you already.'

'And you believed him?' She scoffed at the words and then watched in horror as the man without the earring took something from his pocket. A bottle with the words 'Tincture of Opium' written upon it. When the world lost shape, her last sight was of Alex crying as he heard her pleading groans.

She woke in a room painted dark indigo. As she tried to focus, she realised that the dress she had been wearing was gone, replaced instead by a petticoat, the décolletage falling drunkenly across the line of her nipples.

Swallowing, she held her head very still as jagged lines of ache plundered through her temple, though the locket around her neck swung into view as she moved and her hands came up to release the catch.

They had not taken this? She could barely believe her luck. Alex lay on the bed beside her, asleep. She felt for the pulse at his throat in a sudden dread and was relieved to find a steady and normal rhythm. Just asleep then. Now, if only she could find something to write with. The fire held scraps of newspaper and she stood, carefully walking over to the grate. Already she could hear voices outside and hurried to her task. A piece of charcoal and the edge of paper. And a name.

Property of Thornton Lindsay, Duke of Penborne.

Folding the scrap, she opened the locket and placed it inside. And then she lifted up her son and deposited the trinket in the folds of cloth that swaddled him. *Please, please, God, let someone find it. Because if they didn't, all would be lost.*

The door opened and a middle-aged woman stood there, hair a bright and flaming red and the clothes she wore were the ones that Caroline had come to this place in.

'My name is Clara,' she said quietly, 'and you are in Gloucester. You should bring in a good amount of business with skin like yours, even given the fact that you are no longer a virgin.'

'Business?'

'It's a brothel, my dear. Even a well brought-up girl such as yourself should have an inkling what goes on inside such a place. In four days' time the master of the place will return from London and he will be pleased to have you first.'

'You cannot mean to do this—' Caroline began, but the woman stopped her. 'I would never willingly—'

Her arms were suddenly behind her back, stick-hard fingers opening her mouth and the same bitter tea that she had been forced to drink in the carriage was poured cold down her throat.

'Willingly, nay. But drugged with laudanum, my dear, it's a different story, and after a few months, what man would want you back…?'

'Thorn.' The word was torn from fear and dread and aching love.

And the last sight she saw before her eyes closed was the crone lifting up her son and leaving the room.

She was tired and could not quite use her arms or her legs, but a man was there undressing, one hand making free with her, his cold fingers opening her thighs, pushing in.

Not Thornton. Nothing was right.

'Pleeease…' She tried to beg.

'I'm almost there, my sweetling. How refreshing to encounter such eagerness in a new girl.' When he smiled she saw half his teeth were missing and the rest were yellowed dirty.

His other hand lifted the sheets, the gleam in his eyes easily seen in the candlelight as her breasts fell away from the flimsy lace. As he lay down beside her, the hardness of his sex brushed against her leg. Waiting, but not for long. She saw that in the lust on his face and in the shaking eagerness of his loathsome hands.

And then the door swung open, wide, the sound of anger and hard knuckles against a soft face, shouting and blood on the sheets. Red, red blood.

Hers?

She tried to focus, tried to rise, but she could move nothing. Neither her eyes nor her mouth nor her hands.

Death. Was this it? This heavy lack of breath, and darkness, and a gurgling rattle.

'Caroline?' Her name came from far away through a passage of light. And then she could breathe again as a weight was rolled off her.

'Caroline.' Again. Closer. Worried. She shook her head and the world cleared a little.

Thornton was there, taking in her battered face with a darkening fury. And behind came Tosh and a taller blond man. Somehow familiar?

'Caro?'

Tears gathered and ran in warm silent runnels down her cheeks. Thornton. Beside her. Real.

'He nearly…' she began, looking up as she reached out, and when his arms closed about her strong and true, the horrors of this place broke upon her in a wave.

'Alexander…?' The word was a shrill desperate sob.

'Is at Penleven Castle being well looked after by Morag. Your note was found, sweetheart. He is safe.'

'It…was…your cousin.'

'I know. He shot himself when I confronted him a few moments after you did, but by then you were gone.'

'And Adele?'

'Knew nothing about any of it. Her crime was only that of greed.' Pulling a blanket around her shoulders, Thornton waited as her shaking lessened and Thomas began to explain.

'Mama had asked Adele Halstead as a French-woman living in London to contact the Earl of Wroxham. She gave Lady Wroxham the locket as a way of reminding him of who we were.'

The tall blond man suddenly laid his hand on her brother's shoulder and began to speak.

'I am Maxwell Halstead, Caroline, and I am your father. Perhaps you will allow me to explain it.'

'Father?' Suddenly Caroline could see the lines of the boy from the locket in the face of the man.

Without being asked to, he reached out, taking her

hand in his own. Warm. Big. Solid. A father. No longer orphans and perhaps even loved? The tears in his eyes told her it was so. Her eyes. Deep blue. Dependable.

'Your mother and I were married briefly. We eloped, you see, to Gretna Green but it was only a matter of hours before my parents caught up with us.' The shaking in his voice told of the effort it was taking him to relate the tale. 'I was eighteen, just eighteen, and my mother had a hold on me then that I am now ashamed of.' He stopped, giving the impression of one who was carefully finding words that would be kind. 'Eloise St Clair was a girl who loved anything of value and the money my mother offered her to just disappear was substantial. When she ran away to Europe, the Wroxham gold made certain that there would be nothing said here to tarnish the reputation of the earldom.'

'Yet she had us.'

'I swear I did not know that she was pregnant until Thornton brought Thomas with him yesterday to Wroxham House and I knew without doubt that he was my son. If I had known that, I should have followed her to the very ends of the earth to retrieve you.'

'Your second wife…made no mention…of the locket?'

Thornton broke in. 'Adele Halstead left England this morning, Caroline. She was the one who kidnapped Thomas in Exeter, but who at the last moment could not find it in her to kill him. For that alone we gave her leniency to leave the country and begin a new life elsewhere without the law on her tail.'

Adele Halstead gone and Leonard Lindsay dead. An ending to it all. And a new beginning.

The three men who meant the most to her in all the world stood as one solid wall of muscle and safety and the tension dissipated as she smiled.

'When did you know…about your cousin?' She addressed this question to Thornton and he knelt down beside her.

'After visiting Adele Halstead, I tried to work out who had been around you each time there was an accident. Yesterday morning the answer came to me. It was Leonard, but when I went to confront him in his room he wasn't there. The maid told me he was in the garden and by the time I returned—' He stopped and she heard the shake in his voice. Husky. Desperate.

'I love you, Caroline. If I had lost you…' Her fingers curled about his and she held on.

Like she would for ever.

Generations spanning the years. Her father and mother married!

A circle.

A whole new family and growing bigger all the time. From two had come three and now she was certain that another child was forming.

A girl.

And her name would be Lilly. A sister for Alexander.

Without even meaning to, she began to cry.

Epilogue

'How did you find me, Thorn?'

They lay in bed in an inn in Gloucester later that night. Together and safe.

Beneath the sheets she wound her bare legs around his warmth and smiled as his arm came firmly round her.

'When Alex was deposited in a church by the dock-yards, a priest found your note in the locket and a constable was called. Luck had it that the miscreant who had delivered him to the church was in his cups in a local bar and easily apprehended, and so the whole story came out.'

Caroline shuddered at the memory of everything. How easily it could have turned out differently.

'My cousin will never hurt us again, darling. It was a madness, I think, from the opium he had become addicted to. That, and a jealous envy, made him a lunatic.'

'Just suddenly?'

'No. On reflection it had been coming for a while, and he found it hard to let Penleven go. It had been his home, you see, for the years that I was away and he wanted it for himself. When he saw how much you meant to me and that Alex could become the heir, it tipped him over the edge.'

'Were you his only family?'

She felt him nod rather than saw it. 'Morag and I. His parents died when he was very young and he had about as much time at Eton as I did.'

'So you knew him there.'

'No. He was four years older than I am and our paths seldom crossed.'

She rolled on top of him, a thread of teasing in the movement, and his wicked smile made him look so breathtakingly handsome that Caroline had to smile back. In the candlelight his scars were only shadows and without his patch she could almost imagine him to be healed.

She hoped that he was, by her love.

Leaning down, she kissed his nose, his cheek, his temple.

'If anything ever happened to you, my darling…' His voice was rough.

'It won't.'

'Promise me?'

In response she lifted her locket from the table beside the bed and hung it around his neck. 'Tomorrow I will paint a portrait of us both inside.'

'To keep for ever,' he whispered back, opening his mouth as her lips came down warmly across his own.

REGENCY
Collection

*Let these sparklingly seductive delights whirl
you away to the ballrooms—and
bedrooms—of Polite Society!*

Volume 1 – 4th February 2011
Regency Pleasures by Louise Allen

Volume 2 – 4th March 2011
Regency Secrets by Julia Justiss

Volume 3 – 1st April 2011
Regency Rumours by Juliet Landon

Volume 4 – 6th May 2011
Regency Redemption by Christine Merrill

Volume 5 – 3rd June 2011
Regency Debutantes by Margaret McPhee

Volume 6 – 1st July 2011
Regency Improprieties by Diane Gaston

12 volumes in all to collect!

www.millsandboon.co.uk

REGENCY
Collection

*Let these sparklingly seductive delights whirl
you away to the ballrooms—and
bedrooms—of Polite Society!*

Volume 7 – 5th August 2011
Regency Mistresses by Mary Brendan

Volume 8 – 2nd September 2011
Regency Rebels by Deb Marlowe

Volume 9 – 7th October 2011
Regency Scandals by Sophia James

Volume 10 – 4th November 2011
Regency Marriages by Elizabeth Rolls

Volume 11 – 2nd December 2011
Regency Innocents by Annie Burrows

Volume 12 – 6th January 2012
Regency Sins by Bronwyn Scott

12 volumes in all to collect!

MILLS
BOON

www.millsandboon.co.uk